W9-ADK-201

GEARS OF WAR®

SEP - - 2019

Gears of War novels from Titan Books:

Gears of War: Ascendance by Jason M. Hough

SEP -- 2019

GEARS OF WAR.

ASCENDANCE

AN ORIGINAL NOVEL BY
JASON M. HOUGH

THE
COALITION·

XBOX
GAME STUDIOS

TITAN BOOKS

WILLIAMSBURG REGIONAL LIBRARY
7770 CROAKER ROAD
WILLIAMSBURG, VA 23188

Print edition ISBN: 9781789092615
E-book edition ISBN: 9781789092684

Published by Titan Books
A division of Titan Publishing Group Ltd
144 Southwark Street, London SE1 0UP
www.titanbooks.com

First edition: July 2019
10 9 8 7 6 5 4 3 2 1

Editorial Consultants: Rod Fergusson, Bonnie Jean Mah

This is a work of fiction. Names, characters, places, and incidents either
are the product of the author's imagination or are used fictitiously, and any
resemblance to actual persons, living or dead, business establishments,
events, or locales is entirely coincidental. The publisher does not have any
control over and does not assume any responsibility for author or third-
party websites or their content.

© 2019 Microsoft Corporation. All Rights Reserved. Microsoft, the
Crimson Omen logo, Gears of War, Marcus Fenix, The Coalition, and The
Coalition logo are trademarks of the Microsoft group of companies.

www.gearsofwar.com

No part of this publication may be reproduced, stored in a retrieval
system, or transmitted, in any form or by any means without prior written
permission of the publisher, nor be otherwise circulated in any form of
binding or cover other than that in which it is published and without a
similar condition being imposed on the subsequent purchaser.

A CIP catalogue record for this title is available from the British Library.

Printed and bound in the United States.

Did you enjoy this book? We love to hear from our readers.
Please email us at readerfeedback@titanmail.com or write to us at
Reader Feedback at the above address.

TITANBOOKS.COM

For all the hardworking and talented people who bring the Gears universe to life, and the passionate fans who support and inspire them.

ACT | 1

1 : AN INVITATION

The rock in her hand wasn't much more than a pebble, yet it felt like it carried the weight of the world.

Kait Diaz held the stone in her palm, felt its grit and pores. It had been cleaved in half at some point—when or where was anyone's guess. Maybe in yesterday's battle, maybe a million years ago when a boulder rolled loose down this forsaken hillside. Whatever. It had once been part of something larger, but now it was a separate thing.

"Alone. Like me."

Kait whispered the words so the others wouldn't hear.

She glanced up and studied the pile of rocks that blocked the cave mouth. Even with help it had taken her the better part of a day, building it up, sealing what would soon be her mother's tomb. Just one small opening left. A little window into the darkness. Once she put the rock in place, that would be that. Reyna Diaz would be gone. No light would ever shine on her again.

At the edges of Kait's mind swam memories of her childhood, but for now at least she kept them firmly in that blurred periphery. Later, perhaps, she'd be ready. But not now.

She lifted the small stone and forced it into the gap. Her hand lingered, covering the spot.

It's over, she thought, but she knew that wasn't really true. Reyna would always be a part of her, and she might have found a lifetime of wisdom and comfort in that, if not for the amulet around her neck. The heirloom, the one last thing Mom had given her...

That had really muddied the goddamn waters.

JD and Del approached. They stood on either side of her and each rested a palm on the barrier wall, mimicking her stance.

"She'll be missed," JD said.

"Hell yeah, she will," Del added. "Her and Oscar both. Everyone else those creatures took—"

"Just... *stop*," Kait said. She let her hand fall from the rocks and turned her back on the burial site. "I can't... this is all I can do for now, okay? Let's get the hell out of here."

The two soldiers looked at each other, then nodded in unison. She moved and they parted a little to give her some space.

Seated just a short distance away were JD's father Marcus Fenix, Damon Baird, Sam Byrne, and Augustus Cole. Not one of them had ever met Reyna, but now that Kait moved away from the wall—a wall they'd spent all night helping her build—each of them took their turn to place a hand on the surface and say a silent goodbye.

Kait left them to it. Anyone else and she might have doubted their sincerity, but not this group. Friends of Reyna or not, they'd all fought at Kait's side against the Swarm, and helped her get here in time to say goodbye. She had that at least, and these people had made it possible. For that she would owe them, always.

Some silent agreement passed through the group then—the sort that existed between people who had fought together as they had. Sam kicked dirt over the ashes of their small campfire. Gear was checked and packed. The few extra clips of ammo they carried were divided up and a canteen passed around. They didn't have much left. No one had expected to be stuck out here.

Cole looked to Marcus. "Where to?"

"I'm not in charge," Marcus replied.

Cole shrugged. "You're *always* in charge. Even when you're outranked."

The old soldier shook his head. "We did what we came here to do. Thought I might head home."

Del couldn't help himself. "Your home's a smoldering ruin."

"Maybe so, but it's still home," Marcus growled.

"If there's even one wall left standing, I'd be shocked."

Marcus eyed the young man. "And whose fault is that?"

"Whoa, whoa. Relax." JD stepped in between them. "No need to get into whose fault it was."

"Easy for you to say," Del replied, "since it was really *your* fault."

Marcus grunted. For a moment he regarded Del and his son, then turned back to the larger group.

"Let Baird decide."

"Me?" Baird asked. "That'd be like the blind leading the sighted. I don't know this area at all. Look, we need to find a working comms tower. Do that, and I can get a bird to come pick us up."

At this Kait decided to speak up.

"I might know a place."

They all turned to her.

"It's a bit of a hike, and I'm not sure about comms, but there's supplies. Food maybe."

"Food, huh?" Cole eyed her. "I like the sound of that. Is it on a desolate hillside surrounded by nasty murderous baddies?"

"No, it's—"

"Good enough for the Cole Train, then," he said. "Lead the way."

Each step she took brought a little relief. Distance had a way of doing that, she supposed.

She'd barely slept. Last night a nightmare full of teeth and claws and tentacles, ending with a glowing mouth and that Speaker's voice, had sent her bolt upright and drenched in sweat. Kait had set to work right then and there on the rock wall that would entomb her mother, and the noise of her efforts had woken the others. Within minutes they were all pitching in to help, not a word passing between them, and they'd kept on until the job was done.

By midday they were out of the hills and on to a wide grassy plain, the sun pounding down on their necks. The air vibrated with the sounds of wildlife—buzzing, chirping, and the occasional rustle as something hightailed it out of their path. The tall grass, up to Kait's shoulders, felt like a thousand caressing fingers trying to pull her down into the earth to sleep. Kait found it harder and harder to focus, her vision blurring from exhaustion.

"You okay?"

She glanced around, willing the fog from her mind. JD and Del had come up beside her. It was Del who had spoken, but their faces bore the same expression. Concern. Worry.

"You really want me to answer that?" she asked, instantly regretting her tone, and having pushed them away earlier. They meant well, she knew.

Her friend grimaced and looked away. "I guess not. Just... look, we're here for you, alright?"

"Anything you need," JD added.

Kait couldn't keep the smile from her face, but it was only half formed, struggling to break through the grief just like she was. "Thanks, guys. I mean it. Right now I just need some time. Can you give me that?"

The two men nodded and fell back again. A few steps at first, then farther as the march went on.

When the swamp came into view it was almost a relief.

"Uh, we're going in there?" Cole said. "I take back my comment about desolate hillsides."

"Scared, Cole?" Marcus asked.

"Naw, man, just, you know, hoping for a little R&R after the recent unpleasantness. That... don't look too relaxing."

"The man's got a point," Samantha put in.

All at once the field around them went dead quiet, leaving only the wind that sent waves through the tall grass. Birds, insects... it all just stopped. Kait felt a cool tingle run up her spine and down her arms.

From somewhere behind them came a high-pitched yelp.

Then another, then more.

"Something tells me R&R isn't in our future," JD muttered. They all turned around, and instinctively started to spread apart and form a defensive line.

Alert again, Kait watched the horizon, glancing down only to verify the ammo reading on her Lancer. It was a customized model, pilfered from Marcus Fenix's estate as the walls literally fell in around them. The sixty-round clip was less than half full. When her gaze returned to the undulating field she saw movement at the edges.

The grass was parting, as if invisible objects raced toward them across the surface. Then something gray and mottled bobbed above the grass and, for one ugly instant, seemed to make eye contact with her before dropping back below. Those eyes were white and seemed sightless.

"Juvies!" she shouted. "From the left!"

"And the right!" JD added, already moving in that direction. Del followed him and Kait felt a strong pull to stick with them. Fighting beside them felt natural somehow, like an instinct rather than a conscious choice. As Del once put it, they were simply on the same wavelength.

But she was on the wrong side, nearer to Cole and Marcus. The two veterans moved off left, keeping low in the grass. With no cover here, fanning out was the only option. Kait suddenly found herself in a position to either flank left, or stay in the middle where Baird and his "special lady-friend" Sam stood like wind ranchers preparing to defend their last mill. Sam had a beat-up old Gnasher shotgun resting on her forearm. Baird's weapon was larger, held low. Kait knew that everyone was perilously low on ammo.

Baird braced the weapon against his hip, and Kait recognized it as the aptly named Buzzkill.

"Been looking for an excuse to try this thing," he said to no one in particular. "Time to level the playing field."

"Quit yapping and do it," Sam said.

Kait moved back a few steps, a grin curling at the corner of her mouth as Damon Baird let loose.

There came a whirring *whoosh* as the blade flew out and scythed through the tall grass, which fell in a line straight out from Baird, cut almost exactly in half. Somewhere off in the distance a

Juvie yelped. The bow-shock "V" it made came to an abrupt end.

Pleased, Baird kept firing. In front of him a pattern began to form like a fan—lines in the grass the width of the circular Buzzkill blades, spreading in an arc extending perhaps a hundred yards out. Two more Juvies fell from the salvo, but that wasn't the point, Kait now realized. Baird had created pockets of low grass the Juvies had to run through, revealing themselves in small, naked glimpses that made targeting far easier.

She braced herself and opened fire. Short bursts, the weapon rattling against her armpit each time. One of the scrawny creatures went ass-over-teakettle, limbs flailing. The other just dove lifelessly forward, vanishing into the grass.

From right and left came the bark and thrum of gunfire. Everyone took advantage of Baird's cleared lines to sight from a distance. A few of the creatures managed to get close, only to taste the wrath of Sam's Gnasher. Turning, Kait shielded her eyes to see how JD and Del were faring. Her friends were side by side, their expressions calm and focused.

"More incoming!" Marcus shouted. "Following the paths, disguising their numbers!"

And he was right. It was more intelligence than the little monsters had shown before, but then Kait had never faced them in such a wide, empty space as this. A second wave came rushing forward, not far behind the first, staying low and using the already-trampled grass to their advantage.

The Buzzkill made a sound that told her it was empty. Baird threw it to the ground and drew a Boltok pistol, wielding it with two hands.

"We don't have the ammo for this," Sam said to her man. "Plan B?"

"Melee?" Baird offered. "Sticks and fucking stones?"

Off to Kait's left, Cole grunted a laugh. He slung his Lancer and drew a long hunting knife.

"Trading a chainsaw for a knife, huh?" Kait said.

"Close combat, multiple enemies. Speed is better," Cole replied. "They wanna dance, I'll dance, unless someone's got a better idea. Outta ammo here."

Kait had five rounds left.

Then four.

Three.

For each Juvie she took down, three more seemed to stream in behind it. Fatigue started to grip her again. Where she'd been sweating before, now she was drenched.

"Guys? There's a lot of them," JD said.

"The swamp," Kait shouted. "Now!"

Part of her expected them to scoff at this idea. Not JD and Del, but maybe Cole or Baird, whom she barely knew. Retreat, even of the temporary variety, wasn't part of a soldier's vocabulary—at least not in her experience. This group, though, was seasoned. Practical. The "win by any means" variety that reminded her of Mom.

So instead of arguing they began to move. First a backward walk by those who still had ammo, then a full-on sprint by the whole party as their guns neared empty.

Kait reached the trees first. They were decrepit things, branches drooping and leafless, covered in gray fungus. The smooth grass plain gave way to undulating ground, stagnant water filling every low spot. White reeds poked up from the deeper pools, like bony fingers reaching out from so many graves. No grass to hide the Juvies here, though, and the trees provided solid cover. Kait positioned herself behind the first one with a thick trunk, turned, and aimed.

JD and Del were close behind. For a second they appeared to be in a footrace, which if true would not have surprised her. They bolted past and found their own trunks to hunker behind.

Ten paces behind them came Sam, a faster sprinter than Baird, whose pace seemed to be flagging. Still, he made it. The couple moved even farther into the trees, splashing as they went. Neither, it seemed, had a bullet left to fire.

Kait turned back and squinted, waiting for Marcus and Cole. Neither emerged from the grass, though. Another sound began.

"Dad, c'mon!" JD shouted.

Kait held up a hand for quiet. She strained, hearing yelping Juvies and, there, just below the chorus, the dueling growl of two chainsaws.

Marcus emerged from the grass first, still facing back toward the enemy. He swung his Lancer hard to one side just as a Juvie pounced at him. It was a grotesque, naked parody of the human who had died to create it. Blood and gore sprayed in an arc as the motorized saw cut through the scrawny creature. It fell in two neat halves to either side of Marcus. He stepped back and just had time to heave the weapon back the other way as another Juvie hurled itself toward him.

This one lost an arm and half its head for the effort.

The swing had Marcus twisted to one side. He never saw the third Juvie emerge from the grass. Instead of leaping toward his head, this one went low, diving to its shoulder and rolling into Marcus's calves. The veteran went down, splashing in the blood of his first kill.

Kait raised her rifle and took aim, but the fight became a tangle of limbs. She tossed the weapon to the ground and raced forward, drawing Reyna's broken-tipped machete as she went. Three long strides and she was there. Marcus saw her from the corner of his eye and kicked upward with both legs, sending the Juvie flying off and up into the air. Kait leaned into a slide, raised the knife, and sliced through the creature's gut as it twisted around above her. Hot blood sprayed across her face. She gagged as she turned her slide into a clumsy roll.

Wiping one arm across her face, she pushed herself upward and stood at the ready. Marcus rolled out from under the Juvie she'd just eviscerated. Yelping sounds came from all around.

Then Cole was in front of her, chainsaw revving. He coiled and rammed it toward her face. Kait flinched, heard the growl of Cole's Lancer as it passed by her cheek and struck a leaping Juvie just behind her. Its yapping cry ended in a crunch of bone and teeth.

Together the three of them ran for the trees. Ahead, JD and Del unleashed a deafening salvo on the now completely exposed enemy. As the bullets streamed past her, Kait didn't look back. Judging from their high-pitched cries, just audible over the sudden burst of gunfire, she knew they'd come in overwhelming numbers. Outrunning them wasn't going to happen.

Spotting a dirt trail, she led them to it. Somewhere ahead was the hideout she'd suggested, but she couldn't quite remember exactly how far they had to go through the swamp. Her only visit had been months ago, with Oscar, and she'd spent most of that journey helping her uncle guide his horse Chuzz through the—

"Chuzz," she muttered.

"What?" JD called out, not far behind her.

"I have an idea!" Kait glanced ahead, looking for a familiar tree or bend in the trail that wove through the swamp.

"Whatever it is," Del shouted, "now would be good."

There! Kait recognized a curved branch, and at its midpoint hung a length of rope. She angled toward it and pushed herself into a full sprint. Turning her head she shouted to the others, "Follow my path exactly!"

Just before the drooping tree she turned and made a wide curving path around a dark area on the ground, choked with those bony white reeds. She returned to her original course once the branch with the rope was behind her. Then she came to a stop on a small rise.

The others followed her route with determined precision. Their expressions changed, though, when they realized she'd come to a halt.

Behind, the pack of Juvies poured toward them.

"Last stand?" Marcus asked as he reached her. "Is that your strategy?"

Kait shook her head. "Not exactly." Her gaze remained fixed on the Swarm, almost insect-like in the way they crawled over everything—even one another—to get to their prey.

Just before the tree, they met the same fate Chuzz had.

The first to hit the deep pool just vanished into the reeds as if it had fallen off a cliff, which wasn't far from the truth. Kait heard the splash but didn't see it over the vegetation. It was only when the others followed that splashes of muddy stagnant filth began to spray from the concealed pond. Some of the Juvies seemed to recognize the problem before falling in, only to be bowled over or shoved forward by those behind them.

"I hope they can't swim," Baird said.

Kait allowed herself a satisfied grin. "Let's not stick around to find out."

For an hour they ran, jogged, and waded through the rapidly darkening swamp, with only Kait's memory of the landscape to guide them around the occasional obstacle. By the time the ranch house came into view, they were all bruised, soaked, and exhausted.

At least the Juvies gave up, Kait thought. Sometime after the second water trap their sounds had faded, then vanished altogether. Either they couldn't swim and had all succumbed to the swamp, or the little fuckers were smarter than they seemed and had given up.

"That the place?" Marcus asked. He'd come up beside her, his armor still dripping brown water from the last gully. Somehow he'd managed to keep clean the black skullcap he wore over his head. Clean-ish, anyway.

"Yeah," she said.

"What's it doing in the middle of a swamp?"

Kait raised her voice a little for the benefit of the group. "Used to be a horse ranch, until Windflares emptied a nearby lake, dropping all the water in this lowland. The place never recovered. My uncle knew the owners, traded with them now and then."

"Is this where he got Ugly?" JD asked.

"He was always ugly," Del noted.

"The horse, you idiot."

"Chuzz was his real name, and yeah, this is the place," she said to JD. For a moment she became lost in memories of Oscar. *If only I could have buried him like I did Reyna.* She wondered what had become of him after the Snatcher took him. If one of those Juvies they'd just fought could have been him. Probably gave the thing serious indigestion before the end. Knowing him, probably made the monster a little drunk, too. "The owners left a couple years ago," she continued, "moved south to higher ground. We've been using it ever since as a supply cache and Windflare shelter."

"What sort of supplies?" Marcus asked. "You mentioned comms."

Kait shrugged, glanced down. "Just... you know... stuff we sorta stole from the COG."

To her surprise Marcus laughed. "How much stuff?" There was a flash of admiration in his perpetual glare.

"Let's find out."

She entered first. The house, once grand, felt like an empty shell now. It had been a warm place full of rustic charm and surrounded by picturesque rolling grasslands. All that had gone, though, and the color had bled away, leaving dim gray walls with peeling paint. Dusty floors with patches where thick rugs used to lie. The huge central fireplace was just an ugly black mouth, wind howling somewhere deep inside.

Her shoes crunched on broken glass as she crossed into the great room. The rest followed her in silently, keeping their thoughts to themselves.

"Over here," Kait said, and her voice echoed. She walked to an open doorway at the back corner, leading to a small room full of wood shelving.

"Nice," Del said. "A lifetime supply of dust and cobwebs."

Kait frowned at him. "Not that. Here." She pointed at a discolored square on the floor at the back, three feet to a side, with a recessed handle on one edge. Kait knelt and heaved at the metal pull. "Little help?"

JD stepped up. Together they managed to get the rusty hinges to cooperate, and soon enough the hatch swung upward with a squeal and thudded against the wall in a thick puff of dust. Beneath it was a square of darkness and a wooden ladder of which only the top three rungs were visible.

Leading the way down, Kait felt around for the light switch. By the time she switched it on, Marcus and JD were already on the stone cellar floor, waiting. The single bare bulb cast a wan yellow glow over the area, barely reaching the distant corners.

JD whistled.

Marcus rubbed at his chin, nodding slightly. "This'll do," he said.

Once it had been a wine cellar, but most of the old bottle racks had been pushed to the sides or dismantled altogether, creating a vast empty space. Across this, row after row of semi-organized COG gear had been piled, leaving paths in between for easier access.

Kait walked down one aisle, passing ammo crates and several hard cases labeled with bold warnings of explosives. None of this mattered to her right now. It was at the end of the row that she found what she wanted.

"Rations," Kait said. "Ready to eat."

"Enough for an army," Del said. He and JD were just steps behind her, and when Kait moved aside each grabbed an armful of the COG-labeled packages and headed back for the ladder. Del, she saw, had tucked a dusty old bottle of wine under his arm, too.

She grabbed a protein bar and tore the wrapper away, chewing rapidly and consuming the whole thing in three big bites.

"Over here," Marcus said from somewhere off to her left. "Field comms."

"Ulh gih Ber," she replied through her mouthful.

"Huh?"

Kait swallowed with an effort. "I'll get Baird."

"Nah. Just grab the other handle, we'll move it upstairs where there's some light. And look for power cells, will you?"

Brushing crumbs from her hands, Kait started scanning the aisles. Didn't take long to find a whole pile of the devices. She stuffed a few into pouches at her belt. Only then did it register that she still wore Anya Stroud's armor. Marcus's wife, who died a long time ago. He'd given the armor to Kait in a moment of necessity, as they hunkered down inside his estate while Jinn and her DeeBees shot the place to hell all around them. Over the last few days it had become like a second skin, but standing here now she wondered if it might bother him to see her wearing it. The piece had history, if not serious sentimental value.

Kait looked at Marcus. His back was to her as he wrangled the large comms crate out from under some thermal blankets. All business, all calm professionalism. Would it gnaw at him? Memories dredged up every time he glanced in Kait's direction?

She'd ask about it, Kait decided. Later, when there was no imminent threat. Such a time felt far in the future.

Twenty minutes later the portable comm was set up on the floor in the middle of the great room. While Baird and Sam tinkered with it, Kait sat with Del and JD.

Del picked up an extra mug and poured wine into it from the old bottle. "Try some. It's damn good."

"Should be," Kait said, taking the wine. "Oscar stocked this place." She sipped, aware that Del and JD were watching her. The mention of her uncle had put them on edge. Neither seemed to know what to say, and for her part Kait didn't really want them to say anything. She met their eyes, raised her mug, and drank.

They joined her in the silent toast.

"You're right about the wine," Kait said. "It's very good." After a few more swallows a slight haze settled over her thoughts, pushing away lingering images from last night's dream.

Across the room Cole moved from window to window, constantly scanning the swamp for any sign of the Swarm.

"Do you have to keep pacing like that?" Baird asked without looking away from the comm display. "What are you so worried about?"

"The Cole Train ain't worried, baby," he replied without pausing. "Hoping those little bastards come back for a rematch!" Leaning out of one of the broken windows he shouted, "We're in here, bitches! Come and get some!"

Samantha chuckled. "You really need to get out more, Augustus. So much pent-up energy."

"This is like a vacation for me." The big man sighed. "Hardly ever get outside the walls anymore, you know? I miss it. A little."

The comm made a long series of beeps and pings.

"Here we go," Baird said, holding his hands away from it as if his touch might fry the thing. When the beeping settled down, he leaned back in and tapped away at the controls. Entering an ID code, Kait assumed. Baird shrugged. "Could be a while before the system recognizes my credentials and allocates a bird—"

A crackle of static, then a familiar voice.

"Damon, is that you? Where the hell are you? Report."

It was First Minister Jinn. Kait almost laughed.

Sam *did* laugh. "What the hell, has she been waiting by the console? That's a bit needy, even for her."

Her boyfriend sat back, chin in his hand. "She's probably already got us triangulated," he said, index finger tapping at the corner of his mouth. "Should we talk to her now?"

JD stood. "Better that than when her Command Bot gets here with a fully armed escort. Last time she didn't use words so much as... what was it? Oh yeah. Missiles."

"Agreed." Marcus Fenix nodded. "I'm curious to hear what she has to say for herself." When no one argued otherwise, Baird leaned forward again and picked up the handset. As he did, he activated the video feed, and her face appeared on the screen, looking off to one side.

"First Minister!" he said. "Uh… Lovely to hear from you."

"Cut the bullshit, Damon, and give me a status report." Her voice had a slight nasal quality that made Kait reflexively clench her fists hard enough for her nails to bite into her palms.

Baird glanced at his companions as they gathered around him, then launched into his summary, starting with the events around Tollen Dam. He talked of the creatures they had dubbed the Swarm, that were emerging from the old Locust burial site there. Before he could go into detail, Jinn cut him off. She'd been looking off screen the entire time, but now her gaze finally fixed on Baird.

"Has the threat been neutralized?"

"Not from what we've seen," he replied. "If anything, it's getting worse."

Jinn's mouth tightened and her brow furrowed. She leaned in, squinting.

"Looks like you've got an interesting group with you. Hello again, Fenix."

"Hello—" JD said.

"It's been—" Marcus said at the same time.

They exchanged a silent glance, then Marcus spoke. "Jinn," he said. "It's a goddamn mess out here, and the time you wasted blaming things on the Outsiders and on us didn't exactly help, not to mention what you did to my farm."

It was all Kait could do to suppress her smile. A silence stretched, and Jinn seemed to be looking straight into her eyes—just an illusion of the screen, Kait decided. *Probably.* She waited, tense nonetheless.

"An error in judgment on our part," Jinn replied, forcing a contrite smile, "but understandable given the intelligence we had."

Kait stepped forward. "Understanda—"

A hand on her arm stopped her. Del shook his head, his eyes seeming to say, *"Just wait."* Kait swallowed her anger, something she was getting awfully tired of doing.

"I've already dispatched a large DeeBee force to investigate what happened at Tollen Dam," Jinn said. "In the meantime… I once again request that all of you come to New Ephyra so we can discuss this in person. As is often the case in these situations, lack of communication, of cooperation, has led to operational inefficiencies—"

"You gotta be fucking kidding me," Kait whispered through clenched teeth.

"Relax," JD said. "Relax."

If Jinn heard, she gave no indication, and never stopped talking. "—work together to solve this, whatever 'this' is."

"We just told you what 'this' is," Marcus said.

Jinn raised an eyebrow. "Surely you understand that I cannot base military policy on a single report, no matter how trustworthy the source." She spread her hands. "Look, I'll ask nicely if I must. Please would you all join me here in New Ephyra for a debriefing and consultation."

"A few days ago you were trying to kill us," Kait said. She couldn't help herself.

"Trying to *capture* you," Jinn corrected, "until I had no choice but to escalate matters."

Baird shifted. "Putting lethal weapons into the hands of security robots was a monumentally bad idea, Jinn."

Jinn held up her hands. "We all made mistakes. I admit

it. Perhaps we can put that behind us and focus on the real problem—this 'Swarm'—instead of pointing fingers? I promise immunity while you're here."

"Is she for real?" Kait asked Del.

"Yup."

Kait smirked. "Wow."

Jinn continued with her pitch, but Kait stopped listening. While the others continued to talk, she walked to the window and looked out over the landscape. It took a force of will not to remove the pendant from where it lay concealed under her armor. That last parting gift, given with no explanation.

What the hell did it mean?

Then Kait caught Baird's final words.

"We'll think about it."

"Think quickly, please. Transportation will be arriving before first light."

The link ended, and the screen went dark. There was a moment of silence.

"Well, what do we think?" Baird asked, not addressing anyone in particular.

"I think it smells," Marcus said, "but then this is Jinn we're talking about. Taking her at her word would be a mistake."

Del shook his head. "Even so, we can't leave this Swarm for her to deal with, can we? I mean, that's not an option. Not in my book."

"He's right," JD said. "We have to try. Get her to understand what we're up against here, if nothing else. Assuming she doesn't arrest us the moment we're through the city gate."

Sam gave a small shrug. "Damon and I have learned to work with her. And we have leverage. She relies heavily on DBi. As long as you're with us, I think you'll be okay."

—◇—

"Kait?" JD asked her. "You haven't said anything. What do you want to do?"

She glanced at him, then the others. They were all looking at her, waiting. Kait took a deep breath to gather her thoughts. She wondered what Reyna would do. *Kick Jinn in the face, probably.* Then thank the others for their help, return to the village, and start rebuilding.

But Reyna was gone now. Time to come to grips with that, or at least try.

"I want to make sure what happened to my mother, my entire village, doesn't happen to anyone else. Their deaths should mean something."

Before any of them could respond she nodded toward JD's father. "I agree with Marcus. We can't trust her. And every Outsider bone in my body says going to New Ephyra is moving away from the problem." JD started to reply, but she held up a hand to quiet him. "But you and Del are right, too. She'd make this into an even bigger mess if left to handle it on her own." Now she turned to Baird and Sam. "Jinn can't be trusted, but I feel like you two can. If you say you can force Jinn to keep her word, I believe you."

Cole stepped forward. "So it's settled then. Marcus?"

The veteran glanced at Kait. After a moment he nodded, slowly. "It's settled."

With the impromptu meeting over, everyone turned their attention to getting some sleep, Cole taking first watch. Kait lay in the dark, watching him as he stood silently by the front window. The old house creaked, settled. Wind moaned deep inside the chimney.

She knew what was to come. Fought it as long as she could, but finally her body gave in.

She slept...

...Crusted webbing held her arms and legs, veins coiled around ancient rock pressed into her back. She writhed, tried to cry out. Her mouth would not work, jaw hanging slack, unhinged, blood trickling from her mouth, nose, ears.

Kait heaved against the binding tentacles. No use. No point.

She turned, looked for anything, had to get out, had to run, had to find—

Oscar. He sat a dozen feet away, his back to her. He held a fish in his hands, ran a knife along its length and let the innards spill out. There was a laugh.

She couldn't call to him. He was already gone. The fish fell to the ground, flopped around, whole again but gasping. Not its place. Not its time.

A glow. Warmth on her cheek. Salvation. She turned to it, basked, saw two figures running toward her. Fleeing something hidden in the shadows.

She knew them. Gabe and Reyna.

Father.

Mother.

They ran. Ran to her. Ran at her. Not fleeing. Charging. Taloned hands splayed for—

From somewhere deep inside herself, Kait heard laughter.

Booming, awful laughter.

Kait heard...

KAIT HEARD.

"KAIT!"

2: A DIFFERENT KIND OF HORIZON

"ait!"

She sat bolt upright, breathing hard. "What is it? Snatcher? Juvies?"

"A Raven," JD said. "Our ride." He knelt next to her, holding out a canteen. Kait took it and drank deep, turned, and spat the liquid against the wall.

"What is this?"

"Coffee," he said.

"I beg to differ."

"Didn't say it was good."

She spat the rest of it onto the floor and shoved the canteen back into his hand.

"You okay?" he asked. "Bad dream?"

"No," she said instinctively. "Not... just, never mind. Okay?" She didn't wait for his response. Pushing to her feet, Kait stood and stretched. Sleeping in armor wasn't something she'd done up until a few days ago, and it sucked. The others didn't seem bothered by it, but then they all had a lot more experience.

Finding her way to the kitchen she grabbed a jug of actual water, first washing away the horrid "coffee" taste, then drinking deeply as if she could drown that ugly dream. It didn't work, but it quenched her thirst. Kait pinched the bridge of her nose to will her headache away. Lack of sleep, for the second night in a row. It was going to catch up with her.

Marcus knocked on the door jamb. "You coming?" he asked. He didn't make it sound rhetorical. He was asking, genuinely, if she would stay with them.

"Yeah, I'm coming," she replied. "For now at least." He studied her, and Kait studied him back. "Are you going to tell Jinn about this house? The COG gear?"

He grunted a laugh, shook his head. "Hell no. Outsiders are welcome to it, far as I'm concerned."

Kait nodded. "Thanks."

For two hours the Raven flew.

It seemed as if everyone else thought such transport was normal. They all fell asleep within minutes of lift-off, and for a long time she sat there with her eyes closed and her head pressed back into the wall, pretending to do the same. Pretending this was all normal. Just a little jaunt to the big city for a pow-wow with the First Minister.

No big deal.

A nasty bump of turbulence sent Kait's pulse hammering. Cole and Marcus stirred. The old friends were seated next to each other and began to talk in low voices. Mostly Cole did the talking, and the laughing, but now and then Marcus got a few words in. Once Kait even saw him grin and chuckle at something the other man had said.

Eventually they both drifted off again.

All her life Kait had been with the Outsiders. Born and bred, as they said. Being part of a group, a family, was something she'd always known. She only ever felt alone when she'd go off into the forest to hunt, or to explore the caves behind the windmills. It never occurred to her that she could be part of a group, and feel alone at the same time.

Quietly undoing her harness, she found her footing and walked up to the cockpit, one hand on a strap attached to the ceiling to keep herself steady. It took a few minutes for the pilot to realize she was standing there. The co-pilot picked up on it then, too.

"Something the matter, ma'am?" the pilot asked.

"Nope," Kait said to her. "Can't sleep. Just enjoying the view."

The two women exchanged a glance and the co-pilot shrugged. Kait figured this view was the norm for them. She resisted the urge to ask what the area below was called. A screen on the dash displayed a map, scrolling slowly as the Raven flew, but there were no names on it, just incomprehensible symbols and strings of numbers.

Looking out the windows she had a 180-degree view from here, and really it didn't look that much more impressive than what she'd see after hiking up a mountain with Reyna and Oscar. Endless rolling hills, mountains in the distance, a lake over that way and a forest over there. Somewhere beyond would be deserts, oceans, and more.

The Raven shifted, the tone of the engines rising. The pilot began to murmur into her headset—codified language that was beyond Kait's understanding, save for the most salient fact. They were about to reach the Jacinto Plateau.

"Might want to buckle in," the woman said to her. "We'll be landing soon."

Kait frowned. "Can I stay? I want to see."

"Never been to New Ephyra?"

"Never been to a city."

At that they both turned, looked her up and down, then turned back to their instruments, no further judgment required.

"Suit yourself," the pilot finally said. "But keep a hand on the—"

"I will," Kait replied, cutting her off, already tired of being treated like the ignorant newcomer. She promised herself then and there that she'd take this all in her stride, play it cool, be just like any other soldier—

"Holy shit," she said.

The pilot smirked.

"Holy..." Kait repeated, and then words failed her entirely.

Any of the things they were approaching might have struck her speechless on their own, but all viewed together—all at once—it was overwhelming. She gripped the strap above her tighter and leaned in, willing her brain to focus on one thing at a time.

In the far distance, massive sheer walls of rock rose up to angular mountains, their peaks lost in golden clouds, their valleys lost in deep shadow. Specks of white swirled and spiraled in the air like dust motes in a beam of sunlight. Birds, she realized. Thousands of them, scattering or settling in equal number.

Closest to her vantage point were the ruins. The old city of Ephyra. It stretched across the entire plateau, as thick as the densest forest. All crumbling stone and burned wooden structures, paved roads cratered and strewn with debris. In places the damage from past wars was abundantly obvious. Huge rents in the ground, jagged shards of granite the size of large homes jutting up through buildings, roads, or whatever else happened to be above them when the Locust Horde came up through the ground and savaged this place.

Matching these eruptions of rock were the craters left by dropped bombs or, perhaps, the horrific damage caused by the Hammer of Dawn weapon. Great scorched paths meandered across the landscape, nothing standing in their wake. She glimpsed teams of robots slaving away at the demolition of old ruined structures.

Yet all of this—the majestic granite cliffs and the seemingly endless ruins—paled compared to the new city that had risen up from the ashes. The walls registered first, for she'd seen something like them at Settlement 5. The massive barriers gleamed in the late afternoon sunlight, practically daring enemies to test their strength. They were cliffs in their own right, made by human hand. Or rather, by construction robots built by Damon Baird's DB Industries.

As the aircraft rose to pass over this barricade, she noticed inner walls like spokes of a great wheel, dividing the city into pie-slice sections. They passed over the outer wall, and Kait leaned over to look down. The contrast with the ruins just outside was remarkable. New Ephyra was, in some ways, simply a gigantic version of the settlements she'd been to, which made sense given the automated construction techniques. Still, the scale of it boggled her mind. Buildings by the hundreds, citizens by the *thousands*. The people moved about like ants, strolling on pristine streets or plazas, gathering in squares. Many—rather shockingly many—pushed baby strollers.

There was a terraced garden where elegantly dressed people sat in neat rows watching an entertainment of some kind, quietly admiring the performers. Seconds later a massive arena passed below, where thousands undulated in triumph as bots played

Thrashball before them. Banners streamed for one team color or the other, and the crowd seemed to react to the game as if they comprised a single organism.

"What do you think?" JD asked.

She jumped a little, and wondered how long he'd been standing next to her. Kait tried for an air of indifference.

"Pretty big."

JD chuckled. "You're such a bad liar."

Kait punched his shoulder. "It *is* pretty big, you moron."

"*Huge*, you mean."

"If you insist."

"A lot bigger than Fort Umson, huh?" Her village, he meant. Its historical name. Kait shot him a side eye.

"Somehow I doubt that's a good thing."

The sound of the engine changed, evidence of their imminent arrival. Behind them the others began to stir, and gather their things.

Kait nodded forward. "What's the building in the center?"

JD glanced that way, squinting against the setting sun. "That's Jinn's place." At the swift rise of her eyebrows he went on. "Government offices, I mean. COG central headquarters, among other things. Her home is… actually, I don't know where she lives. Wouldn't surprise me if it was under her desk."

The building dwarfed everything else, domed roofs of blue and gold catching the late-day sunlight, surrounded by white balconies and garden terraces. All roads seemed to lead there, which Kait assumed was some kind of metaphor for power and wealth.

The Raven banked suddenly and turned, skirting the central palace and continuing past it. This side of the city had a grand view of the mountains, and the homes were built higher to take full advantage. With each passing second the mansions grew in size and elegance. It seemed to her that each one strove to outdo the last, and many appeared to be big enough to contain the entirety of the village that had been her home.

The contrast hit her then. The simplicity of her Outsider village, with its functional buildings and meandering dirt paths, everything just close enough together to make it all defensible, but not so close that you couldn't get some privacy. It had grown throughout her life, but always with a mind toward the growth of both the community and the individual. Here it seemed the opposite, as if citizens only hoped to add their own distinctive mark to the place. Perhaps with buildings being so close together, it was a natural reaction to want to find other ways to make them stand apart. It was like a giant, gilded prison.

And there, ahead and below, was the grandest mansion of them all.

"Baird's place," JD said. "We'll be safe there."

Kait thought of the devastation just outside the big wall, and almost called JD out on the truth of his remark, but then she realized he wasn't talking about the Swarm. He was talking about Jinn. They'd spent the last week fighting her as much as the Swarm. Kait herself was an Outsider. An outlaw in the COG's eyes, though the First Minister had turned something of a blind eye to such things—until people started disappearing. The moment that started happening, Jinn assumed only the Outsiders could be responsible, and reacted with a show of force that nearly destroyed Kait's village. The attack had been fought off, but the damage was immense, leaving the place vulnerable to the Swarm.

Despite her "criminal" status, JD and Del had even more to worry about, having abandoned the Coalition in the aftermath of what happened at Settlement 2. By the laws of this government, Jinn had the right to throw all of them in jail for a long, long time. Probably even Marcus. So it definitely wouldn't hurt to be the guests of Damon Baird.

"Not bad, huh?" Baird asked. He'd come up behind them, leaning in between Kait and JD. "A little cramped, but me and Sam somehow manage to get by."

Across the cabin Sam snorted. "So many empty rooms, it's almost like we should fill them."

Baird grinned, shaking his head slightly at the same time. He chose—wisely, Kait thought—not to respond.

"These DeeBees of yours," Kait started.

"They're Jinn's, not mine," he corrected.

"We're not even across the city yet and I think I've seen more of them than actual people."

He nodded, a mixture of both pride and concern on his face. "Jinn's a little obsessed. It started with the dangerous stuff. Policing, defense, that sort of thing. Lately, though, any task with even a small risk of injury seems to be on her list. Construction, maintenance, hell, even Thrashball, though that doesn't take much skill."

"You wanna go, little man?" Cole asked, not asleep after all.

Below, squads of DeeBees patrolled the streets and stood guard at nearly every corner, their Watcher-class brethren floating just above, seeing all.

Baird, ignoring Cole, went on. "The government relies on the bots for just about everything these days. Leaves us human citizens to enjoy our lives, safe from harm or the hardship of any physical effort."

Kait understood the scale of Baird's leverage then. For Jinn to cross him, the supplier of all this labor, would put her plans in jeopardy.

The aircraft cleared the wall of the Baird estate, the ground below giving way to a vast garden. Meandering footpaths flowed around copses of perfectly arranged trees and plants. Kait saw several ponds where fish swam lazily in circles. At the far end of that serene place all the paths converged into a wide, flat lawn, and just beyond that the mansion rose up. Four stories of sand-colored walls lined with white-framed windows and at least a dozen balconies.

"That's weird," Baird said.

"What is?" JD asked.

"Didn't ask for a welcoming party." Baird nodded toward the lawn.

The space that would soon be their landing pad was lined on three sides by mechanical Shepherds, each facing inward, holding Shock Enforcers across their chests. Kait had seen the robots many times in the last few days, and destroyed a good percentage of them. The Shepherd variety were built as peacekeepers, not warriors, and as such didn't have the programming required to deal with an opponent that would fight back.

Still, she couldn't help but feel a knot forming in her gut at the sight of so many of them, and the tone in Baird's voice didn't help, either. Something was wrong.

The Raven settled onto the grass, the whine of its engines immediately receding. Marcus yanked the side door open and frowned at the line of security. There were dozens, all facing them, all in a neat row, all identical save the one in the middle.

Kait had seen this kind of DeeBee before, too.

The robot stepped forward, and the head-sized screen where its face should be lit up with a live image of First Minister Mina Jinn.

"Welcome back, Damon," the woman said through her metallic blue Command Bot.

Baird spread his hands. "What's with the armed greeting? I thought you said 'safe passage.'"

"Precisely," she replied. "They're here to escort you all to my offices." Then she added, "Safely."

"I think we can manage our way there without help." Marcus Fenix folded his arms across his chest.

To Kait's surprise, Jinn nodded, and even bowed slightly, acknowledging the truth of Marcus's words. The machine straightened up and its head turned to take them all in.

"The truth is, I feel it's important that we talk before you have contact with others here in the city," Jinn said. "A lot has happened in the last few days, but news of it has not yet reached New Ephyra. It is my desire to—"

"—to bury it," Marcus finished for her. "Cover it up. Is that it?"

"No," Jinn said patiently. The screen showed her shaking her head. "To make sure we understand what we're facing before the news is released. Whether true or not, tales of a Locust burial site becoming active again after twenty-five years might have a way of spreading and becoming more than tales. Rumors can't be controlled. But rumors *can* cause panic, and panic in an enclosed city like this is not a healthy thing."

Marcus looked to Baird.

Baird looked to Marcus.

JD sighed. "Are we under arrest or not?" he asked.

"Oh, most definitely not," she said, maybe a bit too emphatically. "I merely ask that you refrain from interacting with the general populace before we've had a chance to discuss what happened."

"What's still happening," Marcus corrected.

"Either way, the public should not be informed until we know exactly what we're dealing with. Please, at least give me a few hours. I'm waiting for you here at my office. The Shepherds will, well, shepherd you here."

"We can't even grab a shower first?" Cole asked.

"I'm afraid not."

"Will there be refreshments at least?"

Kait saw the briefest flash of anger cross Jinn's face, but the politician reined it in with practiced speed.

"Of course."

3: BAD MEMORIES

The Shepherds took them through an underground service entrance at the back of the government building. Four elevators waited at the heart of the basement, doors open, DeeBees both inside and out. Kait stood silently as her lift rose up through the palatial structure. In the car with her were Baird and Samantha, who talked in low voices about the mundane issue of which suite of rooms each of their guests would receive once they all returned to the Baird estate.

"Something on the ground floor for me, please," Kait said.

They both glanced at her. Sam nodded.

"Sure thing. Problem with heights?"

Kait almost laughed at that, but managed to hold it in. She, JD, and Del had experienced enough battles and narrow escapes—on ledges, ladders, ropes, and even a giant metal gear—to last a lifetime. She shook her head for Sam's benefit.

The two went back to their discussion.

A few seconds later Baird leaned over to her. "Will, um, you require your own room, or will you be sharing with JD?"

Kait blinked. "Excuse me?"

"Oh!" he leaned away. "I'm sorry. I thought... we weren't sure if..."

Sam elbowed him, hard. "Real smooth."

Baird winced. "How am I supposed to know—"

"A room to myself," Kait said. "Please."

Flustered, Baird held up his hands. "Not a problem."

Mercifully the doors slid open.

Without a doubt the room beyond had been designed to instill a sense of awe, and as much as Kait hated to admit it, the effect worked. She had to be nudged forward by one of the Shepherds before she finally set foot on the gleaming marble floor.

White pillars trimmed with gold and blue lined all four sides of the expansive room. Arches of gold, complete with a sculpted gear motif, sat atop these pillars, holding aloft an open second floor that looked down upon the impressive space. Above that, a huge arched ceiling of glass panels and elegant blue and gold supports rose even higher—at least forty feet above her head, allowing the golden beams of sunset to stream horizontally across the upper portions of the room.

This light caught the very tip of a massive marble statue resting directly across from Kait. The impressive figure held aloft a torch which, being the only part that caught the golden beams, gave it the effect of being lit.

"Continue, citizen," a DeeBee said in its drab, mechanical voice. Kait stepped forward, following Baird and Sam. The rest of her companions emerged from other elevators to either side. Seeming accustomed to this view, they walked without hesitation toward the hallways at the far end, situated to the left and right of the statue.

The room was otherwise empty, and Kait wondered if that was the norm or if it had been cleared before their arrival to ensure there would be no one to hear their discussions. It had to be the latter. *Had* to be. To build a room like this and then keep people out spoke of snobbery on a level Kait found nauseating.

Then an alternative struck her—that in fact the room actually wasn't impressive enough to draw people to it. That there were others that were far more awe-inspiring.

That seemed even worse.

She followed her companions into a hallway. Baird set the pace, which seemed to get faster the farther they marched into the heart of the building. Finally he turned a corner and stopped. Kait came up behind him, on his left. Sam stood to his right.

Two DeeBees stood impassively in the middle of the hallway, blocking access to the door at the far end. The First Minister's office, Kait intuited.

"Step aside," Baird said to the robots, "we're here at Jinn's invitation."

"First Minister Jinn awaits you in the conference room," the robot said. It gestured to its right, toward a pair of double doors. Baird nodded, turned, and pushed through. Sam followed, then Marcus and Cole.

For her own part, though, Kait hesitated just outside, gaze focused on the precipice. A feeling had come to her, in that instant, that entering this room was like a point of no return.

"What's wrong?" JD asked.

"I just… I'm suddenly not sure if I should have come here," she said, more to herself than to him.

— ✥ —

"It'll be fine. We're with Damon Baird, what could possibly go wrong?" He threw in a wide smile for good measure, making light of the situation. The smile quickly faded.

Del put a hand on her shoulder. "What he means is, we're all in this together."

"It's not that," Kait said.

Her friends exchanged a glance, then waited, giving her time.

"I guess I feel guilty about how we left things, back there."

JD raised an eyebrow. "How so?"

"We buried Reyna, but not Oscar," she went on. "Nor the rest of the village. We just left them. I left them."

"Hey hey, whoa," Del said. "None of this is over yet, nothing's been left behind. Look, when the Swarm is defeated we'll go back there, all three of us, and lay the dead to rest. That's a promise."

"Absolutely," JD added.

Kait glanced at each of them, met their eyes, and nodded.

First Minister Jinn sat at the end of a long table of polished stone. It was surrounded by at least twenty high-backed leather chairs. The Coalition of Ordered Governments' emblem had been embroidered on the headrests in golden thread. Kait began to sense a theme.

Jinn had her hands clasped in front of her, resting on a blue folder. A glass of water sat at her elbow. She stood as Baird approached her, reaching out and shaking his hand. It seemed perfunctory.

Even from the far side of the room, Kait could see the swell of her belly. The sight of this stunned her more than the marble and glass chamber through which they had passed, and she couldn't say why. Perhaps because if someone had asked Kait to describe Mina

Jinn in three words, she'd have gone with "cast-iron bitch." The image of a doting, loving mother didn't come to mind. Granted, this perception came entirely from the handful of times Jinn had sent DeeBees to subdue or kill her.

In quick order the First Minister made it through the others, greeting them each in turn. Before Kait could really prepare, she stepped up.

"Mina Jinn," the woman said, hand extended.

Kait shook it. The grip was warm, soft. "Kait Diaz."

"I'm so sorry about your mother," the First Minister said. "I had great respect for her."

The words were delivered with such sincerity that Kait almost believed them. She let the woman's hand go, and managed a small nod. That seemed to be enough, and Jinn moved back to her chair, gesturing for the others to sit.

"I've arranged for dinner to be brought in," she said. "I hope you don't mind."

"Now we're talkin'," Cole responded.

"Can we just get this over with?" Marcus asked. "I've got an entire estate to rebuild."

Jinn stared at the man for a long moment, an expression of genuine regret briefly visible in her features. There was history behind that look, Kait knew. A lot of it. The estate had belonged to Marcus's wife, Anya Stroud, who'd been First Minister before Jinn. In fact, it had been Jinn's fertility program that had allowed Anya and Marcus to have JD. Kait sank back in her chair, feeling out of her depth.

Jinn didn't rise to the comment, though. Instead she sat and opened the folder in front of her, then picked up a silver pen.

"There has been a lot of miscommunication and some…

regrettable misunderstandings... over the last few days," she said once everyone was seated. "I thought we might start with what really happened out there." Her gaze settled on JD, which was all the prompt he needed.

He began the tale at Fort Umson, Kait's village, artfully skipping the part about how he, Del, Kait, and Oscar had raided Settlement 5 and stolen—make that "repurposed"—a fabricator. He spoke of the DeeBee attack on the village, and the accusation by Jinn—via her Command Bot—that the Outsiders had been taking her people.

"It confused the hell out of us," JD said, "until the Swarm attacked later that night. The creatures took everyone."

"Everyone except you three," Jinn noted, somehow making it sound like a simple observation.

"My mom locked us inside the workshop," Kait put in. "We had to watch the whole thing through a goddamned window."

JD nodded. "By the time we got out, everyone was gone. Your missing people, I'm sure, met a similar fate."

The First Minister scribbled a note on her paper, then motioned for JD to continue. He told the rest of it quickly. How they'd found Marcus at the estate, how Jinn's escalation had resulted in the destruction of that serene and beautiful place.

This time Jinn did comment. "Marcus, JD, I want you both to know—"

"Save it," Marcus said.

Jinn went on all the same. "—I deeply regret what happened at Anya's estate. You know how much she meant to me. It was never my intention for events to unfold as they did."

Marcus's jaw moved, biting back words. His gaze went to JD, a slight nod telling his son to go on.

JD spoke of how the group found themselves fighting both

the Swarm and the DeeBees. At that his voice took on a slightly accusing note, which he quickly squelched.

Jinn simply waited, jotting down notes.

JD told of Marcus being taken by a creature they'd dubbed a Snatcher, and later—when they found him alive—the focus shifted from survival to locating Reyna and Oscar, who'd been taken in the same way. Finding Marcus had given everyone hope. They were too late to save Reyna, though, and Oscar was never found, nor were any of the other villagers.

Kait stared at the table, aware that Jinn was watching her. She was determined not to meet the woman's gaze. The conversation turned to the nature of the Swarm.

"They came from a Locust burial site," JD explained.

The amulet Kait now wore around her neck, tucked under her armor, suddenly felt as if it weighed a hundred pounds. She focused on the center of the table, desperately wishing she hadn't come, yet not wanting to show it. She feared questions to which she had no answers.

JD continued. "...some had the same crystal growths. The conclusion seems pretty clear to me."

"Please share it anyway," Jinn prompted, leaning forward.

"The burial sites didn't work," he replied. "They're not dead. They've just... not awoken, but... more like a metamorphosis. Even so, the connection is unmistakable. We saw some that resembled Locust too much to be coincidence."

A brief silence fell over the room, broken by Del.

"That said, there were others, the Juvies for example... I think they were human."

Jinn's eyes narrowed. "*Were* human?"

"Past tense, yeah."

From somewhere far off came the sound of laughter. Kait

glanced up, looked around. No one else seemed bothered by it. The sound grew closer and louder, then vanished altogether. The laugh she'd heard in her dream last night.

The Speaker's laugh.

Kait shivered.

"Is everything alright, Ms. Diaz?" Jinn asked.

Kait forced herself to meet the woman's gaze. "Bad memories," she said. More like hallucinations due to lack of sleep, but it seemed best not to put it that way.

For a long moment Jinn peered at Kait over her glasses. When she spoke next, it was to all of them.

"Well, this is all extremely interesting. Distressing, even. I feel I should tell you that, before you made contact earlier today, I'd already sent out several fully armed squads of DeeBees to gather intelligence from both the Tollen Dam burial site as well as the village at Fort Umson." She spread her hands. "Since we hadn't yet spoken, this had nothing to do with your account, or my belief in it. I simply needed to know what was going on over there, and hopefully locate you, as well."

Damon Baird sat directly across from her. He folded his arms across his chest and looked at the ceiling.

Jinn raised an eyebrow at him. "You appear to have something to add, Damon," she said. "Go ahead."

"Oh, it's no big deal," he replied, sarcasm clear in his words. "I just want to know one thing. Just a teensy tiny little insignificant thing. What... the *fuck*... do you think you're doing?"

"Excuse me?"

"You know what I'm talking about."

"I'm afraid I don't—"

Baird slammed a fist on the table. "Arming my DeeBees. *Lethally,*

I mean. Sure, they've always been armed, but not like this. Lethality, Jinn. That's what I'm talking about. What the *hell* possessed you to do that? You know their programming isn't capable of handling it."

Jinn shrugged. "First of all, *Damon*, you weren't here to provide your 'contractually obligated' consultation on the matter. So I did what I had to do. Secondly, they're not *your* DeeBees, they're mine. This government's, bought and paid for. We can do with them as we please."

"Oh no. No, no, no. Bring in the lawyers if you like, but the contract between DBi and 'this government' specifically states that only non-lethal combat equipment will be built into the D-series subframe—"

"To prevent such equipment from being used against COG citizens," she asserted. "I did not deploy them against Coalition citizens."

"Uh, hello?" Del said. "Seemed that way to me, when they were shooting at my ass."

JD leaned forward. "I can confirm that. My ass was also shot at."

Kait didn't take the cue to pile on. It was all she could do to suppress her smile.

Jinn looked down her nose at the two soldiers.

"So now you're part of the citizenry again?" she said. "Or are you trying to have it both ways? Outsiders *and* Coalition citizens?"

"Whoa, hey," JD said, one palm out. "We never officially, I mean, after Settlement 2 we just—"

"Can we cut the bullshit?" Marcus Fenix asked.

The whole room went quiet.

The soldier—no, the legend—pointed at Jinn.

"You put lethal weapons in the hands of a bunch of walking circuit boards with less brains than your average rock worm," he said.

"That was wrong." Then he pointed at Baird. "You sold them to her. Also wrong."

His finger aimed at JD and Del next.

"You two went AWOL. That was stupid. So was joining up in the first place, but we've been down that minefield already." Finally he shoved a thumb at himself. "Me? I got involved. Wrong and stupid. So here we all are. Now unless I missed something, the goddamn finger-pointing is taken care of. Let's either get on with solving the problem, or go our separate ways."

No one said a word.

It was Jinn who finally broke the silence. "You've all been through a lot, clearly." She stood, pushing her chair back and resting one arm across the swell of her abdomen. "Perhaps bringing you straight here was a mistake. I suggest that we reconvene tomorrow. By then we'll have sorted out the glitches in the DeeBee comms streams, I'll have the reconnaissance data from Tollen Dam and Fort Umson. As Marcus suggests, we can focus on the issues that are facing us, rather than the past." She looked from person to person. "We all want that, I think. Is it acceptable?"

Nods around the table.

Cole raised a hand.

"Does that mean dinner's off?" He waited, expecting a laugh and receiving none. "Damn, y'all really do need a shower and a night's rest. Work the sticks out of your—"

"Thank you, Augustus," Jinn said. "My apologies about dinner."

"Not a problem," he replied. "The Cole Train would rather be at home anyway."

The First Minister's mouth twisted into a frown. "About that. I'd appreciate it if you would keep the details of this situation to yourself until—"

"Yeah, yeah," Cole said. "I get it."

"And the rest of you," Jinn added. "It would be best if you restricted yourselves to the Baird estate until we meet next. Damon, is that alright with you?"

"Don't ask me, ask Sam," he replied.

Sam snorted. "Since when do I have a say?"

"Since about twelve seconds after you moved in."

Sam shook her head, smiling, then turned to Jinn. "They're welcome to stay with us, but we're not prison wardens."

"No one's a prisoner," Jinn replied, perhaps a little too quickly. "I just can't have rumors about this Swarm spreading uncontrolled. Fear is the enemy of a city like this. The stress is… a hindrance to our goals." The woman's hand cradled the child within her body, and Kait couldn't help but wonder if it wasn't her own stress levels rather than those of the citizenry that most concerned First Minister Jinn.

Marcus stood, then. Everyone else followed his lead, muttering their goodbyes and filing toward the door.

"James, Delmont, would you two mind joining me in my office?" Jinn asked. The pair exchanged a glance.

"Sure," JD said. "No problem." He turned to Kait then and added for her ears only, "Catch up with you later."

"Yeah," she said. "Sure thing. Good luck in there."

Kait followed the others out. She had to force herself not to look back. She'd been with JD and Del constantly since they'd joined her village. To be separated from them now felt strange, and she wondered if the choice was deliberate on Jinn's part.

Probably not.

That's what she told herself, at least, as she headed for the elevator.

4: BYGONES

Del followed Jinn through the double doors into her circular office, then stopped and turned to JD. He lowered his voice. "I've got a bad feeling about this. Being separated from the others, I mean."

JD pulled up next to him, eyes still on Jinn. The First Minister had taken a seat at her desk, and was reviewing some papers before her. JD said, "Seems pretty clear she wants to talk about things that don't concern the others. Which means only one thing: Settlement 2."

"That's what I'm saying. We have things to answer for, we both know that, but no one has our back now."

"Hey," JD said. He met Del's gaze. "This isn't their battle to fight. We back each other up, like we always have. We've done nothing wrong."

"Uh, desertion? That's a crime, right?"

"Okay, okay, technically we did something wrong. But morally? We did the right thing."

"I don't think Jinn will see it that way."

"That's on her, then," JD replied, and clapped him on the shoulder. "C'mon. Let's get this over with. We knew there'd be consequences. It's time to face them." He moved toward the desk, and took one of the two chairs that sat on their side of it.

Del hesitated, still not sure what to think. He took his seat all the same, and waited.

Jinn seemed wholly absorbed in the papers that sat in front her. Her head bowed, pen scribbling furiously, she acted as if they weren't in the room.

"So…" JD started.

Pausing, Jinn held up a finger, then went back to signing. Finally, she set the pen down. Lifting the paperwork from the gleaming wood surface, she took a sheet in each hand, then with some ceremony laid one each in front of them.

"Full pardons," Jinn said, "and reinstatement of rank." She placed pens next to the pages, one for each of them. "All you have to do is sign, and you're back in."

JD folded his arms. "Full pardon for what?"

Make her say it, Del thought, *that's good.*

To his surprise, though, Jinn said, "For nothing." A pleased smile graced her stern features.

"Nothing," Del repeated, skeptical. He glanced at JD, but his friend's gaze remained locked on the First Minister.

She said, "Nothing officially. Your record will be clear. This"— she gestured toward the papers—"will be sealed, marked secret, and forgotten entirely."

Del picked up the page, buying time. This wasn't what he'd expected, not by a long shot. Scanned it. "And what will our records say we've been doing for the last few months?"

Jinn smiled at that. "Gathering intelligence." She sat back, looking pleased with her cleverness. "Outsider movements and behavior, that sort of thing."

"What's the catch?" JD asked. "We didn't ask for this. I'm not even sure we want it. Not to speak for both of us," he added, half turning toward his companion.

"Nah man, you said exactly what I was thinking," Del said. "I mean, there's gotta be a catch."

"Definitely," JD agreed. "So what is it?" he asked Jinn.

She looked from one to the other, and seemed to be choosing her words. A light rain began to patter on the broad windows behind her, quickly obscuring the city lights as the drizzle became a downpour.

"No catch," Jinn said finally, "other than the obvious. You'll be back in, get another shot, and I promise you there won't be another document like that"—her eyes dipped toward the papers in front of them—"ever again. This is a one-time offer."

"Back in... doing what?" Del asked. "Cleaning latrines?"

Jinn spread her hands, palms up. "Hardly. I couldn't exactly justify such treatment of two decorated soldiers, especially ones with clean records. No, what I had in mind is something for which you're uniquely suited." Before Del could ask, she added, "Tollen Dam."

"Tollen Dam," JD repeated.

Jinn frowned. "What happened there—this 'Swarm'—is an unknown. That doesn't sit well with me. For your first assignment, I thought perhaps you could take a team of scientists and engineers—plus a full squad of DeeBees, of course—and try to find out what caused this new behavior."

"Right idea," Del said. He sat back, the exhaustion of the last few days catching up to him. "Wrong approach."

Jinn raised an eyebrow.

"What he means," JD put in, "is that understanding Tollen Dam is fine, you should definitely send a team there. The larger issue is whether or not this is an isolated incident."

"We've had no reports of activity elsewhere."

"None?" Del asked.

"Well, fine, an Outsider was reported missing at a village near another burial site, and we've had some communication glitches at the prep-camp for Settlement 6, but these things happen all the time, Lieutenant."

"I'm not a lieutenant. Not 'til I sign that paper."

"Fair enough," Jinn conceded. "The point is, we've had no reports of this Swarm beyond what your group encountered. That may change in..." Her eyes flicked to a clock on the wall. "...an hour or so when the recon teams arrive on-site."

JD cleared his throat. "That's not the point. We shouldn't wait for another village to be attacked, or a new settlement to go dark. You should be sending teams to the other burial sites immediately, before things get out of hand."

Jinn steepled her fingers, staring at the young man for several seconds before she began to nod.

"There are a lot of burial sites, James. To deploy to all of them would be noticed. Rumors would spread, and panic would follow. Not just here, but all across Sera. All for what may amount to be an isolated event." She peered at him, waiting for a response.

"A few of them, then," he replied, "the ones closest to Tollen Dam."

"Even then, our resources would be spread very thin."

JD shrugged. "Your resources are machines. Make more."

At first she didn't respond. For a time, nothing could be heard but the ticking of the clock on the wall, and the rain against the window.

"It's not as simple as that," Jinn said. "As you all pointed out earlier, the DeeBees aren't equipped for military action. Correcting that is *my* first priority. If you're not going to Tollen Dam, then perhaps you can work with Mr. Baird on a plan to upgrade the programming of his robots. For the safety of the citizens of this city, first and foremost, I need the capability to convert our police force into a military one should the situation ever demand it, quickly and with nothing more than a simple command."

"And the Swarm?" Del pressed. "We're going to, what, rely on wishful thinking?"

Jinn shook her head. "DeeBee suppression squads will be deployed. I'm confident they can keep this contained until we have a better understanding of exactly what is going on out there. In the meantime, sign those papers. For now you'll be my direct liaisons with DB Industries."

"Very convenient," Del said, "seeing as we're guests at his place."

"Isn't it though?" Her gaze swung from JD to Del and back as she waited. The silence stretched.

"Uh," Del said, "can we think about it? Give us a day."

Jinn's mouth formed into a thin smile as she shook her head. "I'll need an answer now, I'm afraid."

"At least give us a couple minutes," JD said.

The First Minister hesitated for only a second before she stood, turned, and walked from the room, closing the door softly behind her.

Del turned to face his friend. "I don't know about this, man."

"Seems pretty clear-cut to me."

"How do you figure?"

JD picked up the paper. "Jinn's not going to say it so plainly, but it's the COG or the brig, isn't it?"

"I thought we had immunity here."

"That was a promise. This is a contract. Look, dotted lines and everything."

"Only for us, though," Del said. "What about the others?"

JD paused, choosing his words or maybe just thinking things through. He said, "They're adults. They'll get their minute with Jinn, make their own decisions."

"That's not what I'm saying." Del pointed at the door. "What's Kait going to think if we do this? If we rejoin the organization she's spent her life fighting, hiding from, running from? Hell, man, what's Marcus going to think?"

"I don't need my dad's permission."

Del sighed. "That's not what I meant."

"It kind of is."

"A bit. Sorry. I shouldn't have gone there."

JD took a deep breath, let it out slowly. "Kait will understand. This isn't about us running around waving the COG flag in her face. This is about… it's about doing our part. A path that actually leads to defeating this enemy, and making sure what happened at Fort Umson doesn't happen anywhere else. You, me, and Kait, alone? We can't do that. We couldn't even save Reyna, or Oscar. With or without my dad's help. We certainly can't do anything if we're in the brig, either. But with Jinn's resources, who knows? As Outsiders we'll just rot in jail. As Gears? We might have a chance."

"All Jinn cares about is protecting this city, and letting the people here live in blissful ignorance. She has no idea how to tackle something like the Swarm."

"That's *exactly* what I mean" JD replied. "If we're here, helping, maybe we can guide her. Keep her in check, at least. This is us we're talking about, Del. We're still going to do things our way."

Del thought about that. He saw the truth in it, but it still made his stomach roil.

"Kait's going to be pissed," he said, after a long silence.

"We'll get her to understand," JD replied, a little too confidently, but that didn't make him wrong.

"And your dad?"

At that JD's features hardened. "I'll handle him," he said in a way that left no room for argument. His gaze slid toward the pen.

Worn down by his friend's conviction, and seeing no real alternative, Del picked up his pen. JD did the same.

They signed the papers.

Del put down his pen and sighed. "You get to explain this to Kait."

JD grinned. "We could rock-paper-scissors for it."

"Oh, no. Hell, no."

A child cries. The sound is far away, then close, then far again. Always behind her, no matter which way she turns or how fast.

No, it's the whimpers of a small animal. Isn't it?

Kait calls out. She thrashes, tries to twist her body. Every movement is dulled, slowed. She looks down. Her legs are hidden up to her knees in some kind of mud.

A mud that writhes.

A mud that stares back at her with a million tiny unblinking eyes.

She punches at the muck, then howls in frustration. It has her hands, now. Holds them strong. The ocean of tiny eyes pulls her down. Her elbows submerge. Her shoulders. The eye-filled tar is only inches from her face.

Kait Diaz, jaw clenched in absolute terror, stares into those eyes.

They're the eyes of her mother. They fill her view, a hundred at least. And now here, this close to her, every one of them blinks in unison. A single, terrible blink.

All the while, somewhere near, somewhere far, a child cries.

5: THE GILDED CAGE

Kait flew out of bed, half conscious, mind roiling with visions of blinking eyes and that dreadful sound. Her tank top was damp with sweat, the wood floor like ice under her bare feet.

"Baird's place. I'm at Baird's place."

In the semi-darkness she searched for a light, but found none. She did find the drapes, though, and yanked them aside.

Pale moonlight slid into her room. From the window she had a view of half the city, and much of the rear lawns and paths of the Baird estate, most of which now lay hidden in darkness. Silhouettes of trees, the occasional foot light along some path or another.

The city itself seemed dead asleep, though from here she could not see its roads. Most of the buildings were dark and bereft of activity, that much was clear.

Kait checked the time. Still four hours until dawn, and she was simultaneously wide awake and dead tired. Moving to the bathroom, she splashed ice-cold water on her face and studied herself in the mirror. She tried hard not to look into her own eyes, fearing they'd match what she'd seen in her dream. Instead she looked at the dark bags under them, and the pallor of her skin.

For a moment she debated finding a doctor who could provide her with something to help her sleep. In the end, though, she decided the problem was that she wasn't exhausted *enough*. She needed a long walk under an open sky, surrounded by trees and the sounds of nocturnal creatures. The kind of walk where her feet felt as if they were going to fall off at the end. Hell, right now she'd settle for fresh air, if there was any to be found in a city this size…

The night before a DeeBee had arrived with its arms full of clothes, on loan from Sam, and after selecting something comfortable to sleep in Kait had told the machine to put the rest in the dresser. She rummaged through the items now, pulling out the darkest and most rugged and practical she could find. Black sweater, dark green pants, and black socks.

At her door she stopped, noticing herself in a mirror that hung on the wall. In her haste to dress the amulet had come untucked from her top. She grasped it and considered burying it in the depths of one of the dresser drawers, or perhaps even somewhere in the back of Baird's property, but couldn't bring herself to get rid of it. Not yet. Stuffing it back under her top, she tried to ignore the cold metal against her skin.

Opening the door she stepped through and stood in the dark hallway for a long moment, listening. All was quiet, though the mansion was so big that there could be a raging party going on at the other end and it would just be a whisper here. No light crept out from under any of the other doors.

She made her way to the back of the building and outside, past the chair-lined patio with its immaculate fountains, into the garden. The night air was cool, but not cold.

Mowed grass crunched under her feet. Rather than following the footpath where small pools of light might alert someone to her presence, she made a direct line for the wall. Soon enough she found herself in the trees, clambering through them easily in the darkness. This was a landscaped place, and Kait had navigated true wilderness at night many times in her life. Not so much as a leaf was disturbed.

The wall, though, posed a different problem. From above as they'd flown over it, the height and surface had appeared easily climbable. But now, standing at the base, she realized she'd had the scale all wrong. It was at least twenty feet to the top, and not ivy-covered as she'd assumed, but instead coated with some kind of slick moss. Aesthetically the same, but unlike leaves and vines, this offered no grip at all.

There was a part of her that wondered why such security was needed in such an evidently happy and peaceful city. Both her mother and Oscar had spoken often of the ill-effects of too many people living close to one another, and though she'd never had cause to doubt their words, she'd never really spent much time thinking about the reasons behind it, either.

For the moment, though, she kept that part of her mind firmly in the background. Her focus was on finding a gate, and the search didn't take long. It was in the very center of the rear expanse, and judging by the tracks in the dirt it was used primarily for delivery vehicles. Off to one side there was a low building with three windows in the wall that she faced, perhaps a hundred yards away, and the tracks led there. A mansion so big it needed its own warehouse. This impressed her for a moment—long enough to notice a light in one of the windows of the outbuilding. She could see no movement inside, though, and decided there was no one who might see her leave.

The gate boasted a biometric lock, and much to her surprise it began to creak open the instant she laid her hand on it.

"Too easy," she whispered, but she accepted the gift all the same. The city awaited her. A short tunnel ran through the wall. Kait stepped through and out onto cobblestones, still damp from the earlier rain.

One step, that was all she managed.

One step and she was surrounded by DeeBees. The closest held up a hand.

"No one is permitted to leave the premises without authorization."

Kait wondered what the robot would do if she argued that both options constituted detainment, and thus the choice was pointless. Before she could say anything, however, they began to close in, giving her no choice but to step back into the tunnel.

The DeeBee planted its feet. "No one is permitted to leave the—"

"Okay, *okay*," Kait spat.

Back inside the wall, she stood idle as the gate slowly worked its way closed. The *clang* it made at the end of this process only helped to solidify her feeling of imprisonment.

She stood for a time, debating other ways out. A rope maybe, or scale that warehouse and use the height of its roof to reach the top of the wall. Might work. Might make a lot of noise, too, and if someone was in there...

Uttering a frustrated sigh, she glanced around and decided to walk the gardens for a while. After only a half-circuit that led her back to the house, though, she gave up. Her plan to exhaust herself physically might well have worked, but at least walking out in the city she could let her mind be consumed by all the sights and smells. Here, in the garden, she was alone with her thoughts, and just now that wasn't a great place to be.

"Especially if I'm going to get rid of these fucking nightmares," she muttered.

"Nightmares?"

Kait froze. She'd become lost in thought and had allowed her senses to dull in the safety of the estate. It took her a second to realize it was a voice she knew.

"What are you doing up?" she asked Marcus Fenix.

He sat in one of the patio chairs on the edge of the lawn— one of the few almost completely hidden in shadow. Kait caught the hint of a small glass in his hand, amber liquid swirling inside. A bottle sat on the table beside him and on the ground, at his left, lay a bundle that looked all too familiar.

"Heard you leave," he said, gesturing toward the wall beyond the garden. "I was curious how far you'd get. Drink?" he asked.

Kait shrugged and took the chair beside him.

The veteran poured, then handed her a glass. He made no toast, though. Just set the bottle down and sipped, his dark gaze on the shadowy gardens.

She took a sip. "JD and Del back yet?" she asked, feeling the warmth of the liquor spread down her throat and into her stomach.

"No," he said, an edge to his voice that surprised her.

"Do you think Jinn went back on her word? Arrested them?"

"It's possible, but I doubt it. Mina Jinn is a lot of things, but she's not dumb. She starts breaking promises like that she's going to have bigger problems than the Swarm on her hands."

Kait absorbed that. "You're probably right. It's just… they've been gone a while."

"You worried?"

Kait shrugged. "Someone's got to keep those two out of trouble."

Marcus grunted, settled deeper in his seat. "It wouldn't surprise me if they were sitting in some waiting room, wondering when she'll summon them. Jinn's like that. Head games are her specialty."

There was some history there, Kait knew, but JD hadn't told her much. Jinn had been Anya Stroud's protégé, back when Marcus's wife was First Minister.

The thought reminded her of something. "Can I ask you a question?"

Marcus studied her over the glass. "Fire away."

"It's about Anya's armor. The armor you loaned me."

"Not a loan," he said, "a gift. That answer your question?"

"Yeah. Well, sort of. I wasn't sure if it was awkward for you, to see someone else—"

"We've got a visitor," Marcus said.

"Huh?"

He nodded in the direction of the trees.

Kait glanced that way and saw a man moving toward them in the darkness. The hairs on her arms began to rise. Someone else had been in the garden?

"Evening, Baird," Marcus said.

"Evening yourselves." Damon Baird spread his arms as he crossed the last twenty feet of grass. "What are you doing out here?"

Kait swallowed, unsure what to say.

"Having a drink," Marcus replied. "Join us?"

"Actually," Baird said, "I was coming to wake you." After a second he added, "Kait, specifically."

"What for?" Kait asked, surprised.

"Something you need to see." She couldn't read his expression in the shadows. "Come with me. You too, Marcus. It's starting soon." He turned again and walked briskly away.

"What is?" Kait asked, but Baird was out of earshot already.

Marcus stood. "Guess we'd better go find out."

6: SECRET DOORS

Baird led them through the garden to the low outbuilding. Kait realized that "warehouse" had been too generous, but it was no barn, either. Entry required use of an actual key—the physical kind—which Baird produced from a pocket inside his coat.

With a *click* the door opened and he stepped through to a dimly lit space. Inside were long empty hallways lined by what might once have been stables for animals, but now served as storage. There were haphazardly stacked paintings, crates of beverages in untidy piles, and countless cobwebs.

Their path took them past all this and on to a wooden stairwell near the back corner. At the foot of it, Baird stopped and inserted his key again, only this time into a keyhole barely visible on a wood beam beside him. A deep grinding sound came from within the wall, and then a creak. The stairs, as one, began to rotate, until the upward slope had become a downward one.

"I'm starting to get the feeling you've got too much money," Marcus said.

Baird ignored him. "This way."

"No shit," Marcus replied. He followed his friend down the steps, and Kait came last.

The space below was nearly pitch black, illuminated only by tiny colored lights, many of which blinked in random patterns. Most were of a pale green, though a few here and there were amber or blue. When they reached the tiled floor at the bottom, Baird flipped a switch on the wall and the stairs rotated back up to their original position.

He flipped more switches, and ceiling lights began to wink on all over the basement room, creating pools every ten feet or so. They stood in a chamber roughly square in shape and surrounded on all sides by screens and other bits of electronic gear. Some of it was neatly mounted in rack enclosures. Other components were piled in corners, powered off and forgotten.

The wall toward which Baird now walked featured a bank of screens—six by Kait's count—all mounted and angled to face a large chair that sat in front of them. On a table between were several keyboards and interface devices. Baird slid into the chair in a motion so smooth Kait guessed he'd done it a thousand times. More, probably. The monitors before him bloomed to life with news programs and highlights of that evening's Thrashball game.

"Welcome back, Damon," a soothing voice said over the room's speakers.

"Evening, IRIS. Can you bring up the feeds we discussed earlier? The recon deployment?"

"Of course," the voice replied. "Just a moment."

"This is new," Marcus said under his breath. "When did you teach the AI to talk?"

Baird turned, pleased with himself. "A recent upgrade. Still working out the kinks."

Soon the images began to flip, one by one, to a series of camera feeds. Some were first-person views, and from the graphs and icons surrounding the images it was immediately clear the signals were coming directly from a squad of DeeBees. Two of the screens, though, were taken from an overhead angle, probably from Watchers hovering above the robots. The landscape around them looked familiar.

"What are we looking at?" Marcus asked.

"My village," Kait said breathlessly. "How... when...?"

"This is live," Baird replied. "Right now. Jinn's recon squad just landed. Figured you might want to watch."

Marcus leaned in. "Didn't seem like you and Jinn were on the best terms. She lets you watch all this?"

"Oh *yeah*," Baird replied. "It's all perfectly legit, hence the secret entrance inside my garden shed." He tapped some more keys and the audio portion of the feed began to pipe in through speakers Kait couldn't see. "Of *course* she doesn't know about it," Baird went on, sans sarcasm. "But that's one of the perks of manufacturing her things. Gave myself a secret back door to all their feeds."

Marcus snorted. He seemed impressed, but not surprised. "Hold on, did you just refer to this building as a shed?"

Baird waved him off. "Quiet now, it's starting. Kait, you want the seat?"

"I'm fine," she replied, the only words she could manage. From the moment the village had appeared, her gaze had not left the displays.

On them she saw the ruins of the place where she'd grown up, a place where she'd learned and loved. Carnage spread across six different screens as the robots began to move through the smashed outer wall. Their cameras panned across charred debris, toppled carts, and the bodies of both DeeBees and creatures alike.

"R-11, zoom in on marked entity," a voice said through the speaker. Some controller in the Coalition command and control center, she guessed. One of the DeeBees, with an "R-11" visible in the upper right corner of its display, turned and focused on a lump on the ground. A thin illuminated square appeared around it. The robot walked closer, knelt, and turned the bundle of gore over.

Kait held her breath.

It was a Juvie, half of its face blown off.

She swallowed and then exhaled. Dread began to course through her at the realization of what was to come. The DeeBees were marching toward the central building, the one she herself had sealed before the battle began. Wheeled that giant door into place and told the kids not to worry. The door held, too. She could see it on the display even now, a hundred feet away, still exactly where she'd left it.

The rest of the building had been shredded like paper, though. There were holes big enough to ride a horse through, and total darkness lay beyond.

"Don't go in there," Kait whispered.

Marcus put a hand on her shoulder.

"Sure you want to watch this?"

The children. She could hear the false words as they'd left her lying mouth. *"You'll be safe in there,"* she'd said, and hugged the boy, William. He'd feared the Coalition was coming to take them all away, but it was the Swarm who'd torn through this place and snatched them up. The Swarm who'd taken them into their lairs and turned them into Juvies and who-knew-what-else.

"Kait?" Marcus asked.

She nodded, forcing herself to keep control of the emotions that roiled in her gut and stung the corners of her eyes. Marcus's hand slid away from her shoulder. He turned back to the screens.

"R-19," the controller's voice said. "Pan right. Stop. Investigate."

On another screen R-19's view swiveled and bobbed. It moved without hesitation toward a scorched area by the steps leading up to the great hall, where another creature of the Swarm lay sprawled. Large ridges ran up its back, and it boasted a thick tail with claw-like quills. A Pouncer, from the look of it, though this one seemed smaller than those Kait had faced.

Something else about the image was wrong. Kait squinted, then saw it. Smoke. Little tendrils curling up from the charred ground and burned areas of the creature's flesh.

"That's a fresh kill," she said.

"So it is," Baird agreed.

"Hmm," was all Marcus added.

All at once the screen went fuzzy, as if viewed through shifting fabric. The images blurred beyond recognition, and a buzz of static streamed out of the speakers.

Baird sat up, concerned. "IRIS, what's wrong with our link? It was working fine before."

"What's the problem?" Marcus asked him. "Your secret tap not so stable?"

A second later, IRIS responded. "The interference is in the source footage. Cause: unknown. I will attempt to improve the quality."

"Hold off on that," Baird replied. "I'd rather see what Jinn is seeing." He turned toward Marcus and Kait. "In the meeting, remember? Jinn said that they'd encountered a problem in the Dee-Bee comms streams. Some kind of interference. I'm not entirely sure she meant to reveal that, but there it is. I think this is what she was talking about."

"What's causing it?" Kait asked.

"Not sure yet. It's localized—see? Not all of the streams are affected to the same degree." His fingers thrummed on the keyboard. A DeeBee spoke, the words lost as its voice warped momentarily.

"Hmm." It was Marcus, who'd stepped closer to the screen and leaned in. "I've heard something like that before."

"Oh?" Baird asked. "Don't keep me in suspense."

"It was when Jinn's DeeBee-avatar, whatever you call it, was stabbed by one of the Swarm. Glitched out just like this. Voice went all weird."

"I remember that," Kait said. "She—it—even grabbed JD by the neck, just before it broke down." The memory made her shudder, despite having forgotten all about it until now.

Quietly, Baird said, "Huh. Interesting."

The controller for the recon squad seemed not to have noticed the freshness of the kill. He calmly instructed R-19 to scan the subject creature, and then went back to addressing the other components of the team.

"They're missing what's right under their noses," Kait said. When they both looked at her, she went on. "Something is killing Swarm. In my village. Right now."

Marcus looked at the screens anew, scratching at the stubble on his cheek in a way that reminded her of Oscar.

"There," a voice on the radio said. A new voice, yet one Kait recognized. It was the First Minister. "Focus on that. What is that?"

The controller responded to her query, guiding several DeeBees to track and zoom in on the great hall. Three of the monitors showed the huge door, now only connected to the main structure by a few planks of torn-up wood. In the shadows, to one side, something moved.

Kait gripped the back of Baird's chair, squinting at the display. The blurriness abated, then came back even stronger. Wave-patterns of black and white dots sprayed across multiple screens, bringing a new loud hiss to the speakers. But despite all that, Kait still saw something in the shadow. Something small and white. Oval in shape. Then, beside it, another. Identical, or close to it.

"Looking for us, dumbbells?!" a voice shouted from far off.

"Who said that?" Baird asked at the same moment Jinn voiced the same question through the speaker.

"Kait?" Marcus said. "Recognize the voice?"

She shook her head. "The signal's too corrupted. Sounded... sounded like a kid, to me." She'd heard the term "dumbbell" used among village children when they played pretend raids against COG depots, wielding slingshots as their weapons, hurling rocks at buckets full of old metal scraps that represented the enemy.

These were no buckets, though. The DeeBees all moved toward the source of the taunt, their focus tight and, Kait noted, utterly robotic. Were she in such a situation, with a party of raiders, they'd be behind cover and scanning the nearby rooftops before even sparing a glance at the person who'd spoken. These bots, though, worked on a simplistic set of rules.

"THIS AREA IS DESIGNATED HAZARDOUS! ALL CITIZENS WILL BE EVACUATED TO SAFETY!" one of them stated. As a single organism the squad of robots marched up the steps toward the meeting hall, displaying limited tactical prowess as they scanned the flanks and spread out upon approaching the main door and mangled front wall.

"EVACUATION IS MANDATORY!" the center DeeBee said. Their

weapons were trained on the shadows where the two faces had briefly appeared.

Two faces, Kait thought. *Same shape. Adolescent voice.*

"Oh," she said under her breath. "Oh no. Baird, shut them down. Shut the DeeBees down."

"Impossible," he replied.

IRIS's voice filled the room. "Technically a command override is entirely possible—"

"That's enough, IRIS." Baird turned to Kait. "Anything other than passive access would be noticed, immediately. I... no, we would lose our ability to keep an eye on what Jinn is doing. If she realized there was a back door, she'd close it for good."

"I don't care!" she said. "It doesn't matter! There are two children in there who don't understand what they're up against. Your goddamn machines are going to slaughter them."

He glanced back at her. "They're not my machines anymore, Kait. Jinn pulls the strings now."

"How convenient for you."

His face softened. "I didn't mean—"

"Enough," Marcus said. "Something's happening." On the screen, one of the machines moved up to the door, standing with its back to the barrier, gun at the ready. Standard breach-and-enter pose.

"No," Kait whispered.

"Proceed," Mina Jinn ordered.

The DeeBees rushed in.

A sound too sharp for the speakers to handle blasted the basement room from which they watched. All at once, the screens went white. Blinding white. Then yellow, and ringing, and...

Chaos.

Three of the screens went dark, save for a "no signal" label in the lower center. The other three were *wrong*. One showed wood flooring at a close-up angle, sparks spitting across the surface. Another lay sideways, flame and smoke visible only inches away. The third was spinning wildly. Rolling or bouncing, across the floor of the meeting hall. The head of a DeeBee, Kait realized, severed from the body.

"What the hell?" Kait scanned the displays, baffled.

The rolling footage slowed, then stopped as the DeeBee's head finally came to rest. It showed the wood beams of the ceiling, illuminated by the dancing light of a half-dozen small fires just out of view. The visual was surprisingly sharp again.

Two faces suddenly peered in from the edges of the screen, one right, one left. They moved in unison, oddly as robotic as the destroyed machine they were studying. But these were human faces. Youthful. Twelve or thirteen years old.

Children Kait knew. Twins, in fact.

"Kait?" Marcus said. The third time he'd said it, she suddenly realized. "Do you know them?"

"Eli," she replied. "Eli and Mackenzie." She covered her mouth with her hand and closed her eyes, the events of the attack flooding back in with total clarity. She'd been about to seal in the children, the meeting hall to be their bunker, when one of the kids asked her about Eli and Mackenzie. The twins had been off at South Village, on one of their frequent trading runs. Safe from the COG, safe from the Swarm. It had never occurred to her they might return.

"I know them well," she said.

The two kids smiled down at the severed DeeBee head. Again in unison, they looked up at one another, on the verge of laughing.

"Nice one," Eli said.

"Thanks!" His sister, Mackenzie, smiled brightly.

The picture began to darken at the edges, and static sprayed across the screen in quick bursts. Together the kids squinted at their vanquished foe, heads tilting to one side as they watched it slowly power down. Eli knelt closer. He grinned, almost playfully, and waved at the robot's camera eye.

"Didn't get us all, First Minister," he said, "but you keep trying."

The image vanished.

Static erupted from the speakers. Just before the link severed, in that wash of random noise, Kait thought she heard two words. Faint, distorted so badly she couldn't make out what was said, or who said it. The voice was deeper, though, and carried a menace. A chill ran up her spine. It had sounded a bit like the Speaker that had attacked her mother.

"Looks like there were survivors after all," Marcus said, looking at Kait. She swallowed. For a time she could do nothing but stare at the screens, all of which had gone blank.

"They were at South Village when the attack happened. I never expected... I didn't think they'd be dumb enough to come back, not after the Swarm..."

"Might be they didn't know about it," Baird suggested. "Though I'd bet they do now, given the corpses in front of the hall."

"Agreed. Fresh kills," Marcus added, "but from before Jinn's recent, uh, emissaries landed. Kids or not, they seem to know how to handle themselves."

Sound returned to the speakers. Or maybe it had been there and Kait had just tuned it out. She barely listened as Jinn and her control team sought first to regain control of their destroyed squad, and then as Jinn barked orders for another, larger force to be readied for deployment.

"Now what?" Kait asked.

Baird raised one finger, pointing at the ceiling, indicating the speakers. Jinn was still talking. "Under no circumstances will the children be targeted or treated as criminals," she commanded. "They are to be returned, *safely*, to New Ephyra."

The audio feed ended.

"Close the connection, IRIS," Baird said.

"At once, Damon."

Baird stood and gave Kait a long, compassionate look. "Get some rest, both of you. When the extraction squad arrives on-site, I'll come get you. It's going to be twelve hours at least, maybe even a day."

"What difference does it make, if you won't intervene?" Kait asked—too harshly, but there was no stopping the words. Baird only nodded, though.

"Maybe I can, given some time to prepare. If it looks like a malfunction, we just might get away with it." He locked eyes with her. "I'll look into it. Working until dawn has become something of a habit lately, much to Sam's annoyance."

"I'll stay, too," Kait said instantly.

Baird studied her. "No offense, Kait, but you look ready to pass out."

"I can't just—"

"He's right," Marcus said. "All you've been through? I'm amazed you're even on your feet, Kait. Get some rest."

"Is that an order?" she asked.

Marcus's customary glare was unfazed. "It's a suggestion from a friend, and one you should take."

7: A PARTING OF WAYS

Kait switched on the small lamp next to her bed and stared blankly at the mattress, the soft pillows and thick blankets, tempted by the rest they offered. But in the far back of her mind a single thought darted around, in and out like an angry hornet. The thought of what she would see if sleep found her. The dark places her dreams would take her, if the last two nights were indicators.

The walk hadn't helped. Too brief. And whatever small solace the drink with Marcus might have won her was banished by what she'd seen on those monitors in Baird's secret lab.

An idea struck her and she made her way to the bathroom. The space was larger than the home she'd grown up in. Marble and shining metal from floor to ceiling. Kait rummaged through the cabinets below the sink, finding no shortage of scented soaps and basic necessities, but nothing that might push her brain into a dreamless eight hours of oblivion.

So she turned the shower on instead. As the water warmed,

Kait stared at her reflection in the mirror, uselessly rubbing at the dark patches under her bloodshot eyes.

Along the wall beside the sink was a narrow table with a stack of neatly folded towels to one side. The other half had been empty before, but now her own clothing waited there, cleaned and neatly folded. No sign of the dust, the dirt, the blood, that had caked it before. Kait pulled off the borrowed sweater and pants she'd donned earlier, showered, then dressed in her own clothing.

Some minutes later she lay in the darkness atop the blankets, hands clasped behind her head in lieu of the too-soft pillows. She stared at the ceiling where the shadows of trees danced. Sleep refused to come, held back no doubt by what she feared waited for her there.

After an hour she gave up. Kait wrapped the blanket around her shoulders and went out onto her balcony. She stood at the low wall and watched the lights of the city and the clouds drifting by the mountains. Somewhere out there, Eli and Mackenzie were probably sleeping in the ruins of Fort Umson, wondering what had happened to the village, and why the COG had sent murderous robots after them, never mind the monsters prowling around. It wasn't right. Bleary and tired as she was, Kait could see now that sending more DeeBees would not help their situation.

A sound caught her attention. It came from her left, and when she glanced over she saw the light had come on in JD's room. Back from his private meeting with Jinn, it seemed.

Glad of the distraction, Kait threw the blanket back on the bed and went out into the hall. It was quiet, illuminated only by moonlight coming in through windows at either end and the slim line of yellow glow seeping out from under JD's door.

Kait knocked, quietly, then a bit louder. Footsteps inside.

When the door swung open, she stepped back, a little embarrassed.

"What are you doing up?" JD had a towel around his shoulders and used it to dab the last of the shaving cream from his jaw.

"Couldn't…" She let the words go, unwilling to admit her trouble sleeping. "Still kind of hungry," she lied. "I was going to find the kitchen and saw your light on. Grab a bite?"

He hesitated. "Yeah. Sure, what the hell. Meet you down there."

The huge home was even more of a maze in the darkness, but after only a few wrong turns Kait finally found the kitchen. She raided the pantry, piling anything that looked good onto a polished silver platter. Bread, dried meats, cheeses. The closest thing to Outsider fare she could find.

By the time she emerged, JD had arrived with Del in tow. One was filling glasses with wine, the other turning on the fake fireplace on the far wall. They all met in the middle, where a long wooden table sat between two equally long benches.

Kait sat first, JD taking a place beside her and Del moving to the opposite side of the table.

"Had no idea how hungry I was," Del said, tearing into a roll before he'd settled onto the bench.

JD spoke through a mouthful of his own. "Same. Good call, Kait."

Kait waited, watching them. For several seconds neither looked up from their plates as they shoveled food like starving children.

Then she caught it. The furtive glance as Del looked across to JD, a glance JD studiously ignored.

"Alright," Kait said, a little amused. "You guys are acting weird. What's going on? How'd it go with Jinn?"

"Wasn't what I expected," Del replied.

"What were you expecting?"

"Oh, you know, formal charges."

JD grunted a laugh. "More shouting at the very least."

— 80 —

"Well, what did she say?" Kait asked.

Neither man spoke. Del was looking to JD, while JD chewed a mouthful of bread with deliberate slowness. Finally he swallowed and said, with a small lift of his shoulders, "Full pardon. Clean slate."

Kait waited for the other shoe to drop, but JD kept eating, avoiding both of their gazes. She set her own food down and turned on the bench to face him. "...and?"

One elbow propped on the table, JD held his hand out before him and made a space between thumb and forefinger, small enough that a piece of paper would barely fit between. "There was one little tiny caveat."

"Is tiny the right word?" Del asked. "I think there's a better choice. Oh yeah. Huge. Huge caveat."

"Well, I don't know about huge."

Kait kicked JD's shin, hard. "I'm running low on patience, guys. Out with it."

Still JD hesitated, and that little pause made her gut tighten.

He said, "The full pardon comes with a reinstatement of rank."

"Ah," she said. "I see. Well..." her words faltered when she saw the way Del was staring at JD. Kait raised an eyebrow at them. "You're not seriously considering this, are you?"

The glare Del had leveled on JD grew even more intense, and she finally understood. The knot in her stomach twisted, transforming from a thing of concern to one of anger. Kait turned herself fully on the bench, straddling it, squaring up on the man beside her. She took a hard look at his profile. The tousled brown hair, the square Fenix jawline, the way his eyes were downcast and decidedly not looking at her, or Del for that matter.

"So," she said, drawing out the word, "you already took the deal.

What do I call you now? Is it Lieutenant, or did this come with a promotion, too?"

"It was a take it or leave it kind of thing." He'd started to turn toward her, then thought better of it and spoke to the table.

"Yeah, it's the part where you took it that I'm having a little trouble with."

Del said, "It wasn't really a choice at all, Kait. We'd be in a deep dark cell right now if we'd refused."

"And I'd break you loveable goofs out, with help from Marcus probably, and on the way out the door we'd burn that monstrous building to the ground."

Now JD did turn to her. "And go where?"

"Home," Kait said.

"Dad's estate is a ruin."

"I meant the village. Fort Umson. But it's interesting to hear what you consider home." That wasn't fair, and she regretted the words the moment they left her mouth.

JD winced. "Sorry. I… didn't mean that."

"What did you mean?"

He gave an exasperated shake of his head. "Just that neither place is… Del, help me out here."

"I could get you a shovel."

JD bit back a reply to his old friend and turned once again to Kait. "Listen, we can't just leave. It was different when there were Outsiders to join with, but now we'd just be three fugitives."

"When there *were* Outsiders to join. Past tense."

"You know what I mean."

Del decided to help after all. "Kait, if we leave, or if we're in jail for that matter, Jinn's going to take on the Swarm in her own way. How do you think that will go? At least this way we have a chance to guide her. Keep her honest."

"Know what she's up to at the very least," JD added.

She thought of Baird's shed, his secret access. "Baird is capable of handling that."

To that, Del gestured to the chandelier, the silver utensils. "I think his priorities are a bit different than ours."

"Even so," Kait replied, "what you two seem to be ignoring is that it's a double-edged sword. You keep an eye on Jinn, she keeps a leash on you. You keep Jinn honest, she keeps you exactly where she needs you to be."

"Doesn't have to be that way," JD replied.

A silence stretched, and Kait let it go on, because she knew they both were aware that she was right. That it did have to be that way. But neither man seemed willing to admit it, so she let it go, because something else was on her mind now.

"Where do I fit into all this?"

This seemed to catch them off guard.

"We," Del started, then took another second to consider the words. "We didn't discuss that. Whoa, before you get mad, we didn't discuss it because we wanted to talk to you first."

JD nodded. "I mean, nothing really changes, Kait. The goal is the same. Stop the Swarm."

"But now, instead of the DeeBees trying to kill us, they're on our side," Del said.

Kait looked at him, skeptical. "You say that like it's some kind of bonus."

"Okay, maybe not yet, but if we can work with Baird, improve the robots' decision making—"

He went on, but Kait had stopped listening. Truth was, she understood them. Agreed with them, even. There was no taking on the Swarm without the COG. JD and Del had made the right call, no matter how much it felt like a betrayal of the friendship the three of them had built over the last several months.

But they didn't know what she'd seen on that monitor in Baird's secret room. Didn't know that there was something more important at Fort Umson than simple nostalgia or the prospect of hiding from what was going on in the world.

And in that instant Kait knew with absolute certainty that leaving the fate of those two teens in the hands of yet another squad of robots was the wrong thing to do.

The feeling of being trapped between two choices fell on her like a physical force. What JD and Del had done was the right thing for them, but not the right thing for her. And so she couldn't bring herself to tell them about the twins, because she feared they'd stick by her side. For her they would go AWOL again, despite knowing Mina Jinn would not forgive another desertion. There would be no third chance.

The anger in her gut twisted for the last time, into something worse. Regret, possibly even loss. Yet she knew there was no other way.

Abruptly, Kait stood. Del was still speaking of plans to improve the DeeBees, but he stopped now, and waited. They both did, watching her.

"I need rest," she said simply, lamely. "I need to think."

The relief that passed between JD and Del was palpable.

"Yeah," Del said. "Of course."

"We'll talk in the morning," JD said.

Kait moved away from the table, nodding. "Sure," she said. "Sorry guys, I just… goodnight."

Del gave her a small wave, and as she left the room she could feel them watching her go.

By the time she'd reached her room, a plan had formed in Kait's mind.

She killed the lights, sat on the edge of her bed, and waited. She thought of the twins, her villagev, and Reyna. Anything but the conversation she'd just had with her friends. That would only lead to second-guessing herself, a frame of mind she had no use for just now.

It took them a while to return from the kitchen. Soft footsteps in the hall, some muttered words she couldn't make out, then finally the dull thuds as JD and Del returned to their rooms. Kait waited another half an hour, listening to nothing but the birds outside, the soft and distant creaks that any home makes, no matter how big.

Now or never, she thought.

Despite having just eaten, she used the terminal there to order breakfast to be brought to her room. The DeeBee on the other end didn't question the hour, nor the full pot of coffee for one person.

While she waited she packed her few belongings and donned the armor borrowed from Marcus Fenix. Her boots she left beside the door for now.

The food arrived in due course. She ignored all of it except the coffee, which she guzzled. The hour ticked past 3 a.m.

She wrapped the food in napkins and stuffed it into her small backpack. She filled her canteen from the sink.

Carrying her boots, Kait slipped from the room and found her way through the darkness of the halls to the back patio. She sat on the edge of a lawn chair to lace her combat boots, cringing at their smell. Unlike everything else, these still bore the dirt and grime of battle. At least she'd been able to shower, she thought, as she marched back through the garden and up to Baird's "shed."

Without the key, she could only rap on the door and wave at the camera mounted on the wall above it.

Nothing happened.

She tried again, wondering if he'd gone to bed after all. Five minutes passed before she heard the lock disengage and the handle turn. Baird poked his head out.

"You're supposed to be sleeping."

"Change of plans," she said.

He arched an eyebrow, noticed she wore her armor, then let her inside.

"There's no news yet," he told her as they walked back toward his secret observation room. "Jinn's still organizing a response, and I'm testing some code that might—"

"I'm not here about that," she said. "Not exactly."

"Oh? Then what?"

"Can you help me get out of the city?"

Damon Baird studied her for a long moment. "Maybe we should talk about this." She followed him through the building, down the rotating stairs, and back into his secret control room.

"Can you do it?" she said. "Sneak me out?"

"I'm not sure that's a good idea, Kait."

"Of course it's not," she replied, "but I have to do it. I have to get there before more DeeBees do. Those kids"—she pointed at the monitors—"are all that's left of my home. They're scared and alone, surrounded, and I'm supposed to sit here in the luxury of your beautiful but grossly excessive home while Jinn handles it?"

"I'm not sure 'grossly excessive' is—"

"It is, and you know it."

He held her gaze for a second, then sighed. "I do. You're right, Kait. It sure is nice, though, isn't it?"

"Not debating that. It's just not for me. Not when those kids are back there, in danger, hunted by the Swarm and harassed by... your machines."

"Robots, actually. And they're Jinn's."

"Let's not go there again."

Baird nodded. He slumped into a chair and twisted back and forth in it, thinking. "Okay, look. If you're hoping for some secret tunnel under the city, I can't help you."

Kait waited, sensing he wasn't done.

"Buuuutt... What I can do is screw around with the patrols a little bit. Yeah. Maybe a poorly timed rolling upgrade that just happens to reboot their surveillance routines the moment you happen to be passing." He wheeled the chair back to the terminals, talking to himself now more than her. Once he got going, Baird was like a force of nature. His hands flew across the controls, and the screens around him twitched and scrolled with activity.

"...disable logging and backup data... no, too obvious. But a link outage due to trunking, ahhh yes, you goddamn genius, that could explain..."

Kait stood by for a while, then sat, and even somehow managed to doze off. The nap did little to refresh her, but at least remained too shallow for dreams. An hour passed, perhaps more, before Samantha finally shook her awake. When she'd come in, or from where, Kait had no idea. Sam met her bleary gaze.

"It's time," she said. "You're sure about this?"

"I'm sure," Kait replied.

"Then here's what you need to do," Baird said from over her shoulder, "and you've gotta do it *exactly* as I say..."

8: DAYBREAK

The cold stones of Baird's estate wall pressed hard into her legs. Outside the gate, two DeeBees stood as still as statues, their backs to her and weapons held at the ready. A Watcher hovered above, the blue-gray bundle of engines and cameras occasionally moving off to the left, then back across to the right along a programmed route that seemed to trigger at random intervals.

For five minutes she'd stood there, watching them, waiting for the "go" signal. *"The gates opening, that's your cue,"* Baird had said. Sam had added, *"Once you start you don't stop, got it? Constant speed—as best you can, at least. Otherwise, well… you'll be on your own."*

Her parting reply had been a simple "thank you," and it felt horribly insufficient now. Standing here, on the precipice of striking out on her own, she couldn't shake all the thoughts in her head telling her *no, this is wrong, go back.* She was leaving on bad terms with basically everyone. The argument with JD and Del, and with her talk with Marcus about Anya's armor being interrupted. Cole she barely knew, but somehow felt sure she'd miss. And Baird and Sam, well, no bad blood on that front, but they'd no doubt face questions about how Kait had managed to sneak away. It might even lead Jinn to discovering the back door Baird had built into the system.

There was Jinn and the COG to think about, too. If she wasn't on their list of criminals before, surely this would—

Three things happened all at once.

The Watcher dropped like a stone to the ground.

The two DeeBees went slack, chins resting on their chests, emitting a single mechanical word.

"MAINTENANCE."

Then with a dull *clunk* the gate swung open.

Constant speed, Sam had said. Kait shoved her doubts aside— she had no choice, really—and pushed out into the pre-dawn darkness of the street. Quickly turning left she walked, calmly but swiftly, to the first intersection. Around the corner she heard the heavy metallic footfalls of a DeeBee patrol. *Constant speed*, she reminded herself, and made the turn just as they went slack, muttering "MAINTENANCE" as their heads dipped and their arms went still at their sides.

Kait walked right through the group, eyes forward and feet moving in a kind of rhythm now. She turned down an alley and into shadow just as the bots behind her hummed back to life. The timing of it set her even more on edge. There really wasn't any room for error here. It was all she could do not to break into a run.

Constant speed, constant speed.

The alley stretched a hundred feet or so, ending at a wall barely waist-high. Kait had been warned of the drop-off on the other side, but it still took a mental effort not to let the action affect her pace. She put one hand on the low barrier and swung her legs over, dropping ten feet to a small, perfectly manicured lawn. Playground equipment stood between her and the next street. Kait ducked under a row of metal bars, trying to will the sting out of her feet. The landing on the grass had been harder than she'd expected, and only now did she realize it must be an artificial surface.

Continuing on, Kait passed more slumped DeeBees, strode under Watchers that became preoccupied with other things the instant she got close, and even happened upon a whole herd of the small, spherical Trackers. A sudden and terrifying sight, the rolling robots thundered down a sidewalk as she emerged from between two buildings, only to disperse like frightened insects before she could even gasp.

Kait crossed the road and spared a glance back, just in time to see the machines roll back into formation as if nothing had happened.

On and on she went, and just when she'd begun to see the sky turning the amber hues of dawn out east, she came to the outer wall of New Ephyra. Turning left, she followed the surface for another few minutes before finding the maintenance door right where Baird said it would be. When she was two steps away from it she heard the *click* as its lock disengaged. She gave it a tug, and it came smoothly open. Kait stepped inside, and the instant the door shut she heard the sound of a Watcher buzzing past.

She paused there to catch her breath, but couldn't afford any more than that. The path Baird had given her wasn't quite done yet. Keenly aware that she'd interrupted her pace, Kait jogged through the dark hallways of the barricade wall's interior until she felt she'd made up for lost time. Thirty feet ahead lay another maintenance hatch, this one leading outside the city.

It had only just come into view when Kait heard the lock disengage.

"Shit," she whispered, breaking into a sprint. *"Four seconds,"* Baird had said, that was how long he could keep a door like this unlocked before it would look suspicious. *More* suspicious, anyway. She'd flubbed the timing, back when she took her breather, and could practically hear the clock counting down as she raced for the door.

Halfway there, she knew that she wouldn't make it. Her heavy pack, her exhaustion from three straight nights without decent sleep, and a half-hour of sneaking through the city made her boots suddenly feel heavy as iron.

She began to consider how she might make it back to Baird's house when the door pushed inward. An almost imperceptible change, but the light spilling in left no doubt. When the lock re-engaged, the bolt slid into thin air rather than into the catch on the frame.

Picking up speed, Kait ran on, reaching the door within seconds. She swung it open, and seeing nothing but the murky ruins of the old city beyond, stepped through.

The door thudded closed behind her.

She was out. She'd made it.

"Not bad," a familiar voice said. "Hope you don't mind the assist."

Kait turned to see Marcus Fenix standing there.

She opened her mouth to reply, then closed it. His appearance finally sank in. He had his armor on, and a Lancer slung on his back.

"I'd ask how you knew I'd be here," Kait said, "but the answer's obvious."

"It's not what you think," he said. "Not exactly."

"What, you're here to take me in?" Kait shot him a look. "Then why—"

"I'm coming with you."

The words hung in the air.

Kait said nothing.

"Also, there's been a change of plans," he continued. "Baird had no way to let you know. So I volunteered. I'm an old hand at that."

"What sort of change?" Kait asked.

"Tell you on the way. Right now we need to move. If we don't get through the ruins before daybreak, the Pickers will harass us until sundown."

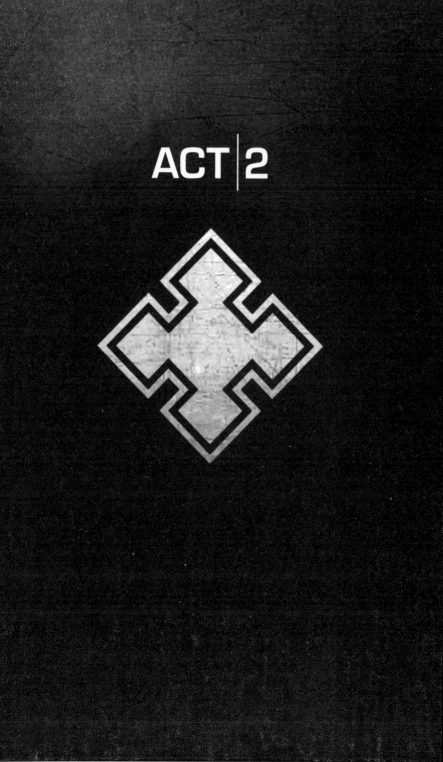

ACT|2

1: BEYOND THE RUINS

He didn't give her time to ask who or what the Pickers were. Once out of the shadow of New Ephyra's wall, Marcus readied his weapon and began to jog toward the north. He kept low, and seemed to choose his path with one part of his brain while the other kept scanning left, right, and forward.

His route favored the shadows. Kait ducked under a half-fallen column and leapt over a copper planter. The walls of the old buildings—those left standing anyway—were black with rot and lined with cracks. But they weren't the worst of it. It was the ground itself that defied belief.

In places the earth and rock had been pushed upward forty feet or more, lifting whatever happened to be above it with ease. Entire buildings lay at sickening angles. Sidewalks and streets alike suddenly became steep ramps that ended in jagged wounds.

They reached a section where the early morning sky was entirely blocked from sight by rubble, fallen together and forming a ruined canopy. All of it was halfway to being reclaimed by nature. Vines and moss were everywhere. Mushrooms the size of Kait's head poked out of the shells of burned-out cars. She couldn't help but imagine being there, three decades ago, when the battle had taken place. The scale of it, as glimpsed on the flight in, had made what had happened in her village seem almost trivial in comparison.

Up close, though, it filled her with a surprising calm.

To see the aftermath of such an attack writ so large, to know that even with all the resources of a capital city a true recovery would take a very long time indeed, the anxiety and guilt she felt at leaving her own village began to crumble away. This place was proof that setting things right was too big a task for one person to handle, and though her mother might have tried, Kait felt a surge of self-confidence concerning her own path.

Rescue those kids, get them somewhere safe.

Small steps, but important ones.

Ahead in the gloom, Marcus approached an arched passageway that led off into shadow. Suddenly he whirled and pressed his back to a wall. Barely ten steps behind, Kait slowed. She had no cover, and couldn't recall if anything behind her would do, so she accelerated to a sprint, aiming for a spot on the wall across from him.

When she was halfway there, someone emerged from the shadow. At first glance she mistook the person for a Juvie, so pale and scrawny, but the figure wore ragged clothes. Shaggy, matted hair that must have gone uncut for years obscured its face. The man—a Picker, no doubt—ran at her with arms stretched, a rusty knife clutched in one fist.

As he crossed under the archway Marcus stepped in, thrusting the butt of his Lancer into the side of the man's head. The scrawny figure let out a single, pathetic yelp before crumpling to one side. Yet Marcus wasted no time. He ducked under the archway and jogged on as if nothing had happened. This time Kait ran to catch up, doing her best to keep beside him.

"Descendants of the Stranded," Marcus said.

"I've heard the term," Kait said, frowning.

"The whole area around Ephyra was devastated by the Hammer of Dawn during the counterattack against the Locust Horde. The Stranded were the ones who couldn't find shelter in time."

Kait took in the ruins once more, chilled by this new perspective.

"Despite what happened, some people still made their way here," Marcus continued. "Whether for safety or to exact vengeance on Prescott for what he did to the planet, doesn't really matter. Some of them had found the limits of their sanity by the time they reached the city, and still manage to scrape out a life here, picking through the ruins to survive."

He reached a fallen beam, lifted it for her, and she ducked under it. Once on the other side, she held it up so he could come through.

"Why doesn't Jinn bring them inside, get them treatment? I thought rebuilding the population was her primary concern."

"I'm sure that's on a list of priorities somewhere," he said wryly. "Probably even has a planning committee." Then Kait understood why Marcus hadn't just shot the man. In fact, thinking back, she realized he'd barely hit him at all. Just enough to daze him and clear the path.

"They mostly keep to themselves," he said, as if reading her thoughts, "but if they get a whiff that something worth scavenging might be out here, they'll come, and in force. I've got no desire to kill them. They don't deserve it."

Kait nodded, and swallowed hard.

"Not much farther now, anyway," the veteran said.

They took a hard left, then a right, and for the first time in ten minutes Kait could see the sky above them through the jumbled rooftops and cleft walls. Dawn had arrived, and against the gray sky above she saw a Raven thunder overhead, going in the same direction they were.

Marcus slowed his pace. "Follow my lead."

"You know," she said, "I wouldn't mind some idea what we're doing out here before I follow any more orders."

Marcus turned to her, his squinting glare as unnerving as ever. She held her ground. Stared right back.

"We don't have time for this." The man's jaw clenched.

Kait folded her arms.

"Alright, alright." He pointed toward a wall ahead. "Beyond that is a COG airfield. You want to get to Fort Umson in time to save those kids? This is your best shot, but we've gotta go now. Baird's made some... arrangements."

"An airfield?" Kait looked in the direction he'd pointed. "Out in this mess?"

"Nowhere else around here would do," he responded. "You'll see what I mean. Now move it—we've gotta run." He didn't wait for her to agree. Scaling the brick wall in front of them, he dropped over the other side, disappearing from sight.

Kait took a glance back toward the ruins, and saw the shadows of several Pickers following at a distance. Beyond them the massive wall of New Ephyra gleamed in the early morning sun, and farther still, the buildings of the city rose. She saw the capital, and thought the windows of Mina Jinn's offices were visible if she squinted just right. She wondered if the woman was in there now, watching them.

Kait raised a hand and made a rude gesture, and then was up and over the wall.

Two things came immediately to mind as she landed hard in the dirt. First, there were a whole lot of DeeBees here.

Second, Marcus had been right about the airfield, and it only took her an instant to understand the choice of location.

The ground here was even, a massive section of the plateau that had survived relatively unscathed by the upheaval of years gone by. Not *wholly* unscathed, however, for though this place wasn't the broken undulating ruin she'd just passed through, it was tilted, as if a whole section of the Jacinto Plateau had cracked free and dipped to one side. The end result was a stretch of land about a quarter-mile wide and a mile long, at a ten-degree slope. At the far end, the land just fell away in a chasm, or something close to it.

Along this massive ramp a runway had been built. Hangars with COG emblems on the sides lined the higher ground here. They'd been constructed on stilts to give them level surfaces inside.

DeeBees were everywhere. Patrolling, hauling gear. A whole platoon of the robots was gathering at the "top" of the runway, lining up in neat rows. Farther away a new hangar buzzed with construction efforts. Several variants of Damon Baird's towering machines lifted twenty-foot-long steel beams into place as if they were twigs.

From the nearest of these buildings came the growing whine of a Condor's four massive engines. The ground itself seemed to vibrate. Marcus was waiting just ahead, crouched and pressed against the back wall of the Condor's hangar. With the growing sound of its engines, though, he began to move toward the corner. Kait rushed ahead to join him, struggling to find her footing on the steeply sloped ground. Reaching the building's corner, she stood behind him and peered past his shoulder.

"Not yet," he said under his breath.

As Kait watched, the Condor eased its way out of the hangar, its nose just coming into view. The roar of the engines became almost deafening as the aircraft wheeled out onto the runway. It taxied and turned until it rested at the highest point, aimed straight down the long incline. There it lowered its rear cargo ramp, and the platoon of DeeBees waiting a hundred yards away moved forward as a single unit, marching in perfect step up and into the belly of the huge vehicle.

"Wait…" Marcus said.

The ramp began to lift. Three feet off the ground, it stopped. In that instant, all around the airfield, the bustle and activity went dead still. Kait heard only the continued drone of the Condor's engines, but nothing more.

"*Now,*" Marcus said, and ran. He made no effort to hide himself, and Kait followed his example. Their path took them straight to the back of the aircraft. Marcus jumped onto the ramp, rolling as he hit the metal surface. He came up on one knee and turned around, facing toward her.

Just then the airfield started to come back to life. The ramp did, too. There was a hydraulic whir just audible under the thunderous engines, and both the platform and Marcus began to move upward. Kait pumped her legs and fists, moving at a full sprint, the best she could manage after three nights with almost no sleep. It wasn't going to be enough. The ramp was over her head already, and still climbing. Kait gritted her teeth, took two long strides, then leapt for it. Reaching out, eyes on the ramp, aware of Marcus inside. He was disappearing behind the rising platform, and for some reason turned away.

She was going to miss it.

Her stomach clenched, her body sensing the fall that was about to come. Then something smacked against her fingers and

Kait grabbed on for dear life. It was the very edge of the ramp, still rising. She barely had it, and already could feel her grip failing.

"Marcus!" she called out, not caring how loud her voice was now. No reply came. It was all she could do to hold on. The ramp continued to move upward. The ground raced by at a blur, ten feet below her now, the distance growing.

She could drop. It would hurt like hell, but it beat—

All at once the airstrip ended.

Kait stared at an abyss. The cliff dropped hundreds of feet into darkness. Reflexively she made a scramble upward, and it only served to loosen her grip even more. She swung her legs up and tried to push off the bottom of the closing door, but to no avail. The muscles in her hands were screaming.

This is it, she thought. She felt a jerk between her shoulders, but it was fleeting. Only the tips of her fingers had the ramp, and it was three feet from closing on her. Even if she could pull herself up, by the time she managed it the door would sever her fingertips. The wind roared all around, buffeting her clothes, pushing her like a leaf in a Windflare.

Kait winced, felt the tears in the corners of her eyes...

...and let go.

She didn't fall.

Instead she hung, suspended and flapping in the roiling air, as the ramp clanged shut. She looked up. Above her was a strip of sturdy cloth, wide as her hand, and it appeared to be connected somehow to the armor she wore.

There was a dull *clang*, and then the ramp started to lower again. Within seconds she felt hands at her shoulders, and Marcus was pulling her inside. Kait tried to help push herself over the edge, but her fingers were numb and refused to cooperate. Her arms weren't in much better shape, every muscle angry with her. So she let him pull, and flopped like a fish onto the metal surface.

Marcus staggered to a control panel on the wall and reversed the ramp's direction. After what seemed like an hour, but was probably less than a minute, the cargo door closed again and they were left in comparative silence.

Pushing herself up to a kneeling position, Kait tried to rub pain from her shoulder where she'd impacted the floor. Her fingers were still numb.

In front of her, a whole platoon of DeeBee Shepherds hung from brackets mounted to the ceiling. They faced forward, heads bowed. Beyond them were a handful of the smaller, spherical Tracker models.

She felt Marcus's fingers tug at her elbow. When she looked at him, he raised a finger to his lips, tilted his head, and moved toward their right. Kait followed. At the wall, Marcus motioned toward two seats folded against the hull. He pulled one down for himself, then strapped in.

"Sorry about that," he said in a hushed voice. "The door was going to close before I could get you in. Had to find something for you to hold onto so I could get to the controls."

Strapping herself in next to him, Kait reached over her head and unhooked a length of fabric. All that had separated her from falling to her death had been a four-inch-wide cargo strap with a yellow S-shaped hook on one end. Marcus had reached over the nearly closed ramp, and despite being unable to see her had somehow slid the hook around the one thing strong enough to hold her in that wind: Anya's armor.

Kait let out a long breath. "No need to apologize," she said when her nerves settled a little. "Thought I was done for." Outside, the sound of the engines grew louder. Seconds later they banked hard. The engines were screaming as the Condor powered upward to clear the mountains. It was all Kait could do to sit there and ride out the turbulent vibrations and spine-jarring course corrections.

The DeeBees didn't care. They hung eerily from the ceiling in perfect columns, reminding her of slabs of meat in a slaughterhouse. Their bodies swayed with the movement of the plane.

"Baird says they'll be like this the whole way," Marcus explained, shouting to be heard over the engines.

"Are they turned off?" she asked.

"Sleeping. His word."

"And when we arrive? What then?"

"They'll be folded up by then, in drop configuration and effectively blind. If we wait here until they're gone, we'll have nothing to worry about."

Kait would have preferred to be on the ground before these walking calculators, but the plan made sense.

"Thanks, Marcus," she said.

"Don't mention it." His words sounded automatic, as if she'd just thanked him for passing the butter, but they weren't dismissive. Kait sat, eyes forward, rubbing her hands together to force feeling back into her fingertips. Eventually the plane leveled out and the engines took on an even, almost soothing note.

After a while she glanced at her companion. He'd fallen asleep, his head lolling with the subtle shifts as the aircraft flew through minor turbulence. The DeeBees swayed on their hooks.

Kait stood and stretched. On the wall opposite her were some equipment lockers. Not wanting to face sleep—not yet, anyway—she crossed through the rows of robots and opened the nearest door. Inside were four pristine Shock Enforcers—non-lethal submachine guns, the standard issue for Shepherds. A serious downgrade from the Lancer Baird had given her.

She closed the door and tried the next. Overkills. Not her favorite. Too sloppy, though they did pack a punch. Kait had a lifetime of experience hunting, and only recently had experienced the kind of combat Marcus lived and breathed. She much preferred to stalk her prey, and fire before they even knew she was there.

The final cabinet contained two EMBAR rifles. "Better," she said. They had the kind of range she preferred, and incredible stability thanks to the electromagnetic delivery of their rounds. The only problem, no scope. They were designed to be carried by robots with zoom-lens eyes. Still, an improvement over what she carried now. Slipping the Lancer off her shoulder, Kait leaned it against the wall, and took one of the long rifles from the cabinet. On a small shelf at the bottom she even found a few canisters of ammunition, and took them.

The other cabinets held only spare parts and extra power cells for the robots. She left these undisturbed and returned to her seat.

Maybe it was the soft hum of the turboprops, or the motion. Maybe it was sheer exhaustion from all that had happened in the last week, but eventually she drifted off, too, and mercifully the sleep was dreamless.

She wasn't quite sure how long she'd been out when her eyes snapped open. Marcus still dozed. The robots still swayed in their bizarre way. But the tone of the engines had changed, and the floor tilted downward now.

Kait nudged Marcus. He yawned, stretched, and then all at once came fully awake.

"We there?"

"Not sure," she said. "Close, I think. We're descending."

"Hmm."

She studied him. "Why'd you come?"

Marcus scratched at his beard. "Getting away from Jinn isn't reason enough?"

"Oh, it is, but you're getting away from your friends, too. And your son."

That seemed to break through his veneer. He eyed her, sidelong, then grunted in bemusement. She thought maybe that had signaled the end of the conversation, but after a time he spoke.

"Jinn talked James and Del into re-upping with the COG."

Kait nodded. "I know. They told me last night."

Marcus leaned his head back against the metal wall, eyes on the ceiling. "She made her pitch when they were the only ones there."

Unsure why, Kait jumped to her friend's defense. "JD's an adult. He doesn't need you—"

"I mean," Marcus corrected, "*you* weren't part of the discussion. Were you?"

Not a question. Kait stared at him, waiting.

"Didn't think so," Marcus added. "That's how Jinn works. She called me last night, too, after talking with James, but she didn't mention their little chat."

"What'd she call about, then?"

Marcus laughed, softly. "Some bullshit about how glad she was I'd returned to the city. How the COG needed the... how did she phrase it… the 'faces of legends to inspire confidence and loyalty.'"

"Shit, really?"

"Word for goddamn word."

Kait shook her head.

"As soon as she ended the call I knew I had to leave. Find some other way to fight the Swarm. James made his choice. It was time for me to make mine, and I couldn't stand the idea of spending another minute 'brainstorming' with our illustrious First Minister."

The aircraft banked slightly, then settled.

"Baird and Sam came to me shortly after you'd left," he continued, "explained how they'd learned of the flight leaving for your village. Figured you should be on it, and asked me to get the new plan to you."

"Did they know you were going to come along?"

Marcus shrugged. "He said he'd make sure there was enough room for both of us. Baird's a smart guy. When he realizes I didn't come back, he'll know."

"So you didn't say goodbye."

"We never do that. Might be we mean it." The tone of the engines fell again. Marcus stirred, glanced at her. "Let's see what's going on."

She nodded, happy for the distraction.

They walked, Kait in the lead, through the swaying forms of the sleeping DeeBee Shepherds. She spotted a few of the slower, stronger DR-1 model in their midst. At the front of the cargo area were two rows of Trackers. The knee-high bots were in their spherical form, ready to drop. She pushed past them and up to the small side-door just before the cockpit entrance. It was the only window. She and Marcus crowded together to look through.

Perhaps a thousand feet below were the tall trees and rolling hills of the area in which she had grown up. It took her only a second to spot some landmarks and orient herself.

"We're about twenty miles out," she said.

Marcus considered this. "Ten minutes. We need to be ready to leave before—"

Off to the northeast, a sudden bright flash interrupted his words. They both watched as a fireball rose up through the trees.

"The hell was that?" Marcus asked.

"No idea. But I know where it is."

"Don't keep me in suspense."

"The road between my village and the next."

"Think it's related?"

Kait thought about it. "Maybe." Her gut said yes.

"Anyone else use that road but Outsiders?"

She shook her head at that.

"Then we should check it out."

Kait opened her mouth to point out the obvious—that they had no way to land the aircraft or even alter its course—but before she could say it Marcus held something out for her. A green backpack with dangling straps and cords.

"What's this?" she said.

"Parachute. A way down. Here, move your pack around the front."

Kait complied, lengthening the straps to account for the bulk of the COG chest plate. As she did so, Marcus put his own parachute on, talking her through it as he went. The harness, the ripcord, the emergency backup. It wasn't that complicated, but she listened intently. Simple or not, this was life-and-death stuff.

He helped get her arms into the gear. There was an urgency to the motions that she understood. They'd be flying over, then past, that explosion. Soon enough the smoke would dissipate, or they'd be too far on the other side of it so as to make no difference. He watched as she snapped the multi-point harness into place, nodding approval.

"We're low," he said, "so once you're clear of the craft you pull the cord. Okay? You can steer a little with the handles at your shoulders. Tug on them both to slow your descent."

"I'm just going to follow your lead," she said as Marcus opened the door to howling wind.

"No you're not," he said, and he pushed her through the opening.

She swallowed back the involuntary urge to scream, and the subsequent desire to curse the name of Marcus Fenix. Tumbling out of control, the wind lashing against her, Kait closed her eyes and waited, suddenly sure she'd be sucked into an engine or hit the tail fins.

When the sound of the Condor receded, she opened one eye.

Trees everywhere, rising up toward her with alarming speed. Kait fumbled for the ripcord and gave it a hard yank. The pack shifted against her shoulders, followed by a fluttering sound. Two seconds later Kait was heaved backward as if lifted by the hand of a giant. She grunted at the strain against her torso, her shoulders, her back. Thankfully it didn't last.

After the pain came the tranquility. Kait floated, lazily. She looked up and marveled at the dark square of blue above her, linked by a dozen long ropes to her pack. Farther up was another square, and set inside it, the form of Marcus. Seeing him reminded her that he'd just pushed her out of an airplane.

Kait decided to let that go for the moment.

There was, after all, the landing to worry about.

2: THE MISSION

The First Minister sat at the head of the table again, fuming with barely controlled rage.

Del paid her little attention, truth be told, as Baird and Jinn exchanged words. She'd briefed them all on what had happened at Fort Umson last night, that survivors had been discovered there. And this morning everyone had awoken to find Kait and Marcus were gone. Del's gaze was locked on the empty chairs where they should be sitting, a pang of guilt in his chest.

He'd thought Kait would come around after a night's rest. With the benefit of hindsight, and knowing now about the discovery of survivors at her village, he felt terrible about how the situation had been handled.

"Del?" JD asked.

The question snapped him back to the present.

"Yeah?" he asked, suddenly aware everyone in the room was looking at him.

"Do you know anything about this?" Jinn asked him, point

blank. "Did Ms. Diaz or Sergeant Fenix say anything to you?"

Del spread his hands. "No. Not a word."

Jinn narrowed her eyes. "Any idea how they managed to get out of the city, unnoticed?" From the tone and the way her eyes darted to glance at Damon Baird, Del almost wrote off the question as rhetorical. Almost.

"You can put anything you want between them and an exit," he said frankly, "if either of those wanted to leave they'd find a way. The two of them together?" He shuddered. "Forget it."

"Assuming they're together," JD added. "Dad might have decided to head home to the estate. And Kait... well, we got into a bit of an argument last night, about Del and me joining back up. It's possible she just needs some time to herself. She might not even know about the survivors. Them leaving could just be coincidence."

Jinn considered this. "The timing implies she found out about it. And they did both leave at roughly the same time. Of course, it didn't hurt that there was a city-wide disruption in DeeBee monitoring capabilities early this morning." This most definitely was not directed at Del.

"Planned maintenance," Baird said, defensive. "Been on the calendar for months."

"Not my calendar," Jinn snapped.

"No, not yours. Mine. DBi's. We do this all the time, part of the service agreement."

"Also," Sam noted, "it was literally on our calendar. The one tacked up in our den. Could be that Marcus or Kait saw it and... well, sensed an opportunity."

Baird stared at her in a way that made Del wonder if there really was anything written on that calendar, or, hell, if the calendar even existed. He almost chuckled.

Abruptly, JD stood. "Del and I will find them. Bring them back."

"Sit down, Lieutenant," Jinn said. "Somehow I doubt you'd arrest your own father. Your friend Ms. Diaz, either."

"Who said anything about arrest?" JD countered. "We'll talk some sense into them."

"Lieutenant, huh?" Baird asked of no one in particular. He looked idly at his hands. "That was quick."

JD glanced at him. "What's that supposed to mean?" Maybe it was the tone, or the way he was looking at Baird, but there was a menace to JD's words that Del wasn't used to.

"Nothing," Baird said. "Congratulations on the reinstatement."

"Do you have something to say, Uncle?"

"I'm sure your father's very proud."

"Alright," Del said, "alright. Everyone take a breath. We're all on the same side here." The tension in the room failed to dissipate, but at least they'd both shut up. Del turned back to Jinn. "We'll bring them back, ma'am. There's no need to arrest them. You have my word."

Jinn waved the comment away. "No, you won't. I'll handle that, but thank you both for the enthusiasm." Before he could protest she added, "I have something else in mind for you two."

Kait's words from the night before echoed through his mind, about how Jinn would keep them where she needed them to be. Maybe she'd been right.

Before elaborating on her plans, Jinn turned to Baird and Sam.

"Damon, Samantha, thank you for the enlightening conversation. At our three o'clock we'll discuss an amended update policy for active-duty DeeBees. In the meantime, I have a mission to discuss with the lieutenants. Do you mind?" She gestured to the door, and waited silently as the couple stood and left without another word.

When the door clicked shut, Jinn favored JD with a thin smile. "I've no doubt your father and Kait can handle themselves. I also have no doubt that it would be impossible to convince them to return unless they decide it for themselves. Marcus Fenix's stubbornness is almost as legendary as his accomplishments in battle, and Ms. Diaz seems to me quite suited as his protégé in that department."

"No argument there," Del said.

JD ran a hand down his face. "Kait probably went to Fort Umson. Even if she doesn't know about the survivors, it makes sense she'd go."

"That is my conclusion, too," Jinn said, "and there is some evidence one or both of them hitched a ride on a Condor headed there, which is why we'll be watching closely when it lands, ready to... address the situation."

Del grunted. "Could you maybe say that in a less menacing tone?"

"If you know all that," JD said, "then why the—"

"To see how Baird would react," Jinn replied. "Anyway, that isn't your concern. Something else has come up." She tapped a control on the table's edge. The lights dimmed, and a screen lowered at one end of the conference room. Shades descended across the floor-to-ceiling windows along one wall, obscuring the view of the city.

"Now, this may be nothing," Jinn said as a map filled the screen, "but I don't like coincidences, and there've already been plenty of those this morning. Either way, this may give us a chance to test your concerns about the Swarm."

Del sat back, orienting himself on the map. It was surprisingly sparse on landmarks or location names.

"What I'm showing you here is considered 'Top Secret,'" she said. "Is that understood?"

Del nodded, as did JD.

"The locations of Locust burial sites are strictly need-to-know, and few people need to know. I expect you both to take this knowledge to your graves."

"Later, rather than sooner," Del suggested.

"We can all hope," Jinn replied with a surprisingly genuine smile. She turned back to the screen. "This site is about one hundred miles southwest of Montevado, deep in the wastelands." The map panned and zoomed in. Satellite imagery began to paint in the features, which still were minimal. It was a flat, barren wasteland for the most part, but as the image zoomed farther still, a circle appeared in the center. Del had taken it for some kind of iconography, but it began to assume a more organic shape. A crater, he realized, and not a recent one, but something from Sera's distant past.

A few small buildings became evident in the basin, and then, finally, the blurry hints of the crater floor's primary feature: a burial-site cap. The dome structure concealed the deep hole that had been dug, within which lay who-knew-how-many crystalline Locust corpses—the strange cocoon-like objects their bodies transformed into after death, interred there more than two decades ago. The solid metal dome was half covered in soil, accumulated over the years by Windflare-driven dust storms. A tall, thin tower protruded from the dome, topped with some kind of metal grating. Ventilation, he guessed.

Del squinted. Either his mind was playing tricks on him, or some of the hazy shapes in the crater basin were vehicles. Haulers or diggers, left to rot when the burial team finished their work.

"Looks undisturbed," JD said.

"The image is several years old," Jinn replied. "But you're right, and that may still be the case. The problem right now is that we don't know what's going on there. Every burial site has a monitoring station, reporting back mostly the status of the cap's seal. The one at this site had been doing just that for decades without fail. Even in a Windflare, we would still get data from it."

Jinn paused, leaned in.

"Last night it went offline."

"Swarm?" Del asked.

Jinn shrugged. "That's what you two are going to find out. Could be anything. A dead power cell, an electrical line that finally fell to pieces after thirty years exposed to the environment. Outsiders raiding for parts."

Del winced at that last, and tried to hide it. He almost got away with it, too.

"I know what goes on," Jinn said without looking at him. "Hence the pardon, gentlemen. The point is, after what you told me yesterday, the timing of this is worrying."

"To say the least," JD agreed.

Jinn went on without pausing. "Take a Condor and a squad of DeeBees. Check with Baird before you go and see what else he might be able to set you up with."

"How about a Hammer of Dawn?" JD asked.

"Absolutely not."

He'd meant it as a joke, Del knew, but the glare Mina Jinn fixed on him just then bled all the humor out of the room.

"Is that clear, Lieutenant?" she added.

"Yes, ma'am."

"Good. You're dismissed," Jinn said. "Report directly to me when you arrive at the site."

In the hall outside her office, Del took JD aside. He glanced both ways to make sure they were alone, and lowered his voice.

"Kait was right," he said. "If not for Jinn we'd be going after her, not to this burial site. No, even better, we'd have gone with her last night."

JD bristled, if only just. "Kait can handle herself. She'll find whoever is out there and bring them back to safety. Besides, if this burial site going dark is what we think it is, that's just as important. Maybe more so."

There was truth to that. Still didn't make it feel right.

"Talk to your dad before he left?" Del asked, after a moment.

JD sighed and nodded. "Briefly."

"And?"

"Let's just say his opinion of our decision-making skills hasn't exactly improved."

"... And?"

"And I reminded him that his opinion of our decision-making skills isn't exactly required. Hasn't been for a long time now."

"Damn," Del said. "I'm sure he loved hearing that."

JD spread his arms. "Doesn't mean I was wrong."

"Think he went with her?"

"I don't know, but the idea of them teaming up against the Swarm... it's better than anything Jinn could send."

They caught up with Baird and Sam in the huge lobby of the capitol building.

"She have anything interesting for you?" Baird asked as JD and Del approached.

Del nodded, lowering his voice despite only a few DeeBees

being about. "A site out in the badlands went dark. We're going to check it out."

"What kind of site?"

"The Locust burial variety," JD said.

Baird nodded gravely. "That's mildly worrying."

"Jinn suggested you might have gear we should take with us."

"She did, huh?" He pretended to think about it until Sam nudged him. "Yeah, I've probably got a thing or two you could bring along. Let's go check out the workshop."

Baird led them from the building, and before the huge door had fully closed behind them an autonomous tram rolled up, uncanny in its timing. They stepped in and he gave the vehicle some instructions. The engines whirred to life and they were off—but not to the mansion. Instead, the car went toward the industrial district on the far side of town, a place dominated by the factories and office buildings of DB Industries.

As it rumbled along, Baird and Sam spoke intensely to each other in hushed tones, Del catching only snippets. "Thermal plating" and "fluid levels." Something about battery efficiency.

"Debating what gear you can lend us?" Del asked.

Sam grinned. "Nah, just figuring out lunch."

With Damon Baird himself on board, the cart rolled straight through the heavily secured gates to the main DBi factory, rounded the building, and came to a stop at an unassuming single-story structure in the back. Baird stepped out first, went to a panel on the wall, and identified himself.

Two huge metal doors began to roll aside, revealing his so-called "workshop." Baird had been a mechanic and tinkerer all his life, a hobby his family had been wealthy enough to indulge. Though he'd inherited a fortune, his wealth had skyrocketed more recently, and the room in which Del found himself was exactly what he'd imagine an ultra-rich engineer would build as his personal playground.

The walls were lined, floor to ceiling, with a mixture of tool chests, cabinets, or shelves of bins containing all manner of spare parts. None of it was labeled, and yet Del had no doubt it was organized precisely as Baird liked it.

On the vast floor of the space were a handful of in-progress builds. The upper torso of a Mech hung from chains mounted to the ceiling, its electronic innards spilling out like guts. Various pieces of testing equipment were linked up to these guts via clamped-on wires. Displays graphed results in pulsating lines. Farther down the floor were similar setups for other models his company produced: a Shepherd, a Tracker, and one of the larger DR-1s, all in various states of disassembly.

"Damn," Del said. "Look at all this…"

"Quit gawking," JD replied. "It's embarrassing."

"What? It's impressive! Tell me you're not impressed."

"This way," Baird said. "C'mon."

Sam parted ways with them there, heading toward the Mech. She sat down in front of a bank of screens and began to study the graphs and figures glowing there. "Don't be long," she said over a shoulder, "we've got a lot of work to do."

"Yes, dear!" Baird replied, striking just the right balance between sincerity and sarcasm. Then he led them through a pair of swinging double doors. The space was dark, lit only by what came through the small windows embedded in the doors. Baird flicked on some lights.

"The warehouse," he said.

To Del it looked more like a DeeBee museum. Row upon row of robot prototypes were lit by strip-lights recessed in the ceiling and floor. They were haunting when seen like this. Silent and utterly still. Baird walked past them without more than a sparing glance, his attention focused on something at the back.

"Been wanting to bring these back," he explained. "Jinn only recently okayed the project, and I think it's far enough along to be useful to you." He reached for a large hard-shell crate, sliding it out from the wall. He thumbed two latches and lifted the lid.

"Del, JD... meet your new best friend... Dave."

He stepped back so they could see. Inside the case, folded into a custom-cut foam bed, lay a small black robot with four dangling limbs and two huge eyes.

"That... I don't know what that is," JD said.

Del did, though. He elbowed his friend. "Marcus used to have a bot like this in Delta Squad. Called Jack, if I remember right. Is Dave the same thing, Baird?"

"Not exactly," Baird said, "Similar, but different. Dave is an evolution of the old Jack, with some upgrades and improvements I've been tinkering with. IRIS, has the latest patch been added to Dave's code?"

"Not yet, Damon. There are still significant issues that require your attention."

"Thanks, IRIS." To Del's confused expression he said, "Don't worry! Field upgradable!"

His confusion was about the synthetic voice, though. It had come from a speaker on a nearby console. "Who's IRIS?" Del asked. "No, scratch that. *Where's* IRIS?"

Baird pointed at a nearby console. "My assistant. Another work-in-progress."

Del grinned. "Man, I could live here. Sure we don't have time for a proper tour?"

"Some other time. Now listen up. Dave's an old model—I want

to stress that. I'm still working on bringing him up to scratch with all the latest schematics and protocols, but even in his current state he'll be useful, especially for interfacing with old COG gear. Where you're going, that could come in handy."

JD rubbed his neck. "Um... I don't mean to sound unappreciative, but I was sorta hoping for a big nasty gun or some new type of grenade."

Baird eyed him. "Neither of which will do you morons any good if you can't get that site back online."

"Can't get it back online if we're trapped in the bellies of Snatchers, either."

"That's a visual I don't need," Baird said.

"What JD means," Del put in, "is thanks. We appreciate it."

Baird let out a breath, then nodded. "Good."

JD closed the case. "Is there at least a manual or something?"

"Just turn it on and you're good to go. An infant could figure it out, so your chances are decent."

3: MIDDLE OF THE ROAD

Thanks to luck more than anything else, Kait somehow managed to land softly in a small clearing. The chute fell ahead of her a few seconds later, wrapping around a tree trunk. She twisted around, trying to work out how to release the damn thing, before deciding not to bother. It wasn't like she'd ever need it again. Kait undid the harness itself and threw the whole pack to the dirt.

Marcus Fenix hit the ground a few seconds later, just twenty feet away. He landed at a jog and released the parachute before it touched soil. The big fabric blob drifted off into the darkness of the forest.

"Why the hell did you push me out?" she demanded. It was cold here, and her breath came out as steam.

Marcus held up a hand, urging quiet. "People get cold feet before their first jump. I've seen it happen many times. Right before the moment they freeze up, stand there, and miss the LZ entirely. Couldn't afford that."

"I would have been fine."

"Which is what everyone says right before it happens to them."

He readied his Lancer. "Are we done talking about this? I'd like to get to that smoke before it's gone."

His words hung in the air for a moment, as Kait considered and discarded a half-dozen responses. In the end she settled for the only thing she could—readying her EMBAR.

"Quarter-mile that way," she said, pointing with the long barrel.

"So it is," he agreed. If he was impressed with her ability to track their target while plummeting from an aircraft, he didn't show it. "You want point?"

"Sure." She marched off, heading due north. They left the clearing, and the forest immediately closed in around them. She ducked under ferns and stepped over fallen branches, looking for exposed soil or soft beds of leaves to quiet her passage.

As they neared the source of the smoke they heard a loud crackling. Marcus dropped back and moved off to the right. He was surprisingly quiet, but not so much that Kait couldn't track the alteration in course without having to look. Besides, the noises coming from in front of her would mask any sounds he might make.

Kait pressed herself behind a tree trunk and chanced a look into the clear area ahead. It wasn't a clearing, but the open ground where the dirt road stretched between Fort Umson and South Village. A twenty-foot-wide scrape of bumpy ground with two well-worn cart tracks running down the middle.

In the center lay the remains of an old wooden wagon, its pieces strewn about and smoldering. The flames licked the air, still spewing dark smoke up into the sky. Kait smelled the burning wood, and something else, too. The stench of cooking flesh.

She swallowed, sure she would see the bodies of the two teenagers lying on the trail, or huddled in a final charred embrace.

What her eyes found instead was the dismembered arm of a Drone, the massive, scaly hand still clutching its weapon. Farther on, a leg, and then finally the torso and head, all steaming in the cold. The pig-like face was snarled in a final expression of anger and agony alike.

Several bodies of Juvies lay nearby, still smoldering.

Kait started forward, ready to step into the road and investigate closer, when something moved on the opposite side of the trail. She could barely see it through the flames. Just a hint of… something. One of the twins?

She hesitated. Whatever it was, it was too tall to be either of the children. And then, through the shimmering heat and smoke, the head swiveled.

A Scion, looking directly at her.

And then it grinned.

For a terrible second she thought it was the Speaker—the very Scion who'd taken her mother and placed her in the hive. But the Speaker was dead. She'd made sure of that with the heel of her boot. This one still had a face.

She could rectify that.

Kait raised the barrel of her EMBAR, sighted down on the huge brute with its ugly, semi-human eyes, and squeezed the trigger. Electromagnetic coils inside the weapon began to whine as the weapon built up a charge to fire.

Before the round went off, though, something fell on her shoulders. Kait collapsed under the weight but somehow managed to roll to her right. She came up to a crouch and swung the weapon like a club, a blind effort that still managed to connect. The Pouncer, tail raised and quills ready to fire, staggered from the impact. The vicious little spikes sprayed outward but went wide. Kait felt the brush of wind as one passed only inches from her face.

She flipped her gun around, but the Pouncer recovered more quickly. It coiled and turned toward her again, leathery tentacles writhing in its mouth, and it was all she could do to dive out the way as it propelled itself forward. The creature's bulk hit her feet, sending her spinning in the air.

Landing on the muddy road, she slid before she could steady herself. She tried to stand but her feet, still stinging from the impact with the creature, weren't ready to cooperate. She took a knee instead, aimed, and it was only for the lack of a scope on the rifle that she noticed the second Pouncer up in the tree behind the first.

Its tail was raised.

Kait had no time to let the weapon charge. She rolled to one side instead, hoping for cover behind a smoldering wooden wheel. Quill spikes thudded into the surface of it a split second later. Several more *thunked* into the ground.

The Pouncer flattened itself on the branch, coiling to leap at her. Just then something moved under it. The creature heaved upward in an eruption of blood and gore. For a second it seemed to float there.

Marcus had come up below it, and impaled the thing with the chainsaw bayonet of his Lancer. He flung the writhing creature into the first one that had attacked, and started to pour rounds into both of them.

Kait's respite ended when the burning cart at her back suddenly lifted up and was tossed aside. The Scion loomed over her, an ugly grin still on its fat face. It raised one massive arm, curled its hand into a fist, and brought it down like a hammer aimed right at her skull.

She dove backward. The ground shook as the impact cratered the spot where she'd just been. Somehow she managed to bring the long-barreled EMBAR up, squeezing the trigger to build a charge before she'd even taken aim. Lying flat on her back, she wielded it from the hip.

The first shot tore through the creature's gut. It barely noticed. The second, though, hit its throat, and blood quickly bubbled from the wound. The Scion grunted, but even this wasn't enough to wipe the grin from its face.

No, that required her third shot.

The round punched right through its clenched teeth and out the back of its head. A spray of hot blood fountained from its mouth, spraying her with bits of teeth and gore. Kait blinked it away.

Pure instinct told her to roll again, and not a moment too soon. The lifeless body slammed into the ground where she'd lain. She remained prone, fighting to get her breathing under control. The memory of the two Pouncers forced her to get up, to ready herself, reload, and fight on.

Marcus stood a dozen feet away, scanning left and right. His arms were covered to the elbows in blood.

"You okay?" he asked.

She spat, then used her sleeve to wipe the gore from her face.

"I think so. You?"

"I'll live," he said. She noticed a cut on his arm then. A nasty one, blood flowing freely from it, but he barely seemed to notice.

"Is that all of them?" she asked.

Marcus let the barrel of his Lancer drop a bit. "The others were dead before we got here. The bomb took care of that."

Kait glanced around, seeing the scene from a different perspective. The burning remains of the cart, the body parts of mangled Swarm in the road.

With the toe of her boot she rummaged through the charred bits of cart at the center of the explosion. Marcus kept on the periphery, eyes never leaving the tree line. Kait found a length of burned wire and held it up in the midmorning light.

"A trap," she said.

"Looks that way. The question is, who set it?"

"Someone from South Village. Has to be. They carved that place out of the mountainside with old mining charges and whatever else they could scrounge up. Any one of a dozen of them could have set this."

Marcus nodded. He'd walked a few steps away, and knelt. "Take a look at this."

Kait glanced in his direction, and immediately spotted tracks in the mud—footprints. She went to Marcus and took a knee beside him, studying the imprints.

"Three sets," she said. "Two kids, one adult." They were heading away from the home in which Kait had grown up, away from the great hall with its huge welcoming fireplace, away from the stables she'd helped Oscar and a dozen others raise so they could have horses. Away from Reyna's belongings, and Kait's own.

Instead, they were headed toward South Village.

She battled back the selfishness. There would be time, later, to return there. Right now finding the twins, making sure they were safe, that was all that mattered.

Another thought came to her then.

She slung her rifle and started to run, keeping to the edge of the road in case more explosives waited.

"Kait!" Marcus shouted after her. He rushed to catch up. "What is it?"

"South Village," she said. "Whether these three know it or not, they're leading the Swarm right to it. I'm not going to let the same thing happen to them that happened to us."

4: CRATER'S EDGE

"This hole in the ground," Del asked, "does it have a name?" The circular rim of its edge came fully into view. They'd be over it in less than a minute, and the Condor was already descending, ready to nose down into the depression.

"Beats me," the pilot replied. She was relaxed, in total control of the aircraft. From his spot at the rear of the cockpit, Del could see her jaw moving as she chewed on a piece of gum. The named on her helmet said Kieho, but she'd told them to call her Yoon the moment they'd come aboard. "They only gave coordinates, which is good enough for me."

JD sat at the navigator's station across from Del, hunched over a nav display. In that moment, with the angle and the light, Del thought he looked a lot like his father, though he'd never say it aloud. He and JD had the kind of friendship where no joke was taken to heart, yet he got the sense his friend was looking for ways to distance himself from his father. Best to let it lie.

"No name on the map," JD said, "but, for all we know, it's

been scrubbed to keep us reliably uninformed."

Del rolled his eyes. Secrecy had its uses, but in his experience it mostly just led to miscommunication, and *that* had no use he was aware of.

"CO-one-zero-six to base," Yoon said into her headset. "We're approaching the landing site."

"Copy that," Control replied. "There is an airstrip in the crater basin, unlikely to have a working guidance beacon."

Yoon popped a bubble. "Understood. One-zero-six out." She turned slightly, eyeing JD and Del from behind her sunglasses. "Likely to be a bumpy one."

"Acknowledged." JD pushed the mic away from his mouth and turned to Del. "So, how mad do you think Kait is?"

"Pretty mad," he replied. "She's got a right to be."

His friend nodded. "I keep wondering if we could have handled it better."

"Maybe," Del admitted. "What's done is done, though. We made that decision without her, and she went back to Fort Umson without us. Fair play."

JD considered this, opened his mouth to reply, but instead swiveled back to the display.

The pilot flipped several switches over her head, then took the flight stick, flexing her fingers as she did so. Her voice was calm. "Crater's edge in three... two... one."

The displays in front of her wavered, graphics going askew. All at once alarms began to go off around the cockpit. Del gripped the arms of his seat.

"The hell?!" He felt sure the craft would plummet to the ground and tried desperately to remember the evac protocols for a Condor, but the cacophony of warning buzzers around him made it impossible to think.

Yoon began flipping switches. She rapped one of the screens with a knuckle, then gave it a hard slap. "C'mon, you piece of shit." Her other hand never left the stick, though, and the craft flew on, straight and true. After a few seconds, the alerts receded into annoying but manageable background noise.

"What the fuck was that?" Del asked.

"A little busy here," the pilot replied, both hands now on the controls.

"Del?" JD said, studying the displays in front of him. "Have a look at this."

Just then getting out of his seat didn't seem like the wisest idea, but Del felt useless, and that was worse. So he undid his harness and moved to a spot behind JD's shoulder.

"Vitals look okay," he said. "Sensors are in the green, too. Except for that. The link to Control, see? Totally dead."

JD tried and failed to get a response from Control.

"It happened as soon as we descended below the crater rim," Del said. "Interference from the rock?"

"Yeah," JD agreed. "That makes sense. No need to panic."

"Who you trying to convince, man?"

Yoon spoke up, voice only slightly strained as she steered the big plane. "Look, you guys are calling the shots here. Do I land or bug out?"

JD studied the displays another second or two. They remained stable, even though the link to Control did not return. "I say we proceed with the landing, check the site, then come back up in ten minutes to report."

"I'm good with that. Yoon?"

"Cool by me," she said.

"How long until the basin?"

The crater was eight hundred feet deep and over a mile across. "Less than a minute," she replied, craning her neck forward to get a better view out the forward window. "Now where the hell is that runway..."

Del tried to recall the layout of the crater floor. The primary feature was the burial cap, with its huge sealed door and tall ventilation tower. Surrounding this were an array of small support structures—power, sensors, and remnants of the infrastructure used to build the site in the first place.

West of all that there was a single, short, unpaved landing strip that had been made for supply deliveries during the cap's construction. It hadn't been maintained since, much less used for a landing. At least, none that he or JD were made aware of.

"Got a visual," Yoon said. "We're good."

"Let's get in back, then," Del said to JD. "Won't be long now."

In the cargo bay, twelve combat-equipped DeeBees hung in perfect rows, swaying from their ceiling racks as the aircraft made minute adjustments on its approach. Weaving between them, Del went to a locker and pulled out his new armor. He laid the heavy chest piece on a bench by the wall and checked each fastener. The piece was brand new, with none of the scars and dents his previous gear had earned. "I wonder how long it'll stay this shiny," he said.

Beside him, JD made the final adjustments on his own gear. "Maybe try getting out of the way next time you're being shot at," he replied, flashing a smile.

Del grimaced. "Hah-fucking-hah."

A speaker overhead crackled, preceding Yoon's voice. "Flight crew to landing positions," she said, sarcastically. As if this were all perfectly normal.

"She's kinda growing on me," JD said.

Del nodded. "C'mon, let's get ready."

They each grabbed Enforcers and some ammo clips. A compact, mediocre weapon designed for DeeBee use, but the aircraft wasn't stocked with anything else. Jinn had insisted.

JD sighted down the short barrel and shook his head. "All of a sudden I'm wishing we'd stood our ground on the weapons. A Lancer wouldn't go amiss right about now."

"Ah, don't worry, man," Del replied, laying on the sarcasm nice and thick. "The DeeBees can 'handle any problems that might arise.'" He laughed and JD laughed with him.

"Next time, we hold our ground. Get her to listen to reason."

Del shook his head. "To her this is being reasonable."

"Sure isn't like it used to be," JD said, testing the gun's aim. "When they sent soldiers to do soldiers' work."

Del gave a single, sharp laugh. "Okay, gramps," he said. "Feel free to join me when you're done reminiscing about ye olden days." He walked aft toward the folded cargo door.

"Hah-fucking-hah," JD said.

Seconds later the Condor's wheels touched earth. The plane bounced once, settled, and began to roll on the uneven landing strip. The engines roared as they reversed thrust.

JD raised his voice to be heard over the din.

"Alright, squad, deploy and form a fifty-foot perimeter, following."

In response the DeeBees all lit up. Status lights on their chests glowed blue, along with the glow from the four "eyes" located at the corners of their faces. Motors in their joints began to hum in preparation for movement. The racks that held them descended, then released, each robot crouching slightly as they took on their own weight. As one they turned on their heels and faced the rear of the craft, weapons up to a ready position.

A moment later the ramp was lowered. Del watched as the distant rim of the crater came into view, the steep slope becoming more and more shallow as the descending ramp revealed it. Nothing but rock and dirt, all the way to the top, where the edge had been scoured almost flat by the violence of the occasional Windflare.

Not a single thing grew in this desolate place. Del could see why they'd picked it as a burial site. When the ramp hit the dirt the DeeBees marched out in formation and began to spread out like spilled liquid. When the last one stepped off the plane, the ramp began to close.

"Shit," JD said. He went to the wall and cranked a hand lever to override the system manually.

"What the hell was that?" Del said. "She expecting us to stay inside?"

As if she'd overheard, Yoon's voice came over the speaker again. "Sorry guys. Been a while since I deployed actual people. Everything's keyed to the DeeBees, but I've switched that off. You're good to go."

"Sign of the times, I guess," JD said. He readied his Enforcer and started down the ramp.

Del followed, then stopped. "Ah, damn it. Hang on."

"What now?"

"Forgot Dave." Del turned and jogged back to the equipment lockers, where Dave's packing crate had been lashed to the wall with yellow straps.

"Do we even need him?" JD called after him. "If we need to tear through a door, the DeeBees should be able to handle it."

"Baird seemed to think he'd come in handy." Del shrugged. "Can't see how he can hurt."

"Try using your imagination," JD replied. "Besides, Baird probably just wants us to field-test his toys."

Placing the crate on the floor, Del cracked it open and activated the packed bot. For a second nothing happened. Then its eyes lit up, glowing blue just like the DeeBees'. A second passed, then all at once the robot unfolded itself and vaulted into the air.

"Whoa," Del said. He stepped backward so fast he almost tripped on his own feet. Dave settled into a bobbing hover next to him, held aloft on a tiny plume of shimmering air. It emitted a series of bleeps that Del figured meant something to Damon Baird, a handful of engineers who worked for him, and perhaps the DeeBees themselves.

"I think he wants to know what to do," JD said. "Eager little guy, isn't he?"

"That's putting it mildly." Composure recovered, Del gestured toward the ramp. "Standard full-spectrum surveillance, please."

Dave rose to head height and darted off in the direction indicated.

"Good," JD said. "He responds to you, so he's your responsibility. Let's move out."

Del took point, marching down the ramp with his Enforcer held casually. At first glance the crater floor seemed dead. Other than some rocks that had rolled over the distant rim and been pushed almost all the way to the basin—no doubt by Windflares—the place looked undisturbed. A fine coat of sand covered everything.

"No lights," JD observed. He gestured with the barrel of his gun. "Even the transmission tower is dark. Maybe it's a power source failure?"

"But it's all solar and batteries."

JD considered that. "Wind could have played havoc with the cabling."

Del wasn't so sure. From the dust coating every damned surface, he suspected the crater's shape protected it from the worst of the winds. Still, some desert critter could have chewed through a cable. Stranger things had happened.

"Could be." He nodded. "I'll check power, you look at the tower."

"Ah, the man's a poet."

"Just… check the tower, alright?" He walked toward the solar arrays as JD ordered the DeeBees—who'd made a nearly perfect circle fifty feet out—to split up and maintain separate perimeters for the two soldiers. Overhead, Dave chirped and seemed to waver between the two parting men as if unsure which to follow.

"Go with him," JD said to the little bot.

But Del had a different idea. "Actually, Dave, can you get up high and get us visuals of the entire basin?"

The bot wiggled slightly as its tiny pulsing engines worked to lift it. It managed about twenty feet of altitude before moving off toward the north.

Pleased, Del left Dave to his task and continued on. The power infrastructure was situated about two hundred feet from where they'd landed. An array of solar panels, all tilted toward the sun, all tinged with a coating of sand. Not enough to render them useless, he guessed, but probably cut their efficiency in half.

"Someone should come out here and maintain this place once in a while," he said over the comms.

"I guess there's not many cleaning crews with the proper security clearance," JD replied.

Del laughed to himself, sure his friend had it exactly right, superficially at least. Deeper down he suspected there was probably a collective subconscious desire for everyone involved to forget about what was buried here, to put it firmly in the past.

He checked the panels first, and it only took a second to

confirm they were working fine. They whirred as tiny motors inside kept them aimed for maximum sunlight. Beside the grid of silvery rectangles was a row of large gray boxes, all linked together with cables as thick as Del's arm. Batteries. He checked these, too, and found that each indicated a charge status of at least half.

"So far so good over here," he said. "How's it look at the transmission tower?"

"Checking it now."

While Del waited, he confirmed the cables linking all the power gear together had not been compromised. Solid links everywhere.

"Weird," JD said in his ear.

"What is?"

A pause. Del waited.

"It's got power," JD finally answered. "In fact, the damn thing is transmitting."

"I don't think 'weird' is the word you want, then," Del replied.

"Oh, that's not the weird part."

"Well, don't keep me in suspense."

JD did keep him in suspense, at least for a few seconds. "It's not that the tower's transmission is getting garbled on the way to New Ephyra," he finally said, "it's that it's transmitting garbage."

"Come again?"

"Just what I said. The outgoing feed is just… gibberish. Something is scrambling the signal."

Del considered that. "Alright, maybe 'weird' might have been the right word after all."

"Told you."

Satisfied the power source wasn't the problem, Del wound his way through the equipment and temporary office buildings left behind from the original construction, headed for JD's position. All around him a group of DeeBees moved to maintain the specified perimeter.

His eyes were drawn to the burial cap, beneath which lay countless crystal-encrusted bodies of the Locust. From this distance the cap appeared to be undisturbed. A ventilation tower rose from it, giving it the vague appearance of a monument, or a grave marker, which was apt.

"Dave, get some close-in footage of the cap itself, will you?" he said. "All the seals, the latches. That ventilation stack. Everything."

The bot chirped, darting off that way.

See, JD? Not so useless after all, Del thought, and made a mental note to thank Baird for the gift when they got back.

He found JD standing next to the base of the transmitter. The tower was about twenty feet tall, with an angled antenna at the top that swiveled on a cylindrical joint, allowing it to stay optimally aimed at the sky.

"Check it for yourself," JD said, stepping aside so Del could study the small status display. The screen was hidden behind an access panel which JD had removed and laid against the base of the tower.

Del leaned in and studied the screen. Sure enough, the queue labeled "outgoing," which would normally list off readings from all the various sensors around and inside the cap, was just garbage names. He tapped one and looked at the contents, only to find more of the same. Random letters and numbers, in seemingly endless succession.

"Huh." Del stood up. "Well, you're right. It's working, it's just getting bad data from the sensors."

"Okay, so, where are those? Can we fix them?"

Del pointed at the soil. "A few hundred feet below us. But don't worry, we don't need to go inside, not yet at least."

"Why?"

"Look at this."

JD leaned in, studying the portion of the screen Del pointed at. "Um. Give me the summary?"

Del tapped it. "The tower's own status is scrambled, too. Whatever this is, it's not just the sensors."

JD turned to him. "We didn't bring a replacement. If this one's circuits are fried…"

Holding up a hand, Del stalled the line of thought. "Dave should have a full set of manuals on this stuff, probably even the right interface port. I'll get him over here, see if we can—"

JD reached into the box, grabbed the big lever marked "MAIN POWER," and yanked it into the off position. The display went black, and an electrical hum emanating from the device faded away.

"What are you doing?" Del asked.

"Turning it off and back on again," JD replied. "What harm can it do? C'mon. You know me and electronics, I've got the magic touch." He threw the switch back into the on position.

Nothing happened.

No power, no display. Nothing.

Del frowned. "Yeah, you've got the magic touch alright."

"Maybe I didn't leave it off long enough… ah, here, see?" A light had come back on. One little indicator, which blinked amber, then went solid green. "Look at that, green! Green's good, right?"

A deep, heavy boom rolled up from deep underground. Something they felt more than heard. Del instinctively looked down at his feet.

"That didn't sound good."

The vibration lingered, then vanished. The two men looked at each other, momentarily relieved and embarrassed. JD opened his mouth to speak, but his words were cut off by another noise, this one much louder. It sounded to Del like a packhorse ramming into a stone wall. Dust shook from the surfaces around them. The very ground itself seemed to buck upward.

Somewhere off in the distance, Dave began to bleep and chirp wildly. The circle of DeeBees, which Del had all but forgotten, acted on some kind of deeply programmed instinct, all turning to face outward, guns raised.

"The hell was that?" JD asked.

With another epic thud from underground, the floor of the crater seemed to buck upward. Del felt himself thrown six inches into the air. He landed hard, stumbling.

"Turn it back off!" he shouted.

JD reached for the handle. His hand missed as the world tilted sideways. Another pulse boomed through the earth beneath him. This time the thunderous noise was accompanied by a horrific rending sound. Del looked in time to see the massive steel door of the burial cap bulge outward.

JD reached for the handle again.

"Forget it!" Del shouted. "Back to the Condor, now!"

They both turned to run. At that moment the "permanent seal" on the burial site exploded outward in a hail of metal debris. Del dove to the right, tackling JD and taking him to the ground between an empty shipping container and an abandoned earth mover. Chunks of metal the size of fists whizzed through the air, slamming into everything. The sound of it was deafening. The container behind him rattled with a dozen impacts. Dust flew up in a thousand small clouds as shrapnel tore the crater floor to shreds.

Something larger flew over them. Del heard it first. A *voomp-voomp-voomp* of something big tumbling end over end. He glanced up in time to see a slab of fractured metal door arc through the sky, fall, and plow straight into one of the Condor's four engines. The propeller blades snapped off like twigs, the engine itself crumpling under the impact as the wedge of solid steel embedded itself into the front of the motor like a well-thrown dart.

The impact was so great it twisted the entire aircraft, leaving it sitting askew on the runway, cargo ramp still in the down position.

Shrapnel had punched holes in several places along the wing, the fuselage, the cockpit.

"Oh, hell," JD said.

In the center of the canopy there was a ragged white gap in the glass, cracks radiating outward from it. And behind, just visible through the shattered window, Yoon sat motionless in her seat, head down, chin resting on her chest.

Electricity rippled across the surface of the aircraft and then, all at once, its landing lights winked out.

"No. No no no!" Del came to a knee, ready to run to her despite knowing instantly she was dead. He was stalled by JD's hand on his shoulder, pushing him back to the dirt. Del rolled as the sound of a dozen Enforcers, fired in unison, rattled through the basin and up the distant crater walls.

Del thrust himself against the side of the old container, Enforcer at the ready, but there was too much dust and confusion in the air to know in which direction the enemy lay, or if there was even an enemy at all. For all he knew, some gas buildup inside the burial site had just been ignited by the power surge to the sensors.

This theory lasted all of three seconds, though. Somewhere off to his right he heard a DeeBee.

"YOU ARE UNAUTHORIZED TO BE IN THIS—"

Then there was a loud metallic *clang* as something heavy

knocked the robot aside. The attacker roared in triumph, a sound so loud it shook the ground beneath them.

"Swarmak?" JD asked.

"Whatever it is, it's big and pissed," Del replied. He held up the Enforcer in his hands. "These are gonna be worthless."

"We need cover," JD said. Then he snapped his fingers. "Foreman's office. Saw it as I was walking over here. Seemed to be intact. Maybe we can hole up in there until we figure out what the hell's going on."

"Okay. Which way?" The air was choked from all the chaos. Del couldn't see more than ten feet, a distance dropping by the second.

A shape emerged from the dust. Despite what he'd just said, Del aimed his Enforcer, then eased off as Dave floated in through the shadowy haze.

"Dave," Del said, "have you got a map of this place?"

The robot bleeped an affirmative.

The mangled torso of a DeeBee slammed into the container only feet from Del's head. It slid down into a heap of broken metal and wires, uttering, "Cease and desisssssss…" as the electronic life bled out of it.

"The foreman's office," Del said to Dave. "Lead us there."

The bot floated off instantly, almost too quickly to follow. It zigged and zagged through the random bits of equipment and construction detritus, pausing now and then for reasons Del could not follow—perhaps it was linked into the DeeBees' sensors and was using them to its advantage. Whatever it was doing, it worked, in large part because of all the fine desert sand and dust that had been kicked into the air. Del could barely see three feet in front of his face, and put all his focus into following Dave.

"Just hope they can't smell us," JD said from right behind him.

The foreman's office, really just a retrofitted cargo container that could be dropped at any COG construction project, emerged from the dusty air after so many twists and turns that Del had no idea where in the basin they actually were. Dave moved aside as the door came into view. Hovering, waiting.

Del tried the door. The handle refused to turn.

From somewhere across the crater floor there came a bloodcurdling howl, so loud he felt it in his bones.

The call was taken up by another creature, off to Del's left. Then a third. A fourth.

"Swarm," JD said. "No doubt about it."

"Unlock the door, Dave," Del said, aware of the hint of panic in his voice. "Now would be good!"

He and JD flanked the bot as it accessed the security panel and sprung the old lock. It felt as if the process took an hour, though in reality Del figured five seconds was more accurate.

He moved inside first, grateful for the clean air. Once JD and Dave were in behind him he shut the door, forcing himself not to slam it closed and alert the entire Swarm to their presence. It clicked softly shut. Del sank to the floor and pressed his back against the flimsy barrier, hanging his hands over his knees.

"Now what?"

"Blinds," JD said.

Before Del could ask what that meant, his friend started moving methodically down the length of the container, activating the metal shutters, covering all four windows as he went. They whirred closed, turning the already wan light into a series of thin yellow lines.

Confident the door wasn't about to burst open behind him, Del stood and dusted himself off. He and JD met in the middle of the container, standing over a pathetically small conference table.

Old papers were strewn about its surface, long forgotten.

"Another shitty situation we find ourselves in," Del said.

"Yeah," JD sighed. "We seem to be pretty good at that, don't we?"

Outside, the deep thuds of a giant's footsteps began to rumble through the floor and walls of the temporary office. Del gripped the table, his eyes on his friend as they both waited for whatever beast was outside to find them. Del imagined a massive clawed hand tearing the roof off their shelter, and then a world of fangs before the end came. The footsteps continued, growing louder. The thin lines of light coming through the slatted blinds vanished from one window, then another, before reappearing.

The footsteps grew quieter.

Del let out a breath.

"Fucking hell," he whispered. "Yoon. I think she…"

"I know. I saw. We'll mourn her later, but right now we need another way out of here. Loss of our pilot aside, think the Condor will fly?"

"One engine down?" Del grimaced. "Hard to say."

"If the other three—"

"Won't matter if the wing was compromised. Or if the electronics were fried. Or a hundred other things. I mean, we left the damn ramp open—and by 'we' I mean 'you.' If one of them gets inside and starts yanking on cables…"

JD took the jab earnestly, sitting silent for several long seconds. "Look, our first priority is to report back to Jinn, right? They need to know about this. It's the proof we came for."

Del nodded. "Get her the footage that's inside Dave, too."

"The question is, how? Crater's blocking transmissions, and I don't think climbing out is going to go unnoticed."

To JD's surprise, Del shook his head. "The crater can't be

blocking transmissions," he said. "Or at least, that's not the whole story here."

"What do you mean? Think back, the moment we passed over the rim. Total loss of contact."

"True, but remember, this place has been here for years, providing an unbroken stream of data that entire time. All of a sudden there's interference from the rock? I don't buy it."

"What, you think the Swarm figured out how to fuck with our comms?"

Del lifted his shoulders. "Stranger things have happened. I mean, you saw the screen on that tower. The data itself was corrupt. Getting a signal out of this crater was already a challenge, I'm sure, but there's something else going on here."

The sounds of enemy activity began to lessen. Del took a chance and crossed to one of the windows. With two fingers he spread the shutters apart.

"See anything?" JD asked.

"Dust," Del replied. "Dust and shadows, but one thing's for sure, it's not our dutiful escort wandering around out there."

"You sure?"

"I'm sure," Del said, watching the shifting forms move about in the choked air beyond the window. DeeBees didn't move like that.

They didn't prowl.

5: THE MOUNTAIN ROAD

One arm raised to shield her eyes, Kait focused on the rutted trail barely visible now under the ice. It had gotten worse the farther they traveled. Her breaths came out in steamy eruptions, and with each subsequent icy inhalation her worries about the Swarm were superseded by a deeply ingrained instinct to get to shelter and warmth.

If the weather bothered Marcus Fenix, he didn't let it show, and Kait would be damned if she'd complained first. She'd grown up out here, after all. Maybe not in the mountains, but in the wilderness. So she marched on, putting every ounce of focus she possessed into keeping her footing, shaking her hands to quell the numbness in her fingers.

The mountain road, really just a cart track at this point, was months past its regular summer use. Rain and wind and snow had left it a lumpy, uneven mess, made all the more treacherous by the carpet of white powder and ice crystals hiding the deepest of its scars.

"When we get to the peak," Marcus said, "we oughta plant a

flag on it." Kait grinned, unsure if the quasi-gripe was honest, or just meant to crack that door open a little for both of them.

"We're not going quite that far," she said.

Neither of them mentioned stopping, or even slowing the pace, for the other feature the mountain road displayed was the tracks of the Swarm, and a lot of them.

In a narrow pass they found more mangled bodies of Swarm, and another blackened circle where a charge had been triggered. This time the trap had claimed three Juvies and a Pouncer. Not bad, Kait thought, but not good enough. The footprints of those not killed by the blast continued ahead.

She picked up her pace.

South Village sat atop a high cliff, only a few hundred feet below the peak of the mountain upon which it perched. Some ancient calamity Kait didn't care to imagine had cleft that mountain nearly in two, creating a chasm half a mile deep. South Village had been built on a fractured ledge only a few hundred feet wide, at the top of the chasm on the south side.

The north side, almost perpetually hidden in mists that rose from the river rapids far below, was too rocky and sheer to be of any use. Besides, it had its own residents who cared very little for human intrusion.

But on this side a small outpost had been built, rebuilt, and expanded over many years. Outsiders were only the latest to reside there, adding several buildings of their own and reinforcing the old stone wall that guarded against approach by the mountain road, should anyone be insane enough to make the trek up uninvited.

In the center of that wall, a massive wooden gate had been built. Two dozen logs lashed together and sealed with tar and rope. Thick as a horse was wide.

It lay shattered in the snow.

Kait crept forward in a belly crawl, her EMBAR aimed through the wide gap where the gates to South Village had stood perhaps an hour before. She would have killed for a scope. As it was, she could barely see the buildings that lay beyond the smashed barrier.

Damn these clouds.

With her left hand she waved Marcus forward. Still prone, she covered him as he rushed ahead to the wall and took cover on the left side. Poking his head around the corner, he glanced about, then leaned back behind the wall and motioned for her to join him. Once Kait's back was against the wall on the right side, he lifted his chin toward her.

"Place is quiet. I don't like it."

Kait nodded. "They would have taken shelter in the main hall. With any luck that's where they are now."

He considered that. "Sweep the perimeter first," he said. "Something about this feels off."

She knew what he meant, and agreed without hesitation. Kait had visited this place many times, throughout her life, and it had never felt so... lifeless. Despite the harshness of the landscape and the bitter cold, South Village was a singular place of warmth in her memories.

"Is there any other way into the village?"

Kait shook her head. "They use winches to get down to the river and back, but an approach from down there is basically impossible."

"Okay," he said. "New plan. We leapfrog from cover to cover."

She shook her head again. "You take the left, I'll go right. We'll meet at the cliff in half the time."

A flash of annoyance crossed his face. In fact he looked, Kait thought, exactly as he did whenever JD disagreed with him. But the expression fell away.

"We've got a different way of doing things, but this is your place, your people. We do it your way."

"If it doesn't work, please don't say I told you so."

Marcus Fenix turned to the village, eyes narrowed.

"I'll *definitely* say I told you so." And then he was around the corner, moving quickly to the left along the interior of the wall.

Kait peeked around her own edge of the ruined gate, saw nothing, and moved in. She hugged the rock wall until it met a guard tower twenty feet away. The wall took a ninety-degree turn there, then ran straight out to the edge of the cliff, some two hundred feet distant. A few buildings, mostly for storing fish, were huddled in the wall's almost perpetual shadow. The wall itself had been hollowed out ages ago. She'd spent hours inside it as a child, running the candle-lit lengths with a stick held before her as a would-be weapon. She and the other kids all around her played some truly epic games of "swords and shields."

All that had gone away the day Reyna had braided Kait's hair and laid it neatly over her left shoulder, proclaiming to the village and the whole world that her daughter was no longer a child, but a grown adult. Everything had changed that day, but one detail burned more brightly than any other in Kait's mind.

The amulet.

Reyna had been wearing it around her neck even then. Kait had watched it sway slowly as the braiding ritual took place, marveled at how the sunlight glinted off its golden edges, wholly unaware of the awful symbol hidden on the other side.

The very amulet she now hid under her armor.

Kait Diaz halted and shook her head vigorously to force such thoughts away, and banish the extreme fatigue she felt behind her eyes. Once again she ignored the sudden unbearable weight of the object hanging around her neck.

South Village, she told herself. *Focus on South Village.* She glanced at the big open yard that lay between the various low buildings perched along the small plateau. Details began to register. The smashed doors, the overturned barrels and carts. A child's shoe lying sideways in the snow.

The silence.

It's exactly like Fort Umson after the Swarm came, she thought. Another detail registered, not as obvious as the signs of struggle but perhaps more important. A layer of snow had accumulated on that shoe. On the barrels and carts, as well. Whatever had happened here, it had been a day or more ago.

Yet the traps on the road, and the footprints... she felt sure those had been more recent. Perhaps less than a day old.

A scenario began to form in her mind. Eli and Mackenzie, accompanied by one of the adults from South Village, leaving for home, unaware that home was under attack and would be a deserted shell by the time they arrived. They waited, scared and confused, hoping someone would return—but no one did.

Except the Swarm. And Jinn's DeeBees.

She felt a sudden and overwhelming sense of guilt that made her pause and lean on the wall. She'd found Reyna, buried her, and blanked out her mind. Let herself be led to New Ephyra while her own people were still unaccounted for.

Meanwhile, not knowing what else to do, the twins and their unknown companion had turned around and headed back here, only this time they were pursued by monsters. If—no, *when* they made it back to South Village, they found it like this. Another ruin. She could only imagine how the two kids must have felt. How crushing it would be.

Kait lowered her chin and set her mouth in a tight line. She'd find them, she'd make it up to them. Somehow.

Raising the Lancer to her shoulder, Kait sighted down the barrel and jogged forward, checking every corner, every door. Checked and cleared every possible hiding place without making so much as a whisper herself. Across the plateau she saw Marcus doing the same.

They met at the cliff, empty-handed and breathing hard.

"Clear," he said, voice low.

"Same on this side."

Her attention swung back to the great hall, in the center of the plateau.

"Kait," Marcus said. "This the way down?" he asked, gesturing to the nearest winch. Beside the machine, thick ropes hung from a swinging arm, descending into the mists.

Somewhere below, Kait knew, would be a sort of basket—a metal frame with taut netting in between, big enough to haul up several bushels of fish caught in the rapids below, plus a few villagers. Another identical contraption stood thirty feet away. Both cargo baskets, Kait noted, were at the bottom just now. She detailed all this for Marcus.

"The cliff on this side has been hollowed out. Tunnels and rooms carved right out of the rock. Most of the villagers live down there, not up here."

"And the other side?" he asked. Kait looked in that direction, seeing only the thick mists that perpetually hid the other side of the canyon.

"There's a species of… birds, I guess. Only much bigger, and fiercely territorial. The villagers call them snapjaws. As long as we stay over here they'll leave us alone."

"Right." He nodded. "We check the hall first, then go down."

"Agreed," she said, taking point when Marcus stepped aside. They approached the hall from the rear, reaching its walls then working around to the side and front. She kept her gun ready and picked a path that allowed absolute silence. A cold wind rose, sending eddies of white icy powder across the devastated plateau. The sudden rush of air made the empty buildings moan.

How quickly, she thought, *a place of warmth and happiness can become a cold, lifeless shell.*

At the door she glanced over her shoulder. Marcus had fallen ten paces behind, less adept than she was at picking a path through the snow and debris. She waited until he'd caught up.

"I'll go in first," he said, in just more than a whisper.

"Why?"

He shrugged. "My turn," he said.

If for no reason other than the spirit of teamwork, Kait relented and pressed herself against the wall so he could move up.

The doors to the hall were closed. Marcus gave a tentative yank on the handle, and to Kait's surprise the door creaked outward. If the villagers had taken shelter here, they would have barred it from the inside. The fine hairs on the back of her neck began to tingle. Something about this was very wrong.

Marcus paused, perhaps as surprised as she was, but after a few seconds he continued to pull the door open. The creaking noise seemed loud enough to be heard for miles, though given the wind

Kait doubted someone standing fifty feet away would have noticed it. Marcus backed up a few steps as the door opened. He pulled it until it lay nearly flat against the outer wall of the long, low building.

Silence returned, save for the moaning wind rushing coldly through the village. He glanced back at her, nodded, then turned to enter.

Kait kept close, just a step behind him, and hadn't even crossed the threshold when she reached out, grabbed the collar of his armor, and yanked him backward, hard. Marcus almost lost his footing on the icy wood floor. He stumbled back a couple of steps before managing to get his balance under control.

"The hell's the matter?" he demanded.

Kait pointed.

Just inside the door, at shin height, was the barest hint of a fishing line. It was stretched taut across the opening, only just catching the wan sunlight that pushed through the perpetual clouds up here. Kait powered on the lights that were built into her armor, and knelt. She turned and watched the glinting reflection off the string, following it ten feet along the floor before the line wrapped around a wooden pillar. The other direction was the same. Marcus waited as she crept along the length and examined the far side of one of the pillars.

The fishing line was tied around the handle of an excavation detonator, which in turn was wired into six sticks of explosive. The stuff was decades old, but she'd already seen twice today how deadly it could be.

That wasn't all. Taped to the top of the explosives was a bean tin, filled to the brim with nails and other tiny bits of metal. Kait had no doubt the exact same trap would be found on the other pillar, but she checked it all the same.

She returned to Marcus.

"More bombs?" he asked. At her nod he said, "It's time we announced ourselves."

With that simple observation the stress of sneaking through this place vanished. Kait stepped back and swept the beam of her lights across the great room.

"Eli? Mackenzie!" she shouted. "It's me, Kait Diaz! Are you in here?" The words echoed through the room, and then again off the rocky outer wall of the village, and the mountainside itself. *If they're here, they heard that*, she thought, and waited.

Marcus shifted, anxious. He seemed about to add his own voice when something moved in the dark recesses of the room. The barest hint of noise. Kait raised her gun instinctively, but kept her finger away from the trigger.

"Eli?" she asked the darkness. "Mackenzie? Is someone there?"

Her light couldn't reach the far end of the hall. She saw only the long dining table that dominated the space, and all the high-backed chairs around it, askew or even tipped on their sides. Bowls and cups, some still holding half-eaten meals or drinks, were scattered across the great wooden surface.

A mug fell from the table, bounced, and rolled across the hardwood floor, leaving a trail of stale beer to mark its path. Kait swung her beam back to the table in time to see two yellow eyes gleaming back at her.

The cat walked casually to the edge of the surface and hopped to the floor, where it began to lap at the spilled drink, its little pink tongue darting into the amber liquid as it stared suspiciously back at Kait.

"Ummm," Marcus said. "If it panics and runs into that fishing line..."

Kait stepped over the line and knelt a few feet from the animal, holding out a hand in a gesture of trust. The feline eyed her, took one last sip of the beer, then darted off back into the darkness.

Marcus rested his Lancer on his shoulder.

"I'm thinking maybe we try the cliff."

Keeping her disappointment in check, Kait led the way back outside and moved toward the winch at the cliff's edge. She left the bomb trap armed and in place in the meeting hall, confident the cat would be too busy with all the food left behind, and hoping the bomb might provide an early warning system if the Swarm were around.

Reaching the cliff she found the reverse lever for the winch, flipped it, and turned the old motor on. The thing wheezed to life and began to spin, coiling the thick rope onto a spool as it hauled the car back up the cliff. Between the rumbling, coughing old winch motor, and the sound of the rapids rising up from below, all other sounds were quickly drowned out.

"Down!" Marcus shouted.

He pushed her to one side even as he dove to the other. Only then did she register the high-pitched whine of the approaching projectile.

6: LONG WAY DOWN

The Dropshot round came from somewhere by the gate, and once over their heads it activated. Its payload shot straight down, exploding between them in a shower of rock and dirt. Kait rolled with the blast, felt the heat and debris scour her back and legs as she went. Her weapon became trapped beneath her, so she rolled further. A good thing, too, as another Dropshot round whistled above, stopping in mid-flight as its payload was propelled straight downward.

Whoever had fired it had missed this time. The explosive bolt went screaming off down the cliff face. Kait was on her feet and running when the explosion came—a muffled boom from somewhere far below.

As she ran she fired a round blind into the misty air, in the general direction of the gate. She could barely see the opening, and had the vague sense that there were three of them, maybe four.

Finding an overturned wooden cart she dove behind it, knowing it wouldn't help against a well-aimed salvo from that

Dropshot, but seeing no alternative. She glanced to where Marcus had been. He'd come to his feet as well, and was rushing off in the opposite direction to the one she'd taken, instinctively giving the enemy two targets to deal with instead of one. Smart.

She caught a flash of movement from the corner of her eye. "On the left!" she shouted to him as a Pouncer first leapt onto a stone bench, then flung itself toward her companion. Marcus hit the dirt when the creature was in midair and unable to change course. The monster lashed out with claws and tail as it flew past him, but only managed to scrape the back of his body armor as it sailed by.

Its trajectory led it straight into the second winch, and its weight was too much for the old wooden beams that supported the rope. There was a thunderous crack as the wood snapped in half with a shower of splinters.

The Pouncer twisted in the air, clawed uselessly for purchase. Kait had yet to judge the intelligence of the creatures, but this one seemed only to realize it was doomed once it had fully cleared the edge of the cliff. As it and the remains of winch number two went tumbling over the edge, it made one last attempt to damage its prey. The large fanned tail curved upward and fired its array of quills toward Marcus an instant before it vanished over the cliff.

The barbs, sharp as nails and each as long as Kait's forearm, sprayed outward and *thwacked* into the ground in a half-circle around where Marcus lay. He grunted and rolled, one of the barbs poking out of his leg. His face contorted into an uncharacteristic grimace as he yanked the projectile out of his flesh, and Kait saw blood spray out onto the icy ground.

She pivoted, squaring her shoulders to run to him, when a second Pouncer landed atop the cart behind which she hid. The weight of the beast shattered the old wood, the cart half collapsing.

The long barrel of her EMBAR was pointed the wrong way, so she did the only thing she could and swung it like a club. The weapon cracked into the side of the Pouncer's tentacled maw. Streams of hot saliva flew from suddenly bared fangs as it grunted from the impact. Its tail came up, barbs aimed right at her face, but as it unleashed them the cart gave in under its weight and collapsed fully.

The quills sailed to her right, one whooshing only inches from her ear. Emboldened, Kait took enough time to aim and fire. At this range the EMBAR was devastating. Her shot blasted a fist-sized hole in the creature's head. Brains and bone sprayed behind it as it collapsed to the ground.

A lucky shot, and Kait knew it.

She ran left, back toward the stone wall along which she'd originally scouted, hoping to draw the enemy away from Marcus. One quill he could likely shake off, but she'd seen the blood spray when he'd pulled it out, and feared it might have done more damage than even someone as tough as he was could take and still fight.

Another Dropshot round sung overhead. Kait turned ninety degrees an instant before the ground in front of her erupted from the payload's explosion. The great hall was directly in front of her now, and she powered toward it. Perhaps fighting out here in the open wasn't the best idea, despite her sniper rifle. She needed darkness, and the building's low roof might keep that cursed Dropshot from firing at all.

It was when she reached the back edge of the structure that the Scion came into view. The massive brute strode confidently forward. Smugly, even. Its black lips were curled up in a wide, savage grin.

Maintaining her pace, she raised her weapon and squeezed off a poorly aimed shot. The Scion twisted as the bullet ripped into its shoulder, but the smile remained—along with the confident stride. She doubted she could beat it to the front of the building. It had the better angle, after all, being on that side of the hall already.

From somewhere behind and to her right, Kait heard familiar rapid thunderclaps as Marcus let loose with his Lancer. She couldn't see his target, or what state he was in, but at least he was shooting. That was something.

Ahead the Scion stopped, extended its arms, and roared at the sky. In that moment, from either side of the bastard, Kait saw new shapes emerging from the mist beyond the gate.

Drones. Two of them, and all the more dangerous as the Scion's cloud rallied them like a potent drug. The two scaly figures lowered their massive shoulders and charged straight at her, coming around either side of their leader.

Kait had no choice. Kneeling, she brought the weapon up and aimed. She chose the Drone on the left, for it was a step ahead of the other and angling in. Aiming not at the heart but the knee, she pulled the trigger and watched in grim satisfaction as the leg folded backward under the force of her shot. The Drone shrieked and tumbled forward. As she had hoped, the second was forced to skid and alter its path, angling sideways, blocking the path of the Scion behind it.

This bought her the precious seconds she needed.

Jumping to her feet she took off at a sprint, rounding the front of the great meeting hall and charging through the open doors. She plunged into the building's darkness and dove high and forward, rolling in the air to land on her shoulder, neatly clearing the tripwire that still stretched between the two columns just a few feet inside the doors.

Continuing her roll until she was standing again, Kait took two running steps deeper into the building, then dove again, this time twisting in the air so that she landed on her back, sliding under the great dining table, her EMBAR aimed down the length of her legs, back toward the door.

She skidded to a stop and waited.

Between her feet and over the barrel of the gun, Kait saw the Scion lumber up to the entrance. Dropshot at the ready, the giant took a step into the building, ducking under the frame of the door. It swiveled its head from left to right, squinting at the darkness. She took aim, knowing its eyes would adjust any second, knowing she was trapped where she lay. Her finger remained hovering over the trigger.

The Scion raised its foot to take another step, then paused. It was looking down, and Kait knew it had spotted the tripwire.

She moved her finger to the trigger.

Just then, the other Drone came rushing through the open doorway, powering into the building, drunk on the strange war-gas the Scions emitted to bring their soldiers to a state of blood lust. It came in so fast it tore right past its leader. The Scion stretched out one massive arm in a failed attempt to stop its soldier. The Drone plowed on, and Kait heard the snick of the fishing line being broken by its legs.

She rolled onto her stomach as the explosions shook the room. Even though her face was pressed against the floor, the flash of the twin explosions still whited out the inside of her firmly shut eyes. A blistering heat crashed over her body. From all around came the sounds of impact of several hundred bolts, nails, and other random bits of metal that had filled the canisters set on top of the improvised bombs. They tore into everything. Wood. Stone.

The flesh of the two Swarm creatures.

But not Kait. She'd remembered their placement, on top

of the bombs rather than beside or beneath. The floor was the safest place, and the thick table above her shielded her from any secondary shrapnel, of which there was plenty.

Ears ringing, eyes still awash with yellow-orange light, Kait crawled deeper into the building. An instinctive move, and one that saved her life. Only seconds after the explosion, a heavy wooden chandelier came crashing down from above. The ropes that held it aloft must have been severed by the powerful nail bomb. The heavy fixture slammed onto the table so hard it levered the entire long wooden surface upward like a child's seesaw.

All the half-eaten bowls of soup and stale mugs of beer were catapulted toward her enemies, and it was almost enough to make Kait laugh. Later, maybe. More immediately she feared the whole building might collapse around her.

Shielded by the angle of the table, Kait stood fully upright, then ran to the side of the building where an interior door frame led to a small antechamber. The door itself had been torn from its hinges and lay in splinters against the back wall of the tiny storage room. Kait dashed in, put her back against the wall beside the door, and waited for the great room just outside to go quiet—or collapse, whichever came first.

Quiet, as it turned out. Tentatively, she took a glance around the corner, then stepped back into the dining hall.

The place was a broken, pockmarked mess. Almost everything save the floor had been shredded by the two bombs. The huge wooden pillars to which the devices had been affixed were simply gone. And in the main doorway lay the smoking, nail-ridden corpse of a Drone. Kait took a few tentative steps toward the body. Nails and bolts were embedded in every inch of its exposed skin. The sight of it made her stomach clench, and she forced her eyes away.

Where was the Scion?

She had no idea. Vaporized, if she was lucky. Blown all the way back through the gates, maybe. She couldn't imagine a scenario in which it could have survived such a blast.

From somewhere outside, toward the cliffs, she heard more gunfire.

"Marcus," she muttered, putting all else out of her mind. Running out of the utterly destroyed front of the once-great hall, she raced along the side of the building to the rear, then crossed the open space that preceded the cliff's edge.

Sound to her left.

Kait pivoted and lifted her EMBAR, only to realize she'd already fired her last round. She jogged ahead anyway, tossing the weapon aside and drawing the machete she wore at her hip.

Marcus stood twenty feet on, Lancer held loosely at his side. The chainsaw blade attached under the barrel dripped with gore.

Lying in heaps around him were three bodies. Two were Pouncers, but the third… Kait shook her head in disbelief. It was a Snatcher, the same kind of creature that had grabbed him and taken him into the Swarm's hive, less than a week ago. The kind that had taken her mother and uncle from her. She'd fought a few herself, before finally finding Reyna, and even with JD and Del at her side the monsters had been fiendishly difficult to kill.

Marcus had sliced its bulging abdomen open from top to bottom, spilling the phlegmy contents all over the snow.

Luckily, no one had been inside.

Kait came up next to him. He was staring blankly down at the dead creature, unsteady on his feet.

"You okay?" she asked him. It was only then that Marcus seemed to come out of whatever trance the fight had put him in.

He blinked, his gaze drifting from her to the carnage around him. Gradually, his breathing came under control.

"I'll live. You?"

Kait nodded.

"Heard the bomb go off," he noted.

"Whoever put it there knew what they were doing."

"Hell of a blast."

She dipped her chin, took in the three enemies that lay around him. "I can't be sure, but there's probably more coming, and I'm out of ammo."

"Let's get below, then. And Kait?" He paused dramatically. "Told you so."

She just shook her head.

Together they walked back to the first winch. As the battle had raged all around it, the wheezy old machine had dutifully hauled its fish basket up the cliff. Without a word or any hesitation, Marcus leapt over the low railing and moved to the far side of the taut netting that served as the floor of the thing. It swung away under the uneven weight. When it returned to the cliff face, Kait hopped onto it.

The rope that held it was attached to a set of wheels about ten feet above the platform. From there, four more ropes came down diagonally, knotted expertly around the corners of the frame. Marcus grabbed one of these and tugged on it.

"Damned sturdy."

Kait found her balance, turned, and reached out for the winch control arm, pushing it into the down position. The basket began to move, and with aching slowness it descended into the mists.

Kait glanced at Marcus's leg. "How bad is it?"

He didn't even look. "Had worse." He'd sprayed it with a

wound sealer, standard COG issue, and that would hold for a few days. With any luck, it would be enough.

The cart ambled down.

"This place," Marcus said, "how many lived... uh, *live* here?"

"Two or three hun—"

A shadow was all the warning they got.

The Scion, ridden with bolts and nails, landed with a deafening howl on the platform, sending it swinging wildly to one side.

Kait grabbed for the nearest rope and just managed to hold on as the metal frame tilted almost fully sideways, then swung back in the other direction. The Scion, weaponless and bleeding from a thousand small wounds, swung at her. The backhanded attack caught her full in the face. Her grip broke as stars exploded in her eyes and the world tumbled around her.

She fell hard on the metal frame. Kait rolled, wanting distance between her and the creature. Dazed from the punch, she'd lost her bearings, and soon felt the edge of the frame and the cool damp open air beyond. Somehow she had the sense to grab the edge of the frame and stop herself going over.

Spitting blood, she lifted her head and heaved herself back onto her feet. Battered by the explosion in the hall, dazed by the blow she'd just taken to the face, she shakily came to her feet only to stagger as the whole basket tilted again. Fighting for balance, she blinked away the pain and the ice-cold air and tried to focus.

There.

Opposite her, Marcus and the Scion squared off. The creature stood almost twice as tall as him, and both were weaponless. Kait had no idea when or how he'd lost his Lancer, but the only weapons he had now were his fists. Tough as he was, Marcus stood no chance against the beast that towered over him. Its arms were as thick as his chest, and it had the wild look in its eyes of a monster hell-bent on revenge. Easily knocking aside Marcus's first punch, wearing that same black-lipped smile she'd seen at the gate, it coiled its own fist back.

Her action came without thinking. Kait crossed to the center of the basket, dove, and rammed her shoulder into the Scion's midsection.

The last thing she saw was the Locust emblem on its belt. A perfect match for the one she wore around her neck.

Pain exploded across her shoulder and all the way down her arm. It was like running at a full sprint straight into a tree. Only, not exactly. Eyes clenched, her one good arm wrapped around the enemy, Kait understood too late that she'd timed her attack a little too well. She must have caught it off balance.

Hard as the impact was, she kept on going.

The Scion toppled with the force of her tackle.

"NO!" Marcus roared.

The Scion bellowed.

Her foot scraped the edge of the platform as she went over. Kait opened her eyes to see her opponent falling away from her, grasping at her wrist. She yanked her arm back, making brief eye contact with the monster. It regarded her with cool rage.

Something locked hard on her ankle, and for a brief instant she thought another of the creatures had entered the fray. A Juvie perhaps, biting down on her leg, accidentally saving her life. The grip of it whipped her around in midair, forestalling her plunge into the rapids. Instead, she swung under the platform and smacked into the wooden subframe. She winced, swung back, and finally managed to glance up.

Marcus stared back down at her, one hand firmly clasped around her ankle, just above the boot.

"I've got you," he said through clenched teeth. He reached with his other hand and held it out. Kait grasped it, and held on as he hauled her back up onto the netted floor.

For a moment she just lay there, struggling to breathe in enough air, letting the sounds and cold spray of the rapids wash over her. After a few seconds she sat up. Marcus was seated next to her, hands hanging over his knees.

"You saved my life," he said.

"I guess we're even, then," she replied. "Thanks for the grab."

"Any time."

He started to push himself to stand. The platform lurched suddenly, dropping a foot before snapping to a stop. It began to swing again.

"The hell was that?" Marcus asked, looking up.

Kait followed his gaze. From high above, distant but echoing down the chasm walls, came the hoots and cries of several Juvies. The platform began to bounce and twist erratically. Small, sharp movements.

"You've gotta be kidding me. Are they cutting the rope?"

Marcus looked down, pointed. Through the mists it was just possible to make out the rocks that poked up around the thundering rapids. His gaze moved back to her.

"Too far to jump. Ideas?"

"Swing the platform," she said, standing and moving to the opposite side. "Get to the cliff and grab something. It's the only way."

"Good," he said, moving to the edge on his side, looping one of the support ropes around his forearm.

Kait did the same. Together they began to sway, extending the motion of the platform. She had become so disoriented that she'd forgotten which side of the ravine belonged to South Village, and which to the nesting snapjaws. There was a fifty-fifty chance they'd be attacked by the giant birds, but those odds still beat the alternative.

So she swayed. Back, then forth. Back, then forth. Timing her motion to the platform, watching Marcus to keep in sync.

Vibrations came down the rope and Juvies hooted from somewhere above. Sawing at the rope? Trying to climb down? There was no way to know.

Behind Marcus she glimpsed a hint of rocky wall through the thick cloud of spray. It was covered in white streaks. Bird shit.

"My side," she said, and turned herself around.

"Grab anything you can," Marcus shouted over the noise of the rapids.

Kait gritted her teeth, eyes scanning left to right, hoping against hope for a protruding root or jut of rock that wasn't already scoured smooth and slick with cold river water.

There. Something dark in the gray fog. She leaned out, reached as far as she could. Fingers stretching.

The dark thing took shape. It wasn't a branch or a stony edge.

A gloved hand.

Reaching for her.

Scion, her mind screamed, and she pulled back. But the swinging platform pushed her closer. Even as her brain told her the hand was too small to be a Scion's, the body came into view and Kait felt the whole world tilt beneath her.

The face emerging from the mist was one she knew.

"Oscar?!"

7: REUNITED

"Wh... Kait?" came the reply of her bearded, ugly, beautiful uncle.

So complete was her shock at seeing him alive, she completely missed his hand. It was his left hand he held out to her, the angle awkward. His right was tucked up against his body, the arm in a makeshift sling. He lunged toward her, but too late. The platform started its backward swing.

"Kait!" he shouted.

Something shouldered her aside. Marcus. Holding onto the support rope with one hand, he leaned out as far as he could and clasped his hand around Oscar's forearm. Oscar twisted and grabbed onto Marcus as best he could with his left hand. Both men grunted with the strain as the heavy platform tried to swing away.

For several seconds the fish basket hung there, as if frozen in time. Kait stood, still awestruck by the sight of the uncle she thought she'd lost, the platform holding precariously steady, Oscar and Marcus clasping forearms, staring at one another as if in some summer-fair contest of strength.

"Kait," Marcus breathed, straining. "Off."

She could not move. Oscar was alive. Oscar was *here*.

"*Off*, Kait," Marcus said, voice level but tight. "*Now*."

The word cut through the fog in her head. She leapt from the platform onto the rocky ledge where Oscar stood. There she grinned at her uncle, tears welling in the corners of her eyes.

"Little help?" he asked her.

Her smile did not waver as she turned and helped him heave Marcus over to the cliff. As he stepped off the platform, four Juvies emerged from the mists above, crawling down the rope and onto the platform.

"Eli!" Oscar shouted. "Now!"

From above, just audible over the roar of the river, there came the loud *crack* of a rifle shot, followed an instant later by a sharp snap. Suddenly the fish-hauling basket went plunging straight down into the rushing waters, Juvies and all. They yelped as they fell, the sounds abruptly cut short when the entire contraption smashed into the rocks and speeding water below. Kait winced at the sound of splintering wood and bone as the river swept it all away.

She glanced up, but saw only cloudy air.

"Eli did that?" she said.

Her uncle nodded. "Kid's got the eye, Kait. A natural sharpshooter, and his sister... hell, you just wait. She learned a lot from the cavediggers, I'll say that much."

As she processed that, Oscar pulled her into an awkward one-armed bear-hug embrace. She let herself be enveloped by his arm, throwing her own around him and squeezing hard.

"You're alive," she breathed into his chest. "I can't believe it. I never thought..." Her words trailed off, washed away by guilt. Guilt for not looking for him with the same zeal with which she'd sought out her mother. Guilt for not thinking he'd survive the Swarm as Marcus had.

"It's okay, it's okay," he said quietly.

"I'm sorry," she managed to get out through her tears. "I should have come sooner."

"Kait... where's Reyna?" Oscar asked, still holding her.

She eased him back, met his gaze, and found she couldn't say it. Her silence was answer enough, though. She could see it in his eyes.

All her life Kait had loved the way her uncle wore his heart on his sleeve. She'd admired the hell out of him for it, in fact. So full of life and love, so unafraid to let himself shine through those squinty eyes. She thought she'd seen every emotion he'd had to offer, but the grief that fell across his face now broke her heart all over again.

"The Swarm," she whispered, searching his eyes, wishing she had a different tale to tell. "Mom didn't make it."

He grimaced, looked away.

Kait swallowed. "We thought you... I thought..."

"It's okay, Kait," he said. "I... I need to sit down. You two better come inside." He turned and walked away before she could say another word. She and Marcus exchanged a glance, and followed.

The ledge became a tunnel carved into the cliff wall, about six feet high and three wide. It curved and widened into a room about ten feet to a side. Low chairs piled with furs surrounded a wooden table with a half-eaten meal spread out across its surface.

Oscar lowered himself heavily into one of the chairs, his good left arm cradling the right. For a moment he just sat there, staring blankly at the floor, left hand absently massaging his right bicep and shoulder. Kait waited, unsure what to say or do.

Then Oscar squeezed his eyes shut, shook his head once, and abruptly stood. "Kait, sit. Are you hurt? Hungry? And your friend...?"

She gestured to her companion. "Oscar, this is Marcus Fenix."

Oscar blinked at that. Looked around. "JD and Del," he said, suddenly urgent. "Please don't tell me—"

Kait held out a reassuring hand. "They're fine. Busy with… well, we'll get to that."

He nodded, satisfied, then faced Marcus. The two men sized each other up. Oscar finally ran his good hand down his tattered vest and crossed the room.

"My manners suck. Forgive me! Uh, can't shake your hand properly though. It's nice to meet you," Oscar said.

Marcus regarded him, shaking the offered hand without hesitation. "Same. Are you sure we haven't met before, though?"

"Don't think so." Oscar scratched at his cheek. "Probably fought in a few battles together back in the day, but not side by side."

The old soldier nodded. "Nice meeting you too, then."

Oscar waved the comment off, gesturing to the chairs, doing anything but meet Kait's eyes. "Let's find you guys something to eat, eh? Fish stew is all we have, I'll get you a bowl." Turning, he shouted, "Young ones!? Come meet our guests!"

"Let me help you," Kait said, stepping forward.

Oscar half turned and gestured emphatically toward the chairs with his good arm. Then he lumbered down a short passage that led deeper into the face of the cliff, and began to bang around in what Kait assumed must be a small cooking area. Within seconds she could hear the clatter of bowls and spoons.

Her mouth began to water. Her stomach rumbled audibly. She sat, looked at Marcus, and inclined her head toward the chair that sat opposite her. He hesitated, but finally sat down. It looked as if he was about to say something when the two children emerged from the same passage Oscar had taken.

Kait had last seen the twins less than two weeks earlier, when they'd left on their usual trading run to South Village—a journey they'd made once a month for the last year. It was a task their parents had been responsible for, but they'd both succumbed to disease when the twins were still babies, and the village had raised them. About a year ago the twins had gone to Reyna and asked to take on the role their parents used to fill. She, Kait, and Oscar had escorted them on their first "mission," and been impressed by their skill in wilderness survival. After a few successful trips, Eli and Mackenzie had begun to make the trip alone.

Here, now, they looked like they'd aged a year or more since Kait had last seen them. She had to remind herself they weren't yet adults, that Mackenzie's hair had not yet been braided.

"Kait!" they exclaimed in unison upon seeing her, and she had no time to stand and greet them. The fair-haired children rushed to her and hugged her right where she sat. Mackenzie, face burrowed in Kait's shoulder, spoke in a quiet voice.

"We thought everyone…"

"I know, I know." Kait squeezed them tight. "I thought the same. I'd hoped you two were safe here, though."

"We went back," Eli said.

"We didn't know about what happened," Mackenzie added.

"It's okay," Kait said. "You did fine. I'm sorry I wasn't there. I didn't…" But her words trailed off. She didn't what? Didn't think to check on them? Didn't care about anyone but Reyna? Didn't want to face the aftermath? Kait battled back a wave of shame.

"Oscar was there," Eli said brightly. "After a few days, anyway."

"God he smelled terrible!" Mackenzie added. "Covered in snot!"

Kait's uncle strode back into the room, steaming bowls

precariously held on his damaged right arm. The room filled instantly with the fragrant smell of cooked fish. He handed one to Marcus, then shooed the kids aside before giving Kait hers.

"Snot. Hah. That's true," he said. "Head to toe. Smelled a bit like the stew, come to think of it."

"A Snatcher got Marcus, too," Kait said, and lowered her gaze as another wave of shame hit her. Marcus had survived, but she'd never guessed Oscar might have.

"Snatcher, huh?" Oscar asked. "Good a name as any."

Marcus nodded. "We've taken to calling their kind the 'Swarm'. I came to in their hive. Not even really sure how long I was there before Kait, JD, and Del found me."

Oscar plopped into the remaining chair. He started to speak, then looked to the twins. "Eyes and ears, kiddos! It's your watch, so get back to it!"

They grinned and ran off, taking separate tunnels. Oscar watched them go, an almost fatherly pride shining in his eyes.

"Your arm," Kait prompted.

Oscar waved her off. "Bruised, not broken. The twins made the sling. Did a damn good job, too."

"And the traps on the road," Kait said. "Yours or theirs?"

"Mackenzie's," he said in quiet disbelief. "Seems like she picked up more than just mountain survival coming here all those times. South Village is... *was*... populated by some of the best old miners and sappers around, and they taught her well, that's for sure. A real artist."

"And who taught Eli to shoot? You?"

Her uncle shook his head. "No, no. That's raw talent. When I found them at Fort Umson he nearly took my head off. Gave him quite a lecture on safety."

At that Kait had to laugh. "The only thing you know about gun safety is how to turn the safety off."

He managed a grin of his own. "Laugh it up, niece. He's turned into a fine little marksman, almost overnight. Hell, the fact that both of them still have all their fingers and toes reflects quite well on me, I think."

She couldn't help but return the smile. It *did* reflect well on the cantankerous old son of a bitch, whom, before today, Kait had never seen interact with the children of the village beyond growling at them so they'd leave him alone.

"How'd you survive?" Marcus asked. "The Snatcher, I mean."

Oscar shrugged, nonchalant. "I suppose I gave it indigestion." At Kait's skeptical gaze he amended the story. "Okay. Truth be told, I cut my way out—that's a kind of indigestion. Speaking of which, I recommend eating that while it's hot. Eat fast, too, so you don't notice the taste."

Kait had something more important on her mind, though. "Oscar, where are the rest of the South Villagers?"

He met her gaze. "Gone," he said simply. "They were all here when the twins left to return home, unaware of what had happened to us. I found Eli and Mackenzie at Fort Umson and, after a day of fighting those... *things* and DeeBees, we decided to come back here and warn them. Help defend the place." His eyes fell. "We were too late."

There was silence then, save for the muffled sounds of rapids and wind outside.

"This 'Swarm'," Oscar said, drawing the word out as if deciding how well it fit, "what do we know about them? What hole did they crawl out of?"

"A Locust burial site," Marcus said. "Tollen Dam."

Oscar sat back, digesting that. He let out a long sigh.

Marcus added, "They won't be satisfied until every last one of us is in their hive."

Oscar considered that. Finally he said, "I'm sitting here wondering if you mean the Swarm, or the fucking COG. No offense, Marcus."

Marcus arched an eyebrow. "None taken."

Kait answered her uncle's question before thinking better of it. "The DeeBees were there to help, Oscar. That first attack, that was a misunderstanding."

"Was it now? How do you know that?"

The landscape of the conversation suddenly became a minefield. Kait decided to leave JD and Del out of it as long as she could. "I spoke with Jinn herself. In fact, we've just come from there."

"There?"

"New Ephyra."

The warmth in his eyes drained like water from a bath. "You were in... you..." The words eluded him. "A meeting with the First Minister. Reyna would be so proud."

"That's not fair," she said, knowing full well it was entirely fair.

He shook his head and stood. "I need some rest. You two eat. We'll talk more in the morning." With that he went back to the kitchen.

Kait remained rooted in place, unsure why she'd just defended the First Minister. Worse, she'd just admitted to traveling to the capitol instead of coming straight home. Why had she done that? How could she explain that to Oscar when she didn't understand it herself?

Marcus downed the last of his fish stew, then rose from the chair. "Going to find a bunk and crash. You should do the same."

"I will," she said, and she meant it. The only thing less inviting than Oscar's fish stew were the nightmares waiting behind her eyelids. At the same time, if she didn't get some decent rest, she'd be of no use to these children and her uncle.

She's falling through clouds.

Gives the ripcord a yank.

Stares at the frayed end of it.

She twists, wants to see the ground, to judge how long…

Only clouds. Everywhere, clouds.

No. Not everywhere. A cliff, rushing past. Rocks and nests and snapjaws that eye her hungrily.

She twists further, looks up. Clouds that way, too, and a rope going up, disappearing far above.

It's attached to her waist, looped there, unspooling before her eyes. It'll reach its end soon. Snap taut. Tear her in half.

Only seconds left.

No knife to sever the cord.

No way to stop it.

She twists more, looks down.

Only clouds.

Clouds and a darkness. A shape. Rushing up as she rushes down. Lunging to meet her.

A Swarmak. Jaws wide. And riding it, the Speaker. He howls with glee as Kait descends toward the open, stinking maw.

In a fit of rage she tears the pendant from her neck, coils to throw it into the creature's waiting jaws.

The Speaker leans forward in its saddle. Shouts to her.

"That's not what it's hungry for, girl!"

8: OLD STORIES

The dream jerked her awake. The untouched bowl of stew sat at her elbow, reeking. At some point someone had thrown a blanket over her. Oscar, she guessed.

Kait stood and wrapped the square of heavy wool over her shoulders. It was a short walk back out to the ledge, the very place where she'd swung for the cliff only to find Oscar standing there, waiting for her.

The air, cold and brisk, helped to drive back her fatigue, but only a little. Something would have to change, Kait thought, and soon, or she'd be little more than a catatonic mess. No use to anyone, least of all the kids she'd come here to save. Though, she mused, it didn't sound like they needed much saving. Even without Oscar's presence, the twins appeared to be much more capable than they'd ever let on.

She took a seat on the ledge above the roaring mountain river and let the water spray over her. After this, she thought, a warm shower. Food that wasn't Oscar's fish stew.

High above she could just make out a thin, jagged patch of sky.

Stars surrounding a half-moon. Snapjaws wheeled, their wings spread wide, hunting in the night or perhaps just looking for more comfortable nests.

With a heavy sigh, Kait pulled the pendant from under her armor. She held it out and tilted it, momentarily forgetting everything it signified and instead simply allowing herself to be mesmerized by the way the moonlight glinted off its golden edges. The thing was old, she realized. Worn and scratched, the color of the metal dulled over many years. She wondered how Reyna had come to possess it. Could it be that the only reason she passed it on to Kait was because her own mother had handed it to her—perhaps also at the moment of death?

She laughed softly. Some family tradition that was.

"She didn't leave you entirely empty-handed, eh?"

Kait jumped, and couldn't have hidden the pendant if she'd wanted to. She'd been so deep in thought that she hadn't heard Oscar come up behind her. The rush of water not forty feet below her didn't help, either.

He took a seat next to her. He'd removed his sling at some point, and even as he lowered himself to sit he was rolling the shoulder and flexing his hand. In his other hand was an old Gnasher shotgun, its wooden stock wrapped in dirty cloth, and deep scratches all along its snub barrel. He set it on the rock beside him and rubbed his hands together, breathing in the night air. Their shoulders touched, and Kait leaned into him. Then she smelled the wine and decided, for once, not to give him grief about it.

"Couldn't sleep either?" she asked.

"Sleep? Did that earlier. I'm on watch now."

Was I out for that long? she wondered, and she glanced at him. "Doing a hell of a job."

Oscar grinned. "Trust me, nothing's getting down here with

both platforms destroyed. Not without tripping some of Mackenzie's little surprises, that is. We'll know in plenty of time."

Kait started to ask how they would get back up to the cliff top when the time came. Then she decided against it. For a time they both simply sat there, watching the snapjaws flap out from their side of the ravine, wheel, then dive back and resettle in their shadowy homes. Finally, Kait got up the nerve to ask the question. She flipped the pendant over and let the moonlight flash across the Locust symbol on the back.

"Did you know about this?" she asked. "Do you know where she got it?" He stared at it for a moment, then held out his hand. Grudgingly, Kait passed it over.

"She got it from her mom," he said.

"I thought I remembered something about that," Kait noted.

Oscar stared at it for a long time, occasionally flipping it from one side to the other. "All I know is that it was important to her—and your grandmother, too. Reyna wore it all the time. Was wearing it the day my brother introduced me to her." He took a longer look at the back. With a sudden swiftness he handed it to her.

They were both gone now, which meant the answers probably died with them. Kait held the amulet for a long moment. Sitting on that ledge she teetered metaphorically on another. Throw the damn thing into the rapids and forget about it, or tuck it back under her shirt and stop fearing an inanimate chunk of metal.

There seemed no real debate.

Kait pushed it back under her shirt. Desperate for a change of subject, she turned her focus to the present.

"So, we have no way out of here?"

"The twins said they have an idea, but they wanted to check it out before they showed me."

"I hope the idea isn't 'blast through to the other side of the mountain.'"

"Very well might be." Oscar chuckled. Then it was his turn to put on the quizzical look. "If we get out, what then?"

Kait answered without thinking, and instantly regretted it. "We take them somewhere safe. New Ephyra."

"Safe? A COG city, run by that hag?"

"I was there, Uncle. It's—"

"There for, what, a day? You saw what they wanted you to see." He turned to face her. "I've seen cities like that laid to waste, Kait. Right before my fucking eyes."

"Then where?" she asked, anger rising. "Here? Hide in this cave until the fish—or the booze—run out? Was that your plan? You think this… this hole in the ground is safer than a fortified city?"

Oscar's eyes went wide. The words stung, and Kait regretted them but was too angry to take them back.

"Everyone from our village is dead, Kait," he said. "Everyone… except us and those kids. I'll hide here as long as I have to, and then… then I'll get them far away from this bullshit."

"Hide and run away. This doesn't sound like you at all, Uncle."

"It's not about me!" He poked her with one stubby finger, and whether on purpose or by accident, pressed the amulet under her shirt. "It's about the twins now. They're what matter."

"Hiding might not be an option for long."

Kait turned at the voice. Marcus stood in the mouth of the cave.

"This is a private conversation between family," Oscar said.

"Save it." Marcus waved him off. "Not interested… but you two need to come see this."

"See what?" Kait asked.

"A problem."

9: OLD GEAR

Trapped inside the foreman's office on the crater floor, they waited for the enemy's numbers to dwindle.

And waited.

And waited.

"If anything," Del said, on his second turn keeping watch at the window, "there's more of them now." JD joined him, and needed only a second to reach the same conclusion.

"I think we need another option, or we'll die of thirst in this dusty old box."

Del had been thinking the same thing. Problem was, the little room was nearly pitch black, and turning on a light would definitely draw attention. Finally he said, "Find some tape."

"Tape?"

"Yeah, man, tape. Like duct tape. Let's seal the edges of these windows so we can turn a fucking light on."

The plan seemed to jolt JD out of the funk into which their

botched arrival had put him. He took one end of the room and Del took the other.

Searching took what felt like ages. The light was so damned dim, Del had no choice but to rely on his fingers to probe the many cabinets and drawers. One mistake and he'd send a pile of reports tumbling off a desk or knock over a stack of hardened safety helmets.

"Anything?" JD muttered.

"Not yet," Del replied. "I've got rope, but no tape. You?"

"Nothing. Why couldn't we end up in the supply bunker?"

Del grinned, despite himself. "Some bean counter at HQ probably insisted that be hauled out. A bunch of paperwork, though? Who'd ever look at any of it again?"

He was arm-deep in a stack of files when JD let out a barely constrained yelp.

"Yes!"

"What is it?" Del could just see him in the dim room.

"Tape. A whole roll. It was in the pocket of the jacket hung over the desk chair."

Del shook his head, smiling. "Of course it was. Fucking hell, okay. Bring it over here."

Passing the roll back and forth, the two of them set to work fixing the edges of the blinds to the walls. Each time a length of tape was yanked away from the rest of the roll, Del cringed and waited for the Swarm outside to come rushing in at the noise. They never did, though, and this was a useful bit of knowledge. Not only would they block light from getting out, they wouldn't have to be quite so damned quiet, either.

The work finally done, JD reached to switch on the lights embedded in his armor.

"Whoa, whoa," Del whispered. "Way too bright, it'll still

illuminate these blinds. Plus every time we turn around shadows will be swinging all over the place, too. That's bound to get noticed."

"What's the point of all this tape then?"

Instead of answering, Del felt his way to the desk and took the lamp from its surface. He moved it to the floor, shoving the office chair aside, and put his thumb and forefinger on the switch.

"Here goes," he said.

The light winked on. Thankfully at its weakest setting. The glow barely lit the underside of the desk, but to Del's dark-adjusted eyes it seemed as bright as the summer sun. He waited there, not moving, for any sign that the enemy had spotted their hiding place.

Nothing happened.

JD gave him a thumbs-up. "Leave it there," he suggested. "Our eyes will get used to it."

"Agreed." Del started to crawl out from under the desk, then froze. "Holy shit."

"What is it?" JD asked.

"A bit of luck," he answered.

Beneath the desk, in a holster that had been nailed in place decades ago, a rusty old Boltok revolver had been hidden away. Del tugged it free of the cracked, aging leather and held it up for JD to see.

"Seems like our foreman expected trouble here."

"Yeah," JD said, "but from the Locust or the workers, I wonder."

Del had no answer for that.

"Is it loaded?" JD asked.

Del swung the cylinder out to check. There were six rounds inside. "Absolutely."

"Well that's something, then."

"Sure is. If they'll line up in rows, and we bag twenty per bullet, there'll only be a hundred left to deal with."

"Okay, smart-ass—it's better than nothing," JD amended. "Keep looking. There had to be a security detail here, maybe even an armed response team. They didn't know what they were dealing with back then, burying the Locust, and should have been prepared for anything."

For Del's part he thought JD was right, but that it wouldn't matter. This room reeked of contractor, not COG, and if Del's experiences in the Coalition taught him anything, it was that the soldiers would have taken every last scrap of their equipment with them when the job was done.

On a table behind the desk, sandwiched between more stacks of faded reports, was an old computer terminal.

"Dave," Del said, and he waited for the little floating robot to come to his side. "See if this still works. Maybe you can access it." To JD he added, "Might have a manifest of what parts they had on hand."

"A detailed layout of the site would be helpful, as well."

"Good call. Dave? Look for that, too."

Though it was ancient tech and covered in dust, the machine sprang to life the moment Dave plugged his little adapter arm in. Graphs and lines of green text bloomed across the screen, brighter than the lamp below the desk. Del quickly moved in front of the image and fumbled at the dials until he found one that dimmed the display. He waited again, as did JD, expecting the Swarm to come crashing through the ceiling. But the seconds ticked by, and the room remained intact.

"Is it working?" JD asked.

Del nodded. "He's in."

Dave went too quickly for Del to follow the readouts. He turned his focus instead to the pile of documents next to the computer, thumbing through them and looking for... he didn't know what exactly, just that he'd know it when he saw it. Only he reached the bottom with no eureka moment. It was just a bunch of useless status reports.

"Here we go," JD said from across the room. He stood in front of a massive board that was fixed to the wall. Most of it was covered with a giant calendar that had hundreds of handwritten notes on it. JD held one corner of the paper between his fingers, lifting it up so he could peer underneath. He lifted it all the way, then tore it off and dropped it on the floor.

Beneath was a top-down drawing of the entire crater basin.

"That what I think it is?" Del asked.

"Yup. And hey, this place does have a name: Orzabal Crater."

"Construction plans or just topography?"

"Even better," JD replied. "Engineer's schematic." He leaned in, tracing one index finger over the lines. "Power. Comms. Drainage. The works. Now to find something we can use."

Del figured Dave would let him know if the computer turned up anything useful, so he joined JD at the map. His friend pointed to a rectangular object.

"We're here."

"Okay, and?"

"That's all I've got so far."

Del frowned.

"Just... c'mon, help me out here. Go to the window, I need landmarks. Hell, I don't even know which direction we're facing."

Del went to the opposite wall and tore some of the taped window-blind away from it. The tiniest of gaps. He leaned into it and cupped one hand around the side of his head to stop any light from leaking.

"What do you see?" JD asked.

"A lot of dust and shadow," he replied, truthfully. But after a moment all of those glimpsed shapes in the swirling air started to add up. The picture began to reveal itself. "Okay. I see... I see another mobile bunker like this one, maybe twenty feet off."

"Same orientation as us, or edge on?"

"Edge. Just a short wall, no windows."

"Anything else?"

"Couple of Haulers and a Behemoth—the civvie version, I mean. They're all caked with dust."

"Motor pool," JD said. "Okay, that helps. I think I've got it."

Del taped the blind back down and returned to the map. JD picked up a pen and drew a cone emanating outward from the foreman's office. Within it lay the mobile bunker Del had seen, and a vague area simply marked "MP"—presumably where the vehicles were kept.

"That puts our bird here," JD said, tapping the end of the lone runway that was on the left side of the map, "and the burial cap entrance... here." His finger landed on a circular structure off to the right. When the dust cleared, it would just be visible from the window. Part of it, anyway.

"Once the Swarm stops kicking up so much dirt," Del said, "we'll get some decent footage of the cap, the mangled door. If Jinn can see that—"

"I'm not sure we can wait that long."

"Well, I'm not sure we have any choice."

Dave emitted a brief chirp, as if weighing in on the matter. It took Del a moment to realize that it wanted his attention. The computer screen displayed a basic site overview, something the foreman probably kept on at all times so he or she could check on the project's status at a glance. Useful back then, maybe, so Del couldn't fault the robot for thinking so, but just now it all showed "offline."

"Appreciate the effort, Dave," he said.

Del started to turn away, then stopped. Something caught his eye, but what? He read the screen again. Nothing stood out, nothing had changed. Everything was offline, or the system that was able to connect to them all was offline, which Del thought was more likely.

"Anything?" JD asked.

"No. Just a bunch of… wait a sec." There it was. Just below the readouts for a series of four fuel tanks, there was a small button marked "Remote vehicle control." He tapped it. A new screen appeared, listing the three vehicles he'd seen through the window, plus several more he hadn't. Then his enthusiasm drained.

Offline, every last one.

"Fuck."

"What is it?" JD raised his voice, just a bit.

Del didn't answer, reading the entire display instead. The vehicles might be offline, but there was something useful there after all.

"Think I might have something."

"Me too," JD replied.

They faced each other across the desk.

JD went first, pointing at the map. "Remember that ventilation tower above the cap? Well, there's a service gantry, runs all the way to the top."

"Should give the Swarm a nice view of us," Del said.

"Yeah, maybe, but look—there's another antenna up there. That one on that transmitter we looked at was just a backup. The main one is up at the highest point. Question is, can we use it?"

Del lifted his eyebrows. "Not us, but Dave probably can."

They both looked at Dave, then back at one another. JD said, "That just leaves how to get over there without dying. Any ideas?"

"In fact I do," Del answered, "but it's risky as hell."

"Risky how?" JD asked. "Riskier than making a run into the heart of a Swarm encampment with no ammo and no way out?"

"Uh, no," he admitted. Del hadn't thought to look at it that way. "But close."

"Well, anything's better than waiting here and hoping they'll leave."

So Del laid out the idea. For a moment his friend just stared at the desk that sat between them, eyes moving back and forth as he weighed the few options they had. They were only going to get one shot at this, and so it came down to either getting out of this crater, or fulfilling their mission by getting a transmission off to New Ephyra.

JD ran a hand over his head. "I'll do it," he said. "I'll climb the tower. You get as far from here as you can. Find a way home."

"Nuh-uh," Del replied. "No way. We stick together, man."

"I could order you."

"We're the same rank, jackass." He held up a hand to cut off whatever JD was about to say. "Look, man. We're in this together, and we both know the mission comes first. If we try to sneak out of this crater, we still have to cross that desert. It'll be what, two... maybe three days before we can find a way to contact control? You think we'll last that long? You think our message will still matter if we do?"

"Too much time," JD agreed.

"This thing, whatever's going on here, it'll be impossible to contain by then."

"Exactly. Which is why one of us needs to stay and climb that tower."

"No," Del corrected, "it's why we *both* need to climb that tower.

We can't leave it to chance, and you know it." A silence started to stretch between them, but Del didn't let it take hold. "You know I'm right."

"Yeah," JD said. "I don't have to like it, though."

"Never said you did."

JD bowed his head slightly, then nodded.

"Okay. You win. Let's get started."

10: KNOCKING ON THE DOOR

"**E**asy," Del whispered. He lifted his edge, eyes locked with JD the whole time to ensure their timing was perfect.

The section of roof rose inch by inch, and once vertical it locked into place. They waited for several seconds, but no cry of alarm went up from the enemies around them. Del could feel their presence, though, like he could feel the other people in a crowd even if his focus was elsewhere.

"Give me a boost," JD said.

Del complied, cupping his hands together. They both stood on the heavy foreman's desk, which had been moved to the far corner of the office beneath the small access hatch built into the ceiling. A way to reach the equipment on the roof—air conditioning, solar panel, and so forth. A way out that wasn't the front door—that was the part that mattered.

He lifted JD until his head was halfway through the opening. Then JD gripped each side of the square exit and held himself in place, turning his head slowly back and forth. After a sweep he looked down.

"Can't see much," he whispered. "Going to climb out and look from the edge." Del nodded, and lifted as JD pulled. Up and out he went in one smooth motion. Del waited, watching the square patch of sky above.

After a few seconds, JD's face appeared. "Send Dave up."

"You sure?"

"Yeah."

Dave made his own way, approaching the hatch. JD caught him and ordered him to turn off his thrusters. Inert, Dave weighed quite a lot, and it was only with Del's help from below that JD was able to wrangle him out onto the roof. Finally, JD leaned back into the opening and held a hand down for Del to use. Del grasped it, jumped, and scrambled up to the small exit.

The roof was dominated on one side by the air conditioner, and on the other by an angled solar cell held up by a metal scaffold. Steel pipes of varying sizes filled the spaces between the two. A small lip, perhaps six inches high, ringed the entire rooftop, broken every few feet by one-inch holes that Del presumed were designed to allow rainwater to drain.

Dust coated the entire area, half an inch thick. A manageable thing to walk around in, but lying in it made Del want to sneeze.

"I'd kill for a helmet right now."

"Shh," JD urged. They crawled to the edge. Del held a hand over his mouth and nose, then lifted his head just enough to peer over the six-inch-high perimeter wall. The dusty air had settled, and that came with pros and cons. Del could see the enemy more clearly now, but they would also be able to see him.

Swarm were everywhere. Muscular Drones, almost human in the way they lumbered about, arms swinging casually at their sides. Pouncers creeping around like oversized scorpions, bodies low to the ground as if ready to spring at anything that might move. Farther off, still obscured by lingering dust, were others. Larger shapes. Snatchers maybe, or worse. Del tried to make sense of their seemingly aimless movement. They didn't appear to be searching. More like they were wandering, or just waiting. The only logic he could apply to their movements—or lack thereof—was that they were clustering in groups. Not squads exactly, it was too disorganized for that, but with only a glance it was obvious to him they weren't just randomly dispersed. Something, be it a leader or just an instinctual thing, was organizing them.

He had about three hundred feet of visibility, and when JD pointed off toward the Condor, just barely visible at the edge of that range, he assumed it was the subject of his concern. But as he watched he realized that wasn't the case. JD was pointing at the extreme edge of the Swarm's numbers.

The groups at the periphery were moving outward, away from the crater basin. The enemy were leaving, and in little clusters of mixed types. Del saw one group made up of a Boomshot-wielding Scion, several hulking Drones, and a bunch of Juvies. Another group consisted of a small horde of varying-sized Pouncers, all walking as if in escort of the Snatcher in the center.

"It's like an army deploying for a battle," he whispered.

"My thought exactly," JD replied. "Only, they seem to be leaving in every direction."

Del considered that. "It's like they don't know where the war is."

"...or they intend to fight it everywhere," JD added.

Though he couldn't say why, Del wasn't so sure. They were the *Swarm* after all, a name given in battle as a first impression, but nevertheless it had always proven accurate. And maybe that clouded his mind, but he felt sure that once one of these groups found what they were looking for, the others would change course to join the party. Almost like ants or, more aptly, locusts of the insect variety.

He wondered, briefly, what they would do if he and JD went into the burial site. He imagined the whole bloodthirsty lot of them piling back in. If only there was a way to seal it up again, but after seeing that door blown open Del figured a whole mountain would have to be dropped in this crater. Even that might not be enough.

And then, what difference would it make if a dozen others around Sera were about to pop?

"Are we gonna do this?" JD said.

"Hell, yeah," Del replied, trying to force confidence into his voice and mostly succeeding. "Got the rope?"

JD did. He unshouldered the length they'd found in a cabinet and, lying on his side, started to tie it around Dave.

Working ever so slowly, JD and Del lifted the bot over the edge of the roof and lowered him inch by inch to the ground. They'd discussed allowing Dave to float down from the roof on his little thruster, but while the motor was quiet, it wasn't completely silent, and on top of that it produced a small blue jet of propellant. All of which might draw the Swarm's attention—not just to Dave, but to the roof itself. All it would take was one Pouncer to leap up and investigate and the plan would fail. This way, at least, Dave would be at ground level when he started his journey, and perhaps able to avoid detection.

Once Dave lay in the dirt, JD took a knife from his thigh holster and severed the rope.

"Okay, Dave," Del said. "Time to do your magic."

The urge to watch was overpowering, but somehow Del managed to keep his head down and let the little guy do his thing.

He could hear it lift off and go into a hover, though the sound was obscured by the noises of Swarm activity now filling the crater.

Though he couldn't see Dave, Del's head was right next to one of the drainage holes along the base of the roof's lip, so he put one eye to that. With his limited field of view he could see the adjacent container-turned-bunker, and some other abandoned machinery that lay beyond. One of the clusters of Swarm stood in between, and Del's focus went to a Grenadier Drone, which had stopped its machinations and abruptly turned sideways.

It seemed to be looking directly at Del.

He froze, not even daring to blink.

Below and off to the left, the sound of Dave's movement also halted. Several seconds passed. The Drone tilted its utterly bald head, and Del realized it wasn't staring at him—it was staring at Dave. Whether it recognized the robot for what it was, or had simply spotted its motion, the Drone eventually lost interest and went back to whatever it was doing.

"Dave," Del muttered, "keep going. Nice and slow."

The hovering robot gently whirred back to life. Through his peephole, Del could see him now. He watched as Dave inched his way painstakingly across the dusty ground toward the motor pool.

"So far so good," JD said.

"It's the next part I'm worried about," Del replied.

The bot's journey lasted several minutes, and drew no further attention from the enemy.

Del moved away from the peephole and nodded to JD. "Dave's at the Hauler."

"You're up, then. Good luck."

Nodding, Del crawled backward to the opening in the roof and lowered himself back down. At the computer he accessed the screen for the remote vehicle control and found the display for the Hauler, which now glowed bright green instead of the dark gray it had been only minutes before. That was Dave's ability to interface with old COG gear, as promised. He reminded himself to thank Baird when they got back.

An image appeared on the screen, showing a forward view from the Hauler, along with some graphs indicating the poor state of its internals and fuel supply. Del ignored all of those. As long as it moved, they wouldn't need much.

They'd agreed not to risk the comms, so Del grabbed a broom leaning against the wall and used it to tap once on the ceiling above him. From above, JD responded with a thump of his boot.

"Here we go," Del said, and he powered-on the Hauler.

The old vehicle had a two-motor setup, one powered by fuel for longer journeys or heavy loads, and a second, smaller unit that ran entirely on batteries. As long as they kept the speed below eight miles per hour, the fuel engine would remain off. Less chance of being heard, but the pace made the process infuriatingly slow as he drove the Hauler across the open space.

JD thumped the roof with his boot, and Del stopped the vehicle, waiting for another thump before driving on. The process was repeated several times. A thump from above, another pause, then moving again.

In the corner of his eye Del caught the indication that Dave had accessed the second Hauler. Good, but one thing at a time. He focused on the task at hand, gingerly guiding the lumbering vehicle until it was parked right next to their bunker.

Wiping sweat from his brow, Del repeated the process with vehicle number two, forcing himself not to become complacent and go too fast. After what felt like an hour, but in reality was only a few minutes, the two hulking trucks were in position, parked one behind the other, parallel to the bunker.

Clambering onto the desk, he climbed back up to the roof.

JD was already on the move. He'd climbed off the roof and was crawling slowly across the top of the first Hauler. Del waited until his friend had crossed the gap between the two trucks, settling into the cab of the second one. He gave a thumbs-up, which Del returned.

Then he went to the edge and studied the still loitering Swarm. Once the nearest Drone turned its back, he swung his legs over the side and lowered himself down to the ground between building and vehicle, dropping the last foot to limit the noise. He couldn't see anything now but the side of the truck, so he focused instead on JD, just visible in the cab behind. JD's eyes were on the Swarm, and after a moment he motioned for Del to proceed.

Tugging on the door handle, Del winced as the old metal creaked open. *Fuck it*, he thought. Time to stop worrying about stealth—wouldn't matter in a few seconds anyway—so he heaved the door open and jumped inside. His hands went straight to the controls, powering on the bigger motor and activating the path-assist mode. As the screen went through its startup routine, Del stomped on the accelerator and wheeled left. The engine roared to life as if it had been used just yesterday. Dirt flew from the big knobby tires. COG vehicles were ugly as sin, though Del couldn't help but smile at the beast's reliability.

He aimed for the dome shape of the burial-site cap. The massive door had been blown wide open from the inside, creatures of the Swarm lumbering out slowly as if in some practice evacuation. Once the entrance was dead center in front of him, Del activated the driver assistance lever and set it for maximum speed. The engine roared in response and the big truck began to accelerate.

Reaching for the door and preparing to exit, Del stopped. There, fixed at an angle between the two seats, was a length of wood and metal he recognized. He'd dismissed it before as a simple "oh shit" handle, but now the shape of it sank in. Del reached out and grasped it, pulling it free.

A Breechshot rifle. The Locust-created bastard cousin to the trusty old Markza, complete with an axe blade attached at the base and in front of the trigger. Held by the barrel it would make a formidable melee weapon. Del had only seen a few such weapons before, and was surprised this one had a scope, perhaps added by the driver of the Hauler as a customization. Like everything else here it was coated in dust, but looked well enough maintained. Whoever drove this truck must have pinched it from one of the Locust bodies and, for whatever reason, left it behind when the site had been vacated.

Not whatever reason, Del thought. He checked the clip, and found that there wasn't one. "Of all the fucking luck!" he shouted at the damned thing.

On a whim he checked the chamber.

A single bullet gleamed back at him.

"Perfect," he grumbled. "Just perfect. The hell am I supposed to do with this?" Still, he swung the relic onto his back. If nothing else, he could use the axe blade mounted under the barrel.

Ignoring the noises of the Swarm around him, Del leaned out the door; they'd been oblivious until now, but no way would the big roaring Hauler escape notice indefinitely. Throwing caution to the wind, he leapt from the cab, rolled, and came up at a sprint. The vehicle was already moving faster than he could run, but that was okay. Part of the plan, in fact. While it accelerated away he shifted focus to the second Hauler, coming up just behind, matching the speed of the first but allowing for a gap.

All around, the Swarm began to shout with alarm.

JD leaned from the cab, door open, his hand outstretched. Running hard, Del reached for and grasped his friend's arm. He jumped as JD heaved, landing neatly on the step that ran along the cab below the door.

"Follow mode activated," JD said. Then he nodded at the customized Breechshot, "Nice find."

"Not really. Damn thing only has a single round."

As the Haulers picked up speed, the two made their way up to the roof of the cab, where Dave waited. The shouts from the Swarm were joined by gunfire as the enemy realized something was up. Del went prone, as did JD. Bullets and quills began to slam into the sides of the truck.

If they were smarter they'd aim for the tires, Del thought.

As expected, though, the Swarm weren't clever enough for that. Their fire focused on the cab windows, which would have made sense if they hadn't been empty. They concentrated almost entirely on the lead vehicle, too, which played right into the plan. Del lifted his head enough to see the barrage sparking off the thick steel walls of the lead Hauler's sides. From off to the right a Pouncer jumped into the air, its high arc landing it on the roof of the cab. The monster plunged its clawed feet into the thin metal roof, tearing aside great chunks, but did nothing to slow the vehicle's progress.

The din increased. The Hauler rocked on its axles as a Drone went under the huge tires, limbs flailing as the body was crushed. Seconds later Del felt the second Hauler roll over the corpse. More enemies were being smashed aside or crumpling beneath the massive tires of the truck in front. Juvies leapt and grabbed onto the sides of the cab, clawing and punching at the windows already ridden with bullet holes.

"Get ready," JD shouted, barely heard over all the noise.

The entrance to the burial cap loomed close. A dome of iron plating thirty feet high, with piles of dirt and rock reaching halfway up in places. In the center, dead ahead, was a jagged hole where the sealed door had stood only hours before.

Around the base of the dome were dozens of cement or metal housings for all the various pipes and ductwork that ran down into the facility. One of these in particular was an airlock of sorts. A small cube-shaped cement-block structure beside the door that had allowed the final inspection team to enter the facility before the place was finally sealed. Atop this, a stepped gantry barely two feet wide ran up the dome to the ventilation stack at the peak.

Del tensed and forced himself to stay prone. Timing would be everything.

With a resounding *smash* the front Hauler plowed straight into the open mouth of the site cap. Rock and chunks of cement flew in all directions before a cloud of smoke and dust obscured the entire mess. Del saw the arm of a Swarm Drone poking out from the now-filled portal. It fell to the ground, severed by the impact of the heavy truck.

JD came to his knees, then a crouch.

Del did the same.

Their vehicle—still accelerating, engine roaring—bore down on the stalled rear of the crashed truck in front of them. Thirty feet.

Fifteen.

Five.

JD jumped, with Dave hovering just beside him. An instant

later Del followed, only an eye-blink before their Hauler slammed straight into the back of the first. The cab buckled and collapsed. Glass and shrapnel sprayed in all directions. The first truck, already clogging the site opening, was pushed in another eight or ten feet, rending unseen metal and smashing cement walls just inside. The earsplitting noise and shower of ejecta assaulted Del as he flew from the roof of the doomed cab to the top of the cement-block structure beside the opening.

Landing first, JD had tucked into a decent roll and kept going, slamming into the dome with a grunt of pain. Del's landing was even less graceful. The explosive force of the trucks crashing together had sent his legs out sideways. He slid across the gritty concrete rooftop and would have gone right over the other side had there not been a metal railing. His back slammed into the rusty bars, the impact knocking the wind out of him.

Fighting for breath, stars dancing before his eyes, Del somehow got to his feet and stumbled toward JD. A set of rusted metal stairs were bolted to the curved surface of the dome, leading up to the base of the ventilation tower. From there, a ladder ran all the way to the top. JD clanged onto the stairs, hands on the flimsy railings to either side.

He made it three steps before a single shouted word rolled across the landscape, deep and ominous. "Shredder!"

It came from far off. Del glanced over his shoulder and spotted the source: a Scion, maybe a hundred feet away among the solar cells, had spotted them. It raised a Buzzkill and began launching whirring sawblades toward them. The razor-teethed discs ricocheted off the dome, sending up showers of sparks all around.

"So much for losing ourselves in the confusion!" Del shouted.

"Just keep going!" JD replied as more enemies joined the

attack. Bullets began to hiss through the air, clanging off the iron dome. One sparked off the railing just inches from Del's hand as he mounted the steps and began to clamber after his friend.

Another blade from the Buzzkill whizzed over JD's head. It thudded into Dave's metal body. The robot rocked and wobbled, the jet of hot air that kept it aloft flickering.

"JD!" Del shouted. "Grab Dave!"

Dave started to fall, dead weight, only to be nabbed at the last second by JD's outstretched hand.

They climbed the steps two at a time, ignoring the hail of gunfire. As he went Del focused on the dormant form of Dave, tucked under JD's left arm.

"He's slowing me down," JD said over his shoulder. "Going to toss him!"

Del roared back, "No! We need him!"

"He's dead weight!"

Del opened his mouth to concede the point, then his eyes caught something. "Wait. There's a light blinking. He's not totally dead."

The grunt JD made signaled some skepticism on that point, but he held onto the bot and continued up the steps.

From below there came the sounds of scrambling claws and wild yelps that could only be one thing—Juvies, and a lot of them. Del chanced a look back and saw them swarming over the crashed Hauler, then onto the roof of the airlock structure. The first of them threw itself onto the steps and started to climb, just twenty feet behind.

Something tore through the air above. Del looked in time to see a Boomshot round sail over. A terrible shot, way over their heads.

Except...

The explosive round slammed into the top of the steps where

they joined with the ladder at the base of the tower, a dozen feet in front of JD. The whole stairwell shook violently, almost sending Del over the side. The rails in his hands vibrated, sending a painful jolt he felt all the way to his shoulders.

Then the world began to tilt.

The steps had been severed just below the ventilation stack, tilting sickeningly to one side.

"Jump!" Del shouted, heaving himself upward. JD heard him and, as one, they mounted the rail and leapt off onto the curved surface of the dome.

Del slid down the dusty surface, scrambled, and found his footing. Ten feet away, JD lay on his side. Dave was next to him. The inert robot began to roll down the side of the dome.

Del forced himself to move. Scrambling to his left, he planted his feet in Dave's path and curled one arm. He grunted as the robot slammed into him, feet skidding back a full foot before he'd tucked Dave under his arm like an oversized Thrashball.

He scrambled back up the side of the dome, reaching his friend just as he got to his feet. While JD got his bearings, Del took a quick look at Dave's readout panel. The red light there still blinked, but the robot's four blue eyes were dark as night.

"I'll take him," JD said, but Del had already hoisted the bot onto his own back, attaching him there.

"Lead the way," Del said through labored breaths. "At the top I'll—"

The sound of rending metal tore through the air as the gantry stairway broke entirely free, rotating as it toppled down the cap's surface, gaining speed as the curvature of the dome grew steeper. Del stood, frozen, unable to look away.

The broken steps hit the ground with an enormous *boom*.

Those Juvies not thrown free in the fall were crushed under its weight. For every one that died, though, two more were starting to scramble up the mound.

"C'mon!" JD shouted.

The landscape below Del writhed with enraged Swarm.

Keep going, he told himself.

No other choice, really.

11: TUNNEL RATS

"Lead the way, kid," Marcus said.

Mackenzie stood at the mouth of an upward-sloping tunnel that led into darkness, away from the cliff. She held a dim lantern in one hand and gestured toward several others that hung from the wall beside him.

"Grab a light," she told them, with a small and well-earned smile on her face. Kait couldn't fault the girl for that grin. She was still young, after all, and it was difficult to tell how all of this felt to her. Eli, standing nearby, held a long hunting rifle at his side as if it were a walking stick. The damn thing was taller than him, and probably twice as old.

"I'll keep watch down here," he said, the suggestion directed at Oscar.

"Good idea," Marcus replied.

Oscar, who'd been about to respond, closed his mouth and gave Eli a reassuring nod. He took a lantern and handed it to Kait, then grabbed another for himself.

"Let's go," he said.

She dialed the lamp up to half brightness and fell in behind Marcus, with Oscar bringing up the rear.

The stretches of tunnel were short but legion, connecting rooms of varying size and purpose to several caves deeper inside the rock. The walls dripped with humidity, and more than once Kait had to turn sideways or crouch just to fit through the narrow spaces.

Mackenzie appeared to lead them by memory, and though the path seemed random, Kait noted that it generally followed an upward slope. At the sixth connecting tunnel, the girl stopped and held up her hand.

"Careful here. Tripwire." She then stepped over what appeared to be nothing, and walked on. Marcus followed, and when it came to be Kait's turn she knelt and studied the passage. Sure enough, just below knee height was a thin length of fishing wire, virtually invisible in the darkness.

"She coats them with dust," Oscar said, coming up behind, "to hide the reflection."

"Wow," Kait replied. It was all she could think to say. How she'd underestimated these two children.

The traps increased in frequency the farther they went, and though the tripwire was Mackenzie's go-to favorite, there were a few other traps Kait was guided around that impressed her just as much. A short wooden stairwell linked a room to a passage, and it turned out to have a brittle step under which Mackenzie had placed explosives that would detonate when the plank cracked in half.

In another hall, a steel pipe had been laid diagonally across the middle of the passage. Mackenzie moved it aside not by tilting it upward, as one would naturally do, but instead by lifting the bottom and fixing it into a notch carved in the wall.

"Move the top," she said with pride, "and you trigger the six sticks of 'Miner's Friend' packed inside."

At this point Kait's mouth went dry, as this route would have been the likely path for her and Marcus to take had their arrival not been interrupted by the Swarm. Or would it have?

"Where exactly are we going?" she asked, unsure where they were in the overall layout of South Village.

"Almost there," Mackenzie said.

Past one more tripwire, they reached the end of the line. Another room hewn from rock, only this one had a long, low, flat ceiling made of wooden beams that were lashed together. One side of the rectangular ceiling panel appeared to be mounted on large hinges made of iron. Kait opened her mouth to ask, but Marcus quieted her with a raised index finger.

He pointed upward.

Looking up, Kait saw only the wood beams, but it was the sound he'd noted. Scratching. Clawing. The grunts and machinations of monstrous creatures.

"The Swarm," Marcus said, voice barely more than a whisper. He and Mackenzie led them back to the tunnel, then came in close, forming a huddle with her and Oscar.

"That's the great hall above us," Mackenzie said.

"What's left of it," Marcus said. "Your nail-bombs tore the hell out of the place."

Kait saw a flash of pride cross Mackenzie's face, quickly replaced by wide-eyed dread. "You were inside? I'm sorry, I didn't—"

"It's okay," Kait said quickly. "We hit the deck. Not a scratch on us, which is how you designed the trap, right? You did good, Mackenzie."

She nodded, meekly.

Marcus gestured to the ceiling panel. "This some kind of secret door into the hall?"

"Not really secret," Mackenzie said, "but not obvious, either."

Marcus gave a thoughtful nod. "Once one of the big bastards gets in there and really starts pounding on it, that's not going to hold."

"Let them come," Oscar said. "They'll bring the tunnels down on their own heads, seal themselves out."

"And us in," Kait pointed out.

Her uncle shrugged. "So? We've got plenty of food and supplies. We wait until they leave."

"Then, what, dig ourselves out? It would take months."

He waved this comment aside, unconcerned. "Once they're gone I'll scale the cliff and rebuild the winch."

Kait's eyes dropped to his belly, and she grinned. "You'll scale the cliff?"

Oscar matched her smile. "Okay, fine, you can do it."

"You're assuming they'll leave," Marcus noted in his matter-of-fact tone.

Again Oscar shrugged. "No offense to any of you, but we can't be that attractive to them. Eventually they'll give up. Find easier pickings somewhere else. *Like a city.*"

Kait wasn't so sure about that, but held her tongue. She looked to Marcus.

"There's no other way out of here?" he asked the group. "What about the river?"

"Not possible," Oscar said. "It's more like heavy rapids connected by waterfalls. This village doesn't even have boats. No way to use them."

"And these... what'd you call them, snapjaws, on the other side?"

Again Oscar's face scrunched up in protest. "You're welcome to try. They got that name for a reason, though."

Mackenzie spoke up. "There was a kid here once that swung over there to try and get one of their eggs. Some stupid dare."

"How'd that work out?" Marcus asked.

"Beats me." The girl lifted a shoulder. "The rope came back empty."

Marcus dropped his chin, momentarily lost in thought. Finally he looked up. "Kait, you said there was a cache of stolen COG supplies here, right?"

"Supposedly. I don't know where it is, though."

He looked at Oscar, who was in turn looking at the twins.

"Know where it is?"

The girl nodded, suddenly looking sheepish. "It's the other place to hide that we were telling Oscar about. Something the other kids mentioned a while back. We... we found it."

"You're not going to get in trouble," Marcus said. "You can tell us."

Still she hesitated.

"I'm not COG anymore," Marcus added, a bit of annoyance touching his words. "Really, you can tell us."

"Oh," Mackenzie said. "It's not that."

Marcus raised an eyebrow. "What then?"

She wrinkled her nose. "Eli's the only one crazy enough to go there." She looked at Kait, then Oscar, then back to Marcus. Finally, she sighed, as if she were the one dealing with the children. "Let me just show you."

Oscar held up a hand, quieting the group. His eyes were cast upward.

Kait heard it too, then. A distant, deep pounding noise that seemed to come from everywhere. It grew louder with each repetition.

"Something's coming," she said.

"Something big," Marcus agreed. He gestured toward the nearby tripwire. "At least we'll know when they make it through."

The trek back to the base of the cliff went much faster. Mackenzie picked her path in silence this time and Kait, following close behind, admired the kid more and more with each step. She was confident and talented, and with the exception of not being "crazy enough" to venture to the secret supply room, she seemed to be fearless in that way only kids could be.

"These snapjaws," Marcus said when they were near the bottom, "what can you tell me about them, Mackenzie?"

The girl kept her focus on their path as she spoke. "Not much, I guess. There's a lot of them. That side of the cliff is in shadow all year round, and they build nests all over it. From what Becca tells me, they leave everyone over here alone, so long as you stay on this side."

"Hmm," Marcus said.

"Got an idea?" Oscar asked him.

"Saw some old miner's work lights in one of the rooms down here. Just wondering what would happen if we lit that side up. Maybe they'd scatter."

"Orrrr," Oscar said, drawing out the word, "maybe they'd go insane with rage."

Marcus nodded. "Might not be a bad thing, if the Swarm are the easy targets."

"True, true."

In the common room at the base of the cliff, Oscar called

out for Eli to join them. The boy emerged from a side tunnel moments later, hunting rifle slung over one shoulder. Oscar took the weapon from him.

"The COG supplies," he said, "can you show us where they are?"

Eli frowned, and his eyes darted to his sister.

"They already knew about it," she told him.

"And we might need what's there," Kait added.

Eli lifted his shoulders. "Sure, I guess. It's not easy to reach."

Kait exchanged a look with Marcus. "I think we'll manage," she said. The boy seemed skeptical, but sprang into action all the same.

This route didn't go up, but sideways; a series of tunnels and exterior ledges that ran north along the river for about thirty feet. The journey ended on a ledge where, just a few feet away, the turbulent river plunged over a drop-off. The unseen waterfall had to be huge, Kait thought, as she could not hear the water crashing at the bottom.

This was the northernmost point of South Village, she realized, the place where the rooms and tunnels ended. A rope hung over the low barrier wall that ran along the ledge. It was held in place by an iron ring bolted into the ground. She guessed the villagers must have packed the COG supplies in a container of some sort and kept it lowered over the side, hidden from view and impossible to reach via any other means. In a COG raid, the rope could be cut and the evidence washed away in the blink of an eye.

Kind of brilliant.

Only she was wrong. Entirely wrong.

To Kait's surprise, Eli merely pointed at the rope. "Don't touch that, whatever you do."

Kait raised an eyebrow. "Um. Okay."

He turned toward the cliff face and began to climb. From her angle Kait hadn't seen the narrow set of steps carved into the rock, running up about fifteen feet to what looked like another cave. The steps followed a natural seam in the rock, making them almost invisible from where she stood.

"Well, go on," Mackenzie said from the back. "It's not far."

This isn't so bad, Kait thought as she navigated the series of small depressions chipped out of the face of the cliff. At the top there was no cave, but a very small room open to the air on the cliff side, and just barely big enough for the five of them to stand.

There were no supplies. Nothing at all, in fact.

Eli went to the northern edge of the tiny space and reached outside, feeling along the cliff until he found what he sought. When his hand reappeared, it held one end of a thick rope with a hefty knot tied at the end.

"Almost there," he said.

And then he jumped.

He put one foot on the knot, grasped the rope with both hands, and pushed outward with his other foot. Before Kait could grab him or even shout his name, Eli was swinging outward and away to the north. Well out over that waterfall, which meant a drop of hundreds of feet below him.

Marcus, who'd reached to try and stop the boy, was pulled back by Mackenzie.

"It's okay," she said. "Just make sure you grab the rope when it comes back."

Kait took on the task. Ten seconds after Eli had swung away, she heard him shout "Rope!" A moment later the rope came back empty. She caught it only by reaching out as far as she dared.

"Here goes nothing," she said, and she copied the boy's maneuver. A jump to get her foot on the knot, hands clasped above, Kait pushed out with her right foot as hard as she could.

As she swung into the cold, damp air, water droplets stung her eyes.

"Run along the rock!" Eli shouted from somewhere in front of her, obscured by mist. She tried to do so, but in truth it was more of an awkward, white-knuckled stumble and crash. Over in seconds, at least. After just two clumsy steps Kait saw Eli, and then the ledge upon which he stood. There was a handle bolted into the cliff face and wrapped with leather. She grasped it and pulled herself the last two feet before reaching the safety of the cave where he stood waiting.

A natural cave, she realized, as she found her footing on the jagged floor.

Eli took the rope from her and expertly flung it back the way she'd come. Cupping his hands around his mouth, he shouted "Rope!" once again into the swirling misty air.

While she waited for the others to arrive, Kait took a few steps into the cave and let her eyes adjust to the darkness. The rock here was smooth yet showed no sign of having been carved or excavated. This was an ancient place, she realized. The entrance went in about twenty feet, angling down and then up, and that was as far as she could see.

Marcus arrived as the rope swung back. He handed it to Eli and told him to tie it off.

"Oscar and Mackenzie are going to hang back," he explained. "Listen for the Swarm."

"Understood," Kait said. Then, to Eli, "Lead the way." He did so, lifting a flashlight.

The cave turned out to be smaller than she'd first guessed. After the entry tunnel dipped and then rose, it widened out into a large chamber roughly shaped like a half-dome, with thick stalactites hanging from the ceiling. Here some work had been done to alter the natural shape of things, with the floor largely cleared of any bumps or protrusions. It wasn't flat, but close enough. Eli swung the flashlight across the walls before finding a small generator and work light, which he turned on.

Marcus nodded, appreciatively. "Pretty good stash."

The floor was piled with crates and mesh bags of COG gear. A similar scene to the one they'd found in the basement of the ranch house. Similar, but also different. Here the secret cache was more haphazardly arranged, and there was a thin layer of dust on everything. More like the haul of looted supplies her own village had kept—as if the point was more to take it than to actually use it.

Reyna had once explained to her that making use of the stuff implied a need for it, and *that* implied that the Outsiders weren't able to fend for themselves. So, almost by tradition, the gear was thrown in some dusty unused corner, only to be accessed in the direst of situations.

This, Kait thought, qualified—just like when Reyna had tasked her, JD, Del, and Oscar to find and bring back a fabricator for the village to use. There'd been no real options left to their community, short of letting things decline to a truly primitive way of life.

"For all the good it did us," she mused.

"What's that?" Marcus asked.

"Nothing," she said, resisting the urge to screw her fists into her bleary eyes. The lack of sleep was causing her mind to wander. He studied her for a moment, then swung his gaze back to the room.

"Weapons," he said. "Ammo. Not a bad start."

"Plenty of food and water to be had from the river, too," Kait added. "Oscar's right. We could hold out here for a long time, if it came to that."

Marcus moved to the nearest crate and ran a hand along the labeling to clear the dust, then glanced back over his shoulder.

"Is that what you want? To wait things out here?"

She shrugged. "It's tempting. Food, supplies. Defensible."

"I meant wait out the Swarm," Marcus said. "Wait here until it all blows over."

"What I want…" Kait began. She blew out a breath, tried again. "What I want is a good night's sleep before I have to answer that."

The old soldier grunted amused understanding. "About being defensible, though," he said, "this room should be our last resort."

"Why's that?"

"Too small, for one," he said. "Worse, though, is how isolated it is. If they back us all the way to here we'll have no choice but to wait things out. No, we hold the tunnels. That's our best chance."

"Makes sense," she said.

He walked deeper into the chamber, and Kait—not really sure why—decided to stay near the entrance. Somehow it seemed right to let him survey the stolen goods. He knew the markings and what they signified. Hell, he'd probably helped battle-test most of this stuff. If anyone would know what was useful and what could be thrown at the enemy in a last stand, it was Marcus Fenix.

When he neared the back of the room, Marcus crouched down to look more closely at a stack of crates. This put him temporarily out of view. Kait was about to follow him, to see what he'd found, when the room shook. She swayed with the shifting floor, and saw Marcus stand quickly.

"The hell was that?" she asked.

"One of Kinzie's little surprises!" Eli said with pride. "Has to be!"

"C'mon," Marcus said. He pushed a fresh Lancer into Kait's hands, along with three extra clips of ammo. "Sounds like the Swarm have entered the tunnels."

12: A DIFFERENCE OF OPINION

The Condor passed over Fort Umson at the preprogrammed angle of attack. Its DeeBee payload, encased in dodecahedron-shaped drop capsules, prevented Baird from having a firsthand view of the landing. Instead, he relied on cameras mounted on the underside of the aircraft.

The pods fell one after another, fanning out as they went. The aircraft followed a steep descent profile as the pods dropped, a precise angle that would see the entire site blanketed by the simultaneous landing of the robots. It was a pattern Baird himself had programmed, and every time he watched it performed he couldn't deny a little pang of pride. To be an enemy finding him or herself suddenly and completely engulfed by such a force must have been terrifying indeed.

Yet for this deployment, Baird's focus was elsewhere. He watched the feeds, both the one looking back from the underside of the Condor, and the one showing the interior of the cargo bay that faced the ramp, waiting for some glimpse of Kait and Marcus's departure. The plan had been to wait until the DeeBees had fully deployed, count off three seconds more, then jump. This would place them outside the perimeter, and have them leaving the craft when Jinn's attention would be on the DeeBees themselves.

So Baird watched, and hoped to see nothing. Nothing would be good. Nothing would mean no scrutiny, at least for a while. Maybe not even until the pair were back in the city. Wouldn't that be nice.

When he saw the nothing he had hoped to see, Baird leaned forward and tapped the grid view. Instantly his screen split into a pattern of gray squares. Sixteen Trackers and twenty-six Shepherds, and several DR-1s, all looking at the inside of their drop pods.

This was his favorite moment. To see them all crack open simultaneously—or nearly so—implied a perfectly timed landing. No front line against which the enemy could square up, or from which they could retreat. Total immersion in firepower before the enemy could blink, and with virtually no warning. Just the sudden whoosh of the aircraft, gliding at this point to minimize noise, and *wham*! All those angular pods slamming to the ground and their armored payloads rising to their full impressive height—

The first pod opened.

Baird saw teeth, then static.

As the others followed suit over the course of less than four seconds, the result was nearly the same. He watched in growing frustration as each DeeBee emerged into hell.

"LZ is hot," some moron said on the Control frequency, panic thick in his young voice.

"That is abundantly obvious," came First Minister Jinn's annoyed reply.

Baird chuckled, knowing he couldn't be heard. The army might be phasing out human soldiers, but it was the lack of experience in support positions that would most likely eliminate their chance for success.

One after another the robots stepped out of their shells and into a total bloodbath—albeit a bloodless one. He wondered when Jinn would inquire about replacing Control with machines, too, and made a mental note to start teaching IRIS how to do just that. Might as well be ready.

On the screen some of the DeeBees held their own against the Swarm, the DR-1s especially. Unfortunately only a few had been sent. Baird adjusted his view again to show only their feeds. He saw the enemy more clearly in those views—all the screens were distorted or garbled to some extent, which was odd—but the Swarm were clearly visible. Which meant Jinn could see them, too, though she'd made no reaction that Damon could hear.

What he didn't see—what he strained to spot in every one of their transmissions—was Marcus or Kait.

Baird ignored the utter dismantling of the DeeBee squad. The outcome was plain as day, as far as he was concerned. They simply weren't equipped to handle an enemy like this, especially in these numbers. That would have to change, and soon, but right now he wanted confirmation that his friends had deployed. Preferably at a safe distance.

"IRIS, play it back again. All angles, and get rid of as much of that distortion as you can this time."

"One moment, Damon," the AI responded.

When the feeds came up he focused on the cargo bay. "This one here, give me thermal overlay."

IRIS complied at once, and heat signatures appeared over the imagery.

The DeeBees all deployed.

Four seconds passed.

Nothing.

"C'mon, you old bastard," Baird muttered through clenched teeth. "What are you waiting for?"

The image remained unchanged, save for the constant random static IRIS hadn't been able to remove fully. Baird watched the silent bay, the empty racks where the DeeBees had hung. Beyond the open ramp the landscape shifted as the Condor tilted its wings, gaining altitude for its circuit of the battlefield and, ultimately, a place to land.

He watched and watched, dimly aware of the chaos on the Control frequency as Jinn's team announced the destruction of the DeeBee squad, one by one.

"Just shut up already," Jinn snapped after a while. "I get it. We're fucked." Even she'd had enough.

Baird's eyes never left the screen.

Still there remained no sign.

Why not jump? he wondered. Maybe the chutes were never loaded? Had his command to store them on the Condor failed to get through? It certainly wouldn't have been disobeyed; these were robots, after all.

Had they slipped out before the drop proper? He tried to imagine the two of them landing in that ambush without the support of the robots. Marcus could handle a lot, Kait seemed damned capable, too, but that was hell of a, well, swarm.

Maybe Marcus and Kait had changed their minds, deciding to deploy once the Condor landed, going on foot. Hell, Kait might be afraid of heights. Baird doubted that very much, but it was possible. No way to know without being there.

So he waited.

And waited.

Until, after the Condor set down and began to wait for a DeeBee force that would never be coming back, he heard Jinn give the order for the aircraft to abort its mission and return. Baird watched with growing dismay as the ramp folded back up, the engines began their signature whine, and the Condor took off again.

He threw his headphones on the desk and stormed out of the room, heading straight for the gates.

By the time he reached Government House, Jinn had already left Control and returned to her office. Baird brushed past her secretary and the two security guards posted at her doors. They were all used to seeing him approach by now, even without an invitation, and made no move to stop him.

Baird marched into the room and slammed the doors shut behind him. "Well?" he asked.

"Well what?" Jinn replied. She was at the window, standing in profile with one hand resting on her belly, perhaps feeling the baby kick. The sight drained some of his fury.

"I hope that catastrophe is the proof you need. Is it? Are you ready to stop investigating 'this' and analyzing 'that' and get on with the job of ending this threat before it's out of control?"

"Catastrophe?"

"You know what I mean! Fort Umson! An entire DeeBee squad wiped out in seconds. That place was absolutely crawling with... what? Why are you looking at me like that?"

Jinn's face was tilted to one side, an eyebrow lifting. "How do you know about this, Damon? It just happened minutes ago."

He faltered. Felt the proverbial rug as it was pulled out from under him. He was angry at the poor response to the Swarm. He was anxious about the danger his friends were in out there, all just to get concrete proof for this woman because their word wasn't enough. And he'd slipped. Plain and simple, he'd slipped.

No sense in denying it, he realized. The time for games was over. "Okay, so what? I've got a way to monitor my products remotely. It's part of their baseline code. Nothing wrong with that."

"There's a lot wrong with that," Jinn retorted. "I can think of… six laws off the top of my head that it violates. How long has this been going on? No, don't answer that, we'll deal with that issue later. You're here to talk about our defeat at Fort Umson. Go ahead, say your piece."

Baird spread his hands. "Defeat is putting it rather mildly, don't you think? You saw it, Jinn. The Swarm in all their violent glory. What they did to the bots. C'mon, what more proof do you need?"

"Their presence at Fort Umson proves nothing. We already knew they were active there."

"Not this active, Jinn. We got our asses handed to us."

"The DeeBee squad was a standard search and rescue deployment," she said with patience. "There to bring those survivors home. They weren't equipped to handle the situation as we now understand it. That will soon be rectified. A response is already being prepared—"

"No, Jinn. There isn't time to screw around. You need people out there! Boots on the ground. Marcus and Kait weren't equipped to deal with that, no matter how many DeeBees were with them." As he spoke Jinn folded her arms, glaring at him. Too late, Baird realized he'd slipped again.

"Marcus and Kait?" she asked.

"I mean, *if* they were…" Baird trailed off, hearing how pathetic he sounded.

"You lied to me, earlier, didn't you?" she said.

A stony silence stretched between them.

When Jinn spoke again her voice had dropped to not much more than a whisper. "They were on that plane. Just as JD guessed. You told me you didn't know anything about it. That you didn't aid them."

Baird let out a breath and nodded. Might as well get it all out there, he decided. "Fine. You got me. Guilty as charged. And I'm not going to apologize."

She considered this. "Why'd they do it? To rescue those kids?" The conviction in her voice faltered as she spoke. She'd figured it out, answering her own question. "They didn't trust me to handle it," she said, flatly.

"Think of it from her perspective, Jinn. Kait was there when her village was attacked by DeeBees the first time. She saw it all firsthand. Can you blame her for wanting to reach the survivors before you did? And Marcus… well, he decided to lend a hand."

She studied him for a moment. "What aren't you telling me?"

Baird hesitated.

The First Minister lowered her voice again. "Tell me they got off before that… massacre."

"I don't know. That's the truth. They were supposed to jump just after the DeeBees deployed, hide themselves in all the activity, but that didn't happen. Not that I could see, anyway."

"So we have no idea where they are, or what their status is?"

"None," he admitted. "All the more reason to get a team out there. A real team—"

She raised a hand, ending his comment. "No," she said with absolute finality.

"The DeeBees can't handle this."

"Then make me some that can!"

The shouted words echoed around her office, followed by a long, cold silence.

He waited. Forced himself to stay calm.

Jinn seemed to think up and discard a few more shouted words. When she finally spoke again, her voice was calm, yet sharply edged.

"This is exactly what I've been trying to avoid. It was a mistake to send anyone out of the city. Look what we have to show for it. Lieutenants Fenix and Walker are out of contact, condition unknown. I shouldn't have allowed them to go. And now we may have inadvertently dropped Sergeant Fenix and Ms. Diaz into another fiasco, then abandoned them there.

"The whole point of the DeeBee program was to keep our best and brightest out of these situations, Damon. Can you imagine the reaction around here if they don't make it back? Sergeant Fenix is a war hero."

"I know that," Baird said. "Better than anyone."

"Then you understand the blow to morale we'll suffer if he doesn't return."

Baird set his jaw. "Better than anyone," he repeated.

She came over to her desk, but did not sit, resting her hands on the back of the chair instead. "I won't keep sending people out there, Damon. I can't."

"Okay," he said, thinking. "Then go big. Don't send another recon team, send a full suppression squad. Hell, send ten! DR-1s, Deadeyes, Guardians—the works. As many as you can. Start at Fort Umson and keep spreading out until we find them."

"And if we don't?"

"If we don't? If we don't find those two it's because they don't want to be found."

"And the Swarm?"

He gave a small shrug. "We'll have given them the best we've got. I doubt it'll be enough, though."

Jinn's gaze dropped to the carpet. After a moment she turned back to the window, her features now hard as stone. "Thank you, Damon. That will be all."

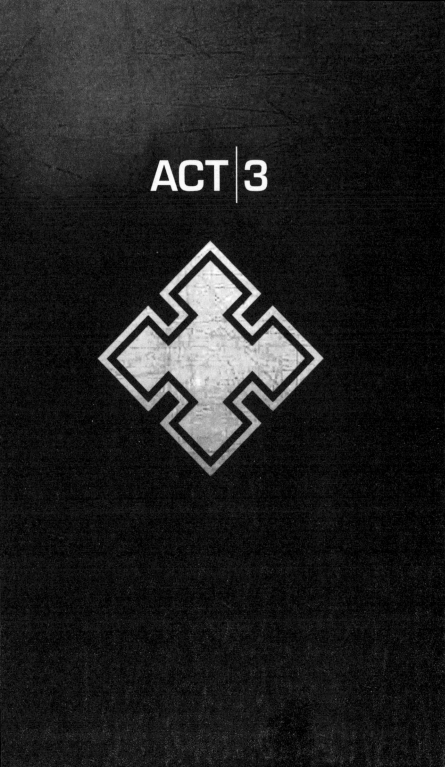

ACT|3

1: SINGING A DUET

Marcus was the last to swing back from the supply room.

"Take this," he said, thrusting a bundle of Lancer magazines toward her.

She took the ammo and set it to one side, reaching out to help Marcus onto the ledge. He hesitated, though, looking back. "I'll make another run. Bring more."

"Is there time for that?" she asked.

As if in answer, two more muffled explosions echoed through the rock, one a few seconds after the other.

"That was the two inner tunnels," Mackenzie said, fear creeping into her voice. "They're already through the first blockade."

Kait recalled the layout in her mind. Mackenzie's first trap was just inside the concealed door the Swarm had been clawing at. That had blown twenty minutes ago, and she'd hoped it would hold them off for a day or more.

Working in from there, the tunnel branched—the main passage, and a narrower side tunnel. Both eventually met at the common room where Marcus had served them fish stew.

"Scratch that question," Kait said to Marcus. "There's no time." She held out her hand anew.

Marcus took it and came over to the ledge.

While Kait tied the rope off, he knelt. "Eli, Mackenzie, come over here."

The twins obeyed.

"You're going to wait here," he said to them, holding up his index finger to forestall their complaints. "We might call for ammo, and you'll need to bring it up to us, quick as you can. Depending on how long this goes on, you might need to go across to the supply cache and fetch more. Understand?"

They nodded in unison.

Kait knelt, too. "You know these tunnels, and move faster in them than we do." All true, but she sensed the real rationale behind Marcus's suggestion. The twins would have a way out, if things went bad. Across to the supply room, where they could hold out for a long time, if needed.

Eli looked to his sister, some silent conversation happening as their eyes briefly met. He turned to Marcus and Kait, nodding. "We won't let you down."

"I know you won't," Kait said.

Marcus stood. "Kait, Oscar? Let's move."

It sounded a little too much like an order, and though he bristled slightly, Oscar still fell in behind Marcus. Kait gave one last reassuring nod to the twins, then followed the two men.

In the common room where they'd eaten fish stew, two tunnels ran off into darkness. Dust and smoke trickled from both, curling up along the ceiling.

Marcus nodded toward one. "You two take the main route. I'll cover the side."

"Makes sense," Oscar said. "We fall back here if things go to shit, eh?"

Marcus nodded, then looked to Kait. "Agreed?"

"Agreed." Before he could go she added, "Good luck."

Kait and Oscar stared down the long, rough tunnel and waited. At the far end, barely visible, she could just make out the jagged edges and pulverized dirt where the bomb had brought the roof down. Mackenzie's trap had done a hell of a job.

"Anything yet?" Marcus asked in her ear. The voice was garbled, either by the rock or the interference the Swarm seemed to generate.

"Nothing."

"Same here. Stay sharp."

"Copy that." She glanced at Oscar and caught him staring at her. "What?" she asked.

Her uncle said nothing, turning his gaze back to the tunnel.

"Seriously," she said, "*what*?"

Oscar sighed. "You sound like one of them."

"Like a Fenix?"

"Like a Gear." He shook his head, rueful. "Coalition army. You sound like I used to."

Kait waited for more, but Oscar withdrew into himself, flexing his injured arm and rechecking his shotgun. There'd been no accusation in his voice, or even disappointment. Just… acceptance. He was right, of course. Her months spent with JD and Del, and her time now with Marcus, had changed her. That was only natural, but she'd never stopped to think about how watching that transformation—as mild as she thought it was—might make Oscar feel.

She tried to think of something to say that might ease his mind, but words failed her just then.

"Maybe you should catch some zees," Oscar said before she could come up with a response. "Could be a while before—"

A single stone shook loose and tumbled down the pile, leaving a trail of dust in its wake. Kait flexed her fingers on the Lancer, pressing the stock into her shoulder but keeping the weapon aimed at the floor... for now.

Just the rock settling, she told herself.

"Activity," Marcus said in her ear.

"Here too," she replied. "Maybe. Stand by."

"Copy that," Oscar said in a light, mocking tone. "Over and out, Sir."

Kait snapped her leg out and kicked him hard in the thigh.

"Ouch! Damn!" He rubbed at the spot, which she thought would have a nice bruise by morning. Or evening. She had no idea what time it was, she realized.

From another part of the cave system, Kait heard the muffled thumps of Lancer fire. The vibrations sent little streams of dust down from the ceiling.

"Marcus?" she asked, and stopped herself before asking him to "report."

"They punched a hole," he replied. "Barely. I'm putting some rounds through... make them think better of..."

The transmission became more garbled. She refrained from acknowledging, lest Oscar throw more stink-eye her way. Instead she turned away from the collapsed tunnel, back the way they'd come, and cupped her hands over her mouth.

"Eli, Mackenzie, be ready. They're starting to—"

The blocked cave ruptured. Rock and dirt spewed in, pounding across Kait like a sideways hailstorm. She fell and landed hard on her elbow, grunting with pain as the debris continued to rain against her armor. The air was thick with dust.

Somewhere to her left, Oscar let out a cough.

She didn't look. Didn't wait to see the enemy coming because by that time they'd be a foot away. Kait just raised her weapon and fired. Full auto. Relying on the hope that the Swarm weren't smart enough to breach and then duck back. They'd come in hard, and she'd make them pay for it.

Oscar's shotgun joined hers, and the two weapons sang a deathly duet.

Juvies rushed through the gap. They galloped and yapped, one leaping up into the wall and then flinging itself toward her. A blast from Oscar's shotgun sent it cartwheeling backward. Kait ignored it, kept firing, the bodies already piling up. Half her shots were blind as dust choked the tunnel. Something bigger, a Drone maybe, fell hard farther back in the hazy darkness, emitting a groan that sounded to Kait more like frustration at not reaching its prey than a cry of pain.

Sorry to disappoint you.

The gun clicked. One of her three clips was already spent. She ejected the magazine and slapped a new one home without even looking, trying to keep the gun's internals at the optimum temperature. That would improve her firing rate, though using up her precious rounds might not be the best idea.

"Sounds like fun over there," Marcus said in her ear.

"Oh yeah," she replied, another Juvie falling lifeless onto the growing pile. "A great big happy reunion." At this rate the Swarm would clog the tunnel with their own dead.

"Halfway through my ammo," Oscar said, trying to sound casual, but there was pain in his voice. She glanced at him, saw he'd moved the shotgun to his left hand.

"Same here," she said. "Let's fall back to the common room."

"Works for me!"

Kait relayed the plan to Marcus.

"Meet you there," he replied.

She turned and ran, making it only a few steps before Oscar called her name. He remained where he'd stood, and for an instant she thought he'd been wounded. But with a quick jerk of his chin toward the wall, she understood.

Kait moved aside, aimed, and let him fall back a half-dozen yards. He crouched there and covered her retreat. The process repeated.

In the common room Kait grinned at him. "Now who's acting like a Gear?"

"Bah," he said. "Just common sense!"

Kait fired off a few rounds at movement deep in the tunnel, then forced herself to stop. Ammo was running low.

"Eli, Mackenzie!" she called out. "Ammo!"

The boy came running only seconds later, the long hunting rifle slung over one shoulder. In each hand he held a Lancer magazine, and Kait could see shotgun shells poking out of his pockets.

"Thanks," she said, taking the offered ammo and directing him, with a quick glance to her right, to take the shells to Oscar.

"Marcus?" Kait called into the radio. "Marcus, can you hear me?"

No reply.

Mackenzie had come in behind her brother, walking instead of running. In her hands were two more of her improvised bombs.

"In case you want to seal the tunnels," she said. "Not that it's doing much good."

"It's slowing them down," Kait told her, "and that's plenty. But we can't set them off yet, Marcus is still in the side passage."

"We can get the main tunnel rigged at least," Oscar said. "We'll handle that. You go get Marcus. Young ones, over here with me."

Mackenzie moved behind Oscar, kneeling to prepare a device. Eli started to unshoulder his rifle, though. He stepped toward Kait, but Oscar used his bad right arm to sweep the teen behind him. "Stay with us, Eli. Kait can handle it." Then, to Kait, "Get going!"

She nodded, and raced off into the narrow side passage.

The passage Marcus had been tasked to watch saw much less use than the main entry to the cave network. Its rough floor and narrow walls were testaments to that.

There was no sound ahead. Kait slowed her pace, straining her ears as she crept along. Far behind her she thought she heard Oscar call out, but not to her. Directing the twins as they went about their task, no doubt.

Something moved ahead. Coming fast.

Kait instinctively dodged left, raising her weapon, the lights embedded in her armor catching the form of a haggard, bloodied figure coming toward her. It cringed at the sudden glare. Her finger brushed the trigger, but then she recognized Marcus.

"Behind me," he managed, stumbling past. Kait pivoted, fired, filling the narrow passage with light and the sparks of rounds ricocheting down the stone hall. A monstrous howl answered her assault. Pain and anger and rage all at once. Something was coming. Something angry.

Beside her Marcus stumbled, went to one knee, grunting with pain. She continued to fire without looking, at the same time offering him her arm and helping him up. Together they staggered back. Kait's Lancer clicked, out of ammo, and with one arm helping Marcus she couldn't reload. She pivoted then, putting her effort into the retreat, helping Marcus.

The Swarm were closing fast. She could hear their steps, their awful growls.

Kait chanced a look behind her. A Drone bore down on her and Marcus, eyes glinting as it smelled victory. Its mouth twisted into a savage grin and it roared.

We won't make it, she thought, turning back, running harder.

Her light caught a shape before her. Something lay on the ground where the wall met the floor. A body.

It was Eli.

Dead, her brain screamed. But then he shifted, and she saw the gun.

Eli lay flat on his belly, hunting rifle extended out before him as if he were lying beneath a hedge, hunting rabbit. The barrel pointed back the way Kait had come.

She saw him too late to slow herself, to try to grab him. It was all she could do to push Marcus to the right and get out of the way herself.

The instant she and Marcus stepped past him, the kid fired.

A single shot.

The sound was deafening in the narrow space, as if she'd lowered her head into an empty barrel and asked someone to hit the side of it with a sledgehammer. It might have been a hunting rifle, but that thing really packed a punch.

Behind her, the Drone's roar was abruptly silenced. Kait heard the monster collapse to the floor.

She skidded to a stop, releasing Marcus. His eyes were clearer now, his jaw set. He gave her a quick nod, leaning against the wall.

"Hell of a shot," he said to Eli.

"C'mon," Kait added, "we've got to move."

With youthful spryness, Eli sprang to his feet. From the lack of fear or concern on his face she wondered if he'd seen the result of the attack, or had fired blind and didn't yet recognize the danger they were in.

An explosion shook the cave. Streams of dirt and rock fell from the ceiling. Kait staggered, found her footing again, and gestured to Eli.

"Get ahead of us," she said to him through clenched teeth. "Clear the path."

He knew as well as she did the path would be clear, but the kid didn't argue. Instead he squeezed past and ran on ahead. As he did so, Marcus seemed to find a hidden well of strength. His weight eased off her, and the two began to jog. Not as fast as Eli, but fast enough. At least, Kait hoped it was. Eli may have taken out that Drone, but more Swarm were behind it.

She stole glances at her companion. A line of blood, already dry, ran from beneath his black skullcap to just above his graying beard.

"How bad is it?" she asked.

"I'll be fine. Thanks for the rescue," he said.

"You'd have done the same."

They pressed on, Kait easing up slightly as the sounds of the approaching Swarm behind her faded. They'd either been temporarily blocked by the fallen Drone, or decided to look for another way around. Neither option felt right, but just then she did not feel like complaining.

A minute later they found Oscar and Mackenzie in the common room, their faces dark with soot. Yellow and orange light flickered from deep within the main hallway, as if it were the outlet for a strange fireplace.

"Be a while before they get through that," Oscar said. "Eli, you run off like that again and it won't be the Swarm you have to worry about."

The boy dropped his chin. "Sorry. I thought I could be more useful with them."

"And he was," Kait admitted. "Very."

"You both did great," Marcus said. "Keep it up."

Mackenzie grinned. It wasn't a grin Kait cared for. At her age she should be proud of winning a race around the wall of Fort Umson, not the effectiveness of her explosives.

The twins were rapidly losing whatever innocence their teenage years still held for them. Just one more crime for which the Swarm would pay. As if they needed any more.

The girl held one last bomb, and now that the group was all together, she and Oscar set about collapsing the tunnel through which Kait, Eli, and Marcus had just emerged. Neither she nor Marcus said a word to stop them.

It was the last way out. With it blocked, they were stuck here for... well, how long was anyone's guess. For the first time it occurred to her that no one knew they were here. It wasn't a huge mental leap to draw a line from Fort Umson to South Village, but only an Outsider familiar with the place would think to search the tunnels below the plateau. As far as she knew, the only four people who qualified were all in this cave.

Mackenzie and Oscar returned. The girl motioned for everyone to cover their ears, and seconds later the whole cave shook again. A plume of dust erupted from the last tunnel, and it was done. The last two remaining passages were useless: one led to the cliff where she'd first reunited with Oscar, and the other headed off to the small chamber that connected them to the secret supply room.

The room shook again, though the source was very distant this time.

"What the hell was that?" Marcus asked.

"One of yours, Kinzie?" Eli asked.

His sister shook her head. "Mine are all used up," she replied, then patted the pocket on her jacket. "'Cept one."

Kait heard distant gunfire. There was a back and forth to the sounds. A firefight.

Marcus turned and rushed out to the cliff as the rest of them listened. After a moment Kait went to join him. He was standing with his hands on the railing, looking out at the eternal mists kicked up by the churned water below, and the shapes of wheeling snapjaws just beyond.

"What is it?" she asked. "See anything?"

"Yeah," he said. "The severed head of one of Baird's robots just fell past."

His words were all but absorbed by the constant roar of the swift river below, but there was another sound, too. Barely audible, almost dreamlike, yet Kait felt sure she'd heard it.

Deep, vile laughter, coming from the top of the cliff.

Kait had heard it before.

2: FAMILIAR FACES

If the hour bothered Augustus Cole, he didn't let it show. Even dressed in civvies, he still carried himself like the world belonged to him and he didn't mind sharing.

"I'd say I'm happy to be here," he commented as he entered, "but cooped up in a room looking at screens isn't really the Cole Train's idea of a good time."

"No?" Baird asked. "Think fast." He threw the Thrashball hard, right at his friend's face. Cole just snatched it out of the air. He held the ball as if it were an extension of his own hand.

"Sam," he said in greeting, nodding toward her. His gaze swung back to Baird. "Where you'd get this?" he asked, twirling the ball on one finger and letting it settle into his palm.

"One of the operators had it on his desk," Baird replied, gesturing toward an empty workstation a few rows away. "It's even got your signature on it."

Cole glanced at it again with renewed interest. "So it does. Damn, how about that. Any of your bots ever get asked to sign a ball? No? Aww. That's a damn shame, isn't it?" He tossed it casually back to Baird.

Sam snatched it out of the air. She grinned at Cole.

"Thanks for coming in."

"Thanks for the invite," he said. "Still not sure what I've been invited to, though. Where's Marcus?" At the glance Sam and Damon exchanged, Cole's face lost its amusement. "Oh shit. What's that old fool done now?"

Baird filled him in on the situation. How Kait and Marcus had left on a rescue op to Fort Umson, but never arrived there.

"But that's not the reason I called you. Not exactly."

"No? What is it, then?"

At Baird's gesture, Cole joined them at the console.

"Take a look at this."

The first thing Baird had done after his meeting with Jinn was return to Control and talk Corporal Hansen into giving him a room to work out of. Then he called Sam and Cole.

He replayed the footage from the ambush at Fort Umson. Cole was quick to understand.

"You're right," he said. "There's no sign of Marcus or Kait."

"It's not what isn't there, friend."

Cole shrugged. "What then? A clue or something?"

"Think big picture," Sam replied.

The man frowned. He twirled a finger for Sam to rewind the imagery and play it again. After a second viewing, he stood and sighed.

"The big picture is we got our asses handed to us. And by 'we' I mean your dumb-ass robots."

"Exactly," Damon said. "Maybe a little too on point, but yeah... *exactly*."

Cole looked at him, then Sam, then back. "Okay, so what then? You wanna send in the Cole Train to clear up this mess?"

"No," Baird said, "but we do need your help."

"Help with what?"

"To make my dumb-ass robots not so dumb-ass."

Cole recoiled slightly. "Say *what* now?"

Baird said, "Jinn and I had the same old argument. Gears versus Bots. No simpler way to say it. You know how I've fought her over this, but I can see the writing on the wall now. She's not going to budge, so instead of sitting by while she yanks out the non-lethality safeguards, we need to get ahead of this."

"Meaning?"

"Teach them how to fight," Sam said. "In the process, maybe we can help our friends, too. And don't worry, Cole, you're not alone on this."

"He roped you into this, too?"

"It's part of the job," Sam replied with a half-smile. "Pull up a chair, Cole. This might take a while."

A sound yanked Baird from his focus on the lines of code in front of him. Sam and Cole were so deep in conversation they hadn't heard it. For two hours they'd been studying the Fort Umson footage, debating how best to enable DeeBees to combat the Swarm. From what he'd overheard, they were still far from a cohesive solution, though a plan was starting to take shape.

The sound came again. A knock at the door.

"Come in," he called out.

The door opened a few inches and Corporal Hansen poked

her head in. "Sorry to interrupt. The Condor is approaching South Village."

He nodded. "Can you put it up in here?"

"Of course." She backed out, letting the door click shut behind her.

"Let's take a break," he said to Sam and Cole.

Seconds later the main screen on the wall winked on. It was connected to the forward camera in the nose of a Condor. Below, dense forest obscured undulating hills. Ahead, a mountain range loomed, one snowy peak in particular dead-center in the screen. Baird sensed more than saw a winding mountain path leading up through the trees.

A screen beside him lit up with a set of controls.

"Thank you, Corporal Hansen," he said to himself, switching to his preferred grid view. Sam and Cole remained at their shared console, but each now leaned back to focus on the screens along the front wall. Most of the displays were nothing but gray squares—the DeeBees, inside their drop pods. This left only the series of cameras mounted on the aircraft itself.

"What was that?" Cole suddenly asked. "Go back. The... the bottom view."

Baird punched up the image from the camera pointed straight down from the Condor's belly, and rolled it back in time.

"There," Cole said.

Baird paused the playback. On the screen, they saw a section of the dirt road winding through the forest. Here, though, the path had been marred by an explosion or fire of some sort. He zoomed in as much as the system would allow. Sure enough, a black scorch-mark extended outward from a cart of some sort, and bodies lay in the dirt around it.

"Swarm," Cole said, walking slowly toward the front of the room, pointing at one of the larger corpses. "Swarm," he repeated, sweeping his index finger to another. He repeated this for each body captured in the image. "Don't see any of ours. Humans or DeeBees."

Baird flagged the image. "We'll show this to Jinn. It's fifteen klicks from Fort Umson, clear proof the Swarm are active elsewhere. Switching back to the live feed."

They all waited as the Condor coasted in toward the mountaintop. With each passing second the ground rose up to meet the aircraft, until finally the wall of South Village came into view beyond the trees. A wall that was, he could now see, rubble.

"That ain't good," Cole said.

Seconds later the images across the display bank began to flicker and bend, their transmissions starting to falter.

"That ain't good either," Cole added. "What's wrong with the signal?"

Baird could only shrug. "Not sure. It happened at Fort Umson, too."

For a moment he wondered if the plan was to land the damned Condor at the front gate to South Village. But at the last second, the bird pulled up hard and disgorged its payload. He watched as the pods fell away from the rear-view camera. As the aircraft climbed, this view also provided a nearly top-down angle on the village proper. There was movement among the buildings. Signs of battle, too.

With breath held, he watched as the DeeBees landed and unfolded themselves, their cameras coming online one after another. Unlike the drop on Fort Umson, this group had been programmed to land short of the village, after which they would march in as a solid unit. Jinn, it seemed, had given up on the containment approach in favor of a more standard attack formation. The question was how effective this would be without proper combat code.

The answer came swiftly.

First in were the Trackers. The rolling machines were nauseating to try and follow via camera, but Baird had spent enough time viewing such footage to know they were moving at top speed. He glanced at the tactical view, which confirmed it. The rolling bots fanned out as they swept in through the gate, forming a line across the wide interior yard. Here they popped open, extending their armored limbs and weapons, instantly creating a cordon wall that bisected the village. Baird had programmed this into their brains a long time ago, to be used for standard crowd-control situations. It worked well enough here, too.

As the Trackers unfolded, their cameras settled into stable views. Eight of them, providing a panorama of the village yard all the way out to the edge of the small plateau. In the center of this combined image was the main hall, which Baird guessed the villagers used for meetings, or meals, or both. The doors to it were wide open, the inside hidden in darkness.

More DeeBees began to march in through the gate, coming up behind the line of Trackers. They moved in clusters, each consisting of a DR-1, a Deadeye, and two Shepherd escorts. Two Guardian-class Watchers hovered above, their glowing shields active.

He felt a little pang of pride at the coordination the force displayed. To an unruly crowd after a Thrashball game, such a display would send people scurrying into the alleys or straight back to their homes. He'd seen it a dozen times.

But this was no gathering of drunken sports hooligans.

A huge beast emerged from the main hall in the center of the village. His first thought was of the Brumak, a foe Baird hadn't seen in decades and thought he'd never see again. Then he saw the monster in full, and understood. It was the Swarm's disfigured abomination of that monster, the creature they'd dubbed a Swarmak. It emerged from the darkness of the great hall, its huge head smashing out a section of wall above the already-massive door frame.

Instantly the DeeBee force opened fire on it, which only seemed to annoy the gigantic, heavily armored enemy. It stood to its full height and roared as round after round of bullets ricocheted off its chest and arms.

The Trackers coiled back into balls, rolling toward the enemy at top speed. As they reached the Swarmak's feet they exploded. The beast seemed barely to notice.

An instant later the Shepherds on the edge of the firing line vanished from the tactical display. Baird saw only flashes of motion and sparks before the cameras went black. Their neighbors turned, moving to re-establish the formation. In doing so, they provided confused glimpses of the left and right sides of the village yard.

"Ambush," Sam said. The Swarmak had been a diversion, and it had worked perfectly. While every DeeBee poured precious ammo into that monster, its smaller cousins had come in from the sides. Baird watched as a Drone swung its heavily muscled arm across the face of a DR-1, knocking the head clean off in a single blow.

"It's another Fort Umson," Cole said.

Baird wasn't so sure. "Hold on. Look, see that?"

The DeeBee troops sent to Fort Umson had been configured for "investigate and secure," but not this time. The remaining DR-1s closed ranks, forming protective wedges around the Deadeyes, kneeling to give their sniper cousins a clearer shot.

Baird felt a flicker of hope. Not that they'd win—the presence of a Swarmak left little doubt of the outcome—but that they might at least do some damage.

He saw Juvies rush toward one squad, mouths snapping as they galloped on all fours. The DR-1s tore them apart. Drones came next, lumbering and confident. Like oversized people, really, and that was something with which the DeeBee programming could work. They began to fall as the Deadeyes found their aim.

Then the Swarmak hurtled in among them. It swept one hand across the line, scattering Shepherds and Deadeyes like leaves.

Above it, a Guardian opened fire, strafing as its rotary canon blazed.

Baird watched in quiet amazement as a Juvie ran up the Swarmak's back, leapt, and collided with the Guardian in midair. The flying robot tumbled to the dirt, unable to stay aloft, and its mechanical innards were torn out by the enemy.

The tide had turned.

He saw a DR-1 glance upward just in time to be crushed like a tin can under the Swarmak's foot. A Pouncer unleashed its salvo of tail quills at the second Guardian, knocking out its shields and camera in one fell swoop. Blind, the machine was as good as useless.

The line broke. Baird knew the DeeBee ruleset better than anyone, having written most of it himself, and in such a situation they switched to an every-man-for-himself scenario. Coordination went out the window, as did the in-built desire to remain in formation. A few began to back away toward the gate. Others rushed ahead, but only one of these made it past the enemy line. A Shepherd. Baird watched as it sought to gain cover behind a stone well. It slid in behind the little column of rock, turned, and raised its weapon.

At this point it was the only DeeBee still transmitting, and with all the interference there wasn't much to see. What Baird did glimpse was almost inevitable at that point, but he couldn't look away. The Swarmak had chased the robot. It ignored the Shepherd's gunfire, or perhaps didn't even notice it. With one massive hand the huge creature wrapped its fingers around the mechanical, lifted it from behind the well, and tossed it over the side of the cliff.

The view became nothing more than the blurred wall of rock as the DeeBee picked up speed, plummeting to the waterway below. It hit the surface with a flash of white, a burst of static, then that all too familiar "no signal" screen, which, by this point, every display showed.

"Well, that didn't go well," Baird said.

Sam replied with an astounded, distressed laugh. "It's data, I guess. But… holy hell, what a bloodbath."

She was right, of course. "If we could get them to recognize the enemy, understand how each of them moves, they'd stop anticipating human reactions. Did you see how they did against the Juvies? The Drones?"

Sam nodded, deep in thought.

Cole still stood at the front of the room, looking closely at the displays. He pointed at the screen where the last DeeBee's transmission had marked the end of the festivities.

"That one," he said. "Go back." Puzzled, Baird complied. He rolled the footage back, seeing the blurry side of the cliff pass by in reverse.

"Too far," Cole said. "Forward… forward… Just before it hits the water. Yeah, now slow it down. Frame by frame, man." Baird did so, squinting at the display as the images ticked through. Blurry rock. Blurry rock. Garbled interference. Blurry rock. The whiteout of impact with churning water.

"What am I missing?" he asked.

Cole kept his gaze on the screen. With one hand he gestured for Baird to roll the images backward again.

"Stop there."

Baird did, then joined his friend at the front. Sam came over, too, slipping an arm around Baird as she did so.

"I see it," she said.

"Show me," Baird replied, seeing only the motion-blurred smear of rock and mist and transmission artifacts.

Cole pointed. "In your head, flip the image over." And just like that, Damon Baird could see it, too.

A figure in the mist. A figure with a particular feature.

"Maybe that's why he always wears that ugly thing," Cole said, smiling at the black shape on the screen that could only be one thing: Marcus Fenix's trademark skullcap bandanna.

"I'll be damned," Baird said. That put the rest of the image in context. Marcus was there, standing in some kind of cave or alcove, watching the DeeBee fall past him.

"Can you enhance it at all?" Cole asked.

Baird shook his head. "We're lucky anything got through. Every time the DeeBees get near the Swarm, the transmission..." he glanced at Sam, and saw that she was looking at him.

"We could counter for that interference," she said, echoing his own thoughts. "Modulate frequencies. Put a high-gain antenna on a Kestrel and fly in ever-growing circles—"

"Why stop at one?" he responded. "Let's deploy the whole goddamn fleet."

She nodded, and he could see her already working out the logistics.

"First things first," he added. "Take what you can learn from this and get me a better set of engagement rules for the bots. Then work on the Kestrels."

"Sure thing," Sam said. "But, listen, a set of combat rules takes time. You know that."

"Time's something we don't have a lot of." She was right, though. Baird added, "Do the best you can. Both of you."

Cole looked at him, dubious. "What are you going to do? Take this to Jinn?"

"Hmm?" Baird said. He'd been lost in thought, and it took a second to realize what Cole had asked. "No. Not yet."

"Why wait? Oh, hang on. You've got that look."

"What look?"

"I know that look," Cole said. "Sam, you see it, right? Baird's got an idea."

"Yep," she said. "He sure does. Spill it."

He held up a hand. "Just... relax. I need to think this through." From the looks on their faces, that wasn't going to satisfy. He decided to think out loud. "This interference we're seeing, it's only when the Swarm are nearby, right?"

They both agreed.

Baird said, "And JD and Del have been offline since they reached the crater. Them, Dave, the DeeBees... all dark. Which means..."

A shadow passed over Cole's features. "Which means they're in some serious shit."

Nobody spoke for a long moment.

When the silence was finally broken, Baird almost didn't recognize the voice.

"Damon?"

He looked around, realized it was IRIS. "Go ahead," he replied, trying to remember if he'd asked her to do something.

"I heard you mention that Dave was offline, but that is not entirely true."

He glanced up, surprised. "Well don't keep me in suspense, IRIS. What do you mean?"

"My understanding is that Dave is based on the original Jack specification."

"Yes. And?"

"Which means he has a Mark One field maintenance subsystem."

"A *what* now?" Cole asked.

Baird waved him off. "Yeah IRIS, so? That's of no use to us. It's only active when he's in field maintenance mode."

"Which is precisely the mode Dave entered," IRIS replied, "exactly forty-seven seconds ago."

Baird sat bolt upright. "IRIS, I might be a little bit in love with you."

"Noted."

His hands went to the keyboard, typing furiously. Over the clatter of keys he heard Cole ask, "You planning to explain?"

Baird spoke as he typed. "The Mark One is old tech! Slow. Outdated. And," he turned to Cole, smiling, "on a totally different frequency. Low bandwidth, sure, but maybe—*maybe*—we can slip Dave a little update. Something I've been tinkering with."

He felt himself become lost in the work as information flew across the screens before him. The work was sloppy, untested, but what else could he do? Optimize, he realized. Trim any fat. He set his mind to it, tasking IRIS with checking his work behind him.

Sam's hand gripped his shoulder, pulling him from his trance-like state. How much time had passed he wasn't quite sure. "Damon, we have to show Jinn what we saw. Marcus is—"

"I know, I know. Just a second. Almost there." He'd been adding a COG equipment update to Dave's interface code, but knew already it was way too much. Working as fast as he could, Baird trimmed out everything except the equipment JD and Del had left with, including the Condor itself.

"IRIS? It's done."

"Would you like me to schedule a—"

"Send it now."

She complied. Baird spun his seat toward Sam and Cole.

"C'mon," he said, "let's go find Jinn."

3: REMOTE POSSIBILITY

Del reached for the first rung of the ladder a few seconds after JD, and didn't bother to spare a look back at the enemy. He could *feel* them. They'd closed the gap and weren't about to stop. At least the others down on the ground had stopped shooting. That may have been to avoid collateral damage, or to conserve ammo—he had no idea and didn't care. All he knew was he needed to climb, and the weight of Dave on his back wouldn't make the task any easier.

"If you're going to reboot, self-repair, or something, Dave, now's the damn time!"

Dave did not reply. Didn't even move.

The ventilation stack extended about a hundred and fifty feet up from the top of the dome. A ladder ran up the entire length, ending high above at a gantry that circled the very top. Del had covered barely thirty feet of this when the ladder began to sway and vibrate. He glanced down to see not Juvies, but a Drone. The ugly bastard had swept its smaller comrades aside and taken the lead. It climbed one-handed, hefting a Hammerburst in its free hand.

As they made eye contact, the creature raised the weapon and cracked off a multi-shot salvo. It hadn't taken the time to aim, though, and the rounds pounded harmlessly into the tower a few feet from Del's face.

Del pulled out the Boltok he'd found under the foreman's desk and aimed down between his feet. He squeezed a single shot off, felt the jolt of it rocket up his arm as the old reliable gun gave a thunderous *crack*. Below, the Drone's face jerked sideways, its head spinning almost halfway around. It dropped from the ladder, fell backward, and disappeared into a crowd of Juvies just below.

It took several of them with it on the way down. That bought him some time.

Four shots left. Plus the one in the rifle.

Del holstered the revolver and threw all his energy back into climbing. JD had opened up a big lead now. Too big, maybe. If he got far enough in front of the pack, Del feared those on the ground would take the opportunity to open fire on him again.

Only, they didn't. Del couldn't understand it.

Do they want us alive? he wondered. Or was it the tower they feared damaging? Why the hell would that—

Then he understood. Or had a theory anyway.

"Speed it up!" he shouted to JD.

"Do I want to know why?"

"We blocked the door, which means this tower is the only way out for them. They're climbing the inside!"

That did it. JD climbed faster. Del—already fifteen feet behind and hauling the dormant mass of Dave—threw all his strength into the task. The rungs began to blur. His biceps and shoulders were like knots of fire by the time he reached for the last one and pulled himself onto the gantry.

The metal-grid walkway was just wide enough for a single person to navigate. It circled the top portion of the tower, about five feet from the highest point. Across from where the ladder connected, there was a short set of stairs that led to the very top, which wasn't an open hole, as Del had guessed, but instead was covered with a steel mesh plate.

JD was a few feet off to the side, standing next to a waist-high gray box. Rising up fifteen feet from this was the high-gain directional antenna. The receiver dish at the very top was covered in rust.

Del approached his friend. He leaned to one side and eased Dave onto the gantry.

"Think that grating will hold?" JD asked, looking at the top of the tower.

Del opened his mouth to reply, but a series of short beeping sounds stopped him. He glanced down.

Despite suffering a direct hit from a Buzzkill, which had left a huge dent in his side, Dave was unfolding his arms.

"Well, look at that," Del said.

"He's functioning again?" JD asked.

"Yeah. Well, his arms at least. Who knows how much damage that blade did—"

Dave suddenly lurched upward, engines whirring. He rose a few feet up in the air and started spinning in a slow circle.

"What's he doing?" JD asked.

Del looked at his friend. "Recording, just like we asked him to."

"Well, shit, perfect timing. Wait until Jinn sees this," JD said.

The crater basin far below looked like a war zone, the ground itself seemingly alive as the Swarm moved about.

"*If* she sees this, I mean. That antenna looks like it's seen about twelve Windflares too many. Think it'll work?"

Del shrugged. "Dave, hook into the antenna and begin transmission, maximum gain." He glanced at JD. "Keep an eye on the ladder, while I check the vent?"

"Works for me," JD replied.

Del circled the gantry until he reached the point where four steps led up to the opening of the ventilation tower. He climbed them and breathed a sigh of relief when it came into view. The tower was capped with a metal grate that looked like it weighed about four tons. Turning to let JD know, he stopped. Off to one side he saw a lump resting atop the grated surface. Del climbed out and walked carefully across the steel grid.

His relief drained away. The lump was a heavy padlock, affixed to a hatch that led down into the tower. Sturdy enough to keep Juvies from pushing through, he thought, but anything bigger and it would snap like a twig.

He rushed back to the small stairwell, then down to where Dave was still recording footage of the scene below them. Del glanced out at the landscape and shook his head in disbelief. For all the Swarm trying to get them off the tower, there seemed to be three times as many making their way out of the crater. They moved in small groups, with no organization he could discern. The plan, if they had one, seemed to be to spread out in all directions, and that scared the hell out of him.

"Dave," he said. "Status? Is it working?"

The bot had plugged itself into a port on the tower's antenna. It made a series of chirps that sounded positive, but remained in place, status lights blinking rapidly.

At the top of the ladder, the first Juvie reached the gantry. JD flipped his Enforcer around and wielded it like a club, smashing the creature's skull. Another came up right behind it, and met the same fate. Then a third. But the climb had taken its toll, and JD's swings were slowing down.

Del rushed over to join him, shifting the Breechshot rifle off his shoulder as he went. He flipped the weapon around to hold it by the barrel, turning it into an axe.

"Let me!" he shouted, sliding in to take JD's place. His friend backed off, breathing hard.

"Check on Dave," Del suggested.

JD didn't acknowledge, he just moved. His boots clanged on the metal walkway, weirdly in sync with the cries of the Juvies as Del brought the axe down. Two fell quickly. A third managed to grasp his leg before he slammed the blade into its nose and sent it tumbling back to Sera.

More were coming, but they weren't his primary concern. Del's heart skipped a beat when he saw the creature now three-quarters of the way up the tower. A full-grown Snatcher, and it wasn't bothering to use the ladder. Its massive talons punched straight into the concrete wall as it scampered toward him, completely bypassing the natural choke-point the ladder had created.

"Things are about to get ugly," he shouted over his shoulder. His mind turned to the single round of ammo sitting in the Breechshot's chamber. Not enough to kill a Snatcher, but with perfect aim he might dislodge it and send it falling to the ground.

The creature seemed to sense his idea. Or maybe some part of its animal brain just realized there was no reason to come straight at him. As it clawed its way up the vertical surface it began to move sideways, making a clockwise spiral and disappearing from Del's view.

"Enough of this," he grunted, and dropped to his back. Lying flat on the gantry, he pressed his palms against the concrete behind him and kicked out with both legs.

The ladder shuddered. The bolts holding it onto the tower—some, anyway—made a brief high shriek. He kicked again, harder, thinking of the corroded metal antenna.

And again. Gave it all the strength he had. The ladder vibrated as a few bolts came free of the tower.

One last push. He closed his eyes and bellowed at the sky as he jackhammered his legs out. Was rewarded by the groan of metal giving way. Del opened his eyes in time to see the surprised face of a Juvie as the top fifteen feet of the ladder slowly bent outward from the wall, then vanished.

Behind him, JD swore. "What the hell?"

"What's wrong?" Del asked, rolling over onto his stomach and pushing himself back to his feet.

"No idea. Dave just… turned off."

"Was he able to transmit?"

"No," JD replied. "I don't know, you're the expert. He just… shut down."

"Out of juice," Del offered.

"Maybe."

Del moved to his friend. "I took out the ladder, but we've got bigger problems."

"Not sure I want to hear them."

Del ignored this. "Snatcher. At least one, climbing up. We don't have long."

JD's face hardened. "The hell do we do? Throw Dave at it?"

"I've got one round in this," Del said, hefting the rifle.

"Against a Snatcher?"

"I was thinking the padlock." He quickly described the access hatch atop the tower.

"Somehow I don't think entering the burial site is wise."

"If you've got a better idea, I'm all ears!"

Before JD could say more, a familiar sound filled the space around them. The tiny thrusters that kept Dave aloft. They both looked as the little robot lifted back up to its usual height and hovered there.

Del checked the panel on Dave's front.

"Did it get through? Tell me we at least achieved something here," JD said.

Del shook his head. "No. Didn't work." He sensed the frustration and anger radiating off JD, but his own disappointment remained in check by what the screen did say.

"Huh," Del managed.

"What is it?"

"He couldn't transmit, but he did receive."

"Received what?"

Del turned to him. "It says 'tactical support upgrade.'"

Before Del could even begin to figure out what that meant, exactly, he heard a series of sharp cracks from the outer wall of the tower.

"Now what?" JD asked.

Del knew the sound, though. He'd been expecting it, and there was no time to explain.

The Snatcher he'd seen coming up the tower had arrived.

He turned and drew his Boltok just as the beast's front legs appeared over the edge. The revolver, old and simple as it might have been, had one redeeming quality.

It packed a hell of a punch.

Del took aim, waiting for the creature to show its face. Another leg came over the edge, its needle-tip slamming down and... and...

The sound was wrong. There was no thud of impact. Just a dull scrape.

Del watched the leg slide left, then right. The Snatcher's body lifted above the rim of the tower, but the leg still moved. Thrashing back and forth now.

It's stuck, he thought, and aimed again, this time the Boltok pointing at the tip of the trapped leg.

He fired two of his four rounds.

The bullets struck home, crunching into the meat of the leg, achieving the desired result. The Snatcher let out a wretched scream, tore its leg violently away from the roof, swayed, and disappeared back behind the wall.

"Nice one," JD said.

Del moved to the railing at the gantry's edge and looked down in time to see the flailing Snatcher land hard on its back. Its legs twitched, and then it went still.

JD joined him there. For a moment they both stared at the scene below. One dead Snatcher surrounded by countless other creatures.

"Hey," JD said. "It's not dead."

Del shook his head. "Naw, man, it's dead."

"Not that. Look there. The Condor."

The aircraft's lights were back on, its engines starting to spin up, audible even from this distance. The only thing the bird didn't do, though, was start moving.

JD activated his comm. "Yoon? Yoon?! Do you read?"

The pilot made no reply, though, and Del didn't think she ever would. "She's gone, JD. Shrapnel took out the whole cockpit when that door blew. No coming back from a hit like that."

"Then what..."

A voice crackled in his ear. "Not... finished... yet," Yoon said, through a storm of static. The pain she was in came through far more clearly than her words. "Can't... move."

Wide-eyed, Del looked at JD. They stared at one another in total disbelief. JD said, "We can't reach you, Yoon. There's—"

"Can't... move," Yoon repeated, "the Condor."

Del looked back at the plane, mind racing.

"One of the engines took a hit," JD replied.

"Not that," the pilot said, her voice not much more than a whisper.

Studying the aircraft, Del understood. "Take this," he said, and tossed the Breechshot rifle to JD.

"Why?" JD started to ask.

"You're a better shot than me. I'll spot for you."

"I don't even know what I'm aiming at!"

Despite the protests, JD followed Del to the edge of the gantry, and the open space where the ladder used to connect. Del took a quick glance down. Three more Snatchers were working their way up the side of the tower. They were already past the halfway mark. He ignored them, for now.

"The Condor," Del said. "Aim."

JD seemed about to argue, then gave in and lay down. He set the rifle on the torn edge of the gantry. The Locust-modified Markza had a sight on it, and JD put his eye to it.

"Del, I swear, if you're going to ask me to end her suffering..." he said, letting the words trail off.

Del crouched and tried to clear his head of the approaching dangers. He scanned the landscape around the aircraft, then spoke calmly. "You've got one shot. It's the cargo ramp, JD. We left it down, and that's keeping the aircraft from moving."

"Shit," JD whispered. "You're right."

"It's clear. The button, JD! For the ramp, now!"

JD exhaled. When he pulled the trigger, the customized Breechshot spat a plume of fire and thunder.

Try as he might, Del couldn't tell if the shot had hit its mark. The answer came a few seconds later, when the rear cargo ramp began rotating slowly into the closed position. JD had hit the manual override switch.

"I'll be damned." For a second Del was speechless. "Nice shot."

"Thanks." JD pushed himself up to a knee. "Yoon," he said into the comm. You're clear. Get as far from here as you can, let Control know—"

"Coming…" the pilot replied, "be ready. Keep Dave… online."

"Pardon?" JD asked, then turned to Del. "Did she just say what I think she said? And what's Dave got to do with it?"

Del helped him to his feet. "I think I know. C'mon!" With that he turned and raced around the tower, reaching the set of steps leading to the grid metal roof. JD followed, looking more and more dubious.

From below, the aircraft's three remaining engines had reached a deafening roar that reminded Del of a Windflare. It was a noise he'd heard too many times to count, as familiar as the sound of Lancer fire. Which is why he knew instantly that something was wrong. The blaring hum should have been smooth, constant, but this was faltering.

"What's wrong?" JD asked.

Del glanced back at Dave, who remained next to the old antenna. "The upgrade. He's accessed the Condor, giving her eyes and ears. Our location. But I think the connection is getting interference."

"'Course it is."

Del crossed the roof and looked down at Dave. The robot hovered above the gantry, five feet below. "Dave, use the tower's antenna to boost the signal!"

Dave returned to the box and connected to it again. An instant later the antenna at the top creaked, but failed to move. They'd pointed it toward New Ephyra when it was built, and over time it had rusted into that angle.

"Forget it," Del said. "Try from up here, Dave."

The robot disconnected and propelled itself up to where Del stood, maximizing its view of the aircraft.

A second later the sound of the engines became smoother. They still seemed off-kilter, but not as much as before.

The aircraft rolled down the runway, moving away from them. Abruptly it turned, a tight one-eighty, and the engines ramped up to full power again. Moving toward them, the bird rapidly gained speed. Then it disappeared again from Del's sight line.

JD moved to the left, stepping up to the edge and leaning out to get a better view. "Del? Why is she flying the Condor toward the tower?"

"I think she's—" he started.

The words were cut off as the access hatch on the roof exploded upward, the padlock shattering. Del shielded his face from the spray of metal chunks. A shape flew through the open hatch, flying ten feet up into the air before it twisted around and landed, all four spiked feet thudding into the metal grid rooftop.

Another Snatcher, tail raised. At the tip a razor-sharp quill gleamed.

It coiled, stepping sideways to keep both JD and Del in sight. It let out a shrieking cry, snake-like tentacles writhing in its mouth. Its tail swiveled from one man to the other, as if trying to decide which to take down first.

JD, still holding the now-empty Breechshot, flipped the rifle around and gripped the barrel with both hands. He swung, stepping in at the same time. The axe blade hissed through the air.

But the Snatcher was too quick. It raised its leg to let the blade swing harmlessly by, then aimed its tail at JD. The pointed tip began to glow as it prepared to shoot one of its incapacitating quills.

Del brought his Boltok up and fired two rounds into the beast's translucent belly. The monster twitched from the impact, its quill firing in the same instant. The projectile cut through the air on a trail of green gas, missing JD's head by inches and slamming instead into the gray box at the base of the antenna assembly with a resounding *clang*.

Del pulled the trigger again, but the Boltok only clicked. Out of ammo.

The Snatcher lunged toward him, spiked feet thrusting at him like spears.

Del dodged just in time, reared back, and threw the empty pistol as hard as he could. The Boltok had some heft to it—a trait that Gears often complained about—but in this instance he used it to his advantage. The overly heavy weapon slammed into one of the Snatcher's four eyes. It howled in pain as it thrashed wildly about on the rooftop.

"JD?" Del shouted. "I'm out of options here!"

The Snatcher gathered its wits—what little it had, anyway. It moved with purpose, righting itself and coming to stand shakily at its full height. Then it swung its head toward Del.

It dipped on its forelegs and prepared to strike, tail glowing as another quill came ready.

Del swallowed. Distantly he was aware of JD's voice, talking to Yoon, and the pilot's garbled response, but the monster before him made their words fail to register. He could only stare into that horrid face, and wait. There was nowhere to go. No option left.

He could hear the growing thrum of the Condor's engines,

and had the sickening realization that Yoon was going to ram the tower. Take them all out instead of letting a Snatcher get them.

Coming from the left, JD tackled him.

Del had no chance to ready himself. No time to understand. One second he was standing on the roof, the next he was falling with JD and Dave, facing upward, watching the Snatcher dive off the roof after them. It spread its legs wide like a spider leaping toward its meal.

Then his peripheral vision disappeared, and they fell through the open side door of the Condor's hull. Above them, the Snatcher was shredded into a blur of gore as it went through one of the roaring turboprops.

Del's head hit the side wall of the Condor's interior, and the world exploded with stars before going black.

The darkness formed into dull shapes and weak colors. Del had no idea how long he'd been out. Sounds were distant, pain nothing more than a vague concept.

Then it all came crashing in.

He'd only been unconscious for an instant, and was laid out against the side wall of the Condor—which currently served as a floor. The *actual* floor was a wall against which his legs were propped. Even as his brain began to comprehend this, the aircraft rolled back to level and Del found himself leaning against the wall, then falling face-first to the floor with just enough time and sense to throw out his arms. Another blow to the head didn't hold much appeal.

Next to him, JD didn't have as much luck. He hit the deck hard, and grunted. The blow served as his wake-up call. Del helped him to his feet, just in time for them both to sway as the aircraft went into another steep turn.

"What the hell is Yoon doing?" Del asked.

"She's not responding."

"Oh, fuck." Del looked toward the cockpit. "We've gotta get to the controls."

"No time," JD managed to growl. "Seats. Harnesses."

"Okay," Del said, and he helped his friend to the fore section of the deck, where several pull-out crash seats waited against the bulkhead.

He'd just buckled himself in when something hammered along the bottom of the fuselage. Along the center of the empty cargo bay a neat row of Pouncer quills poked up through the floor.

The attack seemed to awaken something in the horde of enemies below. From the sound of things, every one of them who held a weapon of some kind opened fire all at once. The whole plane shook. Everything rattled around him—except Dave, who hovered with unnatural stillness.

"Dave," Del said with relief. "You made it! Can you access the flight systems? Level us out?"

An explosion slammed the Condor, rocking it hard to one side. Alarms started to go off.

"Why do I feel like we'd be safer back on that tower?" JD asked.

Before Del could comment, the aircraft went quiet. All engines, down. The sound of bullets thudding against the hull stopped, too. The plane went into a steep climb, though with no engines to push it upward, Del feared that wasn't a good thing.

There came a great crunching sound, grinding against the fuselage from fore to aft, slowing as it went. A moment of terrible silence followed, and then the nose of the plane tipped downward and slammed into what Del assumed was dirt. As crash landings went, it was the gentlest he could imagine.

JD still didn't have time to speak. Before he could, Del had his buckle off and was rushing to the side door. He levered it open and took in the scene outside.

"I'll be damned."

"What is it?" JD asked, coming up behind him.

"See for yourself," he replied, stepping aside. They were resting on the rim of the crater, a thousand yards from the tower.

"Dave!" Del shouted over his shoulder. "Attempt transmission. All of it. Get it to Control, *now*."

The robot bleeped an acknowledgment.

JD tugged at Del's shoulder. "Yoon," he said. "Grab a med kit." Then he raced off toward the cockpit.

Del found a first-aid station and yanked the kit from the wall, then followed. The air inside the cabin was choked with dust and smoke, growing worse as he made his way forward. By the time he reached the cockpit door he could see only a few feet.

JD knelt beside the pilot's seat, eyes downcast.

"She's gone," he said.

Del crouched beside him, put a hand on Yoon's shoulder. She was pinned to her seat by a long piece of shrapnel, the blood around the wound already dry. How she'd survived the strike at all he couldn't imagine. "If only we'd tried to get to her," he said quietly. "I never thought... I mean, she looked..."

She looked like this, he thought.

"We wouldn't have made it," JD said.

They were silent for a long moment.

"Hell of a thing you did for us," Del said to her. "Thank you."

JD was nodding, eyes still closed. Finally, he opened them and stood. "We're still in a lot of trouble here."

"I know," Del said. "At least Dave's able to transmit."

JD continued to nod. He laughed then, a sound laden with grief and dismay. "Mission successful, then, huh?"

Del looked at his friend. "What now? Grab some supplies, head into the desert? Hold out here?"

"Supplies," JD said, sounding only half convinced.

Del gave the pilot's shoulder a final squeeze, turned, and moved back to the cabin. JD joined him soon after, Yoon's COG tags in his hand. He ran a thumb over the gear-shaped emblem, then slipped it into his pocket.

"Was the plan really to jump into the plane?" Del asked him.

"Not exactly. I was supposed to throw Dave in. Then I thought, what the hell, we might as well try."

Del stared at him, impressed and incredulous all at once. "That was one hell of a ballsy move, JD," he said. "Next time you want me to jump off the roof of a building, a little warning would be good."

"Would you have done it if I'd asked?"

"Hell, no."

JD spread his hands, signaling his victory.

A sound outside caught their attention, and Del returned to the open door to look.

Far below, in the basin of the crater, the Swarm remained largely hidden in the dust and smoke kicked up by the battle. Yet Del had no trouble spotting the shift in their movements.

"They're leaving," Del said.

JD joined him. They watched in silence as groups of the enemy streamed outward from the burial site.

"Is it just me," JD asked, "or are a fucking lot of them headed straight for us?"

4: EVERYTHING ON THE TABLE

Marching toward Jinn's office, Baird decided this was a habit he *really* didn't want to develop. At least this time it wasn't anger driving him, but urgency.

"She was just trying to reach you," the assistant at the desk said as he, Sam, and Cole strode swiftly by. Baird acknowledged her with a wave and entered the First Minister's office. He came up short, surprised to find the room empty.

"In here," Jinn said, from a side chamber off to his right. He angled himself in that direction, Sam and Cole right behind him.

He'd always known there were doors on either side of the entrance to Jinn's sanctum, and had assumed they led to restrooms or storage closets. At most a small conference room. Here again, Jinn surprised him.

The side chamber was, in fact, similar to the basement of his "shed." She had an arrangement of screens and control panels that would make even the most senior staffer down in Control proud. Something felt wrong about the space, though, and it wasn't until he'd stepped inside that Baird understood. It was all new. Installed, perhaps, in just the last few hours.

Jinn saw the look on his face. She inclined her head.

"You inspired me, Damon. I realized after our last stint down in Control that a system of my own would be in order. For the more... *delicate* operations."

There was only one chair, and it was not empty. The high-backed seat spun slightly. Corporal Hansen gave him a nod of recognition.

"Unlike you, though," Jinn went on, "I'm not trained in its use."

He shook his head. "Look, that's all fascinating, but we've got... oh hell, what *is* that?"

His eyes locked on the screens.

He, Sam, and Cole all stood perfectly still for several seconds, just staring. The footage was all from a single angle, and short. Maybe thirty seconds' worth, running on a loop. It didn't take long to work out what he was seeing.

Shot from above, perhaps from a hovering Raven, the footage showed a flat stretch of ground, then a crater, though visibility into the distance was limited by a lot of dust and smoke. What at first glance might be mistaken for people fleeing a fire. Baird recognized the shapes in that hazy air.

"Swarm," he said.

Then the camera panned down slightly, and in the bottom corner of the screen the face of James Fenix came into view. The image continued to pan and there was Del, just behind him. The situation became clearer. They stood atop a tower, perhaps two hundred feet above the basin of the crater. Below them, the Swarm formed an unbroken sea of movement.

"Oh, hell."

"Daaaamn," Cole added, drawing the word out. Sam took a step forward, clutching Baird's forearm reflexively. She looked to Jinn.

"When did you get this?" Her question had an edge to it, indicating a suspicion that Jinn had been holding back.

"Only seconds ago," the First Minister replied.

"Came in on an old frequency," Corporal Hansen added.

"The update went through," Baird said, to himself more than anyone. It had worked. Dave was now transmitting on a totally different band.

"Get them out of there, Jinn," Sam said.

Her eyes flared, if only for an instant. Mina Jinn didn't appreciate being ordered to do anything.

"I've already given the order," she said. "A full DeeBee squad plus two Kestrels for support—"

Baird whirled on her, fists clenched.

"Against that?" He pointed at the screen. "You think that's going to accomplish anything? You need to let me figure out a way to bring the Hammer of Dawn back online—"

"*Enough*," she said. "This isn't the time for that old argument."

"It's exactly the fucking time!"

"Damon," Cole said, "even if we could, which we can't, you wouldn't drop that kind of grief on James and Del, would you?"

Baird's lip curled, anger getting the better of him. "Are we looking at the same screen? I mean, am I the only one who sees what's happening here? There's no getting off that tower. They're already dead." This last he directed at Jinn.

She held her ground, though, matching his gaze with her customary quiet, controlled intensity. Then, abruptly, an eyebrow rose.

"If you came here before receiving my summons, why did you come? The three of you were in an awful hurry."

He'd almost forgotten. In fact, for a second after she spoke he couldn't remember. It was Sam who answered her, by simply holding out a piece of paper. A printed image. Marcus Fenix, blurred but recognizable, thanks to his skullcap. Jinn studied it for a moment, then glanced up at them, looking into their faces one by one.

"When was this taken? Where?"

"South Village," Baird said. "Not seconds ago... but close enough."

"And Ms. Diaz?"

He shook his head. "This is all we saw. No idea if she's with him, but it's a good assumption."

"Are you going to suggest that we vaporize that location, too?"

Baird didn't rise to her challenge, though. "Marcus wasn't fighting at the top of the cliff. He's standing at the bottom. My guess? He's trapped down there. Maybe Kait, too. The whole village, for all we know. Might be they can hold out for a while." Again he pointed at the screen. "The crater's the priority, Jinn, and *that* I do suggest you wipe off the face of Sera. Somehow, some way. This Swarm is a bigger problem than just Tollen Dam. Two outbreaks at two burial sites—that's no coincidence. And even if it's limited to only those two places, they're the sources, Jinn. You need to shut them down. Utterly and completely."

He held up a hand, heading off the arguments. "JD and Del are like sons to me. To all of us, you included, Jinn." She'd been in charge of the fertility project that allowed Anya Stroud to get pregnant. The same project that had swollen Jinn's own belly. "But there's no getting off that tower."

To his surprise, Jinn smiled.

"What?" he asked.

"You haven't seen the rest of the footage."

It was Baird's turn to raise an eyebrow.

Jinn nodded to Corporal Hansen. The woman had sat quietly through the entire exchange. She remained so now, knowing what Jinn wanted. Turning back to the console, she rolled the footage forward.

Baird watched in stunned silence as the two men hurled themselves off the tower in what seemed to be a suicidal move. A huge spider-like creature hurled itself after them.

All this from Dave's point of view, falling beside the two men. The robot turned, then, and Baird watched in stunned silence.

A Condor shot into the frame, guided, Baird felt sure, by the diminutive robot. When the aircraft reached the tower, it rolled ninety degrees and the side door popped open. Dave, JD, and Del all fell through with the precision only a machine could plan. A split second earlier and they'd have fallen to their deaths. A split second later and they'd have been sucked into one of the turboprops.

The timing was perfect, though. The maneuver got them off the tower, but not much farther. One engine appeared to be down, and they were taking heavy fire. The plane didn't quite have the thrust needed to climb out of the crater. It crashed against the rim, fell, and lay in ruin, perched precariously on the crater's edge. Static filled the view for a moment. Just as Baird was about to tell Hansen to turn the footage off, the video feed returned.

Dave had moved to the side door, which still hung open. He gave them a clear view of the entire crater now. Smoke and fire and dust... and Swarm.

"They made it out," Baird said. "They made it out! They're clear! Jinn, c'mon. That's all the more reason to can an airstrike *or twelve* on that basin at the very least—"

"Absolutely not." Jinn's answer was sharp as a sword this time. He wouldn't have thought it possible, but somehow her expression hardened even more. "Not until we know our people are safe. There has to be another way."

It was Sam who offered the solution.

5: THE END OF THE ROPE

She sat between the twins, who both dozed. Their heads lolled on her shoulders.

Kait's own extreme exhaustion had turned into a weird sort of hyper-awareness. The second wind, as Oscar called it. Really the third, she thought. Maybe the fourth. She'd lost count.

She was wired, felt a buzz of electricity behind her eyes that she knew would keep sleep at bay no matter how much she needed it. That was fine by her. Sleep would just bring more nightmares, and given that she was trapped in the middle of a nightmare, she was happy to draw a line against more.

For some time her focus had been on the muted sounds of battle from the plateau high above. She strained her ears the whole time, waiting for that deep ugly laugh and hoping against hope it wouldn't come. But the rock was too thick, the cliff too high, to hear specifics. There was a battle, that much she knew, but individual sounds were too hard to make out.

The party hadn't lasted long, though. Aside from the severed

DeeBee head Marcus had seen plummet into the rapids, and the laugh of what she knew was a Speaker, the duration and conclusion took only minutes to play out to its inevitable conclusion. DeeBees were no match for the Swarm.

She wondered how Jinn would react to that news.

Whatever had been in Mackenzie's explosive had burned for an impressive amount of time, and had kept the Swarm at bay, but it had been growing slowly dimmer as the twins slept. When it went out, the "real fun" would start. Oscar's words.

So the sudden heat and brightness came as an unwelcome surprise. Kait raised a hand uselessly, trying and failing to block out the flare of light and the uncomfortable warmth. In the process she almost blocked her view of the flaming, reeking form of a Juvie leaping into the room at full gallop.

It screamed as it barreled into the space, flames roiling off sizzling skin, the smell of cooking, rotten flesh somehow worse than the inferno preceding it. Kait fumbled for her rifle, but she'd draped her arms over the kids to hold them close. A mistake. Maybe a fatal one—for all three of them.

Oscar barely stirred, his snoring unbroken.

But Marcus Fenix had been awake, standing on the opposite side of the room with his arms folded and his chin on his chest. Not asleep, just... waiting. With the arrival of the intruder, he moved in a blur. A long single step toward the smoldering Juvie. At the same time he grasped a wooden stool with both hands, sidestepped, and swung.

The piece of furniture slammed into the creature's back, shattering into wooden shards. The blow propelled the monster in the same direction it had been running, sending it straight out the far side of the room and, a second later, over the cliff into the rapids.

Marcus stood very still, two broken legs of the stool still in his hands. The twins were up now, moving to stand. Oscar rolled over.

"They've made it through," Marcus managed to say before the battle started. He hurled the two stool legs aside and grabbed his Lancer from the wall. Kait did the same, nudging Oscar with the toe of her boot. Eli somehow found his hunting rifle before she'd managed to collect her own weapon, and was already positioning himself to fire on the tunnel from which the Juvie had emerged.

"No," Marcus said. "Cover our exit route." He jerked his head toward the narrow tunnel that ultimately led to the cache of stolen supplies.

Eli wrinkled his nose. "Aww, but—"

"That's an order," Marcus said.

"C'mon," Mackenzie added, tugging at her brother's shirt sleeve. Reluctantly the boy followed his sister into the darkened passage.

Oscar finally sat up, rubbing his eyes. "Morning already? Is that bacon I smell?"

"It's charred Juvie," Kait told him. "Get up." To his credit, her uncle sprang to his feet, eyes alert and scanning the surroundings.

"Where are the twins?!"

"Told them to cover our fallback position," Marcus said as he flipped a table over and shoved it with one foot toward the wider passage where the Juvie had come in. He knelt behind it.

Oscar joined him there, propping the barrel of his Gnasher on the improvised barricade. Kait crossed to the passage the kids had taken, but only to use the corner of the wall as cover. She leaned against it and readied her weapon, barely having time to check the safety was off before a Pouncer emerged from the darkness.

It galloped hard, crouched, then leapt at the table behind which Marcus and Oscar now knelt.

The two men opened fire before it could land, sending the beast into convulsions as rounds poured into it. Oscar's third shot put a massive hole in the crown of the enemy's head, taking all the life from its limbs in the blink of an eye. But momentum was a powerful thing, and the monster had built up quite a head of steam running through the last of the flames. It fell as a lifeless mass, skidded on the rock floor, and smashed into the wooden table.

The barricade had no chance. It split into two jagged halves, sending Marcus and Oscar diving to either side. The Pouncer rolled before coming to a stop in the center of the room, blood pooling around the limp body. Dead or not, the damage was done.

Kait felt something shoot past her, a narrow miss. The quill thwacked into the wall behind her. Another Pouncer, following the first, shrieking with rage as it leapt into the chamber. She recovered, aimed, and fired.

Across the room Oscar lit into the fresh enemy as well, but together they only managed to drive it off to one side. It shuffled to keep its gaze on Oscar, tail coming up to launch another salvo of quills. In the process, however, it had stepped right over where Marcus Fenix lay.

He powered up the saw on his Lancer and gutted the beast with a diagonal swipe, using the motion to roll out from under it. The move saved him from being covered with steaming innards, as well as avoiding the crushing weight of the fallen creature.

It screamed as it died.

Kait barely had a chance to breathe before the strange almost canine yelps of Juvies poured from the passage; four of them, leaping over one another, bouncing off the walls or running straight along them. They came with inhuman speed, dodging with their erratic movement as Kait went full-auto and put a dozen rounds down range. From the corner of her eye she saw Marcus getting to his feet.

Oscar had no angle on the passageway and moved forward, sliding in behind one of the broken halves of the table. He reached the spot at the same instant the lead Juvie emerged. It tried to vault the obstruction, only to catch the butt of Oscar's shotgun as he rammed it into the creature's miserable, distorted face. Blood and teeth flew as the head rocked back. It fell, lifeless, but another was right behind it.

This one went high, reaching for Oscar as it went. Its claws wrapped around the sides of his head as it somersaulted over him. An instant later the two of them were rolling like two wrestlers. Kait had no shot, so she'd have to let Oscar take care of himself. Swinging her rifle back toward the tunnel, she found the tip of the weapon just inches from the face of a third Juvie.

It ducked as she fired, then sprang up and into her abdomen. Snarling, it snapped savagely at her, all fangs and hot, stinking breath. Kait raised one arm and let her armor absorb the bite. She twisted, tried to throw the thing off, to no avail. Just a couple of feet away, Oscar writhed on the ground in a mirror of her battle. Across the room, Marcus found himself locked in close combat with the fourth of the group, though at least he was on his feet.

A deafening *crack* filled the small space. Kait winced, all sound replaced with a ringing noise that refused to end. The Juvie over her crumpled, half its head blown off. Next to her, Oscar's opponent fell with an identical wound. And, she saw, the one in front of Marcus had a hole in its back, blood trickling out.

It toppled sideways.

Kait turned and looked the other way, saw Eli sighting down the barrel of his hunting rifle. He grinned at her and flashed a thumbs-up.

"Three in one shot," she marveled.

"Told you he's got the eye!" Oscar said, on his feet again.

"And a flair for the dramatic," she added, unable to keep the smile from her face.

Marcus moved back to cover the tunnel through which the Swarm were advancing. He fired blind, putting four rounds into the darkness. "I suggest we retreat before they figure out a way down the cliff, and come at us from both sides."

"Fine by me," Oscar said. "Kait?"

She nodded, then took aim and laid down a volley of suppressing fire as the two men rounded the corner behind her and up the narrow passage to where Eli and Mackenzie waited.

She followed them, walking backward to keep her rifle trained toward the enemy. The ground was uneven, though. She tripped on a protrusion and stumbled. Oscar caught her by the elbow and helped her up the concealed steps to the tiny chamber where the others waited.

"We make our last stand here," she suggested to the group. Marcus nodded.

"Bad idea," Oscar replied, eying the nonexistent fourth wall, open to the outside. It was from here they'd swung over to the hidden supply room. "We should move to the hideout. The rope only carries one at a time—it'll take too long if they've already reached us. We should start now."

As tough as it was to admit, Kait knew he was right. They had to cede South Village to the Swarm. She glanced at Marcus, who dipped his head in reluctant agreement.

"Same plan as before," Oscar said. "Kids, you go first. Cover us as we cross over."

The pair went to the rope. Without a word passing between them they played a quick round of rock-paper-scissors. Eli frowned at his loss, shouldered his rifle, and grabbed the rope. A second later he swung out into the cold mists, disappearing from view.

Kait gave Mackenzie a reassuring smile and took up a position next to her, returning her focus to the only way the Swarm could get in. Marcus and Oscar placed themselves to either side of the tunnel, weapons aimed and ready. They'd decided for her. She'd go next.

The rope returned. Mackenzie hopped on, wrapping the thick frayed cord around one arm. With a little cry of glee that belied the danger they were all in, she pushed off the ledge and out into the swirling vapor.

When the rope returned, Kait followed, only without the cheerful hoot.

She rejoined the twins in the supply room and immediately went to the ammunition crate. A fresh clip in her rifle and two more in her pocket, she went back to the ledge as Marcus came hurtling in. He reached out and clasped arms with her, though Kait had to tug on his shirt as well to get the big man across those last two feet.

He flung the rope back and wiped droplets of water from his face.

They made room, and waited.

And waited.

After a minute or so Kait grew restless.

"Something's wrong," she said. "I'm going back."

"The rope's on his side," Eli pointed out.

Shit, Kait thought. The boy was right.

"I could climb back," he offered.

"Not a chance," Marcus replied, a little too harshly. "But nice try." The kid hung his head. Marcus squeezed his shoulder. "Don't worry, if anyone can handle themselves in a situation like this, it's Oscar."

Kait watched the boy as, in the span of only a few seconds, a half-dozen emotions made their way into his expression. Concern. Loss. Yearning. Then finally fear.

But not of the Swarm, she thought. *He lost everything. His home, his friends, and now he fears losing Oscar, too.* Kait grasped the teen's other shoulder and stood beside him as they waited. She knew better than anyone what it was like to lose Oscar. She understood the look on Eli's face all too well.

A shape moved in the thick air, close to the sheer face of the cliff. She heard a grunt and moved to the very edge, leaning out.

"Oscar?" she called out.

Above, she caught a glimpse of the rope. Just a dark line against a gray fog. It jerked and twisted erratically.

"Oscar?"

The shape in the mist grew more distinct. A human form. It was him, she could tell by the beard. He was against the cliff wall, holding the rope with both hands and trying to walk along the cliff face. His features were strained with the effort of holding onto the slick cord.

"Little help?" he asked in a strained voice.

Kait glanced at the rock face, studied it for footholds and found a crack that might do. Water sheeted off the surface. She kicked her boot into the little crevice and tested her weight on it, turning herself at the same time to face the cliff. With Marcus holding her right hand, she reached out with her left, then extended her fingers and sought out Oscar's own.

He had coiled the rope around one forearm and reached for her with his free hand, his face contorted with the effort.

"A little farther!" she shouted to him. She was all the way out on the cliff now, and keenly aware that forty feet below her the rapids plunged over a waterfall that dropped another four hundred.

Oscar took another careful step. Mountain climbing had never been his thing, as far as she knew.

"Lean back," she told him. "Get your legs extended."

"No… time…" he said, and pushed toward her with one last

grunt. Their hands clasped. Kait suddenly took on all his weight. Her foot came off the toehold, and they were falling.

But Marcus still had her. Somehow he had managed to get both hands around her arm before he had to bear the weight of two people. He dropped to the floor of the cave at the same time, flattening himself to the surface so that the full length of his body could support them. Unfortunately, this also meant Kait and Oscar dropped three feet before snapping to a stop. They both hit the cliff with a teeth-rattling *thud*.

"Well, this is a situation, isn't it?" Oscar growled.

"Can…" Marcus said through clenched teeth, "you… climb?"

Kait glanced around, looking for anything she could hold or put her foot on. There wasn't much.

"I'll try," she said.

Marcus grunted. "Better… hurry."

He'd turned his head back toward the South Village cave system. The rope Oscar had used hung there, limp against the rock wall. But there were other shapes, too.

Juvies were incredible climbers, and they'd picked this opportunity to prove it. Three of them were clawing their way across the span of rock, no rope required. In fact, the lead one went right past the damn thing without so much as a glance. It was only fifteen feet from Marcus and closing. No way she'd get herself up in time, much less her and Oscar, who was clutching her and trying without success to find a foothold of his own.

She glanced up and swallowed. "Let us go," she said, trying to keep her voice low.

"Not a fucking chance," he replied.

"Marcus… the children. Forget us. You've got to save—"

"Not," he repeated, "a fucking chance."

The Juvie was only three feet from the cave. She could see saliva dripping from its fangs. Two more were right behind it.

"Marcus!" she shouted, desperate. "Please!"

The Juvie reached the edge of the cave, an arm's length from Marcus.

It leapt at him.

Just as its feet left the ground, though, something large and heavy slammed into it. A COG ammo crate, on casters, Kait realized. The creature and box alike went plummeting into the waters below, and no doubt over the waterfall itself a second later.

From somewhere in the cave, Kait heard the telltale giggle of Mackenzie. A second after that, Eli leaned out from the mouth of the cave, hunting rifle at his shoulder. With two quick shots he dropped the other two Juvies into the water as well. One fell limp, shot through the heart, while the second had its hand blown off and screamed as it plummeted.

Kait blinked away tears. She found a foothold and, almost at the same moment, so did Oscar. With the burden of their weight removed, Marcus shifted his efforts to helping them up rather than just keeping them from falling. Soon Kait found herself lying on the floor of the cave, heaving in breaths of the cold, wet air, and profoundly grateful for everyone around her.

"Thanks," Oscar said before she could. "All of you. Thanks."

"Don't mention it," Eli said, echoing Marcus's tone.

Kait laughed.

"Uhh, guys?" Mackenzie said, interrupting the moment. "There's more of them. A lot more."

"Thought we'd be able to hide here," Oscar said. "So much for that plan."

Wanting nothing more in the world than to remain lying down,

Kait got to her feet. "What now?" she asked, lowering her voice for only Oscar and Marcus to hear. "Keep shooting them until the ammo runs out?"

"At this rate that'll buy us an hour, tops," Oscar mused.

"New plan," Marcus said. A look of cold determination crossed his features. "Wait here. Hold them off."

For a second she thought he was going to climb back over to the village caves, but instead he turned and went deeper into the secret supply chamber, where he started pushing boxes aside with reckless abandon.

Oscar and Eli took to the task of holding off the enemy. The two were like a pair of hunters picking off badgers, the way they tried to one-up each other and called out their more impressive shots.

Finally, Marcus found what he was looking for and returned to Kait.

"You've got to be kidding me," she said.

"I'm not," he said, and thrust a parachute into her hands.

"We have no idea what's at the bottom of that waterfall."

"A river, probably."

Behind them Oscar cursed as his Gnasher ran out of ammo.

"If you've got a better idea…" Marcus leveled a serious look at her.

She didn't, and he knew it. They put on the parachutes and hooked themselves to the kids while Oscar dealt with another wave of Juvies. Her uncle protested when it came time for him to don the gear, but even he recognized that staying there was ultimately a doomed option. While Marcus took the task of holding off the enemy, Oscar strapped in.

"Okay," he said, testing the shoulder straps. "You just, uh, pull the cord?"

"Yeah," Kait replied, "and steer with these two handles. Try not to fly into the cliff."

"You make it sound easy."

He peered reluctantly over the edge. Off to the right, somewhere in the mists, a bellowing roar seemed to shake the whole canyon, sending snapjaws whirling out of their nests in total panic. Kait could imagine what kind of Swarm monster made that sort of noise, and it chilled her to the core.

Marcus glanced back over his shoulder. "I think that's our cue to leave."

"I don't know." In front of her, Oscar hesitated, scratching at his cheek. "We've still got a lot of ammo—"

Kait pushed him over the edge. Before he could berate her with every swear word in existence, she lifted Mackenzie up and jumped out after him.

Wind screamed in her ears. Soon she was falling beside the torrent, the water moving in sync with her as gravity pulled them both into Sera's embrace. Until she pulled the ripcord. The glider-chute unfurled behind her and Mackenzie giggled, delighting in the sudden serenity of flight after the previous few seconds of abject terror.

Below her, Oscar deployed his glider-chute as well, and after a few erratic turns from one side to the other, he seemed to get the hang of it and more or less floated in the same direction she was going.

Kait glanced up and back, at first seeing nothing except her parachute, but then came Marcus, with Eli strapped to him, expertly guiding their descent. The pair passed Kait and then Oscar, taking the lead. For once, Kait thought her uncle would be more than happy to cede that role.

6: BRIGHT IDEAS

They lay prone on the floor of the Condor's cargo bay, Del at the side door and JD at the cargo ramp, watching the Swarm work their way up the gradually steepening slope that curved up from the basin of Orzabal Crater.

Despite the treacherous terrain, the relentless enemy drew closer by the minute. Juvies waded through sand up to their waists. Pouncers hopped from boulder to boulder. Even bigger shapes lurked in the dusty air beyond them.

It wasn't so much the sight of them that filled Del with gnawing dread, but the *sound*. The baying and yelping, the chorus of growls punctuated now and then by a grunted command from a Speaker, and beneath it all the ground-shaking footfalls of still larger monsters.

Del felt a trickle of sweat run down his forehead. He swiped it away and looked at JD.

"Maybe we should try the desert," he said. "Can't be as bad as you said, can it?"

JD shot him a sardonic look. He'd scouted the desolate

landscape soon after they'd crashed here, returning a minute later, dejected, with fine sand covering his pants up to the knees. "I could barely walk, and there's no cover for miles."

Another stray round punched through the Condor's fuselage with a reverberating *clang*. Del ducked his head reflexively, then glanced at his friend. "Well, this isn't going to be cover much longer. It's starting to look more like a chain-link fence."

"Fair point." He returned fire, the Enforcer submachine gun clattering in his hands. Like Del he'd taken several of them from the Condor's locker, along with a pile of ammo, and laid it all on the floor beside him.

Del turned and studied Dave.

The robot hovered near the far wall, away from the enemy. His transmit light was still on.

"How long until he runs out of juice?" JD asked.

"Not sure, but I'm willing to bet the Swarm will be here before that happens. We need to go, JD. Both options suck, we agree on that, but at least out there we'll have bought a bit more time."

JD made a fist and rubbed at his eyes, clearing away dust or maybe just trying to stave off exhaustion. "Okay," he said finally, nodding toward the enemy. "When they make it past that boulder, the one that looks like a deflated Thrashball, we go."

Del studied the slope and spotted the rock right away. "That one? With the pile of rubble in front of it?"

"Yeah."

Del took aim and started to fire at it.

"What are you doing?"

As the gun clattered, the rubble began to erode from underneath. Within seconds the big boulder shifted in its place, tilting precariously.

"Ahh," JD said. "Think you're clever, huh?" After a few

seconds he shrugged and joined Del's attack on the rocks.

The boulder shifted one more time, then finally broke loose from the dirt and began to roll, quickly picking up speed. Seconds later the avalanche smashed into the enemy. Bodies flew, limbs flailed.

"That was satisfying," Del said.

"It was," JD agreed.

"And hey, look, now they're past the boulder. Can we go?"

JD nodded. "Grab whatever supplies you can. We'll make them chase us as deep into the desert as we can get, away from everything."

Del could picture it in his head. A team of Gears, or maybe DeeBees, finding Dave a hundred years from now, and marveling at the historical value of the data the bot carried. *So that's how the Swarm War started!* one would say, and the others would nod with sadness.

The floor beneath him started to vibrate, and not from the footfalls of the Swarm. This was different. Steady, and growing stronger. He placed his hands on it, hoping it was just his imagination. It wasn't.

"The hell is that? Earthquake?"

"More like a tidal wave," JD said, "made up of the enemy." But as he spoke the words, doubt filled his voice. The two looked at each other, both recognizing the growing sound at the same instant.

"Condor," they said in unison.

Except it wasn't... not exactly. Del tilted his head. The sound kept growing. He jumped up and ran to the cockpit, leaning over the seats to get a view out the window. With the aircraft tilted as it was, he could only see sky, but that was enough.

A Vulture came into view. The larger, assault-capable version of the Condor.

Then, a second later, two more. Three.

"I think they got the message," JD said from just behind him.

"Loud and fucking clear!" Del whooped.

The aircraft roared toward him, plus a few Ravens for support. The cavalry had arrived.

"This I gotta see," Del said. He ran to the back of the Condor and hustled down the ramp, moving to the far left side as he went, hopping out onto the rocky edge of the crater rim where the plane had come to rest. He turned his face to the sky, not caring now if the enemy could see him. A second later JD joined him, and they watched in awe.

The Vultures streaked toward the crater at full speed, spreading out as they came to give the crashed Condor a wide berth. Each carried six machine-gun turrets under their wings, and these lit up in unison. Each barrel spat fire, tracer rounds drawing glowing lines into the crater. Plumes of dust and rock erupted from the ground.

Once over the rim, the Vultures opened and their payloads deployed.

Heart pounding in his chest, Del couldn't help but holler a cheer. He'd never been so happy to see DeeBees drop from the belly of an aircraft. Each plane disgorged itself in full. Dozens of bots. The sky filled with their dodecahedron pods. The blue objects slammed into the edge of the crater and started rolling, like a bucket of marbles thrown into a huge bowl.

It almost didn't even matter that the DeeBees were inside. Their pods did orders of magnitude more damage than the rock Del had sent careening down the incline. Everywhere he looked he saw the Swarm getting pulverized by the chaotic, gravity-powered stampede.

"Holy hell," he whispered. "Talk about overwhelming force."

"Only one problem," JD said, and his voice lacked the same excitement.

"What's that?"

"DeeBees suck at fighting Swarm."

"Oh yeah..." Del said. He'd put that little detail out of his mind. Suddenly the whole scene below him took on a different air. Sure, the drop pods were pulverizing the front line, but once they opened the tide would turn back in the Swarm's favor. All this, and Jinn had only delayed the inevitable.

He watched the first of the pods spring open. Not Shepherds, he saw, but full-fledged DR-1s armed with Tri-shot chain guns. And right away it was clear they were something more than even that. He could see the difference instantly, even from this far away. The first DR-1 to emerge didn't walk dumbly toward the nearest enemy, blasting away haphazardly. Instead, it dropped to a knee and swung its weapon in an arc, clearing a semicircle of the nearest foes as its mechanical squad mates emerged from their own shells.

Five of them were out now, and they formed a defensive circle, choosing their targets tactically. Maybe not exactly the way Del would have done it, but still a huge improvement on the previous versions.

"Damn," JD mused. "I spoke too soon."

"Baird's been busy," Del said, smiling at the display.

"I sure have," a voice behind them said.

He jumped, and turned around. In the spectacle of the assault, he'd completely missed the King Raven settling down nearby. Damon Baird stood in the helicopter's open doorway, with Sam and Cole at his shoulders. They were decked out in new COG armor, and armed to the teeth.

Baird hopped to the ground, doing his best to stride triumphantly forward in the deep powdery sand. Cole joined him, while Sam returned to the pilot's seat.

"Uncle Baird," JD said, grinning.

"Oh, now I get an 'Uncle'? About time."

"You earned it." JD met him halfway, giving him a soldier's embrace.

Del turned his head and shouted back toward the Condor. "Dave? Fall in. We're leaving." Waiting for the robot to emerge, Del turned back to Baird. "I guess you got his message."

"We sure did. Hell of a scrape you got yourselves into."

Del rubbed the back of his neck. "Nothing we couldn't handle."

"Uh-huh," Cole said, kicking the side of the crashed Condor. "Looks like you have everything under control."

Baird went to the crater rim and looked down. For a moment he simply watched the battle raging below. Del and JD joined him there.

"The DeeBees are doing better than I expected," Baird said. "But then I wasn't expecting much."

"What's the plan?" JD asked. "Hold them off while a new cap is installed?"

To Del's surprise, Baird shook his head.

"Actually, we're here to pick you up." There was something in his voice. An urgency. Maybe something more. "The DeeBees will keep the Swarm busy here. We've got other problems to fix just now."

"What's happened?" Del asked.

"It's Kait," he replied, "and Marcus."

A hollow feeling filled Del's gut. He wanted to ask the obvious question, yet feared the answer.

Sensing the concern on both their faces, Baird held up his hands to JD and Del.

"We've lost contact with them, at an Outsider village up in the mountains west of Jacinto. Swarm are active there, too. Look, I'll fill you in on the details in the air, okay? The sooner we get there, the better our chances of finding them."

At that moment, Dave hovered out of the Condor and drifted over, riding low on his jet of blue flame.

Baird knelt in front of the robot, scowling as he ran a finger along the dent made by the Buzzkill blade. "What'd you two do, use him as a shield?"

Eyes downcast, JD kicked at the sand. "That's not far from the truth. Sorry."

Del added, "He saved our asses, Baird. Thanks. Can you fix him up?"

Baird gave the robot a friendly pat, then ushered him toward the waiting helicopter. "I'll let you know. Right now, we'd best hurry." He raised his index finger into the air and made a twirling motion, signaling Sam to prep for dust off.

Hunched over against the wind, Del and JD ran toward the waiting King Raven, while behind them the Vultures circled Orzabal Crater, machine guns blazing.

7: SHELTER FROM THE SWARM

After the waterfall the river widened and calmed, though sheer cliffs still flanked it on either side. The proximity of the rock walls allowed no room for Kait to steer her chute beyond simply following the switchback curves of the river.

With each passing second the waters grew closer. Kait reached around to the parachute pack and groped for the release cord, gripping it in her fist and waiting. To let it go too soon would mean a plunge into the water, which could be shallow or have an undercurrent. Keep the parachute too long, and she and Mackenzie might become tangled in the ropes, unable to swim.

"Deep breath!" she shouted to Mackenzie as the dark surface rose to meet them, only inches away now.

When her boots finally touched the water, it parted from her feet as if she were skiing on the surface. Kait yanked the release and felt herself thrown forward and down as the pull of the parachute abruptly stopped. She twisted her body as the water enveloped them.

Kicking hard, Kait fought the weight of the girl strapped to her front. She broke the surface almost instantly, though, aided perhaps by the buoyancy of the parachute pack's air pockets.

They were floating, riding the current. Though the surface of the river was calm, it moved more swiftly than Kait had expected.

"You okay?" she asked the girl.

"That was *awesome*," Mackenzie exclaimed.

It was impossible not to smile. "You can swim, right?"

"Yeah, I'm pretty good. Eli is better."

"Okay, I'm going to release you. Hold onto me, though. We'll stick together, okay?"

"Sure!"

Kait reached in front of her companion and worked at the buckle. A second later Mackenzie was free and floating along next to Kait, a hand on Kait's shoulder. Thankfully, the river wasn't as cold as she'd expected it to be.

Marcus emerged in front of her, gulping in air and running a hand down his face. He coughed once, spat, then turned until he could see her. He gave a thumbs-up, which Mackenzie returned.

Kait looked back just in time to see Oscar splash down. His head broke the surface a second later, and he coughed out some water, already swiveling to find her. Their eyes locked.

"Why'd you push me, Kait?"

"People get cold feet before their first jump."

She could actually see him composing and then discarding a half-dozen replies, probably all too profane for the kids' ears. In the end he just made a face at her and turned his focus to the river. Soon they were all drifting downstream.

The river here was a hundred feet wide, its edges lapping and frothing against sheer cliffs that rose up on either side at least as high again. They were at the mercy of the current, and Kait decided that wasn't so bad. It was taking them away from the village at a decent clip, and with any luck the Swarm would spend days searching through all those tunnels and side rooms, with nothing to find but the traps Mackenzie had left behind.

She smiled grimly at the thought.

"How far does the river go?" Marcus asked Oscar, who only shrugged. The twins didn't know, either.

"South Villagers kept to their mountain fortress," her uncle said, "long as I can remember. They fished and sometimes came west to trade with us, but usually it was us who went to them."

The kids both nodded agreement. Expeditions from Fort Umson to South Village had been a twice-yearly event for them. She wondered if they yet realized that that part of their lives was over. Their home was gone, their friends... hell, almost everyone they knew. And now the one place they knew almost as well had been all but destroyed.

After a time the current grew slower, the river wider, and the cliffs finally became craggy walls and then just broken boulders and dirt as the river emptied out into a vast lake surrounded by a seemingly impenetrable wall of trees.

The river delta, though slow now, took on a new form of treachery. Its banks were choked with dead, felled trees. Gray, petrified wood that looked as if it had been piling up for decades.

"What's that?" Eli asked, pointing.

And then the horror.

Bodies. Dozens of them, and not just Swarm.

Everything that had gone over the cliff at South Village had accumulated here. Juvies, Pouncers... Kait even saw the Scion she'd shouldered off the fishing platform, glassy eyes staring lifelessly at the darkening sky above. But none of that compared to what Eli had spotted.

"Don't look," Marcus said, turning himself to block the boy's view of the body floating thirty feet away. It was one of the villagers. One of many. Kait counted eight that she could see, and wondered with a gnawing dread if they'd jumped into the rapids on purpose, rather than be snatched up by the Swarm.

She couldn't blame them if they had. Admired such a fate, even, all things considered. But it didn't make it any easier to look at them. She averted her gaze, too, rotating the floating pack around so that Mackenzie was facing away from the spectacle. The girl, though, simply twisted back, wanting to see. Kait glanced at her, and for the first time since finding her in South Village, Kait could see real sorrow in the girl's eyes. It was as if in that moment she finally allowed the reality of all this in. Perhaps she'd still clung to some hope that, like Oscar and Kait, the people of South Village and even Fort Umson were out there somewhere, waiting to be found, burying any doubts through sheer force of will or simple teenage innocence.

For all that sorrow, though, Mackenzie did not flinch or look away, and Kait stopped trying to prevent her from seeing the dead.

Finally they were past the bodies, contending only with the rotten logs now. The air became cloying and still.

"There's a building," Oscar said, suddenly.

Kait followed the direction he was pointing and squinted. Sure enough, a few hundred yards distant on the shore, a building—no, several buildings—stood. They were ramshackle things. Old, but big.

"Logging yard," Marcus mused. "Probably pulled in lumber sent down from the mountain while there were still trees up there, then milled them and shipped them off."

"It's shelter at least," Kait replied, though even as she said it, she wondered how true that would be. The buildings looked as if they'd been built a hundred years ago, and sat disused for as much as half that. Part of one roof had collapsed. Those windows that weren't broken were covered in a thick layer of grime.

Piles of lumber ten feet high lay in uneven rows all around the two structures, the wood now black with mold and dirt. The group drifted close enough that she could see rats darting between the stacks of wood planks and the numerous open crevices in the sides of the nearer building.

Kait tamped down a growing sense of unease. "On second thought, maybe we should steer for the beach."

"Good call," Marcus said.

"Suits me," Oscar replied over the other man.

8: BREAKFAST WITH FRIENDS

Even with the impressive dispersal of DR-1s over the crater, several of the Condors were still carrying a reserve force for the second phase of the mission.

The King Raven flew at the rear of the formation, with six Condors in a wing ahead, flanked on either side by Kestrels. South Village was high in a mountain range made up of perilously sheer rock faces. A full moon provided the only light. Del couldn't see even a hint of civilization in any direction.

The village itself had been built on a sheltered plateau maybe halfway up the range, along a spine of peaks that had long ago been cleft in two by some calamitous upheaval. A river tumbled down this steep ravine.

Sam was at the controls and, as the wall of the village finally came into view through the clouds, she tilted the helicopter to the right and dropped them into a steep dive. The rest of the armada kept going, and Del watched as the DR-1s once again fell like spilled marbles, this time onto South Village.

Just before he lost sight of the plateau, he saw the Kestrels dip their noses and strafe past the target, chain guns blazing away. Then the vertical cliff blocked his view. They were in the ravine, descending, the Raven's rotor blades just feet from the walls on either side. Sam flew with quiet confidence, though, trusting her own senses as much as the screens arrayed before her.

An explosion from above briefly lit the sky in bright orange.

"Damn," Cole said. "Why couldn't we be up there where the action is?"

"I'd be happy to drop you off," Sam replied, "once we've got what we came for."

"Bah," Cole replied. "Marcus can wait. Let's get into the action."

Sam pulled back on the stick. The Raven started to rise.

"Shit, only kidding," Cole said. "Marcus first."

The descent began again.

Del watched the cliff across from the village, which hid mostly in shadow. Winged creatures a little bit like bats were huddled in groups on the meager ledges, occasionally darting off to find better perches. They hissed and cawed at the Raven as it passed, rotor-fueled winds disrupting their peace. Some tried to dart out and make their anger known, but the wash of high-velocity air currents only sent them scurrying back to safety on their rock-wall home.

As the Raven settled into a hover twenty feet above the froth and violence of the river rapids, Del spotted a nest tucked in a deeper cleft. Normally the space would be hidden from view, but their passage had pushed away the mists coming off the waters below.

A dozen of the bat-things were arranged around the nest, holding their wings out and snarling at him. These were bigger than the others he'd seen—full adults maybe, with long fangs and narrow eyes. In the nest between them Del could just make out the shape of a large, single egg.

No wonder they were so agitated.

"You stick by your family," he said to himself, even if that family wasn't related by blood. He thought of the lengths he and JD would go to to help Kait, even if they didn't always get along. The bond shared by Baird and Sam.

Suddenly one of the adult creatures took flight, darting straight out at Del as it extended its jaw and snapped angrily at him, wheeling away just a few feet from his face. It went back, its flight awkward under the harsh force of the rotor.

Movement on the opposite side of the craft drew Del's attention away. Cole and JD dropped down to a ledge at the base of the cliff, and moved inside a cave entrance, guns at the ready.

While he was distracted another of the bird-things snapped at Del, just inches away this time. Two more followed, the second of which didn't bother to turn away but instead darted straight through the Raven's cabin, jaw snapping loudly as it passed Baird.

"Holy fuck, what was that?" the man said, waving his arm as if a mosquito had just buzzed his cheek. Del pointed toward the cliff.

"Big... bat bastards. I don't think they're happy we're here."

"Yeah, well, tell them we'll only be a minute." He leaned out over the waters and bellowed, "Cole? JD? Anything?"

The pair reemerged from the cave. Alone. They climbed back up the rope and into the cabin.

"Whole thing's been sealed," Cole said, "but no sign of Marcus or Kait."

"Maybe they went back up top," Del offered. "Marcus would prefer a stand-up fight to hiding down here." Another bat-creature snapped at his ear, then screeched as Del waved it off.

"Sealed *from this side*," JD amended. "We found some improvised explosives, and spent clips of ammo."

"Let's check up top," Baird said. "Maybe they climbed the cliff, or found some other way up." With a knuckle he rapped on the bulkhead behind him. Sam turned in her seat and nodded when Baird pointed upward. The Raven started to rise.

The higher they climbed, the more the sounds of battle drowned out everything else. Cole took the rotary cannon mounted on the Raven's side and readied himself for what he no doubt hoped would be a crowd of cornered Swarm being pushed toward the cliff's edge by Baird's combat-aware DR-1s.

As the plateau came into view, though, a very different picture emerged.

"Oh shit," JD said.

However well coded the robots were, Baird had yet to instruct them on how to deal with an enemy like this.

Standing amid the DeeBees that remained was a Carrier.

The massive creature towered over the robots around it, twenty feet tall at its heavily armored head. Its dominating features were its forearms, which were like two impenetrable walls. Each was ten feet across—almost the width of its chest—and it had heavy armor plating. When the beast drove its fists into the ground and turned those arms outward, the resulting barrier looked ready to repel anything that could be thrown at it.

Nevertheless, Cole tried.

His cannon began to whir, then scream, before the whole thing became a blur as hundreds of rounds spat from its barrels on plumes of fire. Shouting as he fired, Cole swung the weapon left and right, up and down, trying to find a gap in the Carrier's defenses and failing miserably.

All he seemed to do was annoy the beast.

It noticed the helicopter, and the sight of it seemed to banish whatever thoughts the creature might have had about finishing off the DeeBees that surrounded it.

The Carrier reared back, unperturbed by the onslaught to which Cole was subjecting it. Its chest began to glow. With a roar the beast gave a final heave and its chest opened.

Six smaller creatures erupted upward, trailing tentacles behind them as they lurched into the air and then, one by one, flew like missiles toward the chopper.

Cole adjusted his aim, unleashing a roar of his own as he swung the rotary cannon across the incoming attack. The undulating creatures burst into clouds of slimy orange goo as the bullets tore them apart.

Pulling itself forward on those balled fists, the Carrier used this distraction to its advantage. It rushed the hovering aircraft and leapt at it.

Actually leapt. Del couldn't believe the thing could move its own weight, much less actually get off the ground. It had, though, and it moved *fast*.

Sam heaved on the stick, shouting, "Oh fuck!" as she realized she'd been too slow. One of the Carrier's huge hands came up and curled around the landing skid. The chopper tipped sideways almost ninety degrees, then violently back the other way as it took on the entire weight of the Swarm creature.

The King Raven rocked, then plummeted.

Del fought to keep from being thrown free. Cliffs flew by on either side. The engine roared as Sam fought desperately to compensate for the added weight of the gigantic animal. All she managed to do was slow the inevitable.

Then the Carrier's second hand came up and thrust into the

open cabin. Cole dove backward as groping fingers wrapped around the seat attached to the mounted cannon, tearing it free like a hunk of bread from a loaf. It hurled the seat into the cliff wall, smashing the thing to pieces.

The foul beast bellowed in triumph, its hand coming up again, probing this time. Baird pressed against the cockpit bulkhead. Cole flattened himself beneath the leathery fingers. JD moved to the rear wall, shuffling sideways as a talon scraped along just beside him.

Del went out the opposite side, standing on the landing skid, with no idea what he was doing. He just needed to be away. He looked around for anything that might help, just as one of those damned bats took another pass at him, jaws snapping.

"Dammit, I'm not your enemy here!" he shouted at the thing, watching it bank away toward a perch.

They were almost to the rapids. The helicopter's engine howled under the strain, but it wasn't enough. Would never be enough.

"We're going to hit the water!" Sam shouted. "Brace yourselves!"

Del kept looking around and something caught his eye. Tucked under the small overhang above the sliding side door was a tube with a metal implement sticking out. Rope was coiled up behind it.

A plan formed instantly.

He grabbed the tube, thumbed the latch that held it in place, and heaved it free. Spinning it around in his hand, Del looped his other arm through a handhold on the fuselage and turned his body outward as much as he could. The angle, the position—hell, the whole damn situation—was awkward. He had to make it work though.

Sighting down the length of the tube, Del squeezed the trigger and fired the grappling hook. The pronged metal implement launched outward, leaving a snaking trail of rope along its flight path.

The shot was true. The hook punched right into the very thing Del had aimed for.

The egg.

He pulled back on the launch tube. Across from him, in that little cleft, the egg practically flew out of its nest. All at once the bat-things surrounding it erupted into flight, absolutely frenzied at this assault on the most precious thing in their world.

"Sorry about this," he said, and brought the tube hard downward.

The rope went taut. The egg swung, and in that instant the Carrier seemed to notice it. The beast turned its head and, no doubt pleased with the opportunity, opened its jaws and swallowed the egg whole.

This sent the snapjaws into a berserk rage. Their young—their only young—had just been *eaten* by the huge beast in front of them. Their counterattack was instantaneous and complete. The air around Del filled instantly with hundreds of the creatures, all now insane with animalistic frenzy. They darted and dived, using claws and wild screams, but mostly snapping those huge jaws. The air filled with beating wings and the whip-crack of fangs clamping down on anything they could find.

"Hell yeah, baby! How's that taste?" Cole shouted. "Breakfast with friends, mmm-MMM!"

It was too much for the stunned Carrier, which did what any creature would do. Hell, it did *exactly* what Del had done. It swiped an arm at them.

In its panic, it used the wrong arm.

The arm that, until a moment before, had been holding onto the landing skid, rather than the one rooting around inside the cabin. All at once the Carrier was falling, and the aircraft was rocketing upward, freed of the extra weight.

Hanging on for dear life, Del watched as the beast took one

last desperate grasp at the cliff wall, huge fingers leaving deep scrapes along the rock. Then it was gone, swallowed by the rapids. A huge spray of water lashed upward, buffeting the aircraft. Sam fought to keep them from slamming into the cliff. She couldn't go left or right, and suddenly debris—rocks, and even the bodies of DeeBees—came crashing down from above. The Swarm were throwing anything they could get their hands on at the thing that had just killed their Carrier.

Something knocked hard against the tail section. Another hit like that on the rotor and they'd be done for. Sam dipped the chopper's nose and slammed full power into the engines, throwing them forward. There came a great grinding sound accompanied by a shower of sparks as a rotor blade nicked the cliff beside them.

"Hold onto something!" she shouted over her shoulder.

"Yeah, no shit!" Cole shouted back.

Sam pushed the aircraft to its limit, weaving through the erratic angles of the ravine. Then, all at once, the flight grew calm. The river fell away, over a ledge, the waterfall descending hundreds of feet. Below, a wider, calmer version of the river snaked away into the distance, toward a forest.

"What's that?" JD asked, pointing almost directly below.

Sam nudged the Raven in the direction he had indicated. A blob of… something… stretched between two rocks in the water, tendrils trailing off with the current. To Del it looked like some kind of giant jellyfish, which was impossible. They were nowhere near the ocean.

"Parachute," Cole said. "I'll be damned! That old son of a bitch *did* find a way out."

9: BONFIRE

"I'm going to get a fire going," Kait said. "Who wants to help?"

She held a bundle of driftwood in her arms, and tossed it into an untidy pile in the center of the patch of shore on which they'd collapsed after leaving the river. The sticks made a sound like bones clattering together, sending a chill down Kait's arms.

The kids, seated on either side of Marcus, did not volunteer, and she couldn't blame them. All the excitement of the last few days had to finally be catching up with them. Then had come the sight of the villagers' bodies. Something had changed in both of them, then. She wondered if they'd be able to forget what they'd seen, or if this was it, the moment that would signify their entry into adulthood.

"No one?" Kait prompted.

"You sure that's a good idea?" Marcus asked. For the sake of the kids he didn't elaborate.

Kait glanced back across the water toward the ravine, and the cleft mountain beyond it, just barely visible in the far distance. Without a way to use the river, she figured it would take the Swarm a day, maybe more, to hike around, assuming they even bothered to pursue.

"Just for a few hours," she said. "Maybe someone will see it. But even if not, we need to cook some food and get warm before we try to go on."

Grudgingly, he nodded.

"C'mon," Kait said, "someone give me a hand."

"Actually," Marcus said, "I was hoping to recruit them." There was a brief second when she thought he'd meant "recruit" as in, for the army.

"I need some help to search the lumber mill. Might be they've got a radio," he said, perhaps sensing Kait's disappointment.

The kids perked up, almost back to their old eager selves. "We can do that," Eli said.

"You can, huh?" Kait asked. There was a note of admiration in the boy's voice. Oscar had ventured off into the dark to hunt for some real food, and she was glad he wasn't around to hear it. She couldn't tell yet what her uncle thought of the other man, or the way the kids had taken to him. She forced herself to smile. "Okay, go on with Marcus then. Someone's got to keep an eye on him."

The kids both grinned. Marcus just gave a quiet snort. It was about the most amusement he'd ever shown, at least in the brief time she'd known him. It made her wonder, and not for the first time, what Anya Stroud must have been like, that the couple could have produced the mild-mannered, often smiling, good-natured JD.

"Let's move out," Marcus said, coming to his feet. The twins bounced up and followed him, trying—perhaps subconsciously, perhaps not—to match his soldier's gait.

Kait scoured the beach for more driftwood, finding only a few meager sticks among the massive felled tree trunks that clogged the shoreline. Finally she tried the edges of the logging yard, though most of the planks there were rotten with mildew. Rats scattered from her path as she walked the uneven, leaning stacks of sheet wood and unused fence posts.

There was nothing to be found here—she knew it right away—but her search went on because it afforded her an eye on Marcus and the twins, who'd just reached the main building and entered it like a special ops team. Kait could tell from the moment they'd landed on the shore that only rats inhabited this derelict place. Marcus would know this, too, of course. She smiled to herself. Despite his constant scowl and tough facade, he was making it fun for them.

Somehow the sight of that simple gesture pushed her fatigue and stress to the periphery of her mind. She returned her focus to the simple task of finding firewood and kindling, venturing to the edge of the forest, allowing the moonlight to guide her despite the flashlight built into her armor.

Kait made three trips to the forest's edge and back, and without realizing it she'd built not just a campfire but a genuine bonfire. By the time the flames really got going, they were dancing fifteen feet into the air and sending up a plume of smoke that drifted out over the lake on the mild breeze. Instantly too warm, she pushed back the log on which she'd been sitting, adjusting the ones Marcus, the kids, and Oscar had been using, too.

Minutes passed with only the sound of the flames and the gentle lapping of the lake, the dead logs in the water bumping softly against one another with an almost clock-like precision. She glanced back at the lumber yard and its two buildings. She could see the flashlights carried by Marcus and the kids, sweeping across the murky window panes as they no doubt did a very thorough and systematic search under the old soldier's stern directions.

Her stomach growled.

"C'mon Oscar, speed it up." Kait had been hunting with him many times in her life, and even in the most barren of places he always seemed to find something they could cook. A big lumbering oaf he might be, but when the man wanted to be stealthy, he could.

For a time she let the flames mesmerize her. Let them paint hints of images for her brain to tumble about. First these visions were only of fire. Of battles fought, of camping trips in far-off places and summer festivals at Fort Umson, where the Outsiders danced and celebrated their latest successful raid against the COG. Of the great hearth in Reyna's room, where her mother had first braided Kait's hair and hung it over her shoulder. That wasn't supposed to happen until the ceremony, but Kait had been nervous and Reyna had done a trial braiding in secret. A private moment for them to share, giving a special significance to the wink Mom had given her when the actual day had arrived.

Kait sighed. She missed her mother deeply, and only now did it finally seem okay to admit that to herself. Bottling it up might have been the soldier's way, but it wasn't the Outsider's way, and no matter what, she'd always be an Outsider.

That's what Oscar would tell her, anyway. *Had* told her, when she'd brought up the idea once again of taking the kids to New Ephyra. She knew—*knew*—they'd be safer there than anywhere else, but Oscar wouldn't have it. *"Get them as far away from this place as possible,"* he argued, as if the Swarm would be content with this tiny little corner of Sera.

With no one around, Kait pulled the amulet from beneath her armor and studied it again, as if staring at it even more might suddenly reveal some new clue. Oscar had said how important it was to her mom, but he hadn't said why. And if he had no answers, Kait doubted she'd ever know. There was no one left who could tell her.

"Dinner is served!"

Kait glanced up and saw Oscar come striding into the firelight, a rabbit held aloft in each hand. His grin was proud, sure, but not arrogant.

"That fire, Kait," he added as he set the animals down. "Probably can be seen for miles."

"Relax," she said, pushing the amulet back into her shirt. "We have some time, and deserve a rest. Hell, maybe a patrol will spot it, or some locals who can tell us where we are."

"If you say so." He inhaled deeply, no stranger to the charms of an open flame and the wilderness. Then he looked around, a hint of concern crossing his features. "Where are the young ones?"

Kait had to smile. Until a few days ago he'd called her, JD, and Del the "young ones." She opened her mouth to answer, but the word changed on her tongue. It became a shout.

"DOWN!"

Oscar didn't question this. Didn't turn to see what she was looking at. He simply dropped straight to the dirt, and a scythe tore through the air where he'd been. A four-foot-long serrated blade on the end of a ten-foot pole.

Kait saw the Speaker wielding it, and their eyes locked. Grinning, then laughing, it twirled the huge weapon as if it were a simple baton, then gripped it with both hands and brought it crashing down in a clean arc.

The blow would have cut Oscar clean in two had he still been there, but her uncle had rolled to her left, and even now was coming to his feet, stepping away, spreading the fight out.

Behind the Speaker there was more movement. Two Snatchers that Kait could see. Hints of others in the darkness.

"Where are the children, Kait?" Oscar asked, voice calm.

"Yessss..." the Speaker said, voice like gravel and blood. "Where?"

Kait said nothing. She glanced at Oscar, though, and let her eyes flick to the lumber yard.

Oscar's eyes met hers.

"Go," she said. Her uncle nodded, turned, ran. The Snatchers bounded after him. More took their place.

The Speaker stepped forward. He was directly across from Kait now, their eyes locked on one another with only the dancing flames between. She tried to remember where she'd set her rifle down. Somewhere nearby, but the exact position eluded her. She'd been lost in thought, and consumed with the task of building the fire. She'd let her guard down.

She needed time.

Kait reached back into her shirt and tugged the amulet out. She held it beside her face, the Locust symbol facing the monstrosity across from her. An identical symbol graced its chest plate.

"That supposed to impress me, girl?" The Speaker grinned.

"Just thought you might want to see it." She shrugged, hoping it looked casual, that she'd kept hidden the terror that filled her. "It's all that's left of the last one of you bastards I met." A lie, but it wouldn't know that, would it?

The Speaker tilted its head back and began to laugh. A maniacal, howling laugh aimed at the moon high above.

"A worthless trinket," the Speaker said, "from a worthless human." Something in his tone rattled her to the core. The barest hint that it wasn't referring to her, but Reyna.

My imagination, Kait thought, not quite believing herself. But there'd been a lie in its words, too. Kait affected a bemused look. "If we're so worthless, why come after us with such… determination?"

"Oh," it said, "we need humans, yes, but that's the thing about your species. There are *so many* of you."

Without warning it charged, straight through the flames. One sudden leap that sent embers flying and flaming wood scattering before it. Kait fell back, feeling the sudden rush of heat and then the earth shake as the brute landed just feet away from her. Already she could hear the wicked hiss of its scythe, and she rolled as Oscar had, but to the right, away from the lumber yard.

The blade sank straight through the log on which she'd been sitting, and then down two feet into the soft dirt and sand.

Kait got onto her hands and knees, but not to run. Not yet. Instead, she kicked her leg out hard. Her foot made solid impact, and she felt immense satisfaction as the staff of the scythe snapped clean in two. In the instant of her kick the Speaker had put all its strength into pulling the blade free from the muck—no easy task, anyone could see that. As the shaft snapped, there was nothing to pull, and the creature went over backward, right into the bonfire.

It screamed and writhed, consumed in fire. As it began to roll wildly, the two Snatchers on either side of it—which had been coiling to fire their tail quills—were forced to hop backward, unsure.

It bought her seconds, if that. She glanced around and saw her Lancer, leaning against a rock just a few feet away. She ran for it, reaching out.

Something slammed into her side, sent her tumbling across the sand and mud. Stars swam across her vision. Kait ended up face down, mouth full of grit, lungs emptied of air. She forced herself to stand, spat the dirt from her mouth, and turned back toward the fire.

There was a moment, however brief, when she knew she was

seeing double. That whatever had hit her had caused her eyes to cross. But that couldn't be, because the two Speakers in front of her didn't move in unison.

The bastard on the left, skin charred and still smoldering from the fire, clenched its fists and glared at her.

It was the other, though, that came forward. The twin of the first, it carried no scythe, but a club instead. The head of the creature was studded with crystalline growths, making it look all the more grotesque.

All at once a pain registered up her left side. That club was what had hit her, and if not for her armor no doubt every rib on that side would be broken. They might as well have been, the way she felt. Every breath was white-hot and too quick.

She stepped back, toward the water, toward the logs.

"Get the others," the first Speaker said.

The Snatchers backed off, then turned and darted in the direction of the buildings. Behind them, shadows moved in that direction, too. How many Swarm had come, Kait had no idea, but there were more than these four, that was for sure.

"You too," the charred Speaker said to its companion. "This one is mine."

"No," the newcomer replied. It was all that needed to be said. Something passed between them. Hierarchy or understanding, maybe even kinship. Kait would never know. Whatever it was, the two advanced like brothers.

Like twins.

10: TOOLS OF THE TRADE

Oscar ran hard for the derelict lumber mill, but not too hard. The last thing he wanted was to lose the interest of the Snatchers and see them turn back for Kait. The big brute she could handle, he thought, but add these two galloping nasties? No way. Too much for anyone, unarmed on a beach.

"*Go,*" she'd said. Her eyes had said so much more. She'd looked a damn sight like Reyna, truth be told. Absolute conviction and a willingness to sacrifice.

He hoped it wouldn't come to that, but with that word and the look in her eyes, he knew they were of the same mind on this. The twins were the most important thing here. So Oscar Diaz ran.

A quill thudded into the dirt in front him. He weaved left, almost tripping on a loose rock. Another quill hissed past, cutting the air where his head had just been.

He looked back. The Snatchers were slowing down. One turning slightly, glancing back toward Kait.

Oscar did trip, then. Pain flared across his shoulder, the

days-old wound there tearing open again. He gritted his teeth, got up. Ran on, affecting a little limp just to sweeten the deal. Anything to keep them focused on him. With a quick glance back he thought he could actually see the moment their blood lust overcame the desire to turn back for an easier catch. These bastards were built, designed, wired—whatever—to pick up human hosts and bring them back to the hive, or whatever the Swarm called their hovels.

So come and get me, fuckers. You did once. Almost worked, too. He'd never forget the satisfaction he'd felt when his knife had finally sawed through that creature's abdomen and he'd tumbled out into the dirt.

The lumber yard loomed, dead ahead. Fifty feet to go. The side that faced him had four large openings. A loading dock, with a low concrete deck notched for trucks to back in and be filled with goods. Now it was all dark, abandoned, grimy. The awning above it had partially collapsed, blocking two of the entrances. But the other two were clear. Big openings not unlike the caves of South Village. Somewhere in there, he hoped, were the twins.

And Marcus Fenix.

Another glance back. Good, they were still on his trail, and even closing. Shit, maybe he'd sold it a little too well. Time to let the limp go and hope they were too stupid to notice. Sprinting again, ignoring the flare of pain from his shoulder, he made for one of the openings and, when he reached the waist-high concrete dock, vaulted it. He rolled across the gritty surface and staggered to his feet, almost fell again a step later. His body didn't work like it used to. Too many years, too many beers, someone had once commented.

Ain't that the damn truth.

He picked up steam again as he crossed from moonlight into

absolute darkness, his footfalls echoing in the enclosed, hangar-like structure.

"Drop and roll!" a voice shouted. Marcus Fenix.

Oscar didn't much like the man. Respected the hell out of him, sure, as any warrior respects another, but that was as far as it went. Marcus was like the walking embodiment of everything Oscar hated about the army. Worse, there was the way Kait looked up to him. Mimicked him, even. She was under his wing whether either of them would admit it or not.

Still, he knew when to trust a soldier, so down he went. He slid, laid himself out flat, and just in time, too. Something huge sliced through the air above him, making a sound like an arrow in flight, only multiplied a thousandfold.

He managed to roll to his belly as he slid, and looked back in time to see the first of the Snatchers cleft in two by the massive saw blade. There came a *ker-thunk* sound from somewhere deeper in the building, and another of the five-foot-wide circular saws sang through the air, so close he felt its wake on the back of his neck.

The second Snatcher had been in midair when its brother was cut in half. Sailing over that carnage, it seemed on some instinctive level to sense the danger ahead, and flailed uselessly to change direction. Which, of course, was impossible. At the moment it landed the whirring circle of razor-thin steel ripped out of the darkness and cut the Snatcher's left front and left rear legs off at the knees. Not a kill, but near enough as to make no difference.

The beast toppled to one side, severed legs fountaining blood that steamed as it splashed on the concrete. The animal writhed, howling in rage. Tried to right itself and went down with another scream, this one of abject pain, the moment it placed weight on its newly earned stump.

Oscar came to his feet. He walked to the writhing creature and placed the barrel of his Gnasher against its chin, aimed upward toward the brain, and pulled the trigger. The Snatcher jerked once, then lay there, twitching weakly.

A second later, he felt more than saw the presence of Marcus, Eli, and Mackenzie at his side. They watched the Snatcher kick its last and go silent.

"Nice trick," Oscar said to Marcus with grudging admiration.

"Not my idea," he said. "Thank Mackenzie here."

"She set it up but I aimed it," Eli put in.

Oscar laughed despite himself. "You did good. Both of you. Let's go help Kai—"

The ground shook.

And shook again.

"The hell's that?" Oscar asked.

It came into view, then. First glimpsed through the broken second-story windows above the cargo openings. With each lumbering step the ground trembled.

"Swarmak," Marcus said.

Oscar shook his head. "These bastards don't give up."

The massive creature stood as tall as the lumber mill, baring teeth as big as Oscar's arm. Crystalline growths pushed out from its muscled shoulders like armor. Something was chained to its back—a weapon or maybe a goddamn saddle. Oscar didn't want to know. Each foot was as big as a horse, and the whole building shook as the brute lumbered across the mud and sand to place itself directly between the mill and the bonfire.

It wasn't alone, either. A host of Drones and Juvies ran at either side of the great beast. It pointed, and they turned and rushed the building.

"What now?" Eli asked, and for the first time since Oscar had met the boy he heard fear in his young voice. Mackenzie reached into the tattered jacket she wore, pulling free a small bundle of explosives with a four-inch fuse. It looked more like a firework than a bomb, and he wondered how far that was from the truth.

"It's all I have left," the girl said, as if carrying explosives around was perfectly normal for a child her age.

"Save it, okay?" Oscar told her. "We'll need it, I'm sure, but not yet." He turned to Marcus. "Got any more of those saw blades?"

"Negative," Marcus replied. "Kids? Time for plan B."

"Yes, sir!" Mackenzie said.

Oscar turned to him, an eyebrow raised. Marcus just shrugged.

The kids were already running, deeper into the building and its shadows.

A rickety old stairway led up to a second floor made mostly of gantries that looked down on the workshop below. Oscar followed the same route the children took, zigzagging up the steps two at a time. His eyes slowly adjusted.

Marcus kept his flashlight dark, the better to hide their movements. The only light came from the moon finding its way in through the odd broken window and some cracks in the roof. The bonfire, a hundred yards up the beach, was too far away to help, and anyway the bellowing Swarmak blocked their view of it almost entirely.

They passed a side room full of old machinery. Some kind of paper press, Oscar thought, but it didn't matter really. It was big, old, and useless. And besides, this room had no door.

"Keep going," he urged the kids.

Another set of stairs loomed ahead. Eli went first, zigzagging his way up.

For an instant Oscar hoped the kids were taking a serpentine path to avoid triggering more of Mackenzie's traps, but of course they hadn't been in here long enough to set any. Halfway to the top he saw that the reason was much less helpful: rotten planks. Rusted nails poking out of some. Rat droppings everywhere.

Behind them, Oscar heard the sounds of the Swarm entering the building. Spreading out. Searching. He picked up his pace, and lowered his voice.

"Uh, what exactly is plan B?" he asked Marcus over his shoulder.

"Nothing to get excited about," the man replied. "But it beats the alternative."

"Kait's still out there."

"She can handle herself."

He said it in a way that implied he knew Kait better than Oscar did, and for the briefest of instants, Oscar wanted to turn around and ram a fist into the famous hero's face. How the hell did Marcus Fenix know what Kait could or couldn't handle?

Oscar had spent much of his life helping to raise her, teach her, and keep her out of trouble. This last, usually, because Reyna had made him promise to.

"Going to make a run up to Herzog's Pass," he'd say. *"Thought I'd bring Kait."* And Reyna would allow the expedition only after he promised to keep her safe. It was a promise he'd made every time, and always kept. Until the last, when he hadn't been there to even make the promise—nor had Reyna been there to ask for it. They'd both been snatched up by the Swarm.

Both had failed the girl.

And now, like all those times Reyna asked me to protect Kait, Kait asked me to protect the twins. So fuck it. That's what I'm going to do.

They found a supply room on the third floor, built way off to one side. This room had a door, and no giant machine taking up all the space.

"In here," Oscar said, guiding Eli and Mackenzie in.

Only Marcus had a light, and he switched it on once they were all inside.

Judging from the sounds behind them, the Swarm were all over the bottom floor, and starting to work their way up the stairs. It wouldn't be long now.

"Help me barricade the door," Marcus said, pulling a crate full of resin cans across the floor. Oscar found a large spindle of thick chain and began to lug it in that direction. The damn thing weighed a ton, or so it felt. Eli tried to help but Oscar shooed him off.

"Look for anything we can use as a weapon," he said, and that was all it took. The kids sprang into action, darting off in between rows of decrepit shelving, already whispering to one another as to the combat value of everything they spied.

Sweat pouring down his face, every muscle aching, Oscar finally wheeled the roll of chain in front of the door. He put his back against it and chuckled, softly.

"Find this amusing?" Marcus asked.

Oscar waved him off. "Just... still can't believe Kait pushed me off that cliff."

It was Marcus's turn to laugh. Well, not laugh—that didn't seem to be in his repertoire—but the soldier smiled wryly.

"You teach her that?" Oscar asked.

"How to push people off cliffs?"

"How to parachute."

The smile grew by a fraction. "More or less."

The smile faded with the yelps of Juvies nearby, and then the sound of their footfalls as they reached the top of the stairs and scrambled along the hall toward the door.

Oscar waited. The noise grew. The first Juvie went past the door. The second did, too, but seemed to skid by more than run, as if sensing its prey only a second too late.

The third stopped just outside, then rammed into the door. Oscar pushed his shotgun into a gap in their barricade and fired into the slab of wood. The yelping bray of a Juvie was instantly cut off. Good riddance. "You've taught her a lot in a short time, my friend."

"Kait's a quick learner," Marcus said. Something bigger was clomping down the hall, now. Big enough that the other Juvies seemed to melt away, as if making space. Marcus stepped back from the door and hefted his Lancer. He aimed at the wall, tracing the newcomer's movement with his rifle. He fired on full auto, leaving a neat line of bullet holes along the wall at knee height. The creature outside howled in pain, then crashed to the floor. "But you already knew that."

"She's an Outsider, that's what she is. Always will be." He felt a little guilty with the remark, but had to say it. He could have said more, but the lack of response from Marcus seemed to imply that the point was taken. He could teach her all she wanted, but she'd never be COG.

"Oscar?" Mackenzie said, from behind.

"What is it, young one?" He glanced over his shoulder.

She and Eli stood next to a crate, the top of which they'd managed to pry off. "Found these," she said, and with Eli's help the pair lifted up a thick iron bar, about three feet long. No, not a bar. It was a hook. Like a giant fishing hook, with a handle on one end.

"Used to bring the logs in off the river," Marcus said.

"Too heavy to be a weapon," Oscar told Mackenzie, and saw her disappointment. "But you're on the right track. Keep looking."

The door buckled suddenly. Wood splintered. The massive coil of chain toppled to one side.

It was time to put subtlety aside, Oscar figured, and let loose on the door, not caring how weakened it would get. Marcus had the same idea, and together they pulverized the wood, the walls, maybe even a bit of the ceiling.

Maybe they hit something, too. Or maybe not. All Oscar knew was that there were more out there, bloodthirsty as ever, and the ammo would run out soon.

The door buckled again, exploding inward. Marcus squared himself to the door, the lights mounted on his armor temporarily blinding the Drone that stumbled in through the smashed barricade. It threw up one arm to shield its eyes, and Oscar gave it a shotgun blast to the gut for its troubles. The Drone folded to the floor, blood spurting from its mouth.

"Kids, back," he growled over his shoulder. "Far as you can go."

They didn't argue.

Oscar started that way himself, keeping his body turned toward the door, making himself a shield for the twins. Marcus did the same. The two of them walked slowly backward toward the far wall, firing indiscriminately now. Anything that moved got a round. Anything that slithered got two.

"Almost dry," Oscar said.

"Same here."

It would come to melee soon. "Young ones," Oscar said over his shoulder, "look for another way out. Anything. Roof access. Window. Anything!"

"We're on it," Eli said.

Mackenzie darted off to the left. "You take that way," she said to her brother, and Eli nodded.

Damn good kids, Oscar thought. He'd never forgive himself if this was the end for them. And if they did manage to get out of this mess, he resolved then and there to stay by them, no matter what, until they didn't need him anymore. Until they were grown. Like Kait.

A young Pouncer wiggled in through a hole in the wall. He aimed at it, and pulled the trigger. The gun only clicked, though.

The Pouncer raised its tail, which was fanned out, needle-like quills protruding. It aimed at him. Oscar threw the spent weapon at the beast, and just in time. The quills fired, impaling themselves into the Gnasher's stock and bouncing off its barrel. The gun sailed on and smacked into the Pouncer's head.

Oscar drew the long hunting knife from his belt, twirling it around to hold it handle-forward, a slashing stance that seemed best given the darkness and the cramped surroundings.

Beside him, Marcus's gun ran out of ammo, too, but the man had one more clip and slapped it expertly into the weapon, barely a second of interruption to his shooting. He sprayed the Pouncer, sending it retreating back through the hole in the wall.

"There's nothing here," Mackenzie said. Somehow her voice betrayed no fear at all. "Just my last bundle." The homemade explosive was in her hands again.

Oscar wanted to tell her she might need it to end things, rather than be snatched up by the Swarm, but couldn't bring himself to. So he just shook his head in a way that invited no argument.

"What now?" Eli asked. The two of them were at the center of the back wall, surrounded by crates of miscellaneous junk.

"Just stay behind us," Marcus told them. As if there was

another option.

A Juvie crawled into the room, going up around the door frame and actually sprinting upside down along the fucking ceiling. Oscar jumped forward, bringing his knife over his head in a high arc that gutted the scrawny thing. The body fell on him, but weighed almost nothing. He shouldered it aside and shook the blood from his knife.

"Well," he said, "I hope Kait's having as much fun as we are!"

Marcus snorted.

Oscar took another full step back. The twins were just a few feet behind him now. Running out of time.

"Be ready to run," he told them. "Straight ahead, down the stairs, don't stop for anything." Neither questioned this, despite it being abundantly clear to anyone with a brain that running through this damned swarm was a hopeless exercise.

Marcus's Lancer fired its last bullet. He growled, powered up the chainsaw blade mounted under the rifle's barrel, and took a savage swipe at the next Juvie that came through the door.

Oscar renewed his grip on the knife, ready for his last stand.

Something shook the room. A pulse like... like a distant explosion. Then it happened again, louder. A third time.

No explosion, he had time to think. *Footsteps.*

Without warning the wall behind him was torn away. The whole back wall of the building. Oscar turned, and found himself looking into the eyes of a Swarmak.

11: THROUGH THE FIRE

Kait did the only thing she could think to do. She went for the flames.

As the Speakers came around from either side, she took two long strides forward, then a jump that became a dive. Arms protecting her face. Heat like she'd never known, all around her.

But only for a second. A flash of heat, then the flames were gone and she felt herself hitting the mud and gritty sand, doing her best to turn the effort into a roll and mostly succeeding. She came up on her feet, shaky and singed but alive.

Then she ran.

Not for the mill, but the trees. *Keep these fuckers as far away from the kids as possible*, she thought.

But the Swarm was arriving in force now. In the dancing orange blaze of the bonfire and the cool white light of the moon, she saw them coming down the old road that led from the mill into the forest. A few dozen, at least. Could be a thousand for all she knew. The trees hid their numbers.

Hopelessness began to gnaw at her gut. There was no success to be had here. The best she could do was to buy the others some time. Maybe they'd somehow get clear of this place to find refuge in the wilderness. Oscar and the twins were Outsiders. They knew how to live off the land, how to hide from those who might be looking. She had to trust in that.

Drawing Reyna's machete from the scabbard on her thigh, she took off down the beach, following the lake shore away from the mill. The farther she got from the fire, though, the harder it became to navigate the lumpy terrain. Undulating streaks of soft sand followed by sticky, sucking mud, occasionally interrupted by the thick dead trunk of some long-ago-fallen tree.

There was no need to look back. The Speakers would be on her scent, matching her pace with annoying ease, not yet closing in for the kill but—damn it—*toying* with her. One even laughed, and it was damned close. Then they started to converge. A pincer move.

"Okay, shitheads, two can play at that game." Instead of vaulting the next log, she planted her foot on it, spun around, and darted back the way she'd come. The motion was quick, flawless, and wholly unexpected by her pursuers. One had been in midair, leaping over the same log she'd just used as a turn-around point. It tried to pivot to follow her, skidded in the muck just beyond, and went down.

Its howl of rage made her smile.

Kait made a hard left, pushing off her right foot with as much force as the soft ground would allow, knife coming up. The Speaker there had been slightly behind, not fooled by her change of course at the log, but still clearly expecting her to run away, not toward it.

She went toward it.

It swung a meaty arm at her, but she was too quick, coming in under the assault, slashing at it as she passed, not stopping to engage fully.

Another cry of rage, and this one with a twinge of pure pain, too. Again she smiled. She'd felt the knife go through the thing's side as if she'd been gutting a fish.

The fire was to her right now, the mill a hundred yards beyond it. She could hear shooting coming from inside, but it might as well have been a mile away. Between her and the structure was a phalanx of the enemy. They'd arranged themselves in a line, not so much to stop her from reaching the mill but, she thought, to watch the spectacle as the two Speakers closed in on her. She swelled with pride at having spoiled the show, even if only briefly.

Kait angled away, though, knowing that to try and take on that row of Swarm would be suicide. She sprinted hard, and came to the water's edge before realizing it. The mud was deep there, sucking at her combat boots. Ahead of her the water stretched away, a line of glinting moonlight reflected down the middle. Weirdly beautiful.

Even kind of peaceful.

She turned. The two Speakers were twenty feet away, and had slowed to a casual stroll. Both were grinning at her, unable to contain their wicked glee. She stepped back, reflexively, knee-deep in the cool waters of the lake.

Beyond them, the trees stirred. Then she heard repetitive thumps. Or felt, rather, the waters around her vibrating. Kait could imagine what might make that noise, and her imagination in this case was right on target. The Swarmak that emerged from the trees did not surprise her in the least.

What *did* surprise her—what tied her gut in a wretched knot, in fact—was that it did not march toward her. The gigantic lumbering monstrosity went for the mill.

Now what? she thought. *How do I lure a monster like that—?*

The Speakers advanced, feet kicking water as they strode confidently toward her.

Kait turned, mind racing. Nothing but water in front of her, as far as the eye could see. The lake was miles across. Swim it? Would they follow? Did it matter with that huge disgusting beast about to knock the mill off its foundations?

To her right the water was choked with discarded tree trunks, bleached bone-white on top from years in the sun, black underneath with mold and decay. They formed what looked like an uneven blanket, spanning from her almost all the way to the mill itself.

Telling herself it couldn't hurt to try, Kait hoisted herself up on the nearest log and began a slow, awkward run across the surface, jumping from one to the next, fighting with each step to keep her balance as the logs dipped and rolled under her weight. Again one of the Speakers laughed, a sound straight out of her nightmares. So familiar, in fact, she had to stop and look at the creature, sure she would recognize it.

The pair had not bothered to follow her onto the logs. They were simply pacing her along the shoreline, waiting for her to fall in, or give up and face them. A moment passed as they simply stared at her. Them waiting to see what she'd do, Kait trying to force their faces back into the awful dreams that had haunted her since Reyna died.

She heard their controlled breathing. The roar of the Swarmak at the mill as it finally reached the side of the building. She heard the water lapping against the logs below her. The logs themselves, tapping against one another. She heard the wind and… she heard… she heard…

A thumping. Not her heart. Far away.

A thumping that was… familiar.

It grew astonishingly fast and loud, and Kait did not think. She acted. She pushed the logs below her apart and dropped straight down into the water as the sky above her was torn apart by the roar of an aircraft.

Some part of her brain raged at First Minister Jinn. Another useless load of DeeBees. How much time would they buy her? Thirty seconds?

The last thing she heard as she hit the water, other than the *wump-wump-wump* of the Raven's rotor, was a familiar voice.

"WOOOH!" Cole shouted, and he opened fire.

12: MOONLIGHT AND FLAME

"Put us on the beach!" Del shouted over the roar of the engine and the rattle of Cole's rotary cannon.

Sam expertly twisted the craft, avoiding a banking turn so Cole could keep firing. She turned them until the Raven faced north, then killed virtually all the power to the rotor. The craft plummeted. A second before impact she rammed power back into the engines. Instantly they were hovering.

"Out!" she shouted.

Del didn't need to be told twice.

Neither did JD.

They dropped from either side of the helicopter, fell the last five feet, and landed in damp sandy mud. Del had his rifle up—a Gnasher Baird had brought along—and he quickly started moving forward. Driftwood lay everywhere. Ample cover. The nearest Speaker had gone to one knee under the metal rain Cole had unleashed. Del fired at it, too—twice. There'd been a second Speaker, too, but where it was now he had no idea. Floating on its ugly face among the logs, if there was any luck to be had here.

About time we had some, Del thought, taking cover behind an old discarded tree trunk. Ten feet away, JD moved into position behind a boulder. Their eyes met and JD nodded, hefting the Torque Bow he'd selected from Baird's flying armory.

Behind them Sam wasted no time, pushing back into the air. She used the King Raven's momentum perfectly. Already a hundred feet up and moving forward toward the Mill. Rockets streaked from pods mounted on the helicopter's sides, lancing through the air, curling around one another as they homed in on their target.

The Swarmak stood there, holding the wall of the mill and peering into the darkness of the interior. Explosions erupted all up its back and shoulders. It stumbled under the onslaught, crashing into the building.

The heat and fury of the explosions threw Oscar onto his back. The kids beside him had better reaction time. They'd spotted the aircraft before him and, acting purely on instinct, had moved as far toward the center of the building as they could.

The Swarmak writhed under the sudden cluster of bombs detonating across its back, and stumbled. Oscar sprang to his feet faster than he'd done in... hell, he couldn't even remember. Fast. Damned fast. The four-story mass of crystal-encrusted brutality fell against the mill it had, only seconds before, torn open like a pack of rations.

The floor tilted beneath Oscar, then crumbled and fell away. He jumped, reached, grabbed the jagged edge of flooring planks on the side of the room that had survived. The twins were there a second later, tugging at his shirt, his arms, pulling him up to the last stable bit of floor. That was a sure way for them both to die.

"Run," Oscar shouted at Eli. "While you've got the—"

"No way," Eli said.

Beside him Mackenzie just nodded fiercely.

Oscar swore under his breath and heaved himself up. The children backed off as he finally managed to get up to the floor. Behind him the Swarmak roared, and he tensed for the inevitable. The sound that should have ruptured eardrums and broiled them with heat and carrion stench. Yet none of that happened.

Because it had turned around to face the helicopter. The kids had seen this and knew they had time to pull him up. His heart swelled for these two scrappy little runts.

"Thank you," he said, coming once again to his feet, wondering if this day would ever end.

"Where's Marcus?" Mackenzie asked.

The sound of the explosives ripped through the air, and Del could feel the vibrations despite the distance. Powerful shit, yet the Swarmak seemed only mildly annoyed.

The beast extricated itself from the derelict structure and turned to see what had dared attack it. Facing the helicopter, it flexed its massive arms, hunkered down, and aimed. On its back were a series of its own rocket launchers, and it had chain guns mounted on its wrists. With a roar it unleashed all of this on the King Raven.

If Sam was supposed to be scared by this, she wasn't. Del glanced up to see the chopper dodge expertly off to the right, letting loose a second salvo of rockets. The beast was ready this time, though, and although it was slow, there were a hundred yards separating them. It stepped sideways and threw up one crystal-encrusted arm, blocking four of the eight missiles. The other four vanished into the darkness of the mill, exploding inside. The air around the building filled with splintered, rotten wood.

"Sam," Del said into his comm. "They might be in there."

"Yeah, sorry," she said. "Didn't expect it to move like that."

"Can you keep it busy?" he asked. "Draw it off?"

"We'll try," Baird replied. "Cole, light it up!"

"With pleasure, baby!"

The rotary cannon roared to life. Tracer rounds zipped across the span of mud, slapping dully into the Swarmak's incredibly thick hide. Sam maintained her strafing maneuver, beginning a wide circle of the beast.

For the moment, at least, the Swarmak kept its attention entirely on the aircraft.

"That's our opening," JD shouted. He was fifteen feet away, crouched behind a log.

Del nodded, renewed his grip on the shotgun, and rushed forward.

Moonlight and flame illuminated the murky shallows.

Kait kicked hard, streamlining herself as she swam toward the mill. Above her head was a ceiling of logs, all black with mold and dangling tendrils of moss and decay. Below was an inclined, lumpy floor of mud, barely visible. Old fossilized tree trunks lay down there, bone-white, poking up like skeletal fingers.

She could hardly see, and found it hard to gauge the distance to the mill. Suddenly a series of yellow-orange flashes pulsated around her, seeping in through gaps in the logs above. A split second later came the muffled sound of explosions. The helicopter coming down?

No, she thought. There'd been a rhythm to the blast. Missiles, maybe.

Her lungs burned, screaming for air. Kait kicked twice more, fighting the weight of her armor, angling for the surface. There was no other choice.

But the logs above were packed in tightly. No way up. She pressed against two of them, fire in her chest now. The logs wouldn't budge. Panic started to flood into her mind and Kait pushed back with every ounce of will. She tried two more logs, no luck. Another two.

There, a gap.

Tiny, but enough? She pushed her mouth into the minuscule space, felt her lips break the surface... only just. She heaved in a breath. Air, foul with mold, but still air.

Fighting the urge to gag, she dropped down again. With hands and feet now, she tried to push the logs farther apart, but four inches was all she could manage. She let go and kicked again. Without goggles she couldn't see well. Everything was a blur. There had to be a way up. Had to!

Kait did a hard frog-stroke in the direction of the mill. Angled back up again. There... a gap? She thought she could see the moon above. She kicked one last time, hard. Or tried to.

Something grabbed her by the leg, and pulled her down.

The watery moon vanished above her.

Oscar glanced over the edge and spotted Marcus Fenix. He'd fallen to the floor below. It was the room they'd passed earlier, with its derelict paper press. Two massive iron plates, one above the other, with a large hand-cranked wheel used to force them together. All of it covered in rust. Marcus lay beside it. He wasn't moving.

"Marcus!" Oscar shouted to him.

Nothing. He was unconscious, or worse.

Ten feet away, the Swarmak raised its arm to defend itself against a barrage from the Raven's rotary cannon. Stray rounds slapped into the mill. More splinters and sparks. The kids behind him ducked, instinctively. Oscar debated jumping down to help Marcus, but that would mean leaving the kids alone.

No dice, he thought. The kids were his priority.

Then the man's foot twitched.

"Get up, Marcus," he bellowed. "We're still in this!"

Fenix pushed himself up, shaking his head.

"Faster, you old bastard!" Oscar shouted. "C'mon!"

Then he flinched slightly, feeling a presence at his side. The girl, Mackenzie, holding onto his left arm. Eli was at his right. They were both looking down at the fallen soldier.

"I told you to get back!" Oscar said to them.

Below, Marcus reached out with one hand and grabbed onto the heavy base of the decrepit press next to which he'd landed.

"Idea," Mackenzie said. Then she turned and ran back to the inner wall of the room. "Eli, help," she called out.

Oscar looked back and forth between Marcus and the kids. The twins hefted one of the long iron-bar hooks, which had all spilled onto the floor when the Swarmak tore the building's wall away. They handed it to Oscar. In his hand it wasn't terribly heavy. Like a nice big crowbar, really. He hefted it.

"Prefer my knife," he said.

"Not for that," Mackenzie replied. "Look down there." Before he could answer she turned away, lifting a second hook.

Oscar glanced back down. Marcus was on his feet now. Their eyes met, but Oscar let his gaze flash across the whole room. The machine beside Marcus—and what lay across it. It was the big spindle of heavy chain, the one he'd used to barricade the door. It had fallen down there with him. A length of the thick links had unspooled, snaking across the floor.

Eli nudged him. Handed him a second hook. He looked at it, then looked at the kids. Eli pointed at the Swarmak.

"Think they'll stick?" he asked.

Then comprehension dawned—sort of. Oscar glanced at the beast, which still faced toward the King Raven. The aircraft was strafing the beast in an arc, pummeling it with rotary cannon fire that was having no effect except to act as a distraction. The Swarmak fired back, chain guns on its wrists spitting fire, rockets launching from its back. So far it was having no luck, but Oscar knew that wouldn't last.

"They'll stick," Oscar said. "I'll make them stick." He glanced back down. "Marcus! Throw me that chain. You've gotta throw me that chain, Marcus!"

Marcus stared back at him. There was a line of blood trickling down his face from under his black skullcap. His eyes had that shell-shocked lack of focus. But then he looked dumbly at the chain, and something shifted in his eyes. They narrowed. His jaw set.

Marcus Fenix turned his face toward Oscar. "There's no time," he said. "Throw me one of those hooks instead."

Del rolled, a Pouncer landing where he'd just been. He rammed the barrel of his Gnasher into the creature's mouth, and fired twice.

"Last meal," he said, as the corpse fell. Beside him, another Drone lumbered forward, this one more heavily armored than most. It carried a Lancer, almost unrecognizable under a mess of crude modifications.

Before it could shoot, though, two red lights appeared on either side of its face, converging smack-dab in the center of the forehead.

Del threw himself to the ground as JD's Torque Bow bolt thwacked into the Drone's skull. A second later the explosive tip detonated. Brains and bone sprayed the beach. The decapitated Drone fell backward, its limbs flopping up in a sickly way as it slammed into the mud.

"Nice shot," Del said.

"Any sign of Kait? The others?"

Del shook his head. His eyes went to the mill, though, where the Swarmak remained—as if defending the building rather than itself.

"I've got a pretty good idea, though." He fired his Gnasher to the left, dropping a Juvie that was approaching at full gallop. The creature skidded, lifeless, through the mud, coming to rest at Del's feet. He tapped his comm.

"Sam, any sign of them?"

Her response was garbled. The King Raven was a few hundred feet north, over the trees. More interference?

"Take the shore," JD said. "I'll go by the tree line. We'll meet at the Swarmak and… figure something out."

Del nodded, and took off. It was as good a plan as any.

A huge hand gripped her thigh like a vice. Another wrapped around her foot. They heaved her brutally, yanking her down. The hand pulling her foot released it, only to clasp a split second later around her forearm.

Kait spun wildly, kicking hard, flailing her arms. Anything to break the hold—but it was too late. Within a second she found herself wrapped up in a pair of crushing arms, face to face with the ugly grin of the charred Speaker.

It laughed at her, bubbles shooting upward from its hideous mouth.

They were sinking.

It squeezed her hard. Bubbles escaped her own mouth. Precious breath.

Sinking fast. How far down had it taken her? She couldn't see the surface now. Just darkness. Kait's left arm was pinned at her side. Her right was folded over her chest, hand at her chin, totally stuck.

They sank further, the surface no longer visible. Her lungs were on fire. The Speaker laughed again.

Something cold brushed her right hand. Kait looked down and saw something glimmer there. A golden hue. She grasped at it, and her fingers curled around the square hunk of metal Reyna had given her. The amulet. Kait curled her hand even tighter around the Locust emblem, one corner pointing out between her index and middle finger. She gripped as hard as she could, wondering if Reyna somehow knew a moment like this would come. Was this why she'd given the damned thing to her?

Kait would never know.

It didn't matter.

With the last of her strength, and all of her reach, Kait thrust her right arm upward and out. Then she rammed the sharp corner of the amulet into the Speaker's eye.

"...one," Oscar said, finishing his countdown.

He and Marcus jumped simultaneously from the gaping side of the lumber mill. Oscar, up a floor higher, aimed for the Swarmak's shoulder, at a small gap between a crystalline growth and one of the rocket launchers.

He coiled, both arms back as far and high as they could go, the iron log hook held in a two-handed grip. Then he swung forward with all his might.

The hook sank into the bark-like skin with a sound like a shovel driven into hard earth. He grunted as he crashed into the beast's shoulder. It jerked reflexively, tried to turn its massive head to see what had just hit it. Oscar ignored all that. He pounded on the hook, driving it in another few inches. The chain that dangled from the end of it was suddenly yanked sideways, then pulled taut.

Below, Marcus had landed on the Swarmak's right side, and using Oscar's hook for tension, had begun to run along the monster's midsection.

That's my cue, Oscar thought, and he let go of his hook. He slid down the creature's back, bouncing as it suddenly roared and shook its body, trying in vain to swat Marcus away.

Though Oscar couldn't see the man, he could picture it. Marcus, running bodily along the Swarmak's gut, then bringing his own hook around in a mighty swing that would send it straight into the abdomen. The soft flesh. One could hope.

Oscar was knocked aside, rolled in the air, and brought his

arms up to cover his face as he slammed into the side of the mill building. The wall was brittle here, though, and he crashed through, rolling across a dusty floor.

Coughing, he spat blood. With an effort he struggled to a sitting position. He didn't need to shout for the kids to act. They knew what to do. Smart little rascals. Oscar Diaz grinned as Mackenzie's plan sprang into motion.

The detonation was small. That would be the girl's last hand-made explosive, two rooms away. Marcus had wrapped the chain around that old paper press, looping it through the big wheeled handle at the top. Then Mackenzie had lit her last explosive, and thrown it to him. Marcus had caught the bomb and quickly placed it under the base of the machine. The kids had backed away as Marcus and Oscar prepared to jump onto the Swarmak.

And it had worked.

Above him, the paper press crashed through the hole in the floor the bomb had made. The big hunk of iron dropped into the next floor down, and as it went it yanked on the chain Oscar and Marcus had attached to the behemoth.

The weight of the machine and chain were too much.

The Swarmak's feet went out from under it as it was pulled, hard, to the ground. The earth shook as it landed, writhing, pinned there, one hook slowly tearing sideways through the soft flesh of its stomach.

Its howl shook the earth. The building. Rage and frustration and pain all at once, drowning out everything else.

"Now we run," Oscar thought aloud.

Only he didn't move. Something new caught his eye.

On the Swarmak's bloodied gut, two red lights converged.

And above, from the King Raven, a final salvo of missiles.

Del watched from the water's edge as the Swarmak went crashing down. Only as it lay writhing did he see the hook in its gut, the length of chain leading away from it. And there, on the ground nearby, lay Marcus Fenix, trying to get to his feet.

The others must be there, too. Del started to run, unable to take his eyes off the massive creature. Torque Bow laser sights converged, and somehow he heard JD fire the weapon despite the distance that lay between them. The bolt struck home—a perfect shot, straight into the gash the hook had made.

There was a sickening wet *whump* sound as the explosive bolt detonated somewhere in the Swarmak's gut. It went into spasms, limbs thrashing out. One arm tore into the corner of the mill, and the whole structure made a strange, low groan. It started to tilt toward the creature.

"Oh shit," Del said, sprinting now.

He'd never make it in time, though. Sam wasn't wasting the chance. She unleashed the last of the chopper's rocket payload. The missiles streaked through the air like a flock of angered hornets. Another perfect strike. Eight rockets, all slamming home in and around the hole in the Swarmak's belly. The explosions tore it wide, gore flying everywhere.

The shock wave threw Del back, a burst of heat and debris forcing him onto his ass. He rolled over, blinking away the pain.

And found himself looking into Kait's eyes.

She crawled up from the water, one arm tucked against her side. Mud and blood a confused mess on her face. She was gulping in air, pulling herself toward him, mouthing something Del couldn't hear.

Then she collapsed into the mud.

She lies on her back in an endless gray pool, floating serenely on the gentle water, staring up at pure white sky marred only by a black sun.

An anti-sun.

She feels at peace.

There is no danger here.

There is no time. No future, no past.

Just the warm water, and the cold sun. A world of opposites, unchanging.

Kait opens her mouth, unsure what she's going to say but knowing she must say something.

She decides to say "hello," but the word won't come.

Her mouth is full of sand.

She coughs, spasms, retches.

The cold, black sun above her vanishes, returns.

Moves.

It's no sun, she realizes.

It's an eye.

Kait screams, and punches out at the—

13: FAR TO THE NORTH

Kait opened her eyes to blinding sunlight, and quickly closed them again. The after-image on the inside of her eyelid was that of a black sun. She let out a long breath, then turned her head and tried again.

She was on the lake shore, far from the mill—which was just a ruin now, half a mile distant. Del and JD sat on logs nearby, Oscar across from them, the three of them talking in low, serious voices.

Beyond she could see Marcus, standing with Cole, Baird, and Sam. No seriousness there. Baird was leaning against a King Raven, using his hand to mimic the movements of the helicopter, making explosion noises with his mouth. Sam was laughing, her arm around him. Cole looked on, grinning. Marcus looked on, too, not grinning, but he had that "amused Marcus" face on, all the same.

The twins were… where?

Kait sat up.

Instantly her head filled with bright pain.

"Whoa, easy now," JD said, and he was at her side in an instant, arm supporting her. Del stood by, too.

"The kids?" Kait asked. "Where…"

Then she saw them. They were at the edge of the forest, maybe fifty feet away, each with a stick they'd found, playing "swords and shields" as Kait had so many times when she was that age.

"Everyone's okay," Del told her.

Kait nodded. She lay back down.

"Uh, what he means," JD said, "is everyone's okay… but the Swarm could return any second. Can you… nap later?"

She allowed a wave of nausea to pass, then sat up again, slowly this time.

"How long was I out?"

"Four hours," Del said. "Give or take. We didn't want to risk moving you. Not yet. Not unless they came back."

"Thanks," she said. "To both of you. *All* of you. You got here just in time. I thought Jinn had sent us a bunch of useless DeeBees."

"I heard that!" Baird shouted.

Standing with Oscar at the water's edge, Kait splashed some water on her face. It was clean here. The water cold, invigorating. She drank some.

"We're a sorry sight," her uncle said, chuckling warmly. His head had as many bandages as hers.

"It's weird," Kait said, looking at the water. "Part of me wishes Mom had been here, fighting at our side."

"Who says she wasn't?" Oscar asked. He clapped her on the

shoulder, more gently than his usual self. The gesture turned into a one-armed embrace.

The others waited some distance off, giving them their space, waiting.

For a long moment neither she nor Oscar spoke. In the distance Kait could see the meandering, steep-walled canyon, and beyond that, the barest hint of the high waterfall coming down the side of the mountain. Somewhere farther still, hidden by the perpetual clouds, were the ruins of South Village.

Beside her Oscar fidgeted. He cleared his throat, and glanced back at the others. They were all watching her, waiting. Not to leave, she realized, but to make a decision.

She swallowed, hard. This was the moment she'd been dreading.

"So what happens now?" she asked. "I don't think hiding out in South Village is an option anymore." Not that it ever was, really, but she left that unvoiced.

Oscar sighed. "Riftworm," he said.

"Huh?" Kait turned to him, one hand on her forehead to shield her eyes from the morning sun.

"Riftworm village," he said. "It's an Outsider camp far to the north. Figured we could try that."

Kait studied him. "Why there?"

He shrugged. "*Far* to the north, Kait. Won't be any Swarm there. The twins will be safe."

"You sure about that?" she asked him.

For this he had no reply.

"We should take them to the city," Kait said, and she was emphatic. "New Ephyra."

"We talked about this, Kait. Terrible plan."

"It's not terrible. I've been there."

"And you think the Swarm will leave it alone? All those lovely people to snatch up and use?"

"There's massive walls," Kait said. "Defenses."

In response Oscar simply pointed to where South Village used to be. "That was an entire mountain. Didn't stop them."

"Well, to be fair," Kait said, "Mackenzie did more damage to it than the Swarm."

He glared at her for a second, then gave up. "She really did, didn't she?" He laughed heartily. Kait couldn't help but smile, but it was short-lived.

"Please, Uncle, let's take them to the city."

"I'm going to Riftworm, Kait," he replied. "City life? Hell, *COG life*? That's not for me anymore. Can't do it." He wrinkled his nose at the idea. Then his brow furrowed. "As for the young ones... I say we let them decide. They've earned it. Don't need 'grown-ups' making decisions for them anymore. Hell, they might not want to go with either of us."

She held her uncle's gaze for a long time, then nodded. He put two fingers to his teeth and whistled.

"Kids?! Come 'ere!"

Kait and Oscar explained the situation. It didn't take long, and the twins... well, they were smart. Way too mature, Kait thought, and that was part of the problem.

It was somewhat mesmerizing to watch them confer, silently, just by looking at each other, after Oscar finished his pitch.

Mackenzie finally turned and looked at Oscar. "Will you two come with us, whatever we choose?"

Kait glanced at him, surprised by this question. Her uncle was already shaking his head. "I'm an Outsider, kids," he said. "That's my way. If you want to go with Kait, go to the city, I won't stop you, but I won't come with you, either."

They both turned to look at Kait, implying the same question.

She searched for words. "The thing is…" she started, then paused and regrouped. "This Swarm," she said on her second try, "I believe they're going to keep coming for us. Keep growing. Unless we try to stop them. And I don't think I can help do that by hiding out in some remote village."

"And you want to try to stop them?" Eli asked.

Kait nodded, emphatic. "But I want to protect you, as well. In New Ephyra, maybe I can do both."

"But maybe not," Mackenzie added.

"Maybe not," Kait agreed.

"It'll be dangerous there. Maybe more so. Right?"

"Yes, dangerous." Then she crouched before them, putting herself at eye level with the pair. "You two need to understand something, though. This… life you've been living the last few days. Fighting and making bombs and… killing… that's got to end, no matter what you choose. You're too young for this, even if you don't think that's true. I'm telling you this because I hear that eagerness in your voice, Mackenzie. If you're thinking coming with me is the right choice because you'll be closer to the action, forget it."

Their eyes swiveled to Oscar.

"Don't look at me," he said. "Kait's right."

With that the twins walked a few feet away, and quietly conferred. Oscar and Kait stood by, neither speaking. It occurred to her that, without really saying it plainly, they'd just decided to go their separate ways, each maybe hoping the other would have a change of mind if it meant staying beside the twins.

Would Oscar, though? Change his mind? Come to New Ephyra? Kait knew the answer. He was too stubborn. Too proud.

And what about her?

Deep down she knew the answer to that, too.

The twins came back. They went to Kait, and as one they threw their arms around her and squeezed, and she knew they'd made their choice.

JD suggested they fly Oscar and the twins to Riftworm, but Sam had to nix the idea.

"I'd love to, but we barely have enough fuel to make it back to the city," she said. Then she added, "We can get you away from here, at least."

Kait thought Oscar might decline even this small bit of help, but he surprised her.

"There's an Outsider supply cache north of here, about twenty miles," he said. "Drop us there?"

"That works. But we'll circle it first. Make sure it's clear."

Oscar couldn't argue with that, and climbed aboard.

Half an hour later they set down deep in the forest, where snow-dappled trees surrounded a small clearing, barely big enough for the King Raven and the tiny log hut that had been built there.

Oscar and Kait hopped out and checked the structure, while JD and Del made a circuit of the clearing.

The hut was locked, but Oscar tugged a hidden key from between two logs. When he opened the door they found it full of stored supplies. Food, water, even some weapons.

After gathering some gear, the twins both gave Kait fierce hugs. "You'll visit us when you can, right?" Mackenzie asked.

"Promise," Kait replied, feeling tears well at the corners of her eyes.

They hugged Marcus, too, taking the old soldier a bit off guard.

Twenty minutes after landing they were off, headed north into the forest. The kids disappeared into the dense trees after one last quick wave, but Oscar, a step behind them, stopped and turned back. He stood there for a moment, looking at Kait. She raised a hand to him and he waved back.

Then he turned, stepped into the shadows, and was gone.

She'd thought she'd lost him forever when Fort Umson was attacked. Couldn't believe her eyes when she found him again in South Village. And now this…

At least this time she'd been able to say goodbye.

14: THE COMING STORM

The factory floor buzzed with activity. Every assembly line pushed to maximum capacity, every assembly bot swinging about as parts were moved from supply bins to half-built Dee-Bees. People were everywhere, checking quality, hand-tightening pieces, testing components.

"At this rate," Baird said, his voice raised over the bustle of manufacturing, "we'll be able to produce about fifty DR-1s per day."

First Minister Jinn nodded, her face a mask of studied concentration.

"I'd be happier if it were double that."

"I know you would. That's the best we can do."

She turned to him, but Baird kept his gaze on the work below. A construction Mech walked by, carrying a load of hydraulic interconnects piled in a huge yellow bin, bound for some assembly line that was running low on the part.

Feeding the beast, Baird thought.

They stood on a service gantry, forty feet above the factory floor. At this height the Mech was eye-level with them. Jinn tapped her fingers on the railing, not so much nervous as anxious.

"I need an army, Baird. Not a few squads."

"We're building as fast as we can," he said. "You have my word on that."

"I don't doubt it," she replied. "But it's not enough. It's not what I've asked for. Increased production, enhanced logic—"

"Now there we can help you," he replied. "Making a lot of progress in the brains department."

Jinn waited, eyeing him. She'd been waiting for an update since they'd returned from South Village a week ago, in fact, but he'd held her off until the new combat algorithms were sound and tested.

In that time there'd been a steady flow of reports from all over. Settlements, Outsiders, even one of Jinn's counterparts across the borderlands. Locust burial sites were either going offline, or showing signs of "strange activity." Bodies were being found, or worse, missing altogether.

News of this threat was spreading, and Baird knew—hell, they *all* knew—that the Swarm itself wouldn't be far behind. It was only a matter of time.

"I've been working on a new training method," Baird said.

"Oh?"

He chose his words carefully. Jinn had a battle plan, he knew, but she'd kept it from him. Technically he wasn't on her staff, and now that his remote DeeBee access had been revoked, he couldn't keep tabs on the way his robots were being used.

"Cole's idea, actually. Basically like a Thrashball playbook, but the scenarios are things like 'Burial Site Containment' and 'Settlement Defense.' With some core underpinnings in place, you can layer on the appropriate strategy and drop a force in, ready to go."

For a time she said nothing, and he thought perhaps that was a quiet confirmation. But then she sighed and shook her head.

"Right now I need one strategy in particular." She held up a hand before he could protest. "I'd prefer it if you focused your efforts on evacuation scenarios."

Baird raised an eyebrow. "We're going to leave the city?"

Jinn shook her head again. "Evacuation *to* the city."

"The hell for?"

Sam walked up just then, her inspection of the factory floor complete. The confident expression she wore told Baird all he needed to know: things were going fine. And Sam was smart enough not to interrupt. She took her place at Baird's side and listened.

Jinn turned to them both. "Our population is already critically low. I cannot hope to defend a hundred small locations spread out across the continent. New Ephyra has more than enough space, and defensible walls."

"All your eggs in one basket, Jinn," Baird said. "Bad idea."

"There's no better option. My duty first and foremost is to protect our citizens."

"Even the Outsiders?" Sam asked.

She nodded. "Even them. We'll bring them all here, at least until Settlement 6 is ready."

"Forcibly? I'm not sure they'll come of their own free will."

Jinn's face remained impassive. "Whatever it takes. We'll get them here."

Baird wasn't having it. "The Swarm seems wired to seek out humans, Jinn. You bring everyone here and it's just a nice big beacon for them. Instead of a hundred small battles you'll have one gigantic one."

"With enough of your robots, I think we'll be ready."

"Robots won't be enough, Jinn. Trust me. You saw the footage. You've seen their numbers. If you bring everyone here that'll concentrate the Swarm into one big mass. When that happens you've got to take advantage of it. You could end it in a heartbeat."

"For the last time, I'm not going to use the Hammer of Dawn," Jinn said. "It's offline, inaccessible, and that is how it will remain."

Sam snorted. "A DeeBee solution alone is not going to work. Surely you can see that, Mina."

"It *has* to work," Jinn replied. "The alternatives are unacceptable."

"What's acceptable isn't the issue here!"

"It is to me." Jinn's words were sharp, unambiguous. She eyed both of them. "You have a contract with my government, and I expect you to fulfill it. If that's a problem, I suggest you take a long vacation somewhere far from here. I'm sure I can find someone else to run this place."

The big Mech walked past again, off on another task, and they waited for it to pass.

Baird rubbed at his chin, lost in thought. He could feel Sam looking at him, expecting him to continue the argument. He was going to disappoint her, though.

"Damon?" Jinn asked. "Do you have something to say?"

He gave her a sidelong glance. After a moment he shook his head. "I'm a pretty stubborn guy, but I think we've had this argument enough now for me to know you're not going to change your mind."

Jinn arched an eyebrow.

Beside him, Sam was staring daggers. He held out his hands, palms up.

"We said our piece. You know where we stand. It's time to quit talking and get down to the business of making you some badass robots. Before you take over the whole operation and try to make them yourself, I mean."

Jinn tilted her head, a little surprised.

"Speaking of badass, look who's here," Baird added.

The whole gang had arrived from their tour of the factory, and just in time. Baird stepped away from Jinn and shook hands with Del and JD. Sam pulled Kait into a soldier's embrace. The two had become fast friends in the last week.

"Corporal Diaz," Jinn said, nodding to Kait.

The woman saluted, with a slight hesitation. Not entirely comfortable with the title yet, it seemed. Baird couldn't blame her.

Kait looked... better, he thought. Definitely badass in her own suit of COG armor. She, JD, and Del were truly the new generation now.

Yet her features still hinted at the loss she'd suffered, and then suffered again in a different way when Oscar had left with the twins. There were the dark bags under her eyes. Not sleeping, still.

Hmm.

"What were you all talking about?" JD asked, coming up behind Kait.

"Progress," Jinn replied.

"...toward putting an end to the Swarm?" Del asked. "Please tell me it's that."

Straight to the point, Baird thought. *I like this kid*. He watched to see how Jinn would respond. Her reply was, predictably, a politician's answer.

"Eventually," was the word she chose. At Del's obvious frustration, she held up her hand. All eyes on her now, Baird noted. "We've faced a foe like this before, and the results were... catastrophic for both sides. We need to be smarter this time, but the right response—the sane response—can't happen overnight." She gestured to the extensive factory below them, abuzz with activity. "We're building on more than one front, and I'll need all of your help to do it. Even yours, Sergeant Fenix, if you're willing."

Baird looked at his old friend, who'd been lagging behind the group, and now stood about ten feet away. He was leaning against the railing on the opposite side of the walkway, arms folded across his old battle-proven armor. Markedly not the new, improved version.

"Building?" Marcus asked. "That all?"

Jinn shook her head. "We're going to save as many people as we can. Bring them here, to New Ephyra. Protect them," she said. She locked eyes with him, and added, "If we can convince them."

Marcus said nothing. Which, Baird noted, wasn't a "no." Sometimes with Marcus Fenix that was the best you could do.

EPILOGUE: MORNING STAR

He slipped out the back of the house later that night, after the others had all turned in. The air was crisp, a cold wind blowing in from the south. He walked into the garden, past the trees, then turned left just before the gate. Four DR-1s stood guard on the other side, silent and vigilant as always.

At the shed he produced his key, unlocked the door, and stepped inside. The space was dark and cold, vacant these last few days. He closed the door behind himself, and after a moment of hesitation, bolted it from within.

He moved deeper into the building. The stairway rotated with a second turn of his key. Creaking like it always did. He made a mental note to oil that as he descended into the secret basement chamber.

"IRIS," Baird said. "Lights please. All systems on."

"Of course, Damon," she replied.

The room filled with a soft blue glow. Screens bloomed to life, filling almost at once with blocks of code and various status displays.

"You have not visited at such a late hour in some time, Damon.

Is everything alright? Are you having a dispute with Ms. Byrne again?"

"No, no, nothing like that." Baird took his chair, leaned back into the cushions, and took a moment to clear his mind. He hadn't been back to this room since his remote access to the DeeBees had been exposed and summarily revoked.

He steepled his index fingers beneath his chin and focused on the main display.

"We have a new project to work on, IRIS. Just you and me."

"Very good," she replied. "Allocating a databank—"

"No," Baird replied, a little too quickly. "No need. I've got that covered. In fact, you should disable any permanent storage for this session."

IRIS took a fraction of a second longer than usual to reply. "I am... intrigued."

Inwardly he smiled. She was progressing so fast.

Baird spun his chair around and rolled across the room to a file cabinet on the far wall. He unlocked the bottom drawer and pulled it open. Inside were dozens of data discs, identical in size and shape and none of which were labeled. He rifled through them, looking for the only one that actually mattered. It had a small white dot on its edge, almost imperceptible unless you knew to look for it. The rest were decoys, meant to waste some investigator's time, should that day ever come.

Back at his desk, he slipped the data disc into the machine. "Okay, IRIS. Here we go. Access 'Project Morning Star.'"

"That item is protected by a pass phrase, Damon."

"I know, I set it." He hesitated, partly because of the risk involved in sharing this with IRIS, and partly from the anticipation of having her help. He'd spent countless hours over the years poring over all the files on this disc, and barely scratched the surface of all it had to offer. But with IRIS… he felt almost giddy at the prospect of unleashing her on it. Worth the risk, he decided. "The pass phrase is 'look to the sky.'"

"Analyzing," she said.

He waited. "Any initial thoughts, IRIS?"

She said, "Of the files here, eighty-seven percent are authored by one Fenix, Adam."

"Marcus's dad," he explained. "James's grandfather. The bulk of it is not relevant to us right now, IRIS. I want you to focus on the files pertaining to the Hammer of Dawn."

"What would you like me to search for?"

He kept his voice level. "Anything not referenced in your own databanks. Places, names, that sort of thing." He rolled up his sleeves, muttering to the display. "Been a few years, Dr. Fenix. Ready to give up a few more secrets?"

A list of words began to appear on the display. Most were just obscure things with which IRIS would not yet be familiar. He was looking for the ones *he* didn't know about.

"Hold there," he said, and tapped the screen. "Hmm…"

"Have I found something useful?" IRIS asked.

"Maybe," Baird admitted. "Not sure. Something I missed before. Or ignored. I don't know what it means."

She waited.

Baird read the word aloud. "Azura…"

ACKNOWLEDGEMENTS

My heartfelt thanks to the entire Gears team, especially Rod, Bonnie, and Jerry, for their support and assistance throughout this project. Despite your own intense deadlines you were incredibly generous with your time and energy, and for that I'm eternally grateful.

Many thanks as well to the team at Titan Books, especially Steve, for everything you do but mostly for your patience with me!

Thanks as always to my agent, Sara Megibow, for the tireless effort on my behalf, and to wife and kids, for putting up with my crazy career.

My gratitude as well to the Gears fan community—a wise and wonderful bunch if there ever was one! I'm proud to count myself among you, and hope you enjoyed the novel.

JMH, *April 2019*

ABOUT THE AUTHOR

Jason M. Hough is the bestselling author of eight novels, including *The Darwin Elevator*, *Zero World*, and *Mass Effect Andromeda: Nexus Uprising*, as well as numerous short stories including *Star Wars: Turning Point*.

When not writing he can usually be found either playing with his kids, trying to fix his eternally broken 3D printer, or exploring alien worlds in virtual reality.

He lives near Seattle, Washington.